INDIVISIBLE

KRISTEN HEITZMANN

INDIVISIBLE

A NOVEL

WaterBrook
PRESS

INDIVISIBLE
PUBLISHED BY WATERBROOK PRESS
12265 Oracle Boulevard, Suite 200
Colorado Springs, Colorado 80921

The characters and events in this book are fictional, and any resemblance to actual persons or events is coincidental.

ISBN 978-1-4000-7309-2
ISBN 978-0-307-45908-4 (electronic)

Published in the United States by WaterBrook Multnomah, an imprint of the Crown Publishing Group, a division of Random House Inc., New York.

WATERBROOK and its deer colophon are registered trademarks of Random House Inc.

Library of Congress Cataloging-in-Publication Data
Heitzmann, Kristen.
    Indivisible : a novel / Kristen Heitzmann. — 1st ed.
      p. cm.
    ISBN 978-1-4000-7309-2 — ISBN 978-0-307-45908-4 (electronic)
  1. Colorado—Fiction. I. Title.
    PS3558.E468I53 2010
    813'.54—dc22

                                                                    2009050305

Printed in the United States of America
2010—First Edition

10 9 8 7 6 5 4 3 2 1

To my precious family:
you guys are everything.

One

What therefore God hath joined together, let not man put asunder.

—MARK 10:9, KING JAMES VERSION

Wrapped in a woolen throw, Jonah stared out through moon-silvered evergreen spires. He drew in the clean, sharp air of the rugged mountains, the piercing stars visible to an amazing depth, the sickle moon casting the clearing in stark relief. He had not expected to sleep—didn't dare with memories tugging so hard.

He shut his eyes and let the night enclose him. The chilled tip of his nose stung as he breathed the piquant scents of wild grasses, earth, and pine, a heady overlay with a hint of moisture condensing in the cold and dark.

The beam above moaned with the motion of the porch swing, a rhythmic counterpart to the rushing creek out of sight in the dark except for flashes of white where water struck rock. He felt something brush against his hand and looked down. A white, powdery moth fluttered at the lighted face of his watch. The fluffy *whoosh* of an owl passed, a silent shadow in search of a small, beating heart.

His pulse made a low throb in his ears. He moved the breath in and out through his lungs, filling his senses easier than stilling the thoughts.

Somewhere in the rocky crags a coyote yipped, one of the few predators that had enlarged its range in spite of human encroachment, a bold and canny cohabiter, bearing ever bolder offspring. A long howl sailed into the night, a territorial declaration, signaling roving males to stay away, any females to come hither. He pressed up from the swing and leaned on the rail, trying to get a bead on the coyote's location. After a time, he turned and went inside.

Piper loved morning, the brightness, the cleanness of a new day. But morning started with the sunrise, not when the sky was still black and the room shivery. She burrowed her feet deeper beneath the down comforter, avoiding the inevitable for one more moment. It was too brief a moment.

She crabbed her hand across the lace-covered bedstand and stopped the alarm on the cell phone before it could nag her. She would do her own nagging, as she had ever since she'd realized no one else intended to. Not that they didn't care, just that she was on her own when it came to responsibility, reliability, accountability.

She groomed, and dressed without shedding the film of sleep. Just a few years ago she could have slept all day—if she'd let herself. She slipped on her jacket and turned up the collar, switched on the iPod in her pocket and inserted the ear buds. Enya's "Only Time" accompanied her out the door.

The first gasp of cold air pierced her fog. She drew a flashlight from the other pocket and trudged behind the beam down the steep path, weaving through the pines. Even August nights lost the days' warmth to the thin mountain atmosphere, which the sun would heat once again.

Streaks of deep magenta broke through the black tree silhouettes, announcing dawn, but around her, darkness clung. Over the music, she detected the rushing of Kicking Horse Creek, which paralleled the main street through Old Town. Neither dark and muddy nor sluggish and green, the creek ran frothy white and clear down to the rocky bed.

She couldn't see it from the path even if the sun were up, but its voice carried up the stony crags as she picked her way down the steepest stretch of the path. Her nostrils constricted. She slapped a hand to her mouth and nose to block a putrid scent carried on the sharp air. She swung her light, and the beam caught a furry mound of carnage. She hurried past, gagging.

The path ended behind the Half Moon, but she continued on to the next door, unlocked the bakery, and let herself into Sarge's kitchen. Soon, warm, yeasty aromas tinged with almond, vanilla, and cinnamon banished the dead animal stench in her nostrils. She had memorized the recipes the first week, easy enough as Sarge had served the same eight things since opening the bakery thirty years ago. After twenty years in army kitchens, he saw no need for variety in the mess.

She hadn't baked before, but she'd taken to it, and with a little freedom, the slightest leeway, she might shine. But three weeks into the job, she had yet to sneak a variation by Sarge or convince him to feature anything not indelibly written on the dusty menu board.

She lifted and folded the dough over the plump, rum-soaked raisins, tucking them in like well-fed babies under a fluffy blanket, then put them to bed in the nice warm oven. Down for their nap, just like yesterday, and the day before, and the day before that. Sweet little raisin rolls, just the way Sarge liked them.

She closed the oven, moved to the other end of the counter, and checked the measuring cup in which she had sprinkled yeast over warm water and whisked in sour cream and sugar. Cutting together flour, butter, and salt, she glanced quickly toward the door. No Sarge yet.

She combined the ingredients to make a coarse dough that when properly rolled and folded should bake into lovely light croissants—not something Sarge could envision. The back door banged. He came in, hung his red plaid coat on the hook, and turned his head like a vulture's on the end of his question-mark spine. She did hurt for him. The photo in the front of the store showed a strong, military physique. It couldn't be easy to curl up like a lemon rind in the sun.

"Good morning, Sarge."

"Humph." His sunken eyes peered down his long bulbous nose. Lucky he had rank or his moniker might have been Beak. Or Gonzo. Sarge fit, although he didn't look capable of any spit-flecked rants today. Lately his pain had been bad enough to reduce the rages to sarcastic skirmishes of parleyed insults she could swear he enjoyed. She'd even imagined a glimmer of relief, once or twice, that she was there.

"Are those the currant scones?"

"Already baking. The rolls too."

He toddled toward her, hands bent at his chest like a bald eaglet just out of the egg. He scowled. "What is it this time?"

She checked her surprise. "Gruyère and sun-dried tomato croissants."

"Not in my store." He pushed through the swinging door to the front.

She stared after him. Progress. He'd asked what she was making, not accused her of stealing the ingredients.

———

Breathing the honey scent of beeswax, Tia lowered the candles into the clear amber liquid, curbing her natural impatience. Any pause or jerk would leave a flaw each ensuing dip would reinforce. She worked hard to keep her hand steady. Dipping tapers had trained her in self-control better than any scolding instructor.

She raised the wooden bar looped with six double wicks. As soon as the air touched the wax, it paled to ocher. She fitted the bar onto the side braces to cool the tapers before lowering them again, each plunge having the potential to reclaim with greedy heat what solidity the cool air had bestowed. The life metaphor struck her again. The destructive power of pain; the strength of endurance. She would give them all they needed to stand strong, even though their fate was to burn away, the glow and aroma of their passing a benediction.

A knock brought her out of her thoughts, and she wended through the dim shop where little by little she had replaced the former knickknacks with candles, scented oils, and hand-thrown melting pots. She looked around, satisfied that nothing she saw was made in China. "Just a sec," she called through the door, tangling with the keys since she hadn't opened yet.

"Try this." Piper raised the drooping croissant.

Tia bit into the buttery, melted-cheesy pastry, savoring a chewy tang of sun-dried tomatoes and fresh basil. She leaned her shoulder to the door-jamb and sighed. Not all Piper's creations worked, but this one… "Mmm."

"You like it?"

"Oh yeah."

"You're not just encouraging me because you hope I'll get better if I keep trying?"

"No, it's really—"

Piper snatched the croissant out of her hands, turned the bitten end around in the parchment, and held it out to someone else. "Try something new?"

Tia leaned out far enough to see the person approaching. Lanky in jeans, mountain boots, and brown leather jacket bearing the police department emblem, he looked as ragged as a night spent with Johnny Walker, though she didn't smell it on him, had not, in fact, for years. Even so, every muscle in her hardened—a visceral reflex as automatic as breathing.

He said, "Excuse me?"

His features were edged, and in an instant she realized what day it was.

"The croissant." Piper flashed her sunny smile.

"Oh. No. Thanks."

"One bite," Piper cajoled, a hypnotic maneuver she had mastered. "And your honest opinion."

He took a bite and chewed slowly, the muscles rippling along his jaw. "What are the red things?"

"Sun-dried tomatoes." Piper bit her lower lip.

"Taste a little fishy."

"The gods speak," Tia muttered.

"Fishy?"

"They're not fishy, Piper." Tia folded her arms. "A little tangy maybe."

His gaze flicked over, weighing, measuring her. He must have been doing something in his official capacity, but she didn't care what. Sometimes they went weeks without crossing paths, but every time the encounter arced between them like a chemical adhesion, the two parts of epoxy that did fine until combined, then interacted toxically.

"People who know sun-dried tomatoes will expect that flavor." She spoke to Piper, but her eyes were locked with Jonah's.

"I'm sure you're right." He held the pastry out.

"No." Tia raised her hands. "By all means, finish it." She backed into the shop and closed and locked the door, returning to complacent tapers that had forgotten the burn of the wax.

Jonah winced at the sharp report of the door. Tia. Turning, he caught the look of surprise on the young blonde. He had no intention of explaining. "Here." He tried to return the croissant, but Piper shook her head.

"Do you like it? Would you buy it?"

"You can't sell—"

"If you like it, you could tell Sarge. Maybe he'd let me try a different thing or two."

Now he placed her—Sarge's new baker. No wonder she had the look of a puppy afraid of getting her nose swatted but wanting to please all the same. "Okay." He started past.

"So, hey. Are you a cop?"

"Chief of police. Can I help you?"

"Who's responsible for dead things?"

Caught unprepared, his adrenaline surged.

"There's something on the path between Tia's house and shop. Who's responsible for cleaning it up?"

Some*thing,* not someone. His chest eased. "I'll take a look."

Most days he battled the boredom of policing Redford. This wasn't most days. He turned off the street and cut over to the path. Realizing he still held the croissant, he folded the tissue around it and shoved it into his jacket pocket, then turned upslope until he found what she was talking about by smell before sight.

A raucous white and iridescent blue-black magpie flew up as he stopped several feet from the carcass. A raccoon. But then he realized there were two, only…they weren't.

———

Annoyed when Piper tapped once more, Tia opened the door less magnanimously.

"Oh…my…gosh." Piper all but quivered. "Who is he?"

"Jonah Westfall."

Piper searched her face. "What—did he arrest you or something?"

"Don't be silly." No surprise Piper had picked up on it. His mere presence had curdled her mood.

"There are cute guys in town, but he's smokin'."

No way was she having this discussion. "Does Sarge know you're out here? I can't give you the room for free, so I suggest you don't get fired." Tia started back to her candles.

"Oh, he threatens, but he won't do it."

"I wouldn't be too sure. Sarge has never allowed anyone in his kitchen before."

"I know." Piper followed her. "He's told me about a thousand times. But about Jonah—"

"I have four orders to fill before I open shop."

"Come on, Tia. Tell me."

Tia felt the tapers, then lowered and lifted them once more. "This is a delicate process." One she had done so often she could do it comatose. A bachelor of science and a master's degree, and here she was dipping candles.

Piper watched, then surveyed the workshop as she always did, her gaze roving over the shelves of glass bottles with herbs in oils, dried fruits and berries, blocks of wax and bolts of wick. "This is great. You must love what you do."

"I enjoy it. I wouldn't say love."

"Well, what do you love?" Piper peaked her eyebrows like an imp. "A certain rugged lawman?"

Once again it surprised her how freely Piper barged in. They'd known each other what, three weeks? "You've gone from silly to ridiculous."

Piper leaned her palms on the table. "Why? Is he married?"

Tia slid her a dark glance. "Did he look married?"

"Good point."

Tia straightened. "Now I need to work. And you need to get back before Sarge declares you AWOL."

"I'm going." Piper pressed open the back door but called, "To be continued."

"Or not," Tia called after her.

TWO

In the arithmetic of love, one plus one equals everything,
and two minus one equals nothing.
—MIGNON MCLAUGHLIN

Breathing through his mouth, Jonah deposited the plastic-wrapped animals into the back of his Bronco. Department of Wildlife dealt with off-season poaching and protected species. Raccoons were neither, and if he'd left them, coyotes or cougars would have made quick work of them. Lucky the girl had seen them as soon as she had.

He closed the hatch and entered the side of the municipal building that was the police station. They had one interrogation room, one holding cell used only until they had enough staff to transport a detainee, no forensic lab, and the morgue was in the funeral home. Serious felonies went to the county court. Critical evidence, to the state lab. He had no critical evidence. He wasn't even sure he had a crime.

Passing reception and dispatch, he waved to Ruth, whose narrow head and slender shoulders bloomed into doughy arms and bosom, as though someone had mismatched her body parts. He found Adam Moser writing reports in the cubicle he shared with a second scheduled officer. With a force of five officers plus him, at least one position short in his opinion, they juggled twelve-hour shifts with additional hours on call and still had all the night and some day shifts with single coverage.

The top of Moser's head looked like a polished brown river rock rimmed by a dense black moss with flecks of silver. His long brown neck met straight shoulders, crisply uniformed. His handwriting looked typed. With features more Denzel Washington than Tyler Perry, Moser had it all together.

"Hey, Moser." Jonah gave him a nod.

"Morning, Chief."

"You get anything unusual last night?"

Moser pursed his lips. "Pretty much the norm."

"Nothing about kids playing at cult stuff?"

Moser frowned. "No. Why?"

Jonah told him about the raccoons.

"Two raccoons tear each other up, and why is that our concern?" Moser asked in his measured elocution.

"Because they were connected."

"Tied up?"

"No." Jonah had squatted down and inspected the carnage at closer range than he would have liked. "The animals were sewn together."

"Sewn? With what?"

"Some kind of thread. Through skin and muscle."

"How'd they manage that on two live raccoons?"

Jonah shrugged. "Must have knocked them out. Then they woke up and went crazy, tearing themselves apart. I have them in the back of my Bronco if you want to see."

"I'm good." Moser shifted in his chair.

"I'm running them by the vet."

"Clinic's open again?"

"As of last month."

"I gotta get Marlene down for her shots."

Jonah nodded, unsure Moser had quite grasped the implications of the raccoon thing. People who made animals suffer didn't usually stop there.

He rolled down his windows and drove with as much wind in his face as he could manage while approximating the speed limits to the animal hospital at the outskirts of Redford. He had only heard last week that someone new had opened up, and he hoped they'd make a go of it. Not all the local population was as assiduous about pet care as Moser. Even those who didn't go in for torture.

He braked for a car pulling out of the clinic driveway and turned in. He'd be glad to get the rank package out of his vehicle. No receptionist manned the front desk. The vet would be lucky to cover costs without paying another wage.

He touched the bell on the counter, and a blond woman came out of the back room. Early to midthirties. Average height, decent looks. She appeared to have some kind of hip injury that caused an uneven gait, but she gave him a level appraisal.

"Can I help you?"

The name tag on her white coat read DR. LIZ RAINER. "I'm Police Chief Jonah Westfall. I was hoping you could have a look at something, but maybe…"

"Your horse threw a shoe?"

He pulled a smile. "Actually, my Bronco's got tires."

"Is something injured?"

"It's a little past doctoring. And it's…gruesome."

She drew herself up. "I'm assuming we're not talking human."

"No, I have a coroner for those deaths."

"Okay then." She came through the gate. "Show me." She preceded him out to his vehicle.

"You may want to hold your breath. They didn't die fast." He opened up the back, then, giving her a warning glance, tore open the garbage bag. The smell was a force, excrement and gore. He should have pulled the bag out of the car first. But he didn't want her to have to bend to the ground to examine them. "Can you tell me what you see?"

She pressed her lips together, more sadness than repulsion in her eyes. "The damage seems to be to their sides."

"Look closer. Where the fur is shaved. Sorry. If you don't mind."

"Stitching?" She looked up. Her right eye twitched. "Not a natural predator."

He understood the effort it took her to stay calm. "Have you seen much cult activity with animals?"

"Not really."

"But you'd know what to look for?"

"I wouldn't look for stitching."

He nodded. "That's what I thought too. Well, thanks. What do I owe you?"

She shrugged. "Consider it a service, and pass the word that I'm here."

"I told an officer this morning. He'll be by with his pug, Marlene."

—

Back inside, Liz watched the police chief drive away. He'd seemed sensitive and trustworthy beneath his startling good looks. Most people would not get past the surface, but she always looked inside, searching for the best—and the worst. It was inside that mattered, the substance of a person.

"He's nice."

Though quiet as a ghost, Lucy seldom caught her by surprise, their bond so tight she sensed her before hearing her. Liz nodded without looking away from the window. Lucy was never fooled by appearances. The chief had substance.

"Would you like to meet him?" Liz murmured.

"Don't tease."

"Really." She watched the Bronco stop at the street, then pull out. She'd recognized in Chief Westfall an acquaintance with grief, lodged in the faint lines around his eyes, the creases beside his mouth. Maybe he would understand. "I think you could."

"Not like this. No one should see me like this." The pitch of Lucy's voice rose. "And I'm afraid. So afraid."

"You don't have to be." She turned at her soft crying. "It's all right."

"No," Lucy wailed. "How can it be?"

She hated it when Lucy cried, the way it tugged as though the sorrow lodged inside her as well. "Do you trust me?"

Lucy sniffed. "How can I not trust my own sister?"

How indeed? Raw emotion caught her. "You know I won't let anything happen to you."

She waited, but Lucy didn't answer.

—

Jonah drove with all the windows open to the office and left them open in the lot even though he'd recently cautioned Officer Sue Donnelly not to leave her vehicle unsecured. The smell would be deterrent enough for any thief. He went inside, and Ruth put a hand to her nose.

"Not to be rude, Jonah—"

"I know."

"Moser's on the clock. Why don't you go home and shower?"

He had intended to type his report while the details were fresh, but, as with the smell, he doubted they'd fade anytime soon. He turned around and drove home. The shower took the smell out of his skin and hair but didn't help much with the residual in his sinuses. He changed into a spare uniform and went back to the office.

Ruth sighed with relief as he approached, ending with a giggle.

"Yeah, yeah. Next time I'll let you all handle it."

"I must have heard Moser wrong," she called after him. "I thought he said the raccoons were sewn together."

He entered the office without answering. He'd like to keep that quiet for a while and figured there was at least a ten percent chance he could. He filled in the report and filed it in open cases, animal cruelty—the closest classification he could make.

After he brought his computer out of hibernation, he scoured all the local incidents involving animals, widening his region to include not just the county but adjoining counties as well. The incidents he found involved baiting or neglect. Unlicensed or out-of-season hunting. One wrongful butchering. None mentioned joining.

It could be nothing more than a sick prank, and he'd ignore it except for the eerie nature of the deed. Animal cruelty could indicate dangerous pathologies, and in this there had been intent and premeditation. There'd been surgical prep. The person who did this had not merely intended the creatures to fight but to tear their own flesh apart. He would have the thread analyzed and receive results in a month or two.

He looked up when Moser came in.

"Just letting you know I'm going home."

That time already? No wonder his back felt petrified. As chief, he made his own schedule but often worked longer hours than the others. Determining the direction and strategic mission of the department, managing his people, coordinating assets, and allocating resources kept him plenty busy, but he still maintained hands-on interaction with his officers and the people they protected. He stayed abreast of serious crimes and handled many of them himself.

The raccoon thing was just weird enough to warrant his attention before passing it off. And it took his mind off the rest. The day was almost over, and it wouldn't be back for another year. His hands clenched. His nostrils flared. Not now.

He forced his focus back to the research, but there wasn't that much more he could learn, so he locked up and drove slowly through Old Town. The shops were closed up for the night, but he saw lights at the Half Moon. He parked and stared a long moment, then made his way around to the back and rapped his knuckles on the door. He heard shuffling, then her voice.

"Who is it?"

At least she was cautious.

"Me."

"Could you be more specific?"

"Open up, Tia."

She cracked open the door, frowning. "What?"

"Can I talk to you?"

"As Police Chief?"

"Partly."

She pressed her forehead to the door and pulled it open, the epitome of reluctance. A lambent glow from a dozen candles honeyed her mahogany hair and olive skin. Dark brows arched over onyx eyes, reflecting the flames.

He said, "I don't think you should be working past dark."

Her eyes narrowed. "You're giving me a curfew?"

"I just don't think you should stay here after dark and walk home alone."

"Why not?"

Because someone had ceremoniously slaughtered animals on her walking path? "I saw something that concerns me."

"Something…"

He shook his head. "I'd rather not go into it."

"Look, Jonah—"

"I'm just saying don't be out alone right now."

"But you're not saying why." She braced her hands on her hips. Even with her small frame and stature, no one could mistake her strength. "If you won't give me more than your opinion, I can't make an informed decision."

"You could trust my opinion."

She tipped her head back, forking both hands into her lion's mane, and scrutinized him. "You look awful."

"Yeah, well." She knew what day it was. Because he'd kept up a good professional front, no one else had noticed, at least not commented. But this was Tia, who never withheld comment. "I'll walk you home if you're ready."

"I'm doing my accounting."

"You can do it in the daylight."

Again the hands to the hips. "Tell me why you're worried."

"Can't you ever just take advice?" He matched her glare, then backed down. He was probably blowing it out of proportion. Seeing her this morning had kept her too near the surface, a bad idea on any day. A worse one today. "Fine. Lock the door behind me."

"Of course." Just enough barb to make it sting.

He drove home to his cabin tucked away from both the new, sprawling mansions and the little, old Victorians like Tia's. He removed his jacket and weapon belt, locked his sidearm and backup in the gun safe, then opened the collar of his shirt and entered the den. From the corner shelf he took the bottle of Maker's Mark and rubbed its dustless surface.

He ran his thumb down the label, removed the stopper, and slowly passed the throat beneath his nose. The spirits rose up and constricted his nostrils. His taste buds quickened, saliva glands moistening with anticipation. He imagined the fluid in his throat, remembered the heat like it was yesterday.

Today of all days that heat would comfort, fogging the memories that filled his mind in stark relief. He would welcome the fog, deep, deadening. The voice of desire whispered in his ears.

"You do not control me," he whispered back, closed it up, and set it on the shelf.

In the bedroom he undressed and collapsed onto the bed. Almost over. Just a few more hours.

———

With Jonah's uneasiness pricking her nerves, Tia made her way up the wooded path. Had he invented an excuse to see her alone, or was his concern real? He'd offered to walk her home, a troubling thought at the best of times. She jerked a glance over her shoulder when a pine cone fell from a tree, then expelled her breath.

She moved on, annoyed with herself as much as Jonah. She reached the side street and yelped, pressing a hand to her chest when Piper slipped out of the shadows beside her.

"Sorry!" Piper clasped her hands to her chest. "I didn't mean to scare you."

Her own fault for letting Jonah get to her. "What are you doing out here?"

"Going…home."

Tia released her breath. "I thought you were inside already." Rising as early as she did, Piper had been early to bed as well, like the bright-breasted finches that disappeared at sundown and popped up again with the dawn.

"A bunch of us were playing Cranium at Java Cava."

"Oh." Tia climbed the single porch step. "I guess I'm just jumpy."

"Because of the chief?"

Tia stiffened. "What do you mean?"

"I saw him leaving the shop."

Great. She unlocked the house door. "He doesn't think it's smart to be out alone after dark. He was cautioning people." Except, it appeared, Piper's crowd. Had she been personally targeted by whatever he saw? No, he would have told her that. It was his hypervigilance, and it made her crazy.

Piper followed her in. "Did he say what happened?"

"He didn't give me any details, just said we shouldn't be out. Would you like some tea?" She went to the kitchen and dropped several tight knots of jasmine pearls into two mugs, then put the kettle on to boil. She tucked a strand of hair behind her ear. Jonah had seemed genuinely shaken. As he'd stood across from her in the candlelight, she had glimpsed the rumple-haired boy in a trouble-hardened face.

Her first memory of Jonah was at the top of a slide, knees drawn to his chest, the other kids griping from the ladder for him to go already. His eyes had looked enormous until she realized the sockets from his eyebrows to his cheekbones were bruised purple. He'd looked at her and slid to the bottom, then sprang lightly to his feet.

"What happened to your eyes?"

"Mom stomped the brakes too quick. I hit the dashboard."

"Didn't you wear your seat belt?"

He shrugged. *"Why bother?"*

Years later she'd realized what he meant.

She shook herself. He'd delivered his warning, and she had passed it to Piper. She poured the steaming water over the pearls and handed Piper her mug. Lifting her own, she inhaled the exotic fragrance of the gray-green leaf buds unfurling in the cup.

She looked past her reflection on the window to the black night outside and remembered another blacker night. Lord, it had been grim, had tainted so much afterward. No wonder he'd looked so wretched today. Could she not have been kind?

She shook her head. If she gave him anything, showed any weakening, he would use it.

Piper came up beside her, ghostlike in the glass. "Are you all right?"

"Just tired. I guess I shouldn't work so late." She sipped her brew and savored the mellow flavor. She'd leave at a reasonable hour from now on.

"You could have played with us. I wish I'd thought to come get you."

"I'm too competitive for big group games." As a child she had won at a rate that endeared her to no one. "I prefer Parcheesi with a mug of tea and a fire crackling in the fireplace." Purely the luck of the dice.

"What's the scent on the waxed pine cones?" Piper's eyes glittered.

Tia drew a breath, almost smelling it as she said, "Butterscotch."

"Perfect." Piper laughed.

Okay, it was nice having her, even if she pushed and pried. They sat and talked until Piper's yawns grew contagious.

As Tia went up to bed, Jonah's troubled face pursued her. What could have bothered him enough that he felt the need to warn her? She shouldn't have been rude, not this day especially, but she couldn't stop it. She blamed him for so much. And he deserved it.

Three

The only gift is a portion of thyself.
—RALPH WALDO EMERSON

Stifling a yawn, Piper handed an apple turnover to a man with marble-shaped eyeballs. She'd stayed up so late with Tia, sleeping had felt like blinking, but for the first time they'd been more than landlord and guest, spinning threads of friendship with their words.

"They're just out of the oven," she cautioned, "so the filling might be hot."

Sarge usually served the customers, but a spasm had seized his back, and he'd gone to sit in the warm kitchen. When she first started working for him, he had seemed plain mean, but now she knew it was pain that made him snap, like a dog bruised in places invisible under the fur.

She checked her watch. Two minutes left on the bear claws. She'd get back there before Sarge even thought of bending to remove the sheet from the lower oven.

"Just one second," she told the woman coming in the door, then ducked into the kitchen. The timer had begun to shrill, but Sarge didn't go for it. He lay writhing on the floor.

Piper rushed to his side. "Sergeant Beaker? Sarge?"

He was gasping for words. She lunged for the phone on the kitchen wall and dialed. "This is Piper at the bakery. Sarge is in trouble."

After the emergency dispatcher had taken her information, she hurried back to his side. Yes, she had called him an evil elf, sent withering looks through the wall after his tirades, but that was before. The timer was still shrilling. She jumped up and removed the bear claws, then knelt again and took his hand between hers. "Hold on, Sarge. Help is coming."

His fingers felt like chilled carrots. Piper pressed the back of her free hand to his flushed cheek that felt as hot as hers got leaning over the oven door. He seemed to be trying to order her around, but she couldn't catch a word.

In minutes, Chief Westfall walked through the door, smelling woodsy and looking rugged and more together than when she'd first seen him. "Ambulance is on the way." He crouched down and took the old man's other hand. "Hey, Sarge. Hanging in there?"

Sarge jammed a finger toward her. "You! You interfering—"

Chief Westfall looked up from his crouch. "Go on out front. I'll stay with him."

With one look back at Sarge's face, she carried the tray of bear claws to the case. The shop had been hit by a people wave. *Oh, boy.* She pulled off the oven mitts. "I have no idea who's first."

Two people spoke their orders at once, and a third said, "Where's Sarge?"

"Sarge is…not doing too well." A buzz passed through the crowd as she wrapped a lemon scone and a raisin bun and handed one to each of the two who had ordered together. She scooted to the end of the counter and rang them up.

Good thing Sarge had made her learn the register, but this crowd would wipe out the case, and she wasn't in the kitchen baking replacements or the lunch rolls. How had Sarge done it before she came?

Her head spun with all the demands as people realized they'd get whatever was left if they didn't order first. She threw up her hands. "Make a line. If you don't get what you want today, write it down." She dumped the basket where people could leave their business cards to win a freebie. "Put your requests in here. They'll be half price tomorrow."

She could bake according to the requests. People who didn't come in every day might come twice in a row for a half-price offer. As far as she knew, Sarge had never done half price on anything except the day-old rack, and there usually wasn't much left on that. He might howl if he knew, but the ambulance had arrived, and she'd keep it to herself until he was strong enough to holler without hurting himself.

Tia startled as the ambulance stopped outside the bakery. She had just reached her back door but detoured to Sarge's, praying Piper had not injured herself with a mixer or suffered a burn or cut. She pushed open the kitchen door. Piper was nowhere in sight. Instead she saw Sarge on the floor, with Jonah supporting his head as the EMTs came through from the front.

"What happened?"

Jonah levered himself up, giving them room to work. "Piper called in the emergency. I don't know if he fell or what."

"She's okay?"

"A little shaky. I sent her up front to handle the rush. You know how Sarge is."

From years of experience. He could hardly force words out, yet he was still arguing, purple-faced, with the emergency team. Jonah had removed Piper from the line of fire, and he squatted back down, speaking softly to Sarge, again diverting the tirade.

Tia slipped back to her shop and admitted Mary Carson, who had asked to drop in early to pick up her order. Tia had the tapers wrapped and ready, but Mary would still browse. She always did.

"Is it Sarge?"

Tia nodded, unsure why that hadn't been her first thought. "He's not happy with the fuss."

"Old Sarge will cuss Death right back where it came from." Mary's eyelids reddened. "My Bob was too polite to put up a fight."

Tia touched her arm.

Mary's silver head trembled with palsy. Of the two, Bob had seemed like the strong one, tan and robust, still hiking at seventy-seven while inside his brain a time bomb ticked. Blinking back the tears, Mary ran her finger over the gold aspen leaves on a scarlet, triple-wick pillar candle just inside the door. "My, this is beautiful. You always had an artistic side." Mary was one teacher who hadn't bought into her parents' warnings. She'd let her students prove themselves, one way or another. "This would perk up my living room, give it some life."

"And accent your fainting couch."

"Scarlet with gold threads." She raised her eyebrows. "Did you design it to entice me?"

Tia laughed. "Now there's an idea. Target my designs to my friends' décor. Wish I'd thought of that, but I'm afraid they just happen."

"Well, I'll take it before anyone else does. Kate Maitlan has similar colors."

Tia moved behind the counter where the cubbies were stuffed with tissue and string. "You have a base for it?"

"Oh." Mary snapped her purse. "No, I hadn't thought. I was picturing it across from the planter, so of course it needs a holder." She glanced around the shop.. "Well, I'll have to pick one, won't I?"

Tia carried the six-pound candle around the shop, showing it on the different stands. As they moved to a natural stone pillar near the wall, a stranger came in. Though she hadn't locked the door behind Mary, the business hours were clearly posted.

The man stood well over six feet, his shoulders rounded to minimize that, as with many overly tall people. His brown hair cut straight in line with his earlobes made him look comical. But the white pants, pressed to a crease that could cut paper, and slick blue Windbreaker seemed good quality, and his brilliant white tennis shoes made a squeaky sound on the tile floor, as though they hadn't been worn twice.

"Go ahead," Mary whispered. "He must be lost."

Tia handed her the candle and approached the man, who smelled of hand sanitizer. "Can I help you?"

"No." He spoke crisply. "I don't need help."

"Okay. Just ask if you have questions."

"No questions." He put a shelf between them as though he could hide like the elephant in the cherry tree.

"Okey-dokey," she said mostly to herself and returned to Mary, who raised an eyebrow when the odd customer took a tissue from his pocket to lift and inspect a luminous, melon green ball candle.

"Lovely, isn't it?" Mary addressed him, the former schoolteacher coming out.

He peered over the top of the incandescent ball, looking for all the world like a sea lion who might balance it on his nose.

"She makes all the candles by hand," Mary continued. "You can even see her fingerprints."

His head jerked. "Do you know how many germs are transferred by a single fingerprint?"

"No," Mary said dryly. "How many?"

Tia bit her lip.

Without answering, he set the candle back onto the shelf, held the tissue like a dead rodent, and searched for a trash can.

"Allow me." Tia whisked it out of his hand and deposited it into the bin under the counter. "I doubt you'll find a candle without a fingerprint, except…" She turned. "Maybe the tapers. They're dipped, not formed, molded, or decorated, though I can't say who's touched them since I hung them."

He pulled out another tissue and went to inspect the tapers, actually selecting a beeswax couplet. He plucked them off the peg by the connected wick and dangled them over the counter as she rang up the sale.

"Would you like me to wrap them?"

"No." He pulled out his wallet and retrieved a bill with the long fingernails of his overlarge hand.

"Here you go." She deposited his change into the pouch he opened to receive it and thanked him.

He ducked when the bell over the door announced his exit, then moved away from the shop as though someone might have seen him. Tia narrowed her eyes, pensive.

"What an odd man." Mary set a wrought-iron stand beside the counter. "Imagine being afraid of fingerprints."

"He probably has no control of it." A number of disorders she'd studied manifested irrational fears. And at a time when people kept looking for the next pandemic, avoiding germs wasn't necessarily irrational.

She carried Mary's purchases to the Toyota RAV4 parked in front of the shop. A few steps away, the EMTs were loading Sarge into the ambulance.

Mary shuddered. "It reminds me of Bob."

"I'm sorry."

"It's the suddenness. One minute things are one way, and the next everything is changed."

Tia looked at Jonah, standing with his back toward her, hands at his hips. "I can imagine." She turned away, set the paper-wrapped stand in the back, and closed the hatch. "Is Magna there to help you unload?"

Mary nodded. "I'm stopping by the cemetery first."

"Tell Bob we all miss him."

Mary smiled, tearful again. "It'll go to his head."

Tia looked up and caught Jonah watching. She hesitated, then approached as the driver closed the ambulance doors and climbed into the cab.

"How is he?"

"Too ornery to know what's really going on. I'll check in with him and let you know, unless…"

"That's fine. I'd appreciate it." Sarge had been her business neighbor all the years she'd run the shop, but she had no personal relationship with him. He didn't think much of her, though he'd adored her mother. Actually, that explained it.

He thought the world of Jonah. Which just went to show. She turned and went back to her shop.

———

Jonah jammed his hands into his pockets and headed for the office. He didn't think Sarge was in critical condition, but worry gnawed. The old guy had no one at home to look after him and didn't look after himself. It was only a matter of time before this or something else happened again. But how to tell a man like Sarge he can't take care of himself?

Ruth looked up, her pink nylon tank top accentuating the bulge where her arms expanded. "Nancy Barry wants to make a complaint against Hank Dale. She's having her hair permed, then she'll be back."

"Must be serious."

Ruth giggled. Though in her forties, Ruth had the rosy sort of face that made a giggle work.

"Anything else?"

"Stolen mailbox. Someone replaced it with an old shoe. If this was *CSI*, we'd collect DNA and nail the fool."

"It would only prove who'd worn the shoe, not how it got there or who took the mailbox."

Ruth eyed him. "That's why you're the chief. That rapier mind."

"Flattery will get you everywhere. Anything else?"

"I'm worried about Sue. That husband—"

"Okay, thanks." Sometimes Ruth's gossip yielded valuable information, but Sue was a fellow officer. Sam would become police business when and if they proved he'd committed a crime. The rest was up to them. "I'll be in my office." He had a slew of paperwork.

Hours later, he closed out of the spreadsheet and chewed his pencil. The incident with the raccoons still bothered him. He'd searched every site he could find on rites involving animals. Sickening reading, but he'd not found one instance of animals being sewn together. There had to be significance to that methodology.

He spit a wood fragment and stared at the chewed pencil, memory washing over him of Miss Matthews shaking her head. *"You must be part woodchuck, Jonah."* The other kids had laughed, but he didn't care because her dimples had peeked out when she said it, and he'd needed every smile he got.

"Boy! When I find you..." Jonah pressed his eyes shut, seeing the dark shed, smelling the dust and grease and musty mouse scat. Small enough to fit into the hollows between the junk, he had faced the black widows more readily than the fist that held the belt. His only hope had been to hide longer than the meanness. Still and silent in the dark, he had thought about things like Miss Matthews's dimples.

———

Exhausted, Piper collapsed on a chair in Tia's workshop, in the back room of her store. She pulled the band off her ponytail, and groaned. "How did Sarge do it?"

Tia looked up from the table where she'd been drawing designs. "Have you been at the bakery this whole time?"

"Well, I closed at two like always, but I noticed everything was looking dingy, especially the front, so I scrubbed it down, walls, windows, floorboards, tables, chairs."

"Hmm." Tia closed her sketch pad. "Stress cleaning?"

"I guess I was worried." She let the hair hang between her fingers.

"Sarge is a tough old bird."

"He didn't look tough curled up on the floor." She could still see him writhing. "He made me go out front, but I didn't know how bad the pain was or I wouldn't have left him alone."

"Sarge doesn't allow insubordination."

"But I should have realized…"

"You really couldn't have. Sarge would rather die than admit he needs help."

Piper sighed. "I still don't know if I did the right thing. He was spitting nails."

"I saw."

Piper raised her brows.

"You were out front."

"At least it's over."

She had fumbled her way through the morning rush, baked frantically, and made it through the substantial lunch crowd. Sarge had not told her what to do with the money, and she didn't know the combination to the safe, so she'd stuck the zippered transfer bag in the lower oven and locked the shop. Yeah, it was over. "Until tomorrow." She groaned.

"Shh."

She felt Tia's hand come over her eyes.

"Keep them closed."

The snick of a match left an acrid smell. The air moved when Tia brushed the smoke away and another scent took over.

After a few moments, she said, "Now, breathe."

Piper drew a slow breath in through her nose. The new aroma

smelled soft and mysterious, like a dream she could not quite recall. "That's nice."

"It's called Peace." Tia's cool fingertips pressed into her temples and rubbed, her fingers spreading out, making small circles over the sides of her head.

Piper surrendered her scalp into their care, murmuring, "Peace."

"It's from my Sacred Scents collection." Tia's thumbs moved to the base of her skull. "The insert reads: 'Come to Me, all who are weary and heavy-laden, and I will give you rest.'"

"I like that. How'd you come up with it?"

She could hear the smile. "Jesus said it."

"Like, two thousand years ago?"

"Go figure."

Tia was teasing, but Piper sank deeper into the ministration. *Come to me, you who are weary.* Had it really been so bad? A little rushing back and forth, some rude and disgruntled customers. But she'd managed. Sarge had gotten help, and he'd only yelled at her once. "Can I be you when I grow up?"

"Better to be you, sweetie."

Tia's tone was soft and warm but hinted at sadness.

"The chief sure helped. Without him, I'd have panicked. You could have heard my heartbeat across the street. Then he came in and, I don't know, it felt like everything would be all right." He'd soothed her then, just as Tia's massage soothed her now. "He was really good."

"I bet." Tia didn't hide the edge.

Piper slid a glance upward. "What happened with you and Jonah Westfall?"

Tia's hands slipped away, and Piper regretted the question. Most people wanted to share. Tia was like a mirror reflecting conversation back to others. She listened in a way that made it all about you.

But this was about Tia, and it felt important. "Come on, tell me."

Tia rested her palms on the chair. "He broke my sister's heart."

"Your sister?" She could have sworn it was more personal than that. "Are you close?"

Tia sighed. "We were."

Yet until now she hadn't seen or heard a word about a sister. "Where is she?"

"She moved to Arizona."

"Because of Jonah?"

"Sort of. She got married."

"Then she couldn't have been too heartbroken."

"Ever heard of rebound?"

Piper scratched her cheek, peeling away a shard of caked flour. "Where's the rest of your family?"

"They're all there. Reba had a difficult pregnancy, and my parents went down to help out."

"You didn't?"

"Mom asked me to watch the shop."

"The Half Moon?"

Tia nodded.

"I thought it was yours."

"It basically is."

"How long has she been gone?"

"Nine years."

"Nine years? Did it occur to you she might not be coming back?"

"No, Piper. It never entered my mind." Her tone bit.

"Right. Sorry. It's just a long time to mind someone else's business." She'd obviously hit a nerve, and there was more to it than Tia was saying.

"After the first grandchild, there was the next and then a third."

That could explain the sadness that sometimes crept in. Had they all made a new life and left her behind? Maybe she hadn't wanted to go. "You miss them?"

Tia hesitated. "Yes."

Four

The person who tries to live alone will not succeed as a human being. His heart withers if it does not answer another heart. His mind shrinks away if he hears only the echoes of his own thoughts and finds no other inspiration.

—PEARL S. BUCK

Tia sank onto the chair Piper had vacated. She didn't feel bad for not going out to eat with her. The times they had gone, guys had vied for Piper's attention and even the privilege of paying. Her beauty and high spirits strummed a chord that had the male population humming. Tia half smiled. Only six years between them, but it felt like ages.

She pressed her palms to her eyes, thankful the discussion had ended before she had to cut it off. She had no intention of wallowing. Truth was, she didn't even know how to tell it anymore without sounding pathetic. When was she going to live her own life? How had she forfeited the right? Or maybe she'd never possessed it.

Her parents had borne one perfect child; what did they need with an inferior model? Her colicky, strong-willed nature had acted like a repellent. Her smart mouth had reflected a smart mind, if anyone had cared to notice. Her energy and spirit needed channeling, not crushing.

Her parents had made no effort to hide their feelings from her teachers, her friends and their parents. Here's what you can expect from *that* child. Reba had tried to make up for the glaring discrepancy in affection by buying her lip gloss and trinkets. She adored Reba for trying.

Her cell phone rang, the tone designated for the number on her fliers. She picked it up. "Hopeline."

"Yeah, um." The caller sniffled. "Do you, like, listen and tell me what to do?"

"I listen and pray, and together we consider your possibilities."

The voice was young. "Well. It's my friend. My used-to-be best friend…"

This took her back to Rachel Muerrisey, who through some faux pas had lost her standing at the top of the order. *"What do I do? You're used to no one liking you. I don't know what to do without friends."*

Tia had shaken off the barb with a toss of her head. *"Pretend you're me, a wild pirate child more fleet of foot and deft of hand than any sailor who scaled the masts. You need no one, but seeing your fearsome, spirited ways, they will clamor back to you, seeking your favor."*

It had worked, and in the ruthless way of children, Rachel had no further need of Tia Manning.

Closing her eyes, she emptied herself now and listened, confident that her words would give this caller comfort and courage, while in the back of her mind a voice cried hypocrite. She gave callers hope, helped them forgive others and themselves, yet she could not free herself. No— would not.

Jonah roughed up his hair and stood. His knees felt creaky from sitting so long, but he'd been able to concentrate without being called out more than a handful of times. He checked his watch. Officer Donnelly was late. Jonah frowned. He didn't run things with a heavy hand but expected punctuality. Newly, McCarthy, and even the rookie, Beatty, were fairly reliable. Moser ran like a clock, but Sue…

She rushed in, snapping on her weapon belt. "Sorry. Sorry, Jonah. I had to get Eli to his grandma's."

"Where's Sam?"

"He had a conflict."

Normally he'd let it go at that, but Ruth's comment had stuck. "Of the bender sort?"

She looked up, startled, then down. "He's not drunk."

"Pot? Blow?"

She shrugged.

"Meth?"

"I don't know, Jonah."

"Where's he getting it?"

"He won't say. Obviously." She straightened her shirt. "Anyway, I'm here."

"Need a few minutes to get yourself together?"

"No." She smoothed her hands over her short brown hair and fixed him with her quick, sparrow eyes. "Just fill me in."

She looked a little green by the time he'd finished, though the bulge in her stomach might account for that. He wondered how long she would wait to tell him. Maternity leave would stretch her finances, especially if Sam was using—unless of course he was producing his own.

Time to let the raccoons go. He had a string of petty burglaries and an encroaching drug situation that could be related. The worst used to be marijuana possession. Less than an ounce kept it local; more went to the county. Lately worse substances had been creeping in.

Annexing the Pine Crest development of mansions, golf courses, shops, and amenities east along Kicking Horse Creek—not to mention the soon-to-open ski resort—would raise the population and more than triple the average income if it went through. He hoped, as the council had opined, that the changes would all be for the good. But rising revenues did not guarantee an increase in his staff or budget. All depended on who grabbed first and held on hardest.

He went to the school, used his key to enter the weight room, pumped iron to the point of fatigue, then showered and let himself out. All the officers had this benefit, a thank-you for the work they did keeping the combination elementary, middle, and high school as safe as any in the state. So far they didn't have to work too hard, but he'd glimpsed the first stirrings of gang activity and would not allow it a foothold.

From the early childhood safety programs to middle-school character training and gang awareness courses, he would fight for them. He and his officers served as resources to high-school students and officials in ways he had to believe were making a difference. If he encountered a kid presenting the evidence of abuse that he had, he would not look the other way, no matter who the parents were.

Things happened despite his vigilance, but he did his best. He might have gone into the job for the wrong reasons, but he was made for it. Even off duty, he could be reached at all times, and everyone knew it. It lent him an aura of omniscience if not omnipotence. A strong presence discouraged mischief, true in spite of the man he'd learned it from.

A pride of young males mouthed off to one another on a street corner as he approached, then demonstrated exaggerated bonhomie when he drew abreast. Bunch of goons. He raised a hand, and three of them waved. A glance in his rearview caught one of them with a one-finger salute. He could make it an issue, but the kid was only trying to gain stature with the group, not easy at five feet six with a geeky haircut and a mouthful of braces.

Up ahead, a car rolled past the stop sign, then jerked to a stop when the driver saw his Bronco. Jonah shot him a glance as he passed. The scare of almost getting caught should make the guy respect intersections for a week or two. Redford had only one light, the rest four-way stops. Most people treated the signs like neighbors to nod at.

He normally ate at home, but tonight he pulled into the back parking lot at Bailey's Diner. Breathing the exhaust of charred grease and beef juices, he walked around to the front. Behind the see-through, Richie Bailey looked up from scraping the grill and acknowledged him with a chin bob. Jonah raised a hand, then took a seat at a red Naugahyde booth.

Once upon a time, Richie Bailey had tormented him regularly. Two incarcerations for assault cured his bullying, but you never knew what simmered underneath. Did he take it out on animals in the woods? He looked around the room. Had someone else in there tortured those two raccoons? What did that kind of crazy look like?

Libby Gabaroni slapped down a napkin roll and gave him a grin, no doubt recalling their wrangling behind the high-school gym. Her bouncy bust had amazed him then. Now she took jigglers to a whole new realm.

Jonah opened the menu and chose the burger that topped the list, a half-pound beef patty with pickles, onion, and mustard—no ketchup, they knew. He sipped the icy Coke she brought a few minutes later and tuned in to the conversations around him. The booths were low and good for eavesdropping, not that people hushed up around him anyway, not the way a room had gone silent when the former police chief walked in— people sitting a little straighter, clearing their throats as though they could scrape out anything he might not want to hear.

People nodded and waved, but no one slid in to chat. Jonah swallowed the last of his burger and wiped his mouth. Libby had kept him supplied with refills, but he put a hand over his glass and asked for the check. She had it ready in her pocket, and he handed over the total plus tip.

She looked at the money in her hand. "You want change?"

"It's yours."

She blushed. "No need to hurry out, you know."

He nodded but got up as soon as she had cleared the way. Hanging around would send her a message he didn't want to send.

"Chief."

He turned at the tug on his sleeve.

Merv Brothers pressed a key into his palm. "This'll get you into the you-know-what. You take a look, and tell me there isn't something funny going on."

"How'd you get the key?"

Merv raised pale blue eyes in his whisker-studded, leathery face. "Gave it to me himself, long time ago, when we were speakin'." He ran a hand over his wispy hair. "You watch yourself going in. He says it's wired to blow. Might be for alls I know."

"He told you the shed is wired?"

"He could be lyin'."

"I'd still need a warrant to look without permission. But I'll hold on to this." If Tom Caldwell had booby-trapped the shed between their properties, he didn't want Merv deciding to sneak in himself. "I'll go by and talk to him."

Merv shook his head. "Won't do a spit of good. He'll jump your throat like a junkyard dog sayin' what's his business is none of yours."

"Well, I have to follow protocol." He pocketed the key. "But I'll look into it." He'd made it to the door with Merv still at his elbow.

"Take my word for it. You oughta have you a look without getting his back up."

"I'll do my best." He passed through the door and left Merv rubbing his jaw. He avoided neighbor disputes as much as he could. Open that door and he'd have a continuous stream of whiners. In this case Merv had shared some troubling observations, and it wouldn't hurt to check it out, but not tonight.

Since the officers on duty had the patrol cars, Jonah took his Bronco down the mountain. He had shampooed the upholstery, cutting the stink in half, but only time would fully eradicate it. The medical center that served the surrounding region was about a fifty-minute drive away, so there was no chance he'd hold his breath. Helicopter could make it in twenty, but most people requiring that lift were taken farther down to a larger, better-equipped hospital. It was good Sarge remained at Tri-County—though the staff might disagree. His hollering carried all the way down the hall.

When would Sarge stop needing to give the orders? Jonah stepped into the room. The corners of the old man's lips were white with spit as he reprimanded the nurse who depressed the syringe into his IV. She said nothing, but the tight line of her mouth gave her away.

"Hey, Sarge." Jonah said. "Why're you giving the nurse a hard time?"

She looked up with a little hitch. Sometimes it was about the uniform, but he'd changed clothes before coming. Her cheeks flushed. "Are you a relative?" She meant, *Could you possibly be related to this mean, cantankerous, old snake?*

"Just friends."

An even greater shock. Familial duty she could understand, but voluntary friendship? The nurse gathered the sterile wrappers and discarded the needle. "That should calm you down, Mr. Beaker."

"Sergeant," he growled. "It's Sergeant Beaker." But whatever she'd laced his IV with had softened his fangs.

"It will also help with the spasms." She cast Jonah a smile, the sway of her slim hips in pastel scrubs just enough to show she wasn't all work. "Stay as long as you like, but he'll get dozy."

Jonah nodded and took the seat beside Sarge.

He snarled. "What are you gawping at?"

"One stubborn old goat."

Sarge raised his hands. "I'd like to get these around her little neck."

"The nurse?"

"Not the nurse. That one who tricked me into hiring her."

Jonah crossed his arms. "Why would you want to strangle Piper?"

"For sending me here when it was nothing more than—"

"Sarge, let them decide."

"And just what do you think they can do for me?"

Good point. The way Sarge was twisted up, all sorts of things could be pinched and impinged. He didn't suppose they could put a knee to his back and pull him up straight. "If it's bad enough to lay you out, it's time to have it checked."

"I'm seventy-four years old. I'll decide when I need it checked."

"This spasm had you speechless. We thought you'd had a stroke. Probably scared Piper to death, not hearing you shout."

Sarge tried not to smile, which didn't improve the shape of his mouth. "Who's going to manage the store while I'm lying here?"

"Piper handled things today."

"Hah." Sarge glowered.

"Not as efficiently as two of you together, but people will understand."

"They'll understand me right out of business."

"Now Sarge."

The old man jammed a finger at him. "She serve anything new?"

"What?"

"Try to push her creations on my customers?"

Jonah shrugged. "I think she just tried to keep up. You're lucky to have her."

"Lucky!" Sarge honked through his nose, but his eyes were drooping. "Say that again, and I'll…buzz my pretty nurse to…throw you out."

Jonah laughed. "I can think of worse things."

"I'll bet you can."

"You should take advantage of a little downtime. When's the last time you took leave?"

Sergeant Beaker didn't answer. By the snore that resonated through his commodious nose, the Sarge was at ease. Jonah watched him. He didn't know what could be done for the man. Maybe nothing. But peaceful sleep and relief from pain were sometimes as good as it got.

He flipped through a magazine for the better part of an hour to see if Sarge came to, then went out. Sarge's nurse—Lauren on the name tag—was leaning against a wall, talking with another whose thin, pale ponytail accentuated a broad, pinkish face. The first turned smoky gray eyes on him, her light brown hair clipped back haphazardly.

He paused in passing. "Sarge is…used to being in charge."

She gave her long lashes a slow blink. "It's the pain. He let it go too long."

"He won't admit that."

"He's not the first. Men that age are so reluctant to admit they need help. It's like a badge of honor or something." A hint of dimples indented her cheeks. "Did you come far to see him?"

"Down from Redford."

"You must know him well."

"I do." Sarge had slipped him rolls and raisin buns when it was obvious he'd gone hungry. Not because his family had no means, but as another form of discipline—the sober form that masqueraded as character development but was just as mean as beating.

She slid her hands into her pockets. "I'm taking my break. Want to fill me in over coffee?"

He hesitated, then shrugged. "Sure."

As they moved down the hall to the break room, he described Sarge's military service, then his opening the bakery and the years he'd served the town fresh bread and pastries. "He's a master of efficiency, and anything that curtails him is unbearable."

"That helps to know. Thanks." She handed him a cup of coffee and poured one for herself.

"He doesn't mean half the things he says."

"Oh, he means them." She looked pointedly over the Styrofoam brim of her cup.

Jonah surrendered the point.

"So what do you do?"

"I'm chief of police in Redford."

"You're not."

He rocked back in the plastic break-room chair and cocked his head.

"Sorry. You just don't look like a cop."

"Yeah, well. Sometimes I wear the uniform." Might help if he didn't look like central casting's rogue hero.

She looked at his hands. "Not married?"

"No." He'd already noticed her naked fingers.

"Divorced?"

He hesitated. "A broken engagement. Years ago. I'm not relationship material."

"Says who?"

"Anyone in a position to know."

"What a waste."

A corner of his mouth tugged at her boldness. She sat back, finger-ing her cup. Perhaps, being a caregiver, she had an even stronger urge than most women to fix people. But it wasn't the broken engagement that made him unfixable.

He pushed up from the chair. "Thanks for the coffee. And for look-ing after Sarge."

She didn't get up, just watched him leave the room. The drive back was long and cool, accompanied by classic rock and troubled thoughts.

In her room of the small house connected to the animal hospital, Liz woke with a jolt. Nightmare sweat coated her chest like VapoRub. Her left side throbbed, strange since she had no feeling there at all. Two ailing dogs whined from their kennels, but that hadn't awakened her. She turned her head on the pillow. "Luce?"

"Don't talk to me. I'm sleeping."

Liz turned back and closed her eyes but did not slip like Lucy into sleep. She'd always been the one who cried to be held, cried to be fed. A fighter, Daddy called her. *"Lizzie has spunk enough for both of them combined."*

She didn't feel spunky. She was tired. She wanted to sleep, but she got up and padded to the table, turned on the lamp.

"Unh. Do you have to?" Lucy moaned.

"It's for you, you know."

Lucy sighed. "But it's useless."

"No, it's not. And I won't give up until I find a way."

She sat down at the desk with the three-inch textbook lying open, a stack of note cards beside it, and applied herself to the work until the nightmare dread diminished, leaving her hollow as a pithy reed. Behind her Lucy slept, and Liz didn't begrudge her. She needed it.

Liz rubbed her eyes and turned off the lamp. Dawn was coming in the window, and pets needed tending.

Five

What greater thing is there for two human souls than to feel
that they are joined…to strengthen each other…to be at one
with each other in silent unspeakable memories.
—GEORGE ELIOT

Piper did not believe in God, benevolence being bestowed on her clan
by courts and insurance companies. But when she saw the police
chief duck into the small, stone church five minutes past the time
posted on a greeting board, she walked in behind him.

Dressed in jeans and a black crew-neck shirt, he took a seat in the otherwise empty back pew with enough space on the end for her to slip in too.
She smiled, and his eyes creased in response. They were lined with thick
lashes that lightened at the ends, like his hair, dark underneath lighter
hanks that had to be a natural contrast. She couldn't see him in a salon
getting highlights.

He wasn't a pretty boy. More like the Marlboro Man with a streak of
Wolverine. He looked like trouble, and he looked like salvation. Like a
man who could run cold and could run hot, but never just warm. His
scent was clean and woodsy. She hadn't seen him in over a week, but now
she'd have the whole service to take him in and wonder what he could
have done to upset Tia. The sister thing couldn't be the whole story. People broke up all the time. It didn't make them hateful.

She almost gasped out loud when he reached out and clasped her
hand. Then she realized someone at the microphone had invited them all
to join hands with their brothers and sisters in Christ. Brother and sister
wasn't where her mind had gone. Would she be condemned by these
church people if they felt her pulse?

Someone at the front read a statement. "We are members of the same
body, different gifts, but the same Spirit. If we tug and strive against each

other, we cause injury and disunity. But if we hold tight, bearing each other up, we grow strong, resilient, united. Let us prepare to celebrate this great mystery as one body, one spirit in Christ."

He let go, and belatedly Piper drew her hand back. The service that followed involved standing and sitting and kneeling on the part of the long benches that folded down. Jonah lowered it each time for both of them, and that simple act shot right inside her. Kneeling next to him was the most spiritual thing she'd ever done.

She knew enough not to go forward to the altar. The ceremony had gotten mysterious and solemn, and she didn't want to violate something sacred. But Jonah slipped past her to follow in line to the front where he took what they handed him, then nodded to a golden goblet. He surprised her by not coming back to his seat like the others but continuing straight out the door.

She was on her feet and out almost as quickly as the chief. "How come you cut out early?"

He half turned. "What?"

"You came late and left before it was done."

He glanced at the doors, then back to her. "Are you going to report me?"

She laughed. "Not me."

"Good." He turned back toward the parking lot.

"I've got fig and pine-nut sticky rolls ready to bake. Would you like one fresh out of the oven?"

"Better not." He kept walking.

"Come on. Try something new."

He shook his head. "Sarge will ask, and it's better if I don't know what you're up to." He reached his Bronco and pressed the remote.

Sarge had been out over a week, but she didn't believe for a minute he'd given up control. "You can tell him how much you like it."

"I don't think so."

"Come on. You're not on duty."

"How do you know?"

"It's Sunday. The top guy doesn't work Sunday."

"Another time maybe." His gaze flicked past to the plainer church across the parking lot.

Tia had just emerged. In the sunlight her hair looked molten, attracting an iridescent green hummingbird that hovered above her head for a moment, then shrilled away seeking nectar-bearing wildflowers.

Tia walked down the steps with Eva Gladden, who sold real estate and ordered raisin buns for the whole office on Fridays. They parted with a hug, and Piper turned back to see the chief climbing into his Bronco just as Tia reached her.

"Hey." Tia had a hug for her too. "I didn't expect to see you up early on your day off."

Piper shrugged. "I prepped a few things at the bakery. Want to try my fig and pine-nut sticky rolls?"

"You're opening today?"

"Experimentally. To help Sarge with the medical bills." She'd seen the figures her folks plugged in for hospital costs. "While he's out I want to try as many different things as possible so I know which ones are popular enough to suggest when he gets back."

"Sweetie, Sarge is not going to sell anything new. He's not just set in his ways; he's set in stone."

"I can try." Walking together toward the bakery, she saw Chief Westfall pull up to the stoplight. "Hold on." She couldn't resist one more try. She jogged over and tapped his passenger side window.

He cocked his head, then depressed the window button.

"Tia's brave enough to try my sticky rolls. Why don't you join—"

The driver behind him tapped his horn.

"Gotta go."

Piper stepped back, irritated. The light had changed like a second ago. Her irritation grew when she saw the honking driver was auto sales manager Robert Betters. If ever a name matched a person, it was full-of-himself Bob Betters. He'd hit on her twice even though he had to be as old as, well, the chief. He raised his chunky fingers up from the wheel in a cool-guy wave as he drove by. She could think of a use for the gold chain on his neck.

"Come on." Tia hooked her arm and marched her off.

They met Mary Carson on the street, and Tia invited her in to purchase the sticky rolls, which turned out better than she'd hoped—high altitude schmaltitude.

"I must say, my dear, you have a knack for the unusual."

Piper beamed at the older woman. "I could make a new creation every day and never exhaust the possibilities."

The timer sounded, and she hurried back to the kitchen for her other experimental special. Mitted, she pulled the spinach, goat cheese, and kalamata olive rolls from the oven as yeasty heat waves exfoliated her cheeks. She placed them on a tray and carried them to the front case as a great big guy with a Lego-man haircut walked in. "Can I help you?"

"If you wash your hands."

She looked down, thinking she'd missed a strip of spinach or blob of cheese, then held up pristine fingers for him to see. "They're clean."

"That would be discernable if germs were a million times bigger than they are."

Oh. A germaphobe. She glanced at Tia and Mary Carson, who were watching him and murmuring. Piper turned to the counter along the wall and slipped on a plastic glove, pulled a square of parchment from the box in the case, and held it ready. "Okay?"

Satisfied by her double line of defense, he looked at the tray. His nostrils pinched in as he sniffed. "What is that smell?"

"Spinach, goat cheese, and kalamata rolls straight from the oven."

He looked at the board, and faster than anyone could have read it declared, "That's not on the list."

"Nope." She hadn't dared change the board. "They're the same price as the cheddar rolls." With the more expensive ingredients, she would have to charge more if she got to sell them for real. "I bought the goat cheese fresh this morning from a local source. She's been raising goats and churning cheese for fourteen years."

"Then it's not regulated." The big fella crossed his arms.

"On the other hand, it hasn't passed from farm to packaging to supermarket. Plus, it's been baked."

He frowned. "How long?"

"Long enough to give the roll a golden crust and cheesy, chewy inside." She pulled one from the case, laid it on the parchment, and cut it into bite-sized pieces.

As she set it up on the sample plate, Bob Betters swaggered through the door with a hapless guy who looked like an overgrown baby with downy duckling hair and pudgy cheeks. Bob puffed out his chest. "Isn't she everything I said she was?"

She ignored them as her customer took a sample and chewed slowly. He had a pretty good poker face.

"What do you think?"

"Too much kalamata. The spinach is stringy."

Her spirits sank. "What about the cheese?"

"The cheese is interesting."

Interesting was good. She could work with that. "Would you skip the spinach or chop it finer?"

"Finer. And fewer olives."

Bob's head bobbled back and forth between them.

"Would you rather have the last fig and pine-nut sticky roll?"

The man eyed the two choices, then nodded. With her plastic-wrapped hand and a fresh parchment square, she procured the treat, knowing Bob would have chosen the sweet over the savory. After ringing up the sale, she turned to Bob and his companion, irked all over again that he had cut her conversation with the chief short.

"Can I get you something?"

"I'll take the baker." Bob chortled.

"Oh, that's original."

"One date. I will amaze you."

She looked at his glossy face and plastic-looking teeth. Every hair on his head in its place. "I don't think so."

His companion laughed uncomfortably.

"You haven't taken a test drive." He actually went *vroom-vroom*.

She tried not to gag. "Do you want a goat-cheese kalamata roll?"

"If I buy one, can we have dinner tonight?"

"I have a date." Only a little lie, because the day was young and someone would surely want to hang out.

"How about two, and I'll throw in breakfast?"

"Sorry."

"Then I'll have a lemon scone." He read from the board, not even noticing the empty case, or he thought she had them in back.

"I only have the goat-cheese rolls. I'm not really open for business."

"You served him." Bob thumbed the previous customer hunched over the table closest to the door.

"A pine-nut and fig roll. They're all gone now."

"Well, if you're not open, why don't I take you to lunch?"

She clasped her hands. "How can I say this nicely…"

"Not no, but hell no." The Lego man intoned from his table.

Piper's eyes widened as she resisted a laugh. She didn't want to insult Bob, just stop the assault. Did every conversation have to be in overdrive? Mary Carson laughed softly into her napkin. Piper thought she heard, "Well said, young man," but it might have been, "Watch your language."

Piper cleared her throat. "So…kalamata roll?"

Bob glared. "No, thanks. Not a fan of goat cheese."

"I'll have the regular menu tomorrow."

"Right." Bob walked away, scowling at the Lego man as he passed.

———

After grabbing the bag of nails, Jonah climbed out of his Bronco and strode into the cabin. Attending church was not new; attending voluntarily was. He'd been forced into it every Sunday and resented every minute until he had sunk so low there was nowhere else to turn. It wasn't about proving his piety like the police chief before him, but just the opposite, admitting his need of something bigger.

He'd stopped expecting lightning to strike when he entered, but others probably hadn't, so he kept it uncomplicated, going late and leaving early. Piper was the only one to call him on it. She'd become disarmingly persistent.

Now that he'd crossed thirty, women seemed to think him safe. No longer prowling didn't mean he wasn't dangerous. He still had it within him to wreck someone's life.

He changed from his jeans and shirt into a battered pair of cargo shorts and T-shirt that had passed ratty years ago. Methodically, he set to work on the addition he'd begun at the back of his cabin, doubling its size with a rec room, workshop, two additional bedrooms, and bath. He had the acreage to support the addition, and with real estate values escalating as the very wealthy discovered the area's charm, it made sense to improve his investment.

He had poured the foundation slab, framed and sheetrocked the walls, and now he'd almost finished taping the seams. After a couple of hours, sweating with the heat of the day and the labor, he pulled up his shirt and wiped his face. He had put off the other task long enough. He climbed down, put his tools away, and climbed into the Bronco. After inserting the key into the ignition, he dropped his head back against the headrest and closed his eyes. Then he started the engine and pulled out.

As he drove, he braced himself mentally and emotionally. His shirt was damp and flecked with sawdust, but he never wore the uniform when he visited. That would be like running power to C4.

He parked outside the sprawling, single-level house he'd grown up in, almost seeing his dad sitting out on the long front porch, bottle in hand, leer in place. *If it isn't the big shot. Thinks he can do the job better than the old man.*

Over thirty-one years, Chief Stan Westfall's reputation as the toughest lawman in the county had earned him the respect of its law-abiding citizens. Lawbreakers had respected him too—out of fear. Stan Westfall could chill a man's spine with a stare.

The door opened, and his mother stepped out, face slack. "What do you want?"

He hung his hands on his hips. "Seeing if you need anything."

"Not from you." She had thickened at the waist, and he hoped that meant the ulcers had healed and she could eat. She wore her gray-blond hair loose, having learned the inadvisability of a ponytail early in her marriage. But it made her look old and unkempt.

His brother, Pete, sent her money each month, though he'd gotten as far from Redford as he could. Jonah tried, but she wouldn't take any assistance from him. And he'd made no escape. Redford was in his blood. He cared about the city he protected, the responsibility he'd been given.

He glanced at the empty chair on the porch.

"You questioning me?" His absent dad mocked him.

"What happened last night?"

His father's withering stare. *"None of your business."*

"Someone died. That's everyone's business."

"Walk away now. Just walk away."

"Go." His mother's face crumpled, her tone venomous. "Get out of here."

Why didn't she go live with Pete or her sister? What could possibly hold her to this place? She went inside and closed the door. He stood long moments, knowing she would watch him drive away, every mile he put between them a gift. He retraced his route back to the cabin.

The sound of a saw greeted him when he walked in his door. "Jay?"

Half Cherokee, half Dane, Jay Laugersen came from the back room, safety goggles hanging around his neck. "You can't give it up, can you?" One hazel and one husky blue eye gave the impression of superimposed images, a startling contrast in his dark-complected face. He wore his black hair banded at the nape to form a stubby tail.

Jonah tossed his keys on the table. "She's my mother."

"And you're the Raven Mocker's spawn." A heart-eating soul-stealer's offspring was not far off—literally or figuratively. But only Jay could get away with calling him that. Jay had brought him back from the shadowlands, sweating out the whiskey's poison and spooning broth and other potions between his parched lips. He had taught him carpentry, making him work his way out of the hole. He had taught him self-respect.

Jonah said, "Hungry?"

"Got steak?"

"What else?" The whole Angus steer Lorraine Goetthe had raised would last until she'd fattened another for his freezer. He kept a week's worth of beef, most of it steaks of varying thickness, thawed in the refrigerator to throw on the grill when he got off work, whenever that happened to be.

As the steaks seared, he boiled corn and tore lettuce for a salad. Jay had brought O'Doul's, the nonalcoholic beer that marked you a recovering drunk. They sat on the front porch to eat, these damage-control meals a Sunday afternoon ritual.

They talked and ate and laughed.

The bands around his heart expanded. He might never convince his mother he wasn't responsible. Ultimately he had been, for daring to hold the man accountable. He shook his head. For now—

His phone vibrated, and with a sigh he checked it. Moser. "I need to take this."

———

Hiking up through towering pines along an exuberant, tumbling creek, Tia moved at a brisk pace, planting the walking stick she carried, more to wave at bears or cougars than for assistance on the path. The breeze titillated the trembly aspen and bore the scent of golden banner and Queen Anne's lace. Thorny wild roses drew a few bees in the sunny patches, and flat-leaf ferns burgeoned in the shadows.

On she climbed, pulling with hands and feet over rocky terrain where the trees thinned, and she drew abreast of their spired tips. The sun beat down beneath the brilliant blue sky. She looked up. With a low drumming of its pinions on the air, an eagle mounted the sky from a crag overhead—her destination. She had climbed it only once before.

"No, you can't come; you'll blab it around."

"I won't." She'd zipped her lips.

"That would take superglue. Industrial strength."

She had followed uninvited, but he hadn't gotten mad. When he realized she had made it to the top, he said, *"Well, come on over and have a look."*

She had swelled with the thrill of accomplishment. *"Have you shown Reba?"*

"I want to. But she won't come. The climb is too hard and dangerous."

I made it, Tia thought. But Reba was a girlie-girl, weaving Jonah into her feminine spell until he believed her too dainty for real life. Settling into the saddle of the rock, her arm against his, Tia had looked out and thought how much her sister was missing.

Sweat had collected beneath her breasts, down her spine, in the hollow of her throat. The awareness of him had been as heady as the thin air, the steep pitch, the perilous footing. The hint of danger that lay beneath his calm worked on her like the unfiltered sun, burning into her senses, leaving her breathless with wants she could not articulate.

Clenching the walking stick, she halted, suddenly short of breath. Jonah did not own this mountain. But she turned around anyway, shaking.

Six

Two souls with but a single thought, two hearts that beat as one.

—FREDRICH HALM

Climbing the hill behind Duffy's cabin, Jonah called out so Moser wouldn't shoot him. The warning wasn't necessary. He was in no shape to shoot. "What've we got?"

Moser straightened, still white from puking up the contents of his stomach. "Duffy hiked up here, like he does every day, discovered the kill, and thought it weird enough to call."

This time, the young raccoons were about eight feet apart. They had gotten that far by emptying their body cavities, the entrails having been sewn together. Two of each animal's legs had been removed at the hip and shoulder socket so that together they had only four.

"It's like a wolf in a trap, chewing off its leg." Moser's voice wobbled.

"Only this trap was another animal as frantic to separate as the first."

As he had the last time, Jonah took a number of closeups with the digital camera, holding his gorge with difficulty. It appeared that several of the organs had been divided and joined. A more complete connection than the last time when each beast had been left intact. "Our perpetrator has knowledge of anatomy and surgical skill."

"But why…what…" Moser's question petered off.

Jonah shook his head. "Let's get a team up here, do a ground search. Footprints, maybe something dropped by observers."

"You think it's a sport?"

"Sport, rite, fetish. I don't know, but these creatures didn't get this way by themselves."

He surveyed the location. The steep slope and dense forestation were not a natural choice for a spectator event, though a half-dozen hooded spectators could have slipped in among the trees for their ceremony and slipped away as silently. He saw no circle of stones or ritualistic markings on the trees. Maybe it was one sick individual.

Duffy's property bordered parkland, accessible from several trails. He glanced at the one a short distance above. Both times the animals were released near a path or trail. Was there a pattern? a purpose? Or was it simple expediency?

Newly arrived to help with the search. His steel stomach proved once again impervious to stink or gore, but the blood-soaked pine needles, cones, and twigs did not give up easy secrets. Double-pronged deer tracks marked a soft patch, probably a full-grown buck by the depth. They found no wrappers or cigarette butts, no boot prints, no human hairs.

Jonah sent Newly back to his usual duties and told Moser to ask Duffy for a shovel. The photos would show enough. Not long ago, such a crime would have been considered minor. But animal cruelty had gained recognition, and this took it up a notch. Evisceration was dark stuff.

Hands on hips, he scanned, trying to sense the motivation, gratification, whatever the perpetrator was going for. Footsteps crunched behind him, and he turned, expecting Moser, but saw Tia, hand pressed to her nose and mouth. She had approached on the trail just above Duffy's property from which he guessed the perpetrator may have released the raccoons. He moved between her and the carnage, trying to block both animals. "Don't look. It's grim."

She spoke through her hand. "Dead raccoons?"

"Yeah."

"Isn't that Department of Wildlife's business?"

"Would be, except they were sewn together. This pair had limbs removed and organs joined."

"What?" She searched his face.

"This is why I warned you not to be out alone." What if she had happened upon the sicko having his sport? He looked up the trail. "How long have you been hiking?"

"About three hours. You said not to be out after dark."

Leave it to Tia to find the loophole. He checked his watch. "So you passed here, when?"

"I didn't." Her face shifted. "I cut up toward the aerie."

A reckless hike to take alone. He should never have shown her—not that he'd done so intentionally. The memory came with stark definition. Others may have reached the ledge beneath the aerie, but he'd shared it with no one else. She'd been like a kid sister until that day—or so he'd told himself.

"This is sick stuff, Tia. There's a sadist out there—"

"Which you didn't tell me the first time."

"I'm telling you now. These animals were tortured. And these things escalate."

Her eyes flashed. "How do you escalate from…" She waved her hand. "To people?"

He didn't want to speculate. The anatomical element scared him.

"You have to warn everyone, Jonah. Not just me. Tell them what's happening."

"Put Redford in a panic? I don't know what's happening here." He shook his head. "Besides, giving him the spotlight might encourage a step he wouldn't otherwise take."

"But—"

"Maybe he just hates raccoons."

Her jaw fell slack. "You know that's not it."

"Tia, let me do my job. We're searching this area for evidence."

"Found any?"

"Not much. But sooner or later he'll make a mistake."

"What if it's later?"

He understood her concern. But he was not going to put the town in a panic if it was some sick prank. "If I see people alone I'll caution them, as I did you. Not that it mattered."

"People need to know why."

"Some people just listen." She had no idea how complicated an investigation was. What did she think, he could hang a flier and the guy would turn himself in?

"You might try it yourself sometime." She shook her head and started back down the trail.

He jammed his hands in his pockets and left Moser to bury the carnage.

———

From the bench seat encircling an aspen cluster, Piper watched Tia coming down the trail. She had a mountaineer's physique, toned and slender, sinewy, her tanned legs muscular in cargo shorts and hiking boots. She was not breathing hard, but, by the flush of her face and the set of her jaw, something was wrong.

Piper clutched the paperback to her chest. "What happened?"

"I'll tell you, but let's go inside."

Piper scooped a leaf off the ground and used it as a bookmark, tucked the paperback under her arm, and followed Tia. "Did you see the eagles?"

"I saw something else." Tia leaned the walking stick into the corner of the mud room. "Two raccoons. Jonah said they'd been sewn together, but they had torn themselves apart. It was awful."

"What did he mean sewn?"

"Surgically. Legs removed and organs joined together."

Piper recoiled. "That must be what I saw."

"When?" Tia hung her jacket on the hook.

"The day I met the chief. On our path. I thought it was a dead animal. That was the night he warned you not to be out. Remember?"

Tia slumped. "I didn't know it was right on our path."

"Does he know who did it?"

"I don't think he has a clue."

"Maybe we can help. Ask around." She followed Tia to the parlor, flopped onto the settee beside her. "If we get people talking—"

"Jonah doesn't want whoever it is getting attention."

"But someone might know. People brag. They tell me all kinds of stuff."

Tia slid her a look. "So I've seen."

"I can use that. To investigate."

"Jonah won't like it."

"He doesn't have to know until we have something to tell him."

"Piper, this isn't a game." Tia pressed the skin between her brows as though staving off a headache. "Those creatures suffered."

"I know. That's why I want to help."

Tia shook her head. "Trust me; this isn't the way to get his attention."

"What?"

"Don't think I haven't noticed."

Piper blinked. "He's cute, don't get me wrong." Piper drew up her knees and settled into the corner of the settee. "But he's not interested in me."

"Then he's the only man alive who's not." The corners of Tia's mouth pulled up.

"Guys here are just starved for someone new."

"You think in a year or two you'll be old news?"

"A year or two? What would that even be like?"

"What do you mean?" Tia turned.

"I've never been anywhere a whole year."

"Why not?"

She shrugged a shoulder. "We were sort of like…gypsies."

"Gypsies are not tall, blond Barbie-doll people. You look like you had the all-American family."

"I do?" She had made friends in most of the different schools, but she'd never thought she looked settled.

"How come you moved so much?"

"Let's just say my family couldn't do their thing for long in any one place."

"What thing?"

Out of nowhere, tears brimmed her eyes. She hadn't realized the shame was still so close.

Tia touched her arm. "You don't have to tell me."

"No, it's just…amazing how many things you can sue for."

"Do you mean fraud?"

"Most companies—especially employers—will settle to avoid the hassle. And there's enough of them working together, sharing the big set-tlements, that no name comes up too often. Plus, they don't look like lowlifes. My mom is really beautiful, and when she claims her new boss came on to her, it's believable."

"It might be true."

"What matters is they pay. My aunt specializes in personal injury. My dad and uncle are into auto claims."

Tia leaned back. "Wow."

Piper rubbed the tickle on her nose, a nervous reaction to talking about it. "I'm the oddball, a mutant, genetically incapable of lying. Every time they tried to involve me as a kid, I got so worked up trying to keep the story straight that I puked."

Tia shook her head, bemused.

"I hope you don't think I'm going to rip you off now or something."

"Why on earth would I think that?" Tia untied her hiking boots and slipped them off. "I know what it's like to be the odd one out. In your case it's a good thing."

"I'll bet in your case it is too."

Tia didn't answer. "So you went your own way and ended up here."

Piper nodded. "More or less."

"Well, I hope you've found a place to stay."

Piper smiled. "I'd like that. A lot."

———

Jonah had promised Merv he would check out Tom Caldwell's shed and went there next. He had tried several times before, but Tom hadn't been home. This time there was smoke rising from the chimney. He glanced past the house to the shed.

A trickle of sweat ran down his lower back. He imagined the sting of a spider on the nape of his neck. His hands got clammy, and a cloying rage rose up his throat as he stared at a pine shed way too similar to the one in his memories. His nails dug into his palms. His legs came to a leaden stop.

The door of the house opened, and Caldwell stepped out. "Help you, Chief?"

There was a sneer in the way he said it. They'd gone to school together, Caldwell three years ahead of him. Sometimes it wouldn't hurt to have his dad's reputation, but he didn't want to beat people to earn it. "Heard a report you've booby-trapped your shed. I need to make sure it's not a public hazard."

"Now who would you hear that from, the old suck-up next-door?"

Jonah shrugged. "Just open it up and I'll be on my way."

"The hell I will. Not without a warrant."

"What are you talking about, warrant? I'm just saying show me it's safe."

It wasn't safe. His scalp burned as the hand came down, clawing the hair by the roots, dragging him up. *I'll teach you to hide, you miserable whelp.* He couldn't hear out of one ear for a week. But that wasn't what made the shed a terror.

Jonah shook off the memory and stalked toward Caldwell's shed.

"Stop right there. This is my land, my shed, and I said no."

Jonah turned, sick with relief to have it out of his sight. "If I come back with a warrant and find so much as excessive pesticide, I'll run you in."

Without warning, Merv streaked across his yard with an ax. "This half's across the line." He started hacking at the shed wall that faced his house.

Jonah hollered for him to stop. He didn't know where the properties joined, but this wouldn't settle the dispute. Caldwell charged, and Jonah charged after him. They reached the wall as Merv ripped out a splintered board. Caldwell shoved Merv to the ground hard enough to rattle his teeth. Just inside the hole, a shelf held bags of yellowish-white crystals.

Caldwell kicked at Merv while trying to keep his back against the breach, but Jonah had seen enough. "Face the wall, Tom." He reached for his cuffs.

Caldwell swung, a maneuver embedded in Jonah's reflexes. He twisted, then grabbed the man's arm and bent it up his back. Catching Caldwell's elbow in the ribs, Jonah took him down, pressing his face into the dirt, a knee between the shoulder blades as he locked the cuffs around his wrists. As much as he resisted using physical force, the scuffle did relieve the pent-up tension of seeing his mom and the dead raccoons. And Tia.

After shoving Caldwell into the Bronco, he radioed for the sheriff to send a deputy to secure the site until he returned with a search warrant. As soon as the county car arrived, he told Merv to follow them in, called Sue to procure the warrant, and headed for the station.

Rolling his head side to side in the backseat of the Bronco, Caldwell scrunched up his face. "What died in here?"

A smile tugged the corners of Jonah's mouth.

At the station he pressed Caldwell down onto the metal bench in the booking area and cuffed him to the ring on one end. Caldwell glowered. When Officer Sue Donnelly joined them, Jonah said, "Read him his rights. Might take a few times before he gets it. Have him sign the form when he understands."

Caldwell's nostrils flared, his lip curling up with disgust. "You are making such a mistake."

"Call me when he's through photo and prints." Jonah could have processed the man himself, but handing it over to Sue reminded him that the smirk on Caldwell's face did not need punching.

Twenty minutes into questioning, during which Caldwell mostly smirked at the wall, his attorney arrived. Interesting because Caldwell hadn't made the phone call—unless he'd somehow speed-dialed his cell from the Bronco with his hands cuffed. Gordon Byne was a small man with a big head—literally. It sat on his shoulders like a bowling ball, with close-set eyeholes and an extra large mouth hole.

Crying illegal search and seizure, he claimed Merv's vandalism put whatever they thought they'd seen in plain sight and made the arrest unconstitutional—forgetting, of course, the little matter of assault on an officer.

In the video-conferencing room, Jonah sat at the desk with the computer and looked up at the screen mounted on the wall. Caldwell sat in a chair next to him. When the magistrate had sworn him in, Jonah gave him Caldwell's name and address and laid out the arrest. He listed two misdemeanor convictions, no outstanding warrants.

Then he told Caldwell to raise his right hand, not easy in handcuffs, and Caldwell swore to truthfully tell his side. The assault alone should be enough to hold him over unless the judge believed the spin Caldwell's lawyer had put on it. Harassment and brutality. Uh-huh.

The magistrate held Caldwell without bail until morning in the county jail. Judge Walthrup would probably allow bail the next day since the drugs were found through Merv's alleged trespass and vandalism. In the meantime they had enough to obtain a search warrant for the entire property, and they did.

Merv had fallen asleep waiting for Caldwell to be processed. Because he'd endangered himself by acting rashly, Jonah cited him for destruction of personal property.

"It was on my side of the line."

"Get proof of that and we'll talk."

"He used it for illegal purposes. You saw it."

"I saw. But you had no business interfering."

"Got you what you wanted, didn't I? Got you a look inside."

"And an elbow in the ribs. You're lucky you didn't get your head kicked in."

Grumbling, Merv got to his feet.

Jonah handed him the citation. "Go home. Stay away from Caldwell."

Sue joined him, and they went over together to search Caldwell's house, shed, and pickup. Parked beside the deputy sheriff's vehicle, Jonah pulled on the black fitted gloves designed to protect him from getting stuck by a contaminated needle, the worst part of running their hands under cushions and down gaps in upholstery.

"Where's the deputy?"

He followed Sue's gaze to the house. "The shed, I guess. We'll start there." Adrenaline overrode his issues with the structure. He would do his job.

The shed door was slightly ajar. The deputy must have entered before the warrant arrived, a technical violation, especially if the judge had refused. Unless he'd had cause. Jonah called out so the man would know they'd arrived.

No answer. Sue's worried brow reflected his own concern. Had there been a toxic trap? He motioned her to stand behind him, then eased the door open, watching for tripwire, sensor, or laser that might trigger or have already triggered something.

Deputy Stone lay in a heap, his gun a few inches from his hand, the bloody swelling beneath the graying hair at the base of his head indicative of a blow. Jonah looked up for something that might have been rigged to the door. Nothing. He stooped and felt the deputy's pulse.

The man moaned, rising painfully to consciousness.

Jonah helped him roll to his shoulder. "I'll call you an ambulance, Ray."

Ray Stone reached behind his head. "Just a bump."

"A nasty one."

"Was waiting by the house. Heard someone out here."

"Inside?" Jonah shot a look around the dim shed for potential hiding spots.

"Thought so. But he got me from behind."

"I'll get JT to have a look at you." The EMT with the fire department could better assess the deputy's condition. He made the call.

Sue came back to the doorway. "I've done a perimeter search. No one in the house or yard."

"Was the house open?"

She nodded. "Back door unlocked."

"Could use some air," Ray said.

Jonah helped him sit up. The deputy holstered his gun and got to his feet. Outside the door, he leaned against the shed.

"Do your search," he said. "But I'm not sure what you'll find."

Distracted by the fallen officer, he hadn't searched the back shelves or anything else. Now he stepped inside. Sue followed.

The first thing he noticed were the animal skins—rabbit, fox, and…raccoon. The skins were stacked on two wooden picnic tables and included the heads. No indication they'd been sewn, together or otherwise.

"Nice," Sue murmured. "Think he shot enough bunnies?"

"Not a crime. But it does suggest a weapon."

"Hunting rifle." Sue unloaded and passed it over.

His flashlight illuminated the shelf he'd seen through the damaged siding, a dim rectangle of light already showing what he did not want to see. The shelf was empty.

Byne's surprise appearance should have told him someone else was in the game. They might have been in the house when Jonah arrived the first time, or in close enough proximity to see the arrest go down. With the deputy out front, they could have gone out the back to the shed.

"That's where it was?" Sue's light ran over the empty shelf, drag markings in the dust but nothing else.

"Check it for residue."

He scanned the rest of the shed. He'd half expected to find a lab, but whoever had taken the inventory would not have had time to disassemble the equipment and ingredients and rearrange the clutter. "I'll start in the house." The sooner he left the shed, the better. If he saw a three-legged stool and a shotgun, he'd show Sue a side of himself he hid like leprosy.

The house appeared tossed, but the piles of clothes and trash, empty bottles, and food containers heaped in corners could be how Tom lived. A ratty taxidermied boar stood beside the television. Classy.

Jonah moved systematically through the disaster, searching the sofa and stuffed chairs for torn or loose bottom liners, mattress and box spring for slits. He searched the piles of clothes and the few in closets and drawers, checked in boxes and the file cabinet. He eyed the carpet for untacked edges and found a slack corner in the bedroom closet.

Tugging it up revealed a loose board under which a wad of cash had been secreted. By itself, that meant nothing, but he bagged it in hopes of more incriminating evidence—like the .40 caliber handgun shoved deeper into the gap. He removed the magazine, ejected the round in the chamber, and bagged it.

The smaller of the two fire trucks arrived as he moved to the kitchen. He looked out the window and saw Sue and Ray explaining the situation—Sue, how they'd found him unconscious, and Ray, how it was only a bump. Jonah checked the cabinet and refrigerator contents and found another wad of bills in a bag of frozen peas.

Either Caldwell distrusted banks or had need of ready cash. He found ammunition for the handgun in the flatware drawer beside the steak knives, along with a second handgun, same caliber. He checked and found it loaded like the first.

Sue joined him with a bagged cell phone and charger. "He kept this in the shed. Want me to run down the numbers in his log?"

He reached for the bag. "I'll do that. Anything else?"

"A Bunsen burner and bottle caps."

"So he's using."

"Or it's for clients to test the wares."

Jonah nodded. "Good thought. You're pretty sharp."

"Yeah." She polished her nails on her uniform. "Other than that, they cleaned up pretty well."

"Looks that way. I'm almost done in here. Let's flip for the bathroom."

She sent him a look. "You probably have a two-headed coin."

"In which case you only have to call heads."

She swallowed. "I'll do it."

Gutsy. "Actually"—he tossed her the set of keys from the counter—"you take the truck. I'll tackle the john."

"Sure?"

"Find me grounds to impound."

"If it's there, I'll find it."

He watched her go, then looked at the cell phone. He wondered for a moment if she might have already deleted a certain number. If not, the temptation could have struck when she logged the calls. Except for the potential incrimination of her husband, Sam, he'd have let her handle that task. He put the phone with the other items and hoped it would prove a nonissue.

Without the drugs, none of what they had would be incriminating. Whoever mopped up here knew what they were doing. It occurred to him that could be Sam. Who better than a law officer's spouse to know how to thwart a bust?

When they had gotten back to the station, he said, "You know Sam could get swept up in this."

Sue stared straight ahead. "Do what you have to."

She knew he would, but it mattered that she said it. He stopped her at the door. "If people come forward, there might be opportunities for immunity."

"Some people think squealing's worse than time."

"Some people do." He held her eyes until she looked away. "If you've got things here, I'll run Caldwell down."

He never sent a male prisoner alone with a female officer. Besides, this was hitting her close to home. Inside, he fitted Tom Caldwell with a wide leather belt complete with metal ring through which he threaded the cuffs. Neither of them spoke on the way to the jail or when Jonah turned him over.

He had jailed more than a few of his schoolmates, though usually not for long. Even, sadly, some who'd been friends. Came with the job. Some understood that. He headed home beneath a wan moon, expecting to find his place empty, but the scent of smoke reached him as he approached the porch. "Still here?"

Jay pulled a long drag on his cigarette.

"Those things'll kill you." Jonah mounted the steps.

"I only smoke on Sundays."

Jonah pulled up a chair. He'd escaped the lure of tobacco, but his mistress called. He'd expected it to kick in, given the emotional stress of the day, and here it was. He could taste her in his mind. What he wouldn't give for a glass of sipping whiskey and a slow sad song.

He didn't envy Sam Donnelly. What he'd seen looked like meth, and that was no mistress but a dominatrix from the deepest pit.

He turned to Jay. "How do you feel about a new intervention?"

"Who?"

"Guy I know."

"Has he hit bottom?"

"I don't know."

"Let me know when there's nothing under him but the grave."

Seven

Unity to be real must survive the severest strain without breaking.

—MAHATMA GANDHI

Tia looked up from her detailing as a couple of shoppers peered in. She studied the faces, framed by their palms. She and her wares might be the inner structure of a snow globe they studied. She read their expressions and posture, surmising where they were in life and how they felt about it.

To a practiced observer, there were common streams of experience, doubts, needs, and desires. It remained only to fill in the details. In that, her imagination proved more than adequate. They didn't come in. It was Friday of a slow week, and she hoped it didn't portend a downtrend. But a short while later, a shopper entered, tinkling the bell above the door.

Her mother had hung that bell, ever conscious of potential wrongdoers. Stella Manning gave no one the benefit of the doubt. Those who measured up received her laud. All others need not apply. Tia's infantile transgressions had landed her firmly in the latter camp. A mother would know, wouldn't she, if her child were simply bad?

The blond woman in burgundy scrubs moved awkwardly, not a limp so much as an uncoordinated gait that reminded Tia of the three-legged races on field day. Perhaps a prosthetic limb.

Tia moved toward her, smiling. "Can I help you?"

"Um, I don't know. What's the needle for?"

Tia looked at the syringe in her hand and laughed. "Oh. Ornamentation. I was detailing these pillars." She motioned toward the one she'd set down.

"With a hypodermic?"

"It makes a very fine groove and releases the wax evenly." With the unorthodox tool, she as easily outlined pine needles and columbine as added abstract swirls and dots to coarse or smoothly textured pillars.

"You make the candles?" The woman surveyed the store.

"And all the scent blends and oils. You're welcome to browse, or was there something…"

"I'm looking for a gift. For my sister."

She thought of Reba's gifts with a pang. "Birthday?"

"She's not well."

"Oh, I'm sorry." Would she even know if Reba were unwell? Would any of them tell her? "What does she like? Scents, textures? Is she more visual?"

"Do you have anything with a lilac scent?"

"I have a blend that includes it." Tia led the woman to the shelf. "It's called Hope." She lifted the display dish of scented disks for her to smell. "Melted over a tea light, the wax liquefies and releases the aroma. I also have the scent in potpourri oil and these candles."

The ivory pillars were wrapped with a removable band that read: *Those who hope in the* LORD *will renew their strength. They will soar on wings like eagles. (Isaiah 40:31)*

The woman sniffed the scent, eyes closed. "I think I can detect the lilac."

"I'm sorry I don't have it by itself." She had developed the blends herself, preferring them over the potency of a single scent.

"No, this is nice. I like it." The woman looked up. "Why do you call it Hope?"

"It's part of a collection of scents that soothe or invigorate or calm. The corresponding message is a thought to consider."

"Interesting."

Tia read the name tag on her lapel. "Dr. Rainer. Do you work at the Emergency Care?"

"I'm a veterinarian."

"Oh. I'd heard someone reopened the animal hospital." She held out her hand. "I'm Tia."

"Liz." After a brief, strong squeeze, she took the bag of melts from the shelf. "I'll get these. We have a simmer pot."

Tia wrapped the package and tied it with pellucid lavender ribbon, then affixed the shop sticker that bore a half-moon-shaped honeycomb with herbs and berries. She had designed it herself. Customers frequently told her the wrapping was so pretty they didn't want to open it. Her mother would think it a frivolous expense, but Reba would have liked it.

Tia handed the package over with a brittle smile. "I hope your sister feels better."

Liz Rainer's smile had a brittleness of its own. "Thanks."

———

Liz left the shop and strolled past several others. Lucy would be happy with the gift, especially how Tia had wrapped it. That was a nice touch. She liked her, though ordinarily she was wary of exotic-looking women.

The almost black eyes and dark brows were an unusual match for mahogany hair, but she could tell the color wasn't from a bottle. Mediterranean features and olive skin enhanced the effect. Liz tucked her purse strap higher onto her shoulder, imagining a friendship with Tia the candle maker.

It felt good to meet someone and draw her own conclusions. Heady not to have Lucy's opinions in her ear. What would it be like to make a friend her sister knew nothing about? A business woman with shared concerns. She had intended to tell Lucy who had made the candle melts and wrapped them so nicely. But now—

The chief drove past and raised a hand in greeting. She waved back, wishing she hadn't told Lucy she could meet him. A pang of guilt tightened her stomach. What were these thoughts? She didn't keep things from her sister.

Back at the clinic, she passed through the exam rooms to the kennels. "Lucy?"

Her sister loved to soothe the frightened, ailing pets, but they only had one right now, and Lucy wasn't there. She went through the door to the small house. "Luce?"

The bedroom was dim, the curtains drawn. Lucy lay still, breathing weakly. How could she have thought of denying her anything? Liz dropped to her side. "Lucy, wake up. See what I've brought you?" She laid the package on the bed. "Open your eyes, and I'll tell you about the woman who made these."

Lucy's eyelids flickered and parted.

"Her name is Tia. She has riotous mahogany hair; dark, soulful eyes; and strong, elegant hands." Lucy loved details. "She's an artist." She lifted the package. "See how she wrapped this for you?"

Lucy looked at the package. "Is she your friend?"

"I just met her, silly."

"But she could be."

Liz looked down. "Why would I need a friend when I have you?"

"Do you have me?"

She stiffened. "Why do you say that? I will always have you. You're the only constant in my life."

Her sister's eyes brimmed with tears, and Liz gripped her hand. "Nothing will separate us but death. When you die, I die."

"It might not be that way."

"It is that way." She tore the wrapping off the melts, untied the gossamer bag, and the wax wafers tumbled out. She held one close to Lucy's face. "Smell that. It's called Hope."

———

"Whose birthday is it?" Piper plunked herself down at the kitchen table and looked at the various tins and plastic-wrapped parcels arrayed there. Birthdays had been a big deal in her house, lots of presents and cake and candles. An extravaganza of entitlement.

Tia pulled a wide covered basket down from the top of the refrigerator. "Those are care packages for Sarge. From the ladies at church."

From what she'd gleaned, Tia's church was all about doing stuff. Outreach, Tia called it. But this time, it was going to be wasted. "I'm not sure Sarge—"

"He might curse them for caring, but that doesn't mean they don't." She set the basket down. "They're very good women, and besides, he wasn't always awful."

"Really?"

Tia rolled her lower lip in. "His wife and teenage son were killed on the highway."

"How sad."

"He lost perspective and alienated people. His daughters moved away."

Piper picked up a package of snickerdoodles. She hadn't imagined Sarge with a tragic story. "You're delivering the package?"

"I thought you might like to come along, tell him how the bakery's doing."

"He'll be mad about the specials."

"Tell him people like them."

"That'll make him madder." Piper stuffed the cookies into the basket. "He's been selling currant scones, raisin rolls, and almond bear claws longer than I've been alive."

"People know what to expect from Sarge." Tia hoisted the basket. "Ready?"

"Well." She'd been waiting for a chance to plead her case. Now seemed as good a time as any. "Okay."

The hospital was quiet as they followed the directions to the surgical wing. Even Sarge's room was quiet, because his eyes were closed and his mouth hung slack.

"He's asleep," Tia whispered. "We'll just slip it in there to surprise him."

But as they eased the door open, Jonah Westfall looked up from the bench seat by the window. Piper brightened. This might turn out okay. She followed a reluctant Tia in, and Sarge opened his eyes. Just the sight of her seemed to rev him up. "Hi, Sarge. Feeling better?"

"I am not."

"You look better. And you got your voice back."

"Yeah. And guess what? You're fired."

Her mouth opened. "Then who's going to bake?"

"I'll shut it down."

"You can't do that. People are counting on you."

He pushed up in the bed. "Don't tell me what I can't do. It's your fault I'm here."

"Sarge," Jonah murmured.

"If you'd have minded your business, I'd be minding mine." His monitors started beeping.

"Well, Sarge, you weren't minding yours all that well."

Jonah and Tia startled. Sarge's face turned purple. He jabbed a finger at her. "You're fired, you hear?"

Oh, she heard. She squeezed her hands shut. "There's an oven full of money, but it's not enough to pay your medical bills. You need me."

Sarge looked ready to burst an artery. "Need? You?"

She didn't want to lose the job, to lose the room at Tia's. She didn't want to prove her family right that only fools worked for a living. "We need each other." She raised her eyes hopefully, but Sarge erupted.

Jonah caught him by the chest. "Calm down, Sarge."

Not the reaction she'd hoped for, even if she had sort of expected it. "I better go." Tears washed her eyes as she slipped out into the hall.

———

Tia glowered at Sarge, collapsed against Jonah's chest. How could such a weak old man be so brutal? "She's only trying to help."

"I won't have some kid relieving me of my command," Sarge snarled, the corners of his mouth white with foam.

"She's keeping you in business."

"What do you know?" He glared. "She costs me more than she's worth."

"You pay her hardly anything."

"I trained her from scratch. She didn't know a spoon from a shovel."

"Well, she does now. She has quite a gift for—"

"Strange concoctions. *Goat* cheese and *pine* nuts," he spit the words like bullets.

Tia shot a glance at Jonah. Had he blabbed the details? "What matters is that she has opened the door every day and served your customers

so that you still have a shop to come back to." Was he senile not to realize that?

"I'd be opening it myself if she hadn't put me here."

"Your condition put you here. You're not taking care of yourself."

Sarge chewed his lips, muttering, then thrust a finger at her. "What's
that?"

Tia looked down at the basket. "Something to cheer you up."

"Stuff that girl made?"

"*That girl* is Piper. She's worked for you five weeks now. You should
know her name."

Sarge reddened like a fireplug.

Jonah shifted. "She has a point, Sarge."

She didn't need Jonah's help. She set the basket on the foot of the
bed. "Anyway, they're not from Piper. They're care packages from the
church ladies." She had told them it was a useless gesture, but, longing to
bring him into the fold, if only for his own peace, they'd insisted she play
ambassador.

"Old crows waiting for me to drop dead."

She pictured each of them, baking a favorite recipe, something to
cheer and hearten him.

"No one wants you dead, Sarge." Jonah frowned. "It wouldn't hurt
to show a little gratitude."

"It's themselves they're cheering up, the cackling do-gooders. Fat bid-
dies putting out for some heavenly reward."

Tia's jaw slackened. He made it sound prurient.

"The joke's on them, you hear? The worms will eat them in the grave,
same as me. They'll just be sweeter for all those good deeds."

With a jerk, she upended the basket, dumping the parcels onto the
sheet. A few slipped to the floor. "If you don't want these, give them to
the nurses. God knows they deserve it." She headed for the door.

"Tia." Jonah came out behind her as she searched for Piper. "Wait."

"For what?"

"Let me explain."

She turned on him. "Explain what?"

"They told him today the compression in his spine is inoperable. They also said they'll only release him to the VA hospital or a family member. He can't live alone."

"That doesn't excuse him taking it out on Piper and the others, though I'm not surprised you don't see it that way."

"I've been on the phone with his daughters, and neither is in a position or willing to take him."

"I can't imagine why."

"But you might have an inkling how it feels."

She stiffened. "What do you mean?"

"I don't have to explain."

She jabbed a finger to his chest. "You have no clue how I feel."

"Yeah. You don't know anything about rejection, do you?"

That was like a knife to the heart. "You intolerable jerk."

"Bitterness has driven Sarge hard. You might take a lesson from that."

Her cheeks heated, fury curling in her stomach like a snake. "You're calling *me* bitter?"

"I'm saying look in the mirror before you judge Sarge."

Her breath made a low growl, the animal urge to rake him with her nails a terrifying sensation.

"Tia?" Piper approached wide-eyed.

Tia swung around with the basket, narrowly missing Jonah. "Let's go."

Piper glanced over her shoulder but waited until they reached the elevator to ask, "Are you okay?"

"I'm furious, and I hate it."

Piper searched her face. "Sarge's pain—"

"No." She spun on her as the doors closed them in. "Don't excuse him."

"But you said—"

"Forget what I said. None of that matters, you know why? Because it's still a choice. Everyone gets hurt. It's what you do with it that matters."

"Can you change how you feel?"

"No. But you can change how you act." Tia punched the lobby button as though force would make it respond.

"What happened with the chief?"

"He made excuses for Sarge."

"Why?"

"I don't know. He has…some kind of relationship with the old man I've never understood."

"People care about Sarge."

She knew that. But this wasn't about Sarge anymore. He had sparked her temper, but Jonah ignited it.

The elevator doors split. The main doors parted. Swinging the basket at her side, Tia made for her car.

Piper stayed quiet until they were well on their way home, then sighed. "I guess I won't be staying."

Tia's hand fisted. "I'd hire you myself if I didn't already have Amanda covering my days off." The daughter of a friend from church rang up sales, swept, and dusted. She locked up behind her and showed no initiative. Sarge had a treasure in Piper that he didn't deserve.

Piper sighed. "I know you need the rent."

"I do. But you can get unemployment for a while. He had no grounds to fire you. You've been a model employee."

Piper shrugged. "Maybe I'll find something else."

Jobs in Redford were like lottery tickets. If you hit it just right, you might win, as she had with Sarge—or so they'd thought. Tia remembered going door to door at sixteen, filling out applications, knowing her reputation as a troublemaker preceded her. Finally, her mother had given her a few hours at the shop, where she could both control and ridicule her efforts.

Tia didn't like the merchandise, ceramic figurines and T-shirts with generic mountain town slogans, but she'd sold them. She'd sold them so well her mother accused her of lascivious behavior—she'd had to look that one up—but it was the first indication that Stella thought she had anything someone might want.

Maybe Piper didn't have those strikes against her, but finding a new job would be tough. With its proximity to the ski slopes, kids were less likely to leave Redford than many small towns, and shopkeepers helped keep it that way by hiring locals.

Piper had made her own job when she talked Sarge into it. And she was the best investment he'd ever made. Tia clenched the wheel, furious again. He'd fired her for getting him emergency help? He deserved to lose everything.

"Tia?"

She turned.

"It's not worth it."

"What?"

"Blaming Sarge. Wanting him to pay. My family's made it an art, and I don't think they're happy."

Tia huffed. "Mistreating people doesn't brighten things either."

Piper sighed. "No. But you can't help what other people think."

"You're not upset that Sarge fired you? That he's hollered at you this whole time? That he doesn't appreciate all you've done?"

"Of course I'm upset. But"—she shrugged—"that's how it goes."

"It's not how it should go."

Eight

We cannot be separated in interest or divided in purpose.
We stand together until the end.
—THOMAS WOODROW WILSON

Jonah stood in the hall long enough to contain his anger. Tia didn't want to see the truth. Neither did Sarge. Each clung to their positions, and the world could fall apart around them. Frustrated, Jonah settled back down beside Sarge. The old man looked as though he'd expended all his energy, but he wasn't through.

"That fire-haired she-devil has a nasty temper."

Tia's temper was a force. But they had set her off.

"Gave her mother a terrible time."

"That went both ways, Sarge."

"What?"

"With Stella."

Sarge scowled. "Who asked her here anyway?"

"Don't look at me. But Sarge, she has a point."

"What point?"

"You can't fire Piper."

Sarge narrowed his rheumy eyes. "I did, didn't I?"

"If you want to convince people you can be on your own, you have to make good decisions. Canning the person who's keeping you in business is not sound strategy."

Sarge chewed his lips, looking recalcitrant.

"You followed your instincts in hiring her," Jonah prodded.

"She gabbed her way in."

"But you saw the merit or you wouldn't have gone there." Just as Sarge had with him.

"She's trying to take over."

"She's on your side." He ripped open a package of fudge and put a square in the old man's hand. It tore him up to see the tremor in the pale palm. "What does every good commander do, Sarge? Delegate."

Sarge shoved the fudge into his mouth and sucked it into mush, then nodded. "All right. Tell her she still has a job."

"I think you should tell her." Jonah held out his phone. "You can reach Tia's cell. They're probably still in the car."

Sarge lowered his thunderous brows. "It was your idea."

"You're the boss."

"And I'm delegating."

Jonah sat back. *Wily old man.* "Okay. I'll let her know." But he sure as heck wasn't calling Tia's cell. He stacked the baked goods onto Sarge's rolling arm table and left him sucking fudge.

———

Tia dropped Piper downtown and went home. Why did the best intentions so often go so wrong? If no one bothered with anyone else, would they be worse off or better in the long run? Strife came through interaction. Maybe everyone should just live their own lives and never try to impact another and never let themselves care.

Shaking her head, she went into her house and looked around. She could live alone. A lot of the time she did, renting the guest room to vacationers who came and went as though she didn't exist. Their independence suited her just fine. Maybe she encouraged it. Hard to tell.

Then came Piper. Not a boarder, but a roommate and friend. Would she miss her? She closed the door and climbed the stairs. Yes, she would miss her, and it wasn't fair and it wasn't right. Piper had done so much good.

Tia went into her room and looked bleakly around. It was a single woman's room. No husband's or boyfriend's photo on the bedstand. No children's clutter. The current stack of books to read, candles that seemed oddly pathetic. No keepsakes from a vacation, no sweetheart's roses pressed or dried. It was no mystery why. She was toxic.

She went to the window and looked through the organza to the houses across the street and the others spreading down the slope. She loved the lights in their windows and on their porches, like a cascade of candles. Looking at them now, she felt isolated, as though the single light from her bedroom was lost among them, insignificant.

Then she saw Jonah pull up to the curb. A groan came from deep within her. Hadn't he done enough? His walk to her door had purpose, but he hesitated before knocking. She stepped away from the window. Hesitation gone, he had knocked twice before she reached the door, enough to rekindle her indignation for Piper and his insulting stabs.

She pulled open the door and huffed, "What."

"Sarge wants to keep Piper on."

She leaned on the door. "So?"

That caught him short. "So…I thought she'd be glad to know."

"Glad?" Like it was some favor? From the goodness of his heart?

Jonah rubbed his face. "Is she here?"

"No."

"Do you know where—"

"She's out with friends. Since she doesn't have to work in the morning." She managed not to gloat.

"Well, can you give her the message?"

"If Sarge wants to rehire her, he can do it himself."

"Not stuck in the hospital."

"There's no telephone?" She folded her arms. "Anyway, I advised her to pursue other options."

"What, you're her mother now?"

Her mouth fell slack. "Thank you very much, Jonah. You hadn't quite reached your insult quota." She swung the door, but he caught it.

"I didn't mean you could be. Just you're acting like it." They exerted equal pressure for a few seconds, then she stopped pushing and looked away.

His voice softened. "I'm sorry about before. I was worked up from talking to Sarge's daughters."

She refused to meet his eyes. "Tell Sarge to call Piper when he's ready to discuss terms."

"Terms? Come on, Tia."

"Piper deserves better."

"She won't find a better setup. Sarge might not return in any real way. She'll have the opportunities she's wanted."

"Hah. He'll go to his grave with that bakery in his fist."

"I hope that's a long way off." His voice had an edge.

With a pang, she realized what she'd said. Eyes shut, she released her breath. "Sorry."

"Just tell her—"

"You tell her, Jonah. You be that curmudgeon's mouthpiece. I won't." She stepped back and shut the door. Stiffly she climbed the stairs, found her bed, and curled up in a ball. Jonah had compared her to the mean old man who'd driven away everyone who mattered. "Thank you so much," she bit out.

———

Piper felt a quiver when Chief Westfall entered the Summit Saloon. She'd just been canned in front of him by his good friend Sarge. Now she might have to start over somewhere else, and that hurt, but she didn't want him to see how much. He came to stand behind the stool next to hers—the one Mike Bunyan had vacated for a trip to the john.

She raised her Laughing Lab.

"Are you old enough to drink?"

She flashed her sunniest smile. "Want to see my ID?"

Lucas swept past on the other side of the bar. "I carded her."

She took out her wallet, flipping her license down. The picture wasn't bad. And yes, she could legally drink, barely, though she didn't like to barhop. This wouldn't have been her first choice, but Mike had motioned her in from the sidewalk. "What would you like?"

The chief shook his head. "Nothing, thanks. I don't drink."

"How do you stay hydrated?"

His eyes creased. She liked how they smiled before his mouth.

"I just came to give you a message from Sarge."

She patted the stool. "You may as well sit."

He hesitated, then straddled the stool. Lucas popped the cap on an O'Doul's and set it before him. "Thanks." He took a swig.

"What's my message?"

"Sarge wants you to keep the job."

"He does?" Surprise and confusion mingled with joy and relief.

"He's angry and hurting, but most of all he's scared. He's losing control and doesn't know how to be without it."

"Tia told me about his wife and son."

Jonah frowned. "Best if you don't mention it."

She met the chief's dark blue eyes. "How did it happen?"

He stared a moment into the mouth of his beer bottle. "Marty was just learning to drive. He started to pass someone on the highway and got clipped. It put the car into a spin, and they went through the guardrail. Sarge thinks if he'd been out there, he might have stopped it, but Ellen wouldn't let him teach the kid, said he was too impatient. Given Marty's timid nature, she was probably right, and that's what really eats him up."

"Poor Sarge." She meant it.

"Yeah." Jonah stared down at the bar.

Mike came back from the bathroom ready to contest the stool until he realized it was the chief in his spot. He wiped his mouth and tried to look half as wasted as he was.

Jonah slid Mike a glance. "Not driving, are you?"

"No sir."

She'd never heard Mike call anyone sir.

"Who's your DD?" Jonah's voice was low yet somehow penetrating.

"Uh, MacDonald." Mike pointed to a kid shooting pool in the back of the room.

"Go make sure of that."

"Okay." Mike walked away.

The chief turned back. "Don't get in a car with him." He stood up, tossed a five on the bar, and went out the way he'd come, alone.

———

Jonah went home but not inside. He lowered himself onto the Adirondack chair and stared out into the night. He'd been nine when Marty crashed, was riding shotgun in his dad's truck when the call came over the radio. He might not remember it so clearly if the police chief hadn't ordered him down the slope to see what happened to fools that weren't careful.

He'd been retching under a tree when Sarge arrived. Their eyes met only briefly, a look that said Marty had been the sweet-natured son Sarge didn't deserve, and no one deserved a father like Stan Westfall.

Jonah reached into his pocket and pulled out a harmonica. He raised his feet to the rail and crossed his ankles.

Sarge had given him jobs so the bread wouldn't seem like charity; sweeping, counting inventory, stocking shelves. He always pointed out if the work was shoddy. And if it wasn't, he'd said, *"Well done, soldier. Carry on."*

Even now the words brought a hitch to his chest.

He didn't know what Sarge had seen in him, maybe a replacement for the son he'd lost. But he knew what he'd seen in Sarge, and there was no way the man would be stuffed into a care facility. He brought the harmonica to his mouth and started playing, a soft, poignant melody.

He had not insulted Tia, comparing her to Sarge. They were both incredibly strong, incredibly stubborn, incredibly important to him. He wanted both to move past the hurts that held them captive. Didn't help that he'd played a part in Tia's.

At the sound of rustling, Jonah lowered the harmonica and peered into the darkness. At the fringe of the tree line, a shadow moved. He unsnapped his holster, pulled his sidearm onto his lap, and rested his hand atop. Unless it was human, whatever was there could see him a lot better than he could see it. Smell him too.

Bears, cougars, and coyotes wouldn't naturally approach unless crazed with hunger or rabid. He sensed the creature's uncertainty, imagined its eyes roving over him, nose quivering as it took in his scent. Any moment it would slip away, shielded by the trees from a creature far less dangerous, yet threatening by nature of reason alone.

But the shadow crept closer. Jonah watched and waited. The lack of stealth surprised him. Moonlight reflected off a pair of eyes, low to the ground, then higher. He sensed the animal's fear, saw streaks of black across its side and shoulder.

The animal left the trees, pressing through the scrub and pausing where his lawn began, its motion more canine than feline, definitely not a bear. Bigger than a raccoon. Drawing slow breaths, he waited. If the animal charged he'd shoot, but he hoped he wouldn't have to.

As it stepped onto the grass, he noticed the limp, the hang of its head. An injured coyote. Why on earth was it coming to him? His mournful harmonica some sort of clarion? Pace after pace, it drew near, then lowered itself and lay panting with soft whines. He could see blood clumping the fur of its shoulder, neck, and side.

He holstered the gun, pocketed the mouth organ, then took out and flicked on his flashlight. He sat forward, letting the animal register his movement. It raised its head, bared its teeth, and growled. The effort took energy the creature didn't have, and it lowered its head. Slowly Jonah stood. The coyote whined.

He moved toward it, taking one step down and then another. The animal tensed when he reached the grass, and he waited, letting it sense him. It was a female. And she wasn't a pure coyote. She looked part shepherd. A coydog.

He moved, slowly and quietly, expecting her to spring up and run. As he came within a couple of steps, she reached out a paw and dragged herself a few inches toward him. He looked into her eyes, saw the wild fear but also something close to resignation.

He squatted down and examined her wounds. No cutting or stitching. She looked to have been caught with a shotgun blast. By the matting in her coat, she'd lost a lot of blood. She licked weakly at the wounds stretching from shoulder to distended belly.

Jonah swallowed. She was a wild predator, but he took out his phone and dialed the vet. When she answered, he said, "Dr. Rainer? This is Chief Westfall. I know it's past hours, but I have an animal here that I can't transport. Any chance you can come have a look?"

He described the injuries and gave her directions to his place without mentioning that it was a coyote. Half coyote. Panting, the animal rolled farther to her side. Jonah ran the light over her, looking for anything he may have missed. Her eyes had dulled. Her tongue hung slack. Her ribs rose and fell in shallow breaths.

"Hang in there," he whispered. Slowly, he extended his hand, fingers curled to the palm, letting her get his scent. He brought it closer, rested it on her head. She tensed but couldn't sustain it. He moved his fingers softly through the fur. Odds were good she'd be dead by morning, but she'd come to him. "Hold on now. Hold on." He kept her as calm as he could until the grind of gravel announced Liz arriving.

She approached tentatively, her eyes widening when *coyote* registered. By then the animal's head lay heavily in his cupped palm. She caught the new scent and eyed Liz warily, drawing her lips back and rumbling in her throat.

Jonah felt more than heard it. "I don't think she has much fight, but I don't have to tell you to be careful."

"You want me to put her down?"

That would be the obvious choice, maybe the wise one. More wild than not, when she got strong again, she'd take off and be bolder than before. But he shook his head. She'd come to him for help, conquered her instinct and made herself vulnerable. "I thought we could treat the wounds, stop the bleeding and the pain."

A smile touched Liz Rainer's lips. "Is that what your head's telling you?"

He took the jibe with a glance and shrugged.

Liz ran her eyes over the animal. "She's carrying a litter."

"I thought so."

"Well, let's see what we can do to make her comfortable."

He sat back as the vet worked over her, pinching the fur to insert the needle to sedate her, removing thirteen pellets, then salving the wounds. He went inside and brought out a woolen blanket that he tucked under the animal's head, then laid the remainder loosely over her.

Liz said, "She's not a pure coyote, is she?"

"Coydog, I'd guess. A bolder, cannier predator with less fear of people."

"That's why your scent didn't warn her off." She looked at him in the glow of the flashlights. "Maybe I should take her to the clinic."

"I don't think so. She's still mostly wild."

"What then?"

"Can we get her onto the porch?"

"We can try."

He straightened. "Let me get some more blankets." He piled them in a heap, knowing dogs preferred that to a neatly folded surface. Then he wrapped the other blanket more securely around the coyote so that he and the vet could safely transport her.

The animal's eyelids parted as they lifted, her lip curled. She whined. He noted the awkward position of Liz's hip and took the weight of the animal from her. He carried her up the stairs, then placed her gently into the corner opposite the swing.

Liz looked down at her. "She's easy prey."

"I'll stay out here tonight."

"You're going to sleep on your porch for a wounded coyote?"

"She asked."

Again the smile tugged a corner of Liz's mouth. He didn't explain how that little drag had opened him up.

"Then what?"

He sighed. "She might be dead by morning."

"Would you like me to come check her status?"

"I'll call." He turned toward the door. "Let me get my checkbook."

"This is outside my fees."

"You made a special trip."

"Well, what goes around, comes around."

He eyed her. "At least let me cover the medications."

She nodded. "Okay." She followed him in, told him the charge, and accepted his check. "Ordinarily I'd prescribe a course of antibiotics. If you think you can get them into her, I'll have them at the office."

"We'll play that by ear. Thanks for coming over."

After she left, he settled on the swing with the blanket from his bed. The coydog hadn't moved. He wondered who'd shot her, someone disturbed or frightened by her approach? A sport hunter shooting from a car? Coyotes were fair game, especially if she had seemed off or aggressive.

He closed his eyes and woke at dawn to find her still breathing. His fingers were stiff with cold as he called Jay. "Are you free today?"

"I make my own schedule." Jay's construction and renovation

company kept him as busy as he wanted to be, but being his own boss had its advantages.

"Any chance you can come by? There's something here that needs watching."

"Does it wear diapers?"

Jonah laughed. "Come see for yourself."

He brought out two cups of coffee when Jay arrived, striding casually across the yard. "Hold up."

Jay paused. "What?"

"She's here on the porch. I don't want you to startle her."

"She?"

Jonah indicated the coydog. Jay whistled low.

"Showed up last night. Hurt pretty bad."

"You want me to watch her?"

"Until she can watch herself. I have to work."

"A coyote comes to you, and you have to work?"

"She's a half-breed."

Jay pulled a slow smile.

"I'm guessing you can fix her some kind of mash or something."

"What do you have?"

"Steak?"

Jay snorted. He chopped raw meat and corn, added milk, and warmed and softened and mashed it on the stove, then ladled it onto a saucer.

When they brought it out, the coydog snarled.

"Step back," Jonah murmured.

Jay moved over by the swing. Carefully Jonah inched closer and set the saucer near the animal's head. She watched him with wary eyes, taking his measure with instinct and senses more acute than he could fathom. She didn't move until he'd stepped back two paces, then raised her nose and sniffed. She gave the food a couple of weak licks, then laid her head back down.

He turned to Jay. "That's a start, I guess."

Jay had a strange look on his face. "You know this is important, right?"

"Why?"

"Because she's coyote."

"And…"

"As the story goes, when the coyote-man made the world and all the land, he stuck two sticks into the places he wanted people to live. He named the places and turned the sticks into men and women. Then he and the lizard-man and the grizzly-bear-woman and all the others became animals. The people learned by watching the animals what things were good to eat. They grew wise by observing how the bugs and animals lived."

"Okay," Jonah said softly.

"This coyote finding you is a big deal."

"She has something to teach me?"

Jay shrugged, the corners of his mouth twitching. "Watch and see."

Nine

Go from me. Yet I feel that I shall stand henceforward in thy shadow.

—ELIZABETH BARRETT BROWNING

Liz woke with her mind full of Chief Westfall, the coyote that had conquered her instincts, and the coyote's pups. She imagined them pressed into each other, enwrapped, entangled, sleeping, squirming inside the mother's belly. Separate in their own sacs, not even necessarily squired by the same male but growing, living, drawing nourishment from the same source. Littermates.

Lucy rolled to meet her eyes. "There you are. What happened last night? Where did you go?"

She told her about the coyote, how gently Jonah had carried her to his porch and laid her on the blankets, how the animal neither snapped nor thrashed. But she didn't say she'd wondered how it would feel to be held by him, soothed by his hands.

"Will she live?"

"I have a feeling she might. From the sheer force of Jonah Westfall's will."

Lucy looked at her curiously. "You like him."

"He's a compassionate man."

Lucy's gaze penetrated. "You really like him."

"I hardly know him."

"But you like what you've seen."

"Yes. I told you. I think you could meet him."

Did she say it to silence her sister's questions? They both knew how few people would understand. Yes, she'd enjoyed the time with him, working together to save a creature most would consider a benefit to kill. And of course Lucy saw that.

"He might come by for medicine today. Say yes and I'll introduce you."
Lowering her eyes, Lucy withdrew. As Liz had known she would.

———

Tia settled the sculpture into place, three feet of polished granite composite with five niches to hold candles. She looked up when the fingerprint man pressed through the door, looking side to side. He saw her without acknowledging it. Once again his clothes were pristine and very nice quality. She had assumed him a tourist, but now she wondered. Remembering how touchy he'd been last time she'd offered assistance, she let him peruse the displays without repeating the mistake.

She placed five forest green candles into the hollows of the elongated sculpture, studied the effect, then tried ocher instead. Better. She stepped back. Yes. The ocher brought out the muted tones of the granite. She had consigned several of Lloyd's sculptures, but this was his best so far, and she hoped it sold. He could use the income.

She wouldn't sell it short, though. He was coming into his own with his art, and he'd agreed to let her push the envelope and see where it could go. She placed the card with Lloyd's name, the piece's number, and the price.

"Too many candles," the man said behind her.

She thought he meant the store's inventory, but he was referring to the pillar's five hollows.

"It only takes one candle to keep someone alive in a car in freezing temperatures. That much heat in one holder is excessive. It could be hazardous."

"I think five candles on this piece is jubilant."

He eyed her as though she'd missed the point entirely, then held up another pair of beeswax candles by the joined wick. "I'd like these tapers."

"The others worked out all right?"

"I sent them to my aunt."

"Well packaged, I hope."

"Bubble wrap."

Tia nodded. While she rang him up, Rachel Drake came in and waved. He laid the candles on the counter and went through the process of money retrieval. Wouldn't a credit card be cleaner and easier? But he removed the bills and laid them on the counter.

She gave him—gave his coin pouch—his change. He lifted the candles, but the wick slipped from his fingernails. Reaching out, her hand brushed his. He sprang back, thrusting out his hands, and backed into a display that fell with a crash of merchandise.

The crash panicked him even more, and Tia rushed around the counter. "Please, calm down."

Trying to get around her, he bumped another shelf unit that tipped and went down. If he would just contain himself.

Rachel was on her phone. Tia hurried past her. As the frantic customer rushed for the door, he tipped Lloyd's sculpture. It caught her in the calf and cracked on the floor. Gritting her teeth, Tia sagged against a support pillar.

Rachel rushed over. "Are you all right? I called 911."

"I'm fine." Lloyd's sculpture wasn't. She reached down to right it.

"Don't do that." Rachel touched her arm. "You need to leave things as they are. For the police report."

Now it sank in that an officer would arrive and investigate. "He couldn't help it."

"That doesn't change what happened. You've lost a lot of merchandise."

Tia pushed the hair back from her forehead. She might need a police report in order to file with her insurance, but she didn't want to get the poor guy in trouble. He hadn't intentionally torn things up. He'd lost control. And she'd precipitated it.

She told Rachel about his first visit as they waited. "Touching is obviously a trigger for deep-seated fears. He just panicked."

Officer Donnelly came in and halted. "Wow."

"Yeah." Tia rested her hands on the small of her back. "You got here quick."

"I was just down the street. Is he gone?" The sturdy young woman scanned the shop, a hand covering her weapon.

"He went out. I didn't see where."

"So what happened?" Sue raised her notebook.

Tia and Rachel described the incident. Sue wrote it down. "Were you physically threatened?"

"No." Tia shook her head.

"What happened to your leg?"

She looked down. The skin of her calf was raw, blood forming a bruise from the back of her knee to her Achilles tendon. "The sculpture hit my leg. I just didn't…I hadn't felt it until now."

The doorway darkened as Jonah strode in.

"Officer Donnelly's taking the report," she said, hoping he'd take the hint.

He addressed his officer. "I'll finish here."

She said, "We're almost—"

"You need to go, Sue. Eli fell. Sam's taking him to the emergency clinic."

Her face flushed. "Is it bad? Did he say what happened?"

"Just go."

She handed him the clipboard. Sue Donnelly was not a Redford native. She hadn't grown up with them, had no idea of their history. With news of her injured child everything else had left her mind. As it should.

Jonah watched her out the door, then turned back. "You want to fill me in?"

She didn't, but Rachel did, ending with, "He just freaked out."

Jonah nodded. "Thank you. I'll finish with Tia now."

Rachel tugged her purse strap higher. "I'll come back tomorrow, Tia. I want a bunch for my party."

"Okay. Thanks."

Jonah reviewed the officer's notes. What more could he need?

"Have you seen this guy before?"

"A couple of weeks ago. The day Sarge collapsed. He bought candles."

"Credit receipt?"

"He paid cash."

"Description?"

She pressed a hand to her forehead. "He's quite big, round shoulders. A blunt haircut and very large square hands. He wears his clothes pressed and spotless. He's afraid of germs and fingerprints. And…being touched."

Jonah lifted his pen. "Is that what set him off?"

"It is, and I don't want any wisecracks."

A hint of dark humor touched his eyes, but he refrained. "Did he threaten you?"

"No."

"You're injured."

"He knocked Lloyd's sculpture. It fell against my leg. It wasn't intentional. None of this was." The mingled scents of the broken and spilled packages confused her senses. Or maybe it was Jonah's scent interfering with her damaged creations.

Jonah pocketed the notebook. "You want help cleaning up?"

"No."

"Those shelves look heavy."

"I'll manage."

He clicked his pen and stuck it in his pocket. "I apologized last night."

"So forget it." She wrapped herself in her arms. "Anyway, you're wrong."

"About what?"

"I'm not bitter."

He gave her his cop face. "Okay. So let me help you with the shelves."

"No, thanks." She turned her back.

"You ought to have that leg looked at."

"So they can tell me it's bruised?"

"Ice it then."

It was hurting enough to bring tears if she bumped it. Gritting her teeth, she grabbed one end of the tempered glass shelf lying across the display frame. No way could she move it alone. Jonah came up beside her.

Together they lifted the shelves off the frame. A broken edge had gouged the floor. They raised the frame and inserted the three unbroken shelves. The other display was a single unit. They righted it, and she straightened.

"Can you think of anything else about this guy that might help me find him?"

She shook her head. "I don't want him prosecuted."

"You've got serious damage and personal injury."

"It was an accident." She looked at her leg. "I just need to clean up." She surveyed the shards of glass and broken pottery and crumbled wax. She had intended to make a claim for her insurance, which would require a police report. When had that changed?

"You should close up until it's safe. Last thing you need is someone slipping on a shard."

"Last thing I need is someone minding my business." She hadn't meant to snipe but hated his stating the obvious.

"Yeah. Got it." He looked her up and down, then walked out, turning the sign to CLOSED as he went.

———

Jonah left Tia's shop, scanning for the person she had described. He might be long gone, but if he was still upset about Tia's touching him, he could endanger others or himself. He checked the nearest shops. The kid at the T-shirt store had seen nothing. The man at the Western gallery had heard the crash but not seen anyone.

Jonah went into the bakery, glad to see Piper had forgiven Sarge's outburst and gone back to work—with no renegotiation of terms, as far as he knew. She looked up from arranging items on a tray and said, "Hi."

"Hi."

"Can I get you something?"

"No, thanks. Tia had an altercation next-door. I wondered if you saw or heard anything."

"Just now?"

"Forty minutes to an hour ago."

She shook her head. "The smoke alarm went off in the kitchen. I've been dealing with that."

"Okay."

"What happened at Tia's?"

He repeated an abbreviated version, then described the man.

"That guy?" Piper looked distressed.

"You saw him?"

"Not today. A while ago. I can't believe he'd do that."

"Tia said it wasn't intentional. He snapped."

Piper shook her head. "Poor guy. He's got that Monk thing."

"He's a monk?"

"No, you know the TV show."

Jonah hadn't owned a television in years. Typical mountain reception, and it wasn't worth paying for satellite.

"That guy who has to have everything lined up and spotless."

"OCD?"

Piper shrugged. "He seemed nice enough. A little funny about germs. I sold him a fig and pine-nut sticky roll that could have been yours if you'd come in that time I asked."

He half smiled and got her back on point. "He made no threats…"

"He's not mean, just different."

"And you didn't see him today."

Her silky blond ponytail swung as she shook her head. "Is Tia okay?"

There were too many ways he could answer that. "You can check with her." He palmed his notebook. "Thanks for your help."

Having done all he could with that, he drove to the emergency clinic, found Sue and Sam in the waiting room.

Sue looked to be holding herself together with sheer force of will. "Eli's getting x-rays."

Sam sat, elbows on his thighs, hands shaking. He raised red-rimmed eyes, his face rough with several days' growth of beard. "What are you staring at? Accidents happen."

He was a thin man, narrow across the shoulders and chest, getting a bad-habit belly that made his jeans ride low. Jonah curbed his tongue. The last thing Sue needed was an altercation between her husband and her boss.

"How did he fall?"

"Climbed the railing on the balcony. He knows he's not supposed to go there."

"Where were you?"

"On the couch. Sleeping. He was supposed to be napping too."

"How did he get outside?"

"Gets hot in there. I opened the balcony door. He was supposed to be sleeping." He wrung his hands together, exhibiting remorse, until he muttered, "It's not my fault."

Jonah leaned in. "You're blaming the kid?"

"Back off."

Jonah grabbed his shirt collar. "You're supposed to be his protector, not a liability."

"Get off me." He jerked away.

"Jonah." Sue gripped his arm.

A tech wheeled Eli out of the radiation room. Sue rushed over, Sam plodding behind, indignant and self-righteous. Jonah turned on his heel. A toddler alone on a balcony? Negligence at best. The severity of the injury would determine a lot. He hoped for Sue's sake, and Sam's, that this would be a wake-up call and nothing more.

He climbed into the Bronco, annoyed that he'd vented his frustration on Sam, deserving though he was. Getting physical on the job was his dad's forte. Jonah drove to the animal hospital and went inside. After ringing the bell, he stood for a long time without acknowledgment. Finally Liz came out with a miniature Pomeranian in her arms. She handed the dog to a petite woman who looked just like it.

Jonah didn't know her name, but he'd seen her around town with the dog. He smiled as she passed. She smiled back like a proud grandmother, her cinnamon hair and closely clustered features a perfect familial match. Liz came around the counter, limping without wincing, which led him to believe the injury was not new, maybe even congenital.

"How's your coyote?"

"Don't think we can call her mine. But she's breathing, lapped a little mash, a little water."

"Predators will smell her injuries."

"I called a friend to watch her."

Liz raised her brows. "Does she know not to touch?"

"*He's* good with animals, children, and former drunks." No telling why he'd said it, but understanding dawned in her face.

"Ah."

"I'll try the antibiotics you mentioned."

"Sure." She went through a door and came back with a pill bottle. "Bury these in raw meat, liverwurst, peanut butter, anything that sparks her interest. She should swallow it whole."

He took the bottle. "Thank you for coming over last night, risking contact."

She gave him a knowing look. "I doubt half what I've heard is true."

He stiffened.

She broke into a smile. "Just teasing."

She'd either learned things from people in town or she'd been probing. "What do I owe you for the pills?"

"If you keep her until she bears her litter, I'd like two."

Now it was his turn for surprise. "If a coyote mated the coydog, they'll be wilder than she is. Full grown, two of them could take you down."

A smile touched her lips. "I'll take my chances."

He shook his head. "I can't be responsible."

"I'm sure you can—when you want to be."

"That's not what I—" Again she'd been teasing. Flirting. He sized her up.

"So that's the deal," she said. "If the medicine makes her well, I have my choice of the litter."

He sighed. "We'll talk about it when the time comes." Chances were good the animal wouldn't live long enough to bear pups or would run off to bear them in secret.

As he got into his truck, the radio dispatched a call to the middle- and high-school complex. Arson in the boys' locker room. Someone had lit a heap of sweaty gym socks on fire. Jonah radioed that he was on it. He even had a guess who'd done it.

The fire department had everything under control when he arrived. Standing in the parking lot, while the firefighters removed the soaked and charred material, Lieutenant "Stogy" Sanders gave him the rundown. "The emergency sprinklers extinguished the blaze before it really got going. Little, if any, accelerant used. Not even possibly accidental."

Jonah nodded. It was the kind of thing adolescent boys found funny before their frontal lobes matured. But fire was no toy. They'd bring juvie charges.

Jonah turned to the man beside him. "Any ideas, Coach?"

"Snyder's in my office. I suggested he wait around and talk with you."

"You left him alone in your office?"

"Cozzie's with him."

The girls' softball coach was built like a cannon. Packed about the same punch too, without raising a hand. Jonah went in and relieved her, staring down the kid he'd reprimanded a couple of months ago for luring a stray dog with lunch meat, then tossing cherry bombs. They might be discussing more than arson today.

Ten

So we grew together, like to a double cherry, seeming parted,
but yet an union in partition.
—WILLIAM SHAKESPEARE

Piper pulled open the pantry door and shrieked.

"Shh." Wedged between the wall and shelves, the big guy clamped his hands to his ears.

Heart pumping, she pressed her palm to her chest. "What are you doing?"

"He's looking for me." The Lego man looked miserable, drawing his big knees to his chest.

"The chief?"

One decisive nod.

"Because you messed up Tia's shop?"

"I didn't mean to."

Piper crouched down. "Of course you didn't."

"She touched me. And I bumped the shelves. Then everything was falling." He rubbed his knees. "I can't go to jail with all the germs and dirty people." He closed his eyes and shuddered.

"Why would you go to jail?"

"I saw him. I saw his face." He gave her a pointed look. "He was very angry."

"That's because he talked to Tia. They're always mad at each other."

He clearly disbelieved her. "Why?"

"They have a love-hate thing."

He moaned. "I'm dead."

"You're making this worse than it is. Come out of the pantry."

He shook his head.

Sighing, she reached for the broom. "I'm going to sweep the front.

You can sneak out the back or come up and have something nice and warm from the case."

She went out to the front. The few tables had emptied, and no one waited at the counter. He must have run in when she had the kitchen door propped open to let out the smoke. She wouldn't think such a natty dresser would sit on the floor, but that was probably his least concern.

Starting in the front by the window, she whisked the broom over the floor. A few minutes later, she sensed motion behind her and turned. The man was standing nervously beside the counter, watching her. She pointed toward the case. "What would you like?"

His Adam's apple moved in his neck. "There are no fig and pine-nut sticky rolls."

"No."

"No spinach, kalamata, and goat cheese."

"Sarge doesn't like me doing anything different."

He studied her solemnly, then pointed. "A cheddar roll, if you wash your hands."

She set the broom against the wall. "One cheddar roll coming up." She washed at the small sink, pulled on a glove, and used a tissue to hand him the food. "It's on me."

His brow puckered. "You don't want me to pay? It's free of charge?"

"Yep. But you should tell me your name. If we're meeting in closets and all."

That surprised an uneasy smile onto his face. "It's Miles."

"Like miles to go before I sleep?"

"Like Miles Standish."

"Your last name is Standish?"

"I won't tell my last name. Then you could find me." He jerked a glance over his shoulder, a strange gesture for such a big guy.

"Well, you can find me."

"Only here. At work. Not where you live."

"Okay." She smiled. "I'm Piper."

They didn't shake hands. Standing in front of the counter, he devoured the roll without dropping a crumb.

"So here's what I think, Miles. We should talk to the police chief, let him know it was an accident, and offer to help Tia."

"No. I can't. You didn't *see* him."

She had the other night when he'd upset Tia. He looked hard and edgy. Maybe the chief did have a dark side. What did she really know? "Well, think about it, okay?"

When he'd gone, she took the broom and finished sweeping, straightened the chairs around the tables, and then placed the call.

The chief strode in a half-hour later. "You have information for me?"

"His name is Miles. He didn't mean to cause trouble, and he's afraid of you."

"Of me?"

She nodded.

"He's never even seen me. What are you—"

"He saw you leaving Tia's shop, and you looked mad."

Jonah planted his hands on his waist. "Saw me from where?"

"I don't know. I found him in the pantry."

"What?" The edge was back.

"He was scared."

"Help me understand. He tore up Tia's shop, then hid over here?"

"He didn't mean to do that."

"He injured her."

"What?" She searched his face. "Tia's hurt?"

"More than she's admitting."

Miles hadn't said a word about hurting Tia, not a word. How could he not say anything? "I need to see her." She locked the register and scooted out around the counter.

"Piper." His voice was low and even. "I want to talk to him. If he comes back, you let me know."

She'd have to. "Fine." She motioned him out the door and locked it, flipping her sign, then rushed next-door.

———

Startled by the knock, Tia bumped her elbow on the shelf and rubbed the pain away as she unlocked the door.

"Are you all right?"

"It's just a bump."

"I mean everything."

Tia slumped. "Yeah well, it's kind of a mess."

"Jonah said you're hurt."

"Jonah should keep his mouth shut."

"He's worried."

"It's none of his business."

"Yeah, that's hard when he's in love with you."

Tia straightened as though jerked up by a rope.

"Come on, Tia. It couldn't be more obvious if his forehead flashed neon."

Tia stepped back and winced again.

"Your leg looks bad."

"It feels worse." She grimaced.

"Did you take something?"

"I found an old Percocet in my purse, but it hasn't kicked in yet. Aren't you open next-door?"

"Only to clean up and close down." She fished a pottery shard from under a shelf and added it to the pile Tia had swept up. "Tia, Miles didn't mean to do this."

"Miles?"

She nodded. "The Lego man. His name is Miles. He didn't mean—"

"I know that. But…" She spread her hands, encompassing the scope of it.

"He's scared he'll go to jail."

Tia frowned. "Why would he go to jail?"

"Because the chief of police looked so mad when he walked out of here. I told him you and Jonah get mad every time you see each other, but—"

"No, we don't." Tia leaned on a shelf, taking the weight off her leg.

"You need to put that up. I'll make an ice pack." She returned to the bakery, fashioned Tia a bag of ice wrapped in a towel, then hurried back.

Tia gingerly lowered herself to the stool behind the counter. She bent her knee and positioned the bruise onto the pack. "Thanks. That'll help."

"I'm sorry this happened."

"I'm all right."

"Can I make you some tea?"

"I'd like that."

Piper heated the electric kettle in the back, brewed a cup of strong sweet tea. Wasn't that the remedy for all that ails? "Here you go." She set the cup and saucer next to Tia's leg.

"Thanks."

"Can I do anything else?"

"You should finish up next-door. Just lock up please, when you go out."

"I'll come back when I'm done."

"No need. I'll see you at home."

Tia looked grim, but Piper let it be. She had work to finish, and Tia knew where to find her—if she'd ever ask for help. Piper hated the parasitic tendencies of her clan, but could someone be too self-sufficient?

———

As the heat of her injury melted the ice pack, Tia leaned her head back and closed her eyes. The shop grew dark, and the tea turned cold, but Piper's insight regarding Jonah weighed on her. If she could see it in so short a time, what must others think? Had she only been fooling herself?

Dark thoughts closed around her, skeletal fingers boring into her skull, evil whispers in her ears. She could name the demons. Self-loathing. Regret. Despair. They had no power she didn't give them. But they clung to her now as memories of Reba flowed one into another.

Her beautiful, sweet sister with strawberry blond hair, their dad's fair skin, and a dusting of freckles across her nose and cheeks. Reba didn't hate her freckles. She knew they made her cute, fresh, wholesome. And they had mostly disappeared by adolescence.

Sarge had likened her to Hayley Mills, the young heartthrob of the fifties, Pollyanna bringing sunshine to the world. Then came Tia, favoring her mother's side, with her darker skin and the shape and snap of her eyes. She had none of her mild father, his soft voice and pliant nature. Strong-willed, they'd called her. Tempestuous.

She didn't remember what she'd fought about. It probably hadn't mattered. It was all intangibles, needs that drove impulses and drew reactions. She wished she could say she didn't care. But every slicing criticism had drawn blood that only Reba saw.

Tia closed her eyes. Jonah could have made it right. If he had begged and apologized, Reba would have forgiven him, forgiven them.

Tears came.

She'd spent the years since studying psychology for an explanation—an excuse?—for her behavior. If nothing else, she had to know she would never make such a mistake again. She'd wanted to help others to avoid pitfalls, to understand their fragilities. But even with two college degrees, that desire had come to nothing.

Her leg grew numb. She dropped her head to her chest, letting the fog cloud the memories, then yelped when someone rattled the door. She swung her leg down and peered at the night-filled window. Jonah, hands pressed to the glass, peered back. She prayed he wouldn't see her in the dim security lights concentrated overhead. No luck.

"Go away."

He knocked. "Come on, Tia."

She braced herself against the counter, itching as blood flowed back to her toes. Her calf howled with pain. Limping to the door she freed the lock. "What?"

"Piper called. She's frantic. She tried your cell and both doors."

She had turned off her cell, but how had she missed Piper knocking? Percocet. It must have knocked her out.

"What are you doing here in the dark?"

"I guess I missed the 'I answer to Jonah' memo."

He pulled her onto the sidewalk where the outer lamp illuminated her tears. "Is it your leg?"

"Will you stop butting in?"

"Piper called me. I'm a cop. I respond." He blew out his breath. "I have a psychopath out there eviscerating animals, maybe the same one who tore up your shop because you touched him. And here you are, in the dark, alone."

He had a point.

"It's late, and you're injured. For once, be reasonable. Let me take you home."

She slumped against the jamb. "My purse is inside."

"Where?"

"The back."

He eased her inside the door and let it close, then moved through the shop under the security lights. Her whole body shook. The injury must be worse than she'd thought. The drug had certainly worn off.

Jonah returned with her purse and jacket. She reached for the coat, but he slid the sleeve up her arm and wrapped it around for the other. She closed her eyes as he settled it over her shoulders. Had her dad helped her that way when she was little? All she remembered were her own stubborn assertions, *"I can do it myself."* She tugged her purse over her shoulder.

Jonah supported her elbow as she limped through the door. He half lifted her into the Bronco at the curb, her leg throbbing as she positioned it. Jonah reached for the buckle, but she took it from him. She couldn't let him reach across.

He stepped back and closed the door, walked around, and invaded the space inside with a presence that consumed oxygen. She'd never ridden alone with him. Silence climbed in to chaperon. He parked directly across her front walk. She opened the door, but before she could get her wounded leg to the concrete, he was there holding her arm.

"I can do it."

He closed the door behind her and guided her toward the house. She didn't want him at her door, but there he was. She fumbled for her keys.

He raised her chin. "They don't care, Tia."

A lump filled her throat.

"You're never going to change their minds. Even if you spend your whole life alone."

She didn't pretend to not know what he meant. "Can you imagine the names I was called by my own mother?"

"Yes. Mine can hardly stand to look at me."

"But not because of me, Jonah."

"No." His hand softened on her cheek. "Not because of you." His voice roughened. "You know how I feel."

She closed her eyes. "Don't."

"It doesn't go away."

"You won't let it."

"Tia."

He was so close, and he was right, it didn't go away. She looked into his face. "We made a mistake."

"It wasn't a mistake."

"How can you say that, when it destroyed so much?"

He looked away, his jaw rippling.

"Please, Jonah. Let this go."

Her cheek felt the loss of his hand. She watched his retreat, thankful and aching. He glanced over once, then got into the truck and pulled away from the curb.

Jonah skidded to a stop outside his cabin and was halfway to the steps when he remembered the coyote. He leaned over the railing, his heart sinking at the empty blankets. Earlier, he and Jay had given her a dose of antibiotics in a lump of meat, and he'd thought it a good sign.

Lights were on inside, and the sound of a saw drifted through the open door. He mounted the stairs, closed the door behind him, and headed toward the noise. The air was frigid inside except in his room where the wood-burning stove blazed and in the back where Jay had plugged in the electric heater.

The whine of the saw wound down. Jay pulled the goggles down around his neck. "You're back."

"She's gone?"

"Not quite."

Jonah followed him to the bedroom door where Jay stopped and motioned him in. Jonah scanned the room, pausing when he saw the eyes. From the depth of his closet, two reddish orbs. "What's this about?"

Jay shrugged. "I gave her the choice of staying or going. Took her two hours to come inside, then she walked directly to your room and claimed the closet."

"How am I supposed to change clothes?" Jonah peeled off the department jacket and hung it on the hook, laid his weapon belt across the dresser, and locked the gun into the drawer safe.

"You work that out with her." Jay went back to work as Jonah removed his shirt and pulled on a wolf gray sweatshirt. He slipped his bare feet into well-worn Birkenstocks and sat on the edge of the bed, contemplating his roommate. "Now what?"

Her lip curled, but she made no sound. When he stood up, her eyes followed him to the doorway. She didn't move. In the kitchen, he sliced off a chunk of steak and bored an antibiotic inside. He approached the closet cautiously, knowing as he crouched that she could rend his throat in a single spring. He set the meat down and backed away. Her eyes never left him.

After he and Jay had finished their meal, he went back to the closet and found the meat gone. He located Jay outside by the glow of his cigarette.

"Thought you only smoked on Sundays."

"Sometimes I make exceptions." He tipped his head to the stars, and his breath blew white.

Jonah jammed his hands into his pockets. "Will she kill me in my sleep?"

Jay shrugged. "If your ticket's punched, you'll ride the train, my grandpa always said."

"I'd rather not have my throat torn out."

"No doubt."

"What if she has to pee?"

"Leave the doors open. She got in. She can get out."

"Anything else can get in too."

Jay shrugged. "Do what you think right."

They both knew he'd leave the door open.

Eleven

The constantly recurring question must be: What shall we
unite with and from what shall we separate?
—A. W. TOZER

Lucy didn't want her to go, but Liz zipped her coat and gathered salve
and the kit that held another injection of sedative. "Don't worry. She's
too weak to hurt me."

"Not if you make her better."

"I'll be fine, silly. I just want to make sure her wounds are healing."
And her pups are safe. She didn't say it aloud. It would be a surprise. Two
pups from the same litter.

She kissed Lucy's forehead. "You rest and don't worry about me."

She had reached the bedroom door when Lucy said, "Is it the coyote
or the police chief you want to see most?"

Liz turned. "The chief has the coyote, honey. Otherwise I'd have no
reason to see him."

Lucy searched her face, eyes gulping like fish mouths as she fought
tears. "Don't let him take you away."

"Take me away?"

"From me."

She absorbed Lucy's distress. "Nothing can take us from each other.
You know that."

Lucy sniffled. "I'm afraid."

"Don't be. Everything is going to be fine."

Tears rolled down Lucy's cheeks. "Promise?"

"Promise."

She drove to the chief's cabin, a good distance from any others. Why
was he so remote? Maybe he couldn't afford something closer. She had
used funds from those early interviews and two television appearances to
buy the animal hospital and house, and it had not come cheap.

Jonah's yard was neat, wood stacked to the roof at one sidewall, holly growing along the porch. Several tall aspen encircled the structure that sat in a clearing of taller pines. A broad creek gushed along the mountainous side of the clearing, transforming the static landscape. Lights were on inside, and the door stood open. Was he expecting someone?

As she approached the cabin, she noted with keen disappointment the empty blankets on the porch. If the animal was gone, she would not receive the pups, and what reason would she have to see Jonah Westfall? Lucy's question sprang into her mind, but she pushed it away. Her flirting had been harmless, silly. And yet…

She knocked on the door frame. A man who wasn't Jonah came into view and appraised her with one stunning blue and one hazel eye. She'd never seen that trait in a human and realized she was staring.

He said, "Hi," as though used to it.

"I'm Dr. Rainer. I came to see the chief—the coyote. I came to treat the coyote."

"You're the vet."

She nodded, looking over her shoulder at the empty blankets. "Did she die?"

"Relocated."

"Jonah brought her inside?"

"She brought herself." He turned and started walking. Liz took that as an invitation.

They stopped outside a room that was clearly Jonah's. His department jacket hung on a hook beside the door, and the room carried his scent. Her head rushed. She shook herself as Jonah rose up from his knees near the open closet. Tall, rangy in sweatshirt and jeans, he exuded masculinity. As he turned toward Jay, she observed an ease between them that seemed deeper than friendship. No blood tie, obviously. Were they…

Jay moved aside and Jonah saw her. "Liz."

Her name instead of her title sent a frisson down inside her. "I came to check on the coyote."

He looked toward the closet.

"She's in there?"

"You can't get to her."

"I brought sedative."

"She's calling the shots now—so to speak." He motioned toward the door. "Let's leave her alone." He ushered them into a room with two leather couches and two recliners. Simple but solid wooden tables gleamed with a warm finish, and a stone fireplace with a half-log mantel created a manly place oddly overpopulated with candles.

"Are those from the Half Moon?"

"Yeah. But don't tell."

She raised her brows.

"Long story."

Jay's odd eyes were both watchful and knowing. Protective and intimate.

"How long have you two been…here?"

The men looked at each other. Something sparked between them that ignited laughter.

Jay said. "You think we're…" He waved a hand between them. "Together?"

Jonah's brow lowered. "Jay's my sponsor. He saved my life."

"Oh." Heat rushed to her cheeks. "I'm sorry. I…I didn't really think— it just looked…" She dropped her hands to her sides.

Jonah cleared his throat. "Would you like a drink? Coffee, tea? Coke?"

She shook her head. "No caffeine. My mind is already running away." *Stupid, stupid.*

Half grinning, Jay lifted a jacket from the end of the couch. "I'll just be going. Nice meeting you." He nodded at Jonah. "See you later."

When Jay had gone, Jonah forked his fingers into his hair. "I don't believe anyone has ever questioned my orientation."

"I didn't. Really. There was just something between you."

He expelled a long breath. "Let me take your coat."

"I shouldn't stay. There's no reason if I can't treat the animal."

"You drove all the way out here."

She pulled the coat tighter. "It's kind of chilly."

"Jay had the doors open so she could come and go. I'll light a fire." With easy dispatch he got a blaze roaring up the chimney. Then he went to the kitchen and came back with a mug of hot chocolate. "Minimal caffeine."

"Thank you."

"You're welcome." He sank into the worn leather recliner.

She took the other, feeling like her limbs were made of cardboard. "So Jay helped you get sober."

"He got me sober. Jay found me with more booze than blood in my veins. He used sweats, potions—incantations for all I know. I had shut down."

"How long did it take?"

"Five weeks. He treated me like a baby, spooning gruel into my mouth. He got me on my feet and taught me carpentry so I'd have an employable skill, since neither of us believed I'd get my old job back."

"Your old job?" She blew on the chocolate, then sipped.

"Chief of police." The fire crackled, chasing away the chill.

"You obviously did, though."

"Yeah."

"Weren't people concerned whether you could do the job?"

"They knew I could do it." His eyes turned to flint. "I'd proved it when I took the job."

"I didn't mean to imply…"

"I've been sober six years."

"And Jay?"

"Nine. The longest he'd gone before was three. He'd been close to slipping, but we pulled through together and kind of keep it that way."

"He's a very good friend."

"He is."

She studied him. "Is it primarily a physical craving? Your addiction?" His eyes rose slowly in the shadowed sockets. "Or underlying issues?"

"Call it scientific curiosity."

"The desire is always there. But other things trigger it."

"I didn't mean to pry."

"Confession is part of recovery." He got up and poked the fire, resettling the logs. Flames leaped with renewed vigor. Liz rose stiffly and joined him at the fireplace. He had told her deeply personal things. Did she dare tell him hers?

Rehanging the poker, he slid his gaze to her. A sensation she'd never felt before melted her bones. Eyes locked on his, she moved closer, her skin prickling with the fire's heat. No denying the attraction. He must see and sense it. He knew.

His voice thickened. "We could start something here."

Her weak leg almost gave out. She had never been near a man like him.

"We could, Liz, but it wouldn't be fair."

"Because…" He might lose his sobriety? his heart? Then she saw it in his eyes. "There's someone else."

"I'd stop it if I could. But I just…" He spread his hands.

She could help him, change him. "Does she feel the same?"

"No. Yeah." He shook his head. "It's complicated."

"What isn't?"

He ran his thumb over her cheek. "This."

That gentle stroke opened a pit of yearning. She would do, give, be anything he wanted. "And in the morning? Will it be complicated then?" Why had she said that? Because her own complication had swelled up and choked her. What he would see. What he would know.

Eyes pressed shut, he lowered his hand. "Yeah. It would."

Liz forced the strength back into her legs. "How long have you loved her?"

"I don't know when it happened. I've known her since I was nine."

"Childhood sweethearts?"

"Not exactly. I was engaged to her sister."

Her heart staggered. He'd loved them both?

He gripped his head and turned away. "I need to stop telling you things."

"I'm a good listener." And she wanted to know, to hear how he'd committed to one woman and loved another. Sisters.

He pressed his palm to the fireplace stone. "You should go."

"But—"

"For your sake, Liz. Go." His tone left her no choice.

⚊

Fists clenched, Jonah listened until the door closed and Liz was gone, her defenseless blue eyes no longer searching him. He shook his head in frustration and relief. She'd been willing, even after he'd told her, because something inside a woman made her believe she could change what was inside a man. But what was inside him had nothing to do with her.

Tia's rejection had stung. He'd wanted to assert…some control. He moved toward the shelf, took the bottle down. He opened the lid, breathed the fumes like an asthmatic inhaler. His mouth touched the glass, his tongue the smooth, cold lip.

Sensing something behind him, he turned and saw her watching, eyes glowing red in the firelight. Was she leaving? He closed the bottle and slid it onto the shelf. Her lips drew back in a snarl, a low hum in her throat. He would have to go past her to open the door, but she lowered her head and limped back to the bedroom, her blood-crusted sides heaving. He followed.

She didn't go as deeply into the closet but flopped down on the T-shirt and shorts he'd worked out in the day before. They had to be covered in his scent, but she didn't seem concerned. Maybe she used it to camouflage her own. He sat down on the bed, watching her pant. There was water in the bowl, but she didn't go for it.

She stared hard at him and contracted, curled and contracted, then bent her head around and licked a small, dark wad. She tore away the sac and revealed a wet face. He sank back on his heels, hardly believing she was having the pups in his closet.

He should have let Liz stay. No. He rubbed his jaw. He shouldn't. He'd done the right thing, but his body disagreed. He wanted a drink. He wanted a release from the need that hollowed him. The old song was right. Love hurt. Love scarred. It wounded and marred.

Jonah ground his palms into his eyes. The coyote growled when he stood up, but he eased out of the room, brewed a pot of coffee, then returned. A second wad lay against her belly, receiving the lick-down. He stretched out across the foot of his bed, sipped the black coffee from the mug, and felt humbled by her trust. She'd put her life in his hands when he couldn't be trusted with his own.

———

Piper had left Tia alone in the living room after the chief brought her home, but now she climbed onto the settee next to her. "Are you mad?"

"Mad?"

"That I called him?"

Tia shook her head. "I'm sorry I worried you."

"Between Miles and the animal torturer…"

"I know. Jonah made that clear." Tia pinched the bridge of her nose. "But honestly? I've walked these streets my whole life. I could do it blind."

"Not with your leg like that."

Tia sighed. "You're right. I guess the pain pill knocked me out. Right now, I wish I had another one."

"You should see a doctor in the morning. In the meantime, one ice pack and ibuprofen coming up." She fetched the soft pack from the freezer and a dose of weaker, but hopefully helpful, pain relief.

"You're a good nurse."

"Just a friend, I hope."

Tia smiled. "You are that."

"Or sister. I'd love to have you for my sister." As an only child tugged from place to place she had wished most of all for a sister.

Tia's smile faded. "You wouldn't say that if you knew."

"Yes, I would." She wished Tia realized how much she meant it. She took her hand. "Whatever happened, it wasn't your fault."

Tia closed her eyes. "It definitely was."

"So what if it was? Does that make you a horrible person? Everyone makes mistakes."

"You sound like a *Sesame Street* song."

Piper snuggled in. "I loved *Sesame Street*."

"So did Reba." Tia's grin twisted. "I told her Big Bird had a growth disorder and Grover was a mama's boy."

Piper rested her head on Tia's shoulder. "And Oscar?"

"I kind of liked Oscar. He said it like it was."

Piper giggled, crossing her ankles on the coffee table right beside Tia's. "Want to have a pajama party?"

When Tia got up and limped to the kitchen, Piper guessed she'd pushed too far, but then Tia came back with a bottle of red wine and a box of Godiva dark chocolate. "I bought these truffles for my birthday last month. I think now would be a good time to eat them."

Twelve

Let children walk with Nature, let them see the beautiful
blendings and communions of death and life, their joyous
inseparable unity, as taught in woods and meadows, plains and
mountains and streams of our blessed star, and they will learn
that death is stingless indeed, and as beautiful as life.

—JOHN MUIR

Jonah woke with his head and arms bent over the foot of the bed, his
empty coffee mug lying on the rug, and the coyote watching him over
three live and one unresponsive pup. The last must have come after he
dropped off, when he'd thought she was finished. Had it been born dead,
or had the mother lacked the energy to lick one more to life? Guilt stabbed
as she looked at him with accusatory eyes.

"Yeah? Get in line." He pushed up from the bed, stripped, and showered. He'd navigated troubled waters last night, and though there were
things he could have done better, he'd come through sober and chaste. It
could be worse.

Then he realized it was Sunday. Maybe he should change it up and
see his mother on Wednesday or Saturday or not at all. Or maybe he
should get to church and stop whining. As Jay said, his sentence was self-
imposed. He didn't have to inflict himself on her or her on him. But he
would.

He brooded through the Scripture readings, then stood with the congregation to recite the creed. He did believe in God, the Father Almighty.
Stan Westfall had personified that person of the Trinity, altering the energy
of a room, charging the space around him with a consuming power any
wrong step could unleash. He understood the Son, broken by the Father's
will, sacrificed to redeem the people fallen in their sins. The difference
came in that Jesus had exalted his father, not destroyed him.

Those images were old, and he knew better. He'd encountered the living God. He just couldn't always see through the fog—the glass was still dark. Some days as dark as the base of a bottle of ale.

Instead of going home to gear up, he drove directly to his mother's house. She didn't answer when he knocked. Not home yet, he guessed. She attended church an hour and a half away, so as not to offend her former congregation or the family of the young woman who had died.

With the rush of relief came words like *worthless, gutless, spineless.*

The wood pile was low. He strode over, jerked the ax from the splitting log, and got to work. The brisk air chilled his salty sweat, and his muscles bulged and stretched. He'd always found release in physical exertion, and it cleared last night's frustration and helped him focus. By the time his mother's Blazer pulled in, he had replenished her supply. He sank the ax and turned.

She climbed out, tugging two grocery bags. He could see another pair in the backseat. She walked past without acknowledging him. He grabbed the other two bags and reached the porch by the time she'd come back for them. Smelling of cold cream and mouthwash, she took the bags without allowing him to cross the threshold. He stared at the closed door a long moment before leaving.

He understood the hatred. If he had left it alone, walked away when the inquiry concluded, everything would have been different. If he had ignored what he knew—or suspected—and let the findings stand, his father would be alive. But the girl would still be dead.

He went home, parked outside his cabin, and rested his head on his forearms stretched over the steering wheel. Jay had come over early. How he timed it was a mystery. Jonah didn't ask for explanations. He climbed out and let the sound of the creek wash over him. The summer flow was still strong, carrying melted snows to basins and reservoirs.

He went inside, glanced at the animals in his closet, then found Jay planing a board in the back extension. "How did you get the dead pup out?"

"Mama went outside."

"You have her house-trained?"

"Animals don't foul their dens."

"Yeah, but she could have used the kitchen or—my whole house is her den?"

Jay grinned. "I think she might have spent time with someone before."

"You're saying I'm not her first?"

"Just a theory." Jay slid another curl of wood before the plane, releasing the scent of cut wood. "So did you prove your manhood last night?"

Jonah slid him a look. "I don't have to prove anything. It was your pretty mug that put the thoughts in her head."

Eyes smiling, Jay felt the surface of the board. "So the answer is yes."

"The answer is no. I didn't take advantage of a lonely woman to prove I'm not gay."

"Why do you say lonely?"

Jonah shrugged. "New in town. Never see her with anyone."

"How often have you seen her?"

"Not that often. But she seems…vulnerable."

"Do you mean Liz or you?"

Jonah sighed. "It didn't feel smart."

"You know how smart feels?"

"Vague recollection."

Jay masked a smile. "You had an interested woman, but instead you spent the night with Enola."

"Enola? You named my dog?"

"She's yours?"

Jonah conceded the point. "Why *Enola?*"

"It means solitary. I think maybe the coydog came to you because you're also alone."

"You're one to talk." Jay had been dating the assistant DA's cousin for four years without progress. "At least I know what I want."

"And wanting something you can't have is better than having anything else?"

Jonah sat down in the plastic-sheeted window seat. "It's not a choice."

"Sure it is."

"No." He shook his head. "I just decided which addiction to conquer."

Enola passed the framed wall, staring at him through the wooden skeleton on her way outside once more. Jonah watched her with a sinking stomach. "I let her down last night, falling asleep before that last pup was born."

"What do you think you could have done?"

"Encouraged her to quicken it."

"Nature has her own way."

"Had she opened the sac?"

"No."

"If I'd been awake, I could have torn it open myself."

"Maybe it was already dead."

Part of him knew he was making too much of a coydog pup, but he and Enola had an unspoken pact. She had sought him out, and he'd accepted. They were bound.

His pager beeped. He checked the source and then returned the call. "Yeah, Sue."

"Child protective services took Eli."

"What? Why didn't they call me? I'd've vouched for your being at work when—"

"The x-rays showed other hairline fractures. Old ones. He's been hurt before, Jonah. How could I not know?"

Jonah rubbed his head. When Sue worked, Sam watched the baby. But when she was home, had she never heard him crying? "Was he dosed?"

"What do you mean?"

"Did Sam drug him?"

"No way. He—" Her breath rushed in his ear. "Could he?"

"You should get a tox screen."

"Jonah, the injuries could be accidental. That would be intentional."

Old injuries discovered on x-rays were rarely accidental. "If he was killing the child's pain, you wouldn't have realized Eli was hurt."

"I thought he was just quiet. Placid. Sweet tempered."

"Don't beat yourself up."

"How can you say that? I knew Sam was using. I know the flash of his temper. If he jerked Eli's arm…"

"The important thing is to establish your ability to care for him, to create a safe environment. How likely is it that Sam will put the blame on you, or on your mother?"

"He wouldn't. Would he?"

"You need to talk to CPS. You and your mom. I'll vouch for you."

"You've only seen me at work. You don't know."

"I have some credible experience."

"That's not firsthand knowledge."

His thoughts flew ahead. "If you know that he's using or trafficking…"

"Sam is Eli's father. Am I supposed to tell him I put his daddy in jail?"

"When the DA brings abuse charges, will he give you the same consideration?" He waited through her silence.

Finally she said, "I have to deal with this. Can you cover my shift?"

"Of course." He hung up and told Jay, "I'm going in."

"I can stay for a few hours. But I'm not sure Enola needs it."

"Her wounds might still attract a predator."

"She is a predator." Jay straightened. "Don't forget it."

———

Liz looked up with surprise and a little hitch when Jonah's Bronco pulled into her parking lot.

Lucy looked over her shoulder, querulous. "What does he want?"

To apologize, Liz imagined, to say he'd made a mistake, wished the night had turned out differently. Heat rose in her cheeks. "I don't know." She gripped the leash of the Rottweiler she had neutered and walked him outside to get his legs back under him. With Lucy watching from behind the curtains, she led the dog away from the window. "I didn't think the chief of police worked Sundays."

"I'm filling in."

Their trajectories intersected at the gate to the dog run. She released the offended animal into the long, chain-link tunnel. "Titan is feeling less than himself this morning."

"With good reason, I guess." Jonah noted the dog's tentative motion. He turned, but she didn't see regret, only sympathy. "I want—"

"Don't apologize." Anger rescued her from tears, but she showed him neither. "It was a moment; now it's past."

He let it go, relieved, it seemed, that she'd handled it for him. What had she expected?

"I hope you didn't just come for that."

"The coydog had her litter."

Her breath caught. "How many?"

"Three live, one stillborn."

She nodded. "It could have been injured in the shooting."

"Could have."

"I thought she might have a few more days. If I'd have examined her, I would have seen the swollen milk sacs."

"You just don't stick your head in a closet with a coyote."

Or your heart on your sleeve with a man.

"Liz, I know you wanted one—"

"Two. And I want them immediately. I hope by bottle-feeding to overcome the wild tendencies and form a bond."

He frowned. "I think you'd have better luck one on one."

"I want them to have each other." She had almost said she wanted one for herself and one for her sister. But after last night she couldn't mention Lucy.

"That would only leave her one."

"In her depleted condition, that's probably all she can nourish."

"I don't know." He looked away.

"Timing is essential. When they open their eyes I want them to realize the hand that holds their bottle is mine. It's like patterning with ducklings."

"These are not harmless ducklings. Coyotes bite the throats and suffocate larger prey, crush the skulls of smaller animals. You need to consider the pets brought here as well as your own safety."

"I promise you, Chief, if I can't tame them, I will mercifully euthanize. Then you won't have the issue of brazen predators. But I think I can do this."

He sighed. "It won't help to argue, will it?"

She shook her head. "What will you do with the third?"

"That's up to mama."

Liz smiled. "Who'd have thought you have a soft spot?"

"I take my responsibilities seriously."

"Is she your responsibility?"

"Looks that way."

She allowed a pang of regret. They might have had something lovely. "Have you determined their sex?"

"Haven't exactly gotten that close."

"When the mother goes out, check the pups."

"They'll have my scent."

"They're living in your closet."

"Good point."

"Besides," she said, "it's an old wives' tale that human scent makes animals leave their young."

"Really?"

"Really. So, I'd prefer females, but two of the same gender will do."

He frowned. "I still don't think—"

"Take them while she's out."

"Then what? She comes back and they're gone?"

"That's how it works. She'll make sure they didn't wander off, then forget they were ever there."

He still looked undecided.

"I appreciate your concern, but I want the pups. In this area, my experience trumps yours." She would not take no, and he must have seen that.

He spread his hands. "If you're sure."

"I'm sure."

When he'd gone, she led Titan back inside, murmuring to him, "I know it's hard." He would not procreate, but he would make a fine companion. A deep ache hollowed her as she closed him back into the cage to wait for his master. Companionship never quite…

"You're sad." Lucy's hand on her arm was light and cool.

"I'm sorry for his pain." She looked into the dog's drowsy eyes, imagining he knew his loss and mourned it.

"I know it's not the dog."

"Of course it is. What do you mean?"

"I know how you feel about the chief."

"No, you don't."

"Oh, Lizzie." Lucy slid her arms around her. "You can't hide it. Why would you?"

"He's in love with someone else."

"Because he doesn't know you. If he did, he would love you as I love you. As I'll always love you. My sister, my heart."

Liz hugged her back. "I love you too, Lucy. You're all that matters to me."

———

"You in for Sue?" Moser asked, arriving for his shift in crisp, pressed uniform, his goatee perfectly encircling his mouth and defining his chin.

"How long do you spend grooming, Moser?"

"It's not the time; it's the care you take." He rubbed his long brown fingers over the facial hair, reminding each one to behave. "Or you can go for the scruffy I-might-be-trouble look."

"Now you're talking." Jonah grinned. "I wash up for banquets, though. And when I work with the kids."

"I have seen that and been greatly comforted." Moser looked over his shoulder at the computer. "Still working the raccoons?"

Seeing Liz had kept the raccoons jangling in his mind. Was there someone with a cruel streak taking it out on unsuspecting animals? "You know what bothers me about the raccoons?" Jonah turned. "I see cruelty, but I don't see rage."

Moser moved that through his thorough and methodical mind. "You don't think making two animals tear themselves apart is an act of rage?"

"Maybe. But it seems more calculated." He leaned back in the creaky seat. Shooting a coyote with a shotgun was either self-defense or sport. But the meticulous effort put into the raccoons felt altogether different. "Think about the process. Two animals captured and drugged."

"Or drugged, then captured."

Jonah spread his hands. "Maybe the bait is doped, but it has to be potent enough to keep them out while he cuts them open."

"Pretty grizzly."

"But painless." Jonah tapped his lip with the pencil. "Or they'd be fighting, and he couldn't cut and sew. Certainly not fastidiously. All those neat stitches."

"But the pain when they wake up. Delayed gratification can still be rage, only deeper."

"Very deep. But look at it. The first two were joined superficially, essentially remaining two separate animals. The second pair had four legs between them, organs joined, no longer complete individuals. What's the motivation?"

"I still think torture fits. It's just not a kind we've seen before."

Jonah shrugged. "Maybe you're right."

"Have you looked at the guy who trashed the Half Moon? There could be a connection between weird animal stuff and weird freak-out stuff."

"Yes, there could."

"What about Caldwell?"

"A connection?"

"No. Just anything new?"

"Newly's working it."

Moser nodded. "Well, I'm here now." He hung his jacket and cleared his throat. "Anything more from Sue?"

"No. And I need to keep some distance there."

A call came in, and because Ruth didn't work weekends, Jonah answered. "Redford Police Department."

A young voice said, "There's like…these dead cats."

Another voice stage-whispered, "Tell him they're stuck together."

Jonah took the girls' names and address. He had the number on caller ID. "You've got the station," he called to Moser. "I've got a fresh pair."

———

Piper locked up and started along the back of the bakery toward the path, then shrieked when Miles loomed up beside her. He pressed his hands to his ears, eyes wide.

Taking deep breaths to calm herself, she said, "What are you doing?"

"I was looking for you."

Okay, a little creepy. "What for?"

"Are you alone?"

"Um…"

"I mean is the bakery closed?"

"It's only open until two. Plus, I sold out of everything."

His features drooped with disappointment as though she'd stuck fingers in dough and pulled.

"Are you hungry?"

"I hoped you might have something interesting."

"You did?" If he was conning her, he had the goofiest way of doing it. "I guess I could make something."

A smile flashed. "That would be good. Very good."

She hadn't tried anything new since Sarge had fired her, but there were ingredients in the industrial fridge she'd been meaning to dabble with before the big kibosh. "Come on." She unlocked the kitchen door and let Miles in. It probably wasn't smart to be alone with a guy she knew nothing about. But looking into his face, she saw no hint of malice. Tia wasn't even pressing charges. She said, "Want to watch?"

His face brightened. "Yes. If you wash your hands."

"You wash yours too."

"I do. Every hour and whenever necessary."

"Wouldn't want the germs to grow."

"Are you making fun of me?"

She smiled. "It's called teasing."

"Oh. It sounds like making fun."

"But you can see the difference, if you look."

He gave a slow nod. "I can see the difference."

"Well, come on then. Let's make a mess! Kidding." She laughed, then laughed harder. "I'm *kidding*."

"It was funny." He nodded. "If you were kidding."

Thirteen

The number two hath by the heathen been accounted
accursed, because it was the first departure from unity.
—JOSEPH TRAPP

Jonah studied the cats, brushing the fur away from the shaved flesh where the stitches had torn out. Once again two of each animal's limbs had been removed at the shoulder and hip joints. This time the joined pelvises had not disconnected.

He prodded the guts with his pen. He didn't know much physiology, but it seemed that some of the organs had been connected to serve both animals like two esophaguses—esophagi?—connecting to one stomach. He saw no sign of struggle. Maybe this pair hadn't survived the surgery. Then why dump them here? Taunting?

Jonah leaned back on his heels. The girls who had called still looked out the upstairs window, though their mom had firmly shooed them inside. He wished they hadn't seen it, but the house nestled against the mountain, and Jonah guessed the cats had fallen—or been thrown—from the trail above.

This time they were domestic animals, perhaps someone's pets. That could be considered escalation, the surgical mutations, a refined style of torture. There were documented cases of psychopaths with a medical fetish, Jack the Ripper for one. Maybe the guy imagined himself a surgeon, a Dr. Frankenstein. But why two animals together?

It came back to motivation. Cruelty and killing were rooted in power, the desire to demonstrate ultimate control over a living thing, in this case forcing two creatures to go against their natures or die. There was a very sick mind operating here, and he had no idea where to go with it.

He took out his phone and keyed Liz. She didn't answer. Well, it was Sunday. She had to have some life. Or else she was avoiding him. He bagged the cats and brought them to the funeral parlor morgue.

"You're kidding, right?" Morey Bejoe blinked slowly.

"Nope. I need to keep them cold and unmolested until the vet can take a look."

Morey shook his head, then shrugged. "Okay. You're the boss."

He handed over the cats and headed back through town, down the main street, ready to be home, to wield a hammer, drill, and saw. Nearing the bakery, he thought about Sarge. Maybe he should visit. It had been a few days. He glanced at the bakery as he passed, then slammed on the brakes, put the truck in reverse, and screeched to a stop outside the window.

Piper sat at the front table with a man who by his size and haircut must be the elusive Miles. He pulled the Bronco to the curb half a block up and got out. He strode over and rattled the door until Piper unlocked it, then pushed in and searched behind her.

"He's gone. Ran out the back."

He couldn't be far. Jonah stalked through the kitchen and pushed open the door. Nothing but dim and quiet. He searched the pantry and the walk-in, then went back to Piper and scowled. "Did you tell him to run?"

"Me? I think you're cute. He thinks you're scary."

Jonah looked at the trays set around the tables. "What is this? What are you doing?"

"Baking."

"With…Miles?"

"He says what he thinks. He's the perfect judge."

"He's violent and destructive."

"Not intentionally."

"Does that matter?" he pressed. "One touch can set him off. Then he tears up Sarge's place and where are we?"

"So it's about Sarge?" She folded her arms.

"It's about I want to talk to him."

"I'm working on that."

He eyed her, perplexed. What part of dangerous didn't she get? "What do you mean?"

"I'm working him up to it, little by little."

"Great progress you've made."

She put her hands on her hips. "Look. He's nice. He's funny. I like him."

"Do you know his last name?"

"He doesn't want to say."

"Does that tell you something?"

"So he's paranoid. He probably has reason to be." She reached down for a tart. "Try this?"

"Piper. I'm trying to get to the bottom of some troubling things."

"I know. That dead animal stuff."

He frowned. "What has Tia told you?"

"Only what you told her. I've asked around, but no one else has any idea what's going on."

"You've asked around?"

"You're only one guy."

"I have a department."

"Sometimes people talk to me."

He cocked his jaw. "So what, you crook your little finger and some Joe spills his guts about torturing animals?"

"Maybe." Her eyes were the color of blue cleary marbles and just as guileless.

He moved in close. "Then what? He asks if you want to see his laboratory?" He leaned. "But hey. He might be nice. He might be funny."

She stepped back, breathing quicker. "I was just trying to help."

"You can help by not getting in my way."

Her brows puckered. "Tia said you'd be this way. Guess she knows you pretty well."

"Then learn from her mistake." He turned and went out. The last thing he needed was Piper mucking around in his cases. He slammed the Bronco into gear and got halfway out of town before his phone rang. He activated the hands-free. "Yeah."

"Jonah, can we talk?"

"What's up, Sue?"

"Will you meet me at the station?"

He cocked his jaw and narrowed his eyes. "Yeah. Of course." He slowed the Bronco and made a U-turn, heading back the way he didn't want to go. He arrived before Sue and waited in his office, hoping she wasn't tendering her resignation. When she came in, he went around and sat on the edge of his desk. "What's up?" He'd seen her mad, but this was different.

"You were right. Sam's passing the blame."

"I thought he might."

"I mean, come on. My mother? She weighs ninety pounds. And it's not just about Eli, Jonah." She looked away. "I was going to tell you—"

"I know."

She turned back. "You know I'm pregnant?"

"Congratulations."

She looked down at the floor, then back. "Nothing gets past you, does it?"

He smiled.

"I don't know how I'll make it with another one on the way without Sam's income. But it doesn't matter, does it?"

"Not so much."

She chewed the cuticle of her left index finger, then realized it and lowered her hand. When she'd first started on the job, in the interest of professionalism, he'd suggested she break that habit. She mostly had.

"So this is what I know. There's a man named Greggor. I don't know if it's first, last, or nickname." She gave him what sketchy impressions she had, enough to have someone check it out. "That's all I know, and most of it I only suspect."

"It's a starting point."

She looked down. "He should not have messed with my child."

"Rule number one."

"I know it's wrong, but I wouldn't have turned him in."

"I know."

"I want my son back."

"You'll get him."

She drew a breath. "You said you'd vouch for me."

"I will."

She nodded. "How did you know?"

"That you were pregnant?"

"That Sam would turn on me." She raised her eyes.

"Takes a certain kind of man to hurt a child."

"He's that kind of man?"

Jonah held her eyes.

———

Tia looked around the circle of graying women. One was widowed, one divorced, all with kids mostly grown. She was younger than some by fifteen years and others by more than thirty. Although she cherished each one, if she'd been told her circle of friends at twenty-seven would be these older women, she'd have laughed long and hard.

First, she'd have pointed out, they would not approve of her. She was too wayward, too headstrong. They had little in common, and not one could claim to need salvation as she had. Not that they knew—the details anyway. They had lived quiet, pious lives, reached their middle and elder years with grace. How else could she explain their loveliness?

While there were women her age without kids or permanent relationships in Redford, within the Worship Chapel community she was an anomaly. The question came around to her, and she read the answer she had written the night before. Did they realize how vulnerable she made herself each time she shared an insight, how she slaved over each comment, leaving no opening for criticism?

One of the other women nodded. "Very thoughtful, Tia. Wanda?"

Only one had heard her story in all its ugliness, and she watched mildly from across the table as Tia rested her hands on the small notebook from which she'd read. Carolyn gave her a soft smile. Not a motherly smile—thank God. More otherworldly.

To spare Reba humiliation, her mother had not revealed the damning act to the multitudes. Tia could have kept the secret herself, but she had laid it before Carolyn as proof that she should not be admitted into any fellowship. Carolyn had insisted she was wrong. *"There is no stain that cannot be washed in the blood of the Lamb."*

To have these women look at her without condemnation, she attended services, served on committees, came to studies, kept her vow, a vow she'd made before God in Carolyn's presence. She needed what they had to give, these friends and mentors. She would not disappoint.

"Will you read the next passage?" Carolyn asked.

Tia read, her voice clear, her heart full. She wanted it all to be true. Their discussion lasted two hours. When they had cleared the brownie plates and teacups, gathered their study materials and coats, Carolyn murmured, "Hold on a minute, okay?"

Feeling as though she'd been retained by a teacher for misbehavior, Tia hung back. The day had turned cold, and Carolyn shut the door after the last of the other ladies left. "You seem pensive today."

"Do I?"

"Is your leg hurting?"

"A lot, surprisingly." She leaned on the inner door frame to shift her weight. "Makes me realize I'm not so tough after all."

Carolyn smiled. "Something we all need from time to time. How's the Hopeline?"

"Five or six calls a week. Mostly at night."

"It's been three years?"

"Almost four."

"Repeats?"

"I try not to notice."

"We could be counting that time toward your license."

"I know."

"I hate to see you wasting your education. You'd do a lot of good with a counseling practice."

Tia shrugged. "For now, the Hopeline is enough."

Carolyn hesitated, then said, "Rosemary saw the police chief take you home last night."

Tia's smile faded. "I took a Percocet, and it knocked me out. Piper got worried and called him."

After a while, Carolyn nodded. "If you ever need to talk…"

"Thanks. I will."

"Friends can help."

Something she was only now learning. She had burned out her childhood friends with her energetic nature. Or else their parents had thought her a bad influence. It was laughable the things people had thought she'd done. Cheating, vandalism, scoring boys.

She was one of the smartest kids in the school. Why would she cheat? The vandalism accusation had angered her because she didn't mess up people's things. They had no proof to make it stick, so she hadn't been punished, but the suspicion remained. And boys? Maybe if she had not been so hung up on…

She sighed. "I'm okay, Carolyn, just numbed by the pain meds."

"Of course. I'm so glad you came anyway."

It was expected, wasn't it? She'd committed to the group. "Me too."

They hugged. Tia went out.

Mary Carson was waiting outside. "I noticed that you walked over."

Tia nodded. "I thought walking it out might help."

"Now you know better. I'll give you a ride home."

Tia smiled. There were worse things to have in her life than kind, older women.

Piper looked up from polishing the rocker when Tia limped into the house and sank down on the settee with pain creasing her brow. "Would you light the candles on the mantel, Piper? Turn the MP3 on low."

She did. "Are you okay?"

"I can't believe a bruise can be this big an issue."

"A bone contusion is more than a bruise."

"Still."

"You're usually so fit. You're not used to something keeping you down."

"I guess." What had really thrown her was Carolyn and Rosemary knowing about Jonah. He'd only taken her home, but she could guess how it looked, him holding her arm, cupping her face. Their ardent dialogue.

She closed her eyes as strains of Coldplay softened the mood. "So tell me about your day."

Piper settled onto the settee. "Well, it turns out Sunday's pretty busy. Sarge was missing the church crowd."

"But you don't get a day off."

She shrugged. "If I'm not working, I…"

"Feel like you're taking advantage of someone?"

Piper cocked her head. "Lame, isn't it?"

"Not considering your background. It's compensation."

Piper pulled her knees to her chest. "After I closed, Miles came by. I decided to use up the ingredients I'd gotten to experiment with before Sarge freaked out and fired me. We baked up a whole bunch of different things."

Tia frowned. "You know he's not right."

"Maybe, but tell him to mince and he minces."

Tia laughed.

"Anyway we were sitting down, judging the creations when the chief saw us through the window."

"Uh-oh."

"Yeah. Miles ran out the back."

"Oh, boy."

"I get that Jonah wants to question him about your store, but he's wrong to think Miles has anything to do with dead animals."

"How can you know?"

"I just know. I told the chief I've been asking around and—"

"I'll bet that went over well."

"He got kind of scary."

"He's not a safe man, Piper."

"Except…he is. Even when he gets hard and intense, I know he's protecting me."

Tia stared at the candles. "Just don't confuse protective with safe."

Fourteen

If two lie down together, they will keep warm. But how can
one keep warm alone?

—ECCLESIASTES 4:11

As he headed toward town the next morning in his Lysol-scented
Bronco, Jonah phoned Liz. "I'm sorry to call so early, but I was hoping to catch you before you opened."

"What is it?"

"Another pair of animals I'd like you to examine."

"Like the last ones?"

"Close enough."

"I'm not sure what else I can tell you."

"I'm hoping you can verify something."

After a pause, she said, "Where are you?"

"Can you meet me at the funeral home?"

"The…"

"Morgue is in the basement."

"Okay."

"I'll explain when you get there."

"I'm on my way."

He waited for her outside the two-story Georgian-style house flanked
by tall pines that spread a rusty bed of needles and cones on the sparse
lawn. With a flat, windowed, brick face, it was one of several historically
protected buildings in the town. It had been a funeral parlor for over fifty
years, but was also a residence.

Liz parked and moved toward him with her uneven gait. He wouldn't
ask, but maybe sometime she'd tell him what had happened. She had pulled
her hair into a ponytail, wore minimal—if any—makeup, royal blue
warmups with a yellow stripe down the leg. Obviously not trying to impress
him, which he hoped meant his slip the other night had not done damage.

He liked her, didn't want to complicate things. She greeted him with a measured smile. Polite. Professional. Friendly.

He said, "Thanks for coming."

"You piqued my curiosity."

"Sorry about the morgue. I needed to keep them cold until you could see them, and since I didn't want to use my fridge…" He motioned her toward the door. "Morey agreed to keep them in here. He'll let us have a look."

"Nothing like the morgue in the morning."

Smiling, Jonah rang the bell that brought Morey to the door, his belly protuberant in red silk pajamas. He had told Morey they were coming, but obviously that hadn't inclined him toward dressing. Jonah sent her an apologetic glance.

She raised her eyebrows and followed Morey inside. They passed the viewing rooms to a heavy metal door beyond the black velvet curtains, clambered down the stairs to the morgue. The air was naturally cool, the scent moderately repugnant. Morey pulled one of the metal drawers, shaking his head and muttering.

Jonah said, "Thanks."

"Cats?" Liz put the back of her hand to her nose. They had not been cleaned up, only chilled to slow decomposition. He realized how gory and disturbing it was.

She turned her head to her shoulder. "I help animals, Jonah."

"I know. I'm sorry."

She drew a breath, probably wishing she hadn't. Morey handed her a small, scented cloth.

Pulling herself together, she leaned in. "Two limbs are missing from each, corresponding fore and back legs. They were glued at the hip joint and the shoulder."

"Glued?"

"It's a bone epoxy. You can see where it cracked apart at the shoulder. Maybe from a blow."

"Or a fall?"

"It's possible."

"What about other body parts?"

She studied the cats. "There is not a full complement for two animals. Some are missing, some are joined."

"Why?"

"I have no idea."

"Look at the stomach."

"Only one for both cats. Also two lungs between them."

"So they've been surgically altered."

"I'm afraid so." She looked up. "Is that what you wanted to know?"

He nodded. "Did they die trying to separate?"

"I see no sign of struggle."

"So the surgery killed them?"

"Could be infection. This extreme putrefaction looks antemortem. I've had animals this sick and told their owners nothing could be done."

"So they were sick already. Before someone connected them."

"Maybe. I just don't know."

He pushed the drawer back in and thanked Morey. Outside, they both drew lungfuls of air. Jonah turned. "That was helpful, Liz. I appreciate your coming. Can I buy you breakfast?"

She raised her eyebrow. "Oh well, that was so appetizing."

"Sorry. Guess I compartmentalize."

"Any place in mind?"

"Sarge's bakery is on the way to the station." He checked his watch. "I don't have too much time."

She pulled out her keys. "I'll follow you."

They found easy parking in Old Town since most of the shops had not yet opened. In the clear, bright morning, the sky formed an azure backdrop to the craggy, pine-clad slopes. A paunchy gray jay chirped from the corner of a roof, and another flew to join it. Though the morning chill had not passed, the cloudless sunlight promised warmth, and Liz took a moment to draw it all in. This kind of day anything was possible.

Jonah had chosen the bakery next to the Half Moon candle shop where she'd gotten Lucy's melts. Maybe it would be open by the time they finished eating. She'd like to see Tia, talk to her again.

He held the door for her. Did that make it a date, or were they merely colleagues sharing a meal? He respected her knowledge, consulting her when she didn't sense he often asked for help. He appreciated her sense of humor, responded to her repartee. He wanted to be done with the other relationship—he'd said so. He just needed the right woman. Who better than one who already understood so well?

The girl behind the counter noticed Jonah the minute he walked in. They were fourth in line, but suddenly everything the young blonde did was for his benefit. Or maybe, Liz admitted, she was projecting her own feelings.

A man heading out with his order nodded. "Chief."

"Morning, Don."

"Ma'am."

She smiled.

They reached the counter, and the girl looked up at Jonah with a mixed expression, waving a hand over her wares. "Strictly regulation. Not a contraband item in the case."

"I'm not here on reconnaissance, Piper."

She smiled brightly. "Then what can I get you?"

"Liz?"

She studied the choices laid out temptingly. "I haven't had a bear claw in years."

"That's us," Piper said, "a bastion of the obsolete." She pulled a tissue square from the box.

"Make that two obsolete bears claws," Jonah said. "And coffee, please."

Liz ordered coffee too.

Piper poured and handed over their cups. "How's Sarge?"

"Still touch and go. Things okay here?"

"You kidding? No one yelling at me? Well, except you."

Liz raised her eyebrows.

"I didn't yell."

"Your face did."

"I'll have a talk with it."

Her giggle made her sound half Jonah's age. Piper handed over their pastries. "Seven ninety-five."

Jonah paid, and it felt…nice, Liz thought, warmth spreading through her chest. They took a table for two at the window. She set down her mug and pastry, then braced herself between the chair and the small square table to sit. Jonah didn't comment on her awkwardness.

She tore open a tiny tub of creamer for her coffee. "Nice girl."

Jonah glanced over. "Don't let her sweetness fool you. She's a force. Aside from the odd jobs given to me, Sarge has never hired anyone. Now Piper runs the place."

"Why did you yell at her?"

He sighed. "I need to question someone, and she's running interference. Plus mucking around in the animal investigation."

Liz felt a stab of annoyance. That was her connection. "How is she involved?"

"She found the first pair. But she's not involved. I'm trying to get that across to her." He bit into his bear claw. "And I didn't yell."

Liz quirked the corner of her mouth. "She has a crush on you."

"Don't even start."

She took a bite of her pastry. "Mmm."

"Yeah, she can bake. And you might not think it, but she works hard. Even Sarge admits that much."

"Sarge?"

"I forget you're new here." Jonah took a drink of coffee. "Sarge is a fixture. He's owned this bakery thirty—" His glance went to the window and froze there.

Liz looked from Jonah to the window where Tia hovered a moment, then changed course for her shop next-door. In that moment, it all fell into place. The candles on his mantel. The old flame.

She swallowed. It would take someone like Tia to hold him, someone who ran deeper than one might imagine. She'd sensed it with only one encounter, the way her personality hung and permeated like one of her scents. "You were saying?"

"Um. Sorry." Jonah checked his watch. "I hate to eat and run, but I need to get in."

"Sure." Liz sipped her coffee. "Go ahead."

Something had flashed in Liz's eyes. Surprise, irritation—neither quite fit, although both would be understandable. You don't buy someone breakfast and then leave them sitting there, not without an emergency. Certainly not because Tia had looked startled, stunned, wounded like a bird striking a window.

He went directly into his office, catching a look between Ruth and Newly as he passed. Speculation would fly. What's got the chief in a twist? He closed the door behind him. He had let his personal life intrude—worse, his personal fantasy. Tia wasn't even reality.

What did Tia care if he took Liz to breakfast? He should make it a real date, dinner, dancing—or maybe not with her handicap—then back to his place. Have a drink or two or twelve.

But that was before. Though still tempted, he saw the emptiness of those choices. Getting drunk and sleeping with a woman he didn't love would sicken him, weaken him, plunge him into places he'd been, places of condemnation, of looking into the mirror and seeing his father. But why?

Because he held fidelity above gratification? He pressed his eyes shut and opened himself in silence to God, the higher power, the strength outside himself from whom fortitude and grace emanated. Unlike Jay, he didn't want an excuse to avoid commitment. He wanted stability, completion. God knew that, knew him, the longings, the failings, the faults.

"You're a coward and a fake. When are you going to be a man?"

That wasn't God. Through his fingers, Jonah stared at the wall that still bore the fade marks of photos he'd removed. The last thing he'd wanted was the old man staring at him while he did the job.

"You act tough, but you're soft as pudding inside, softer than your mother. You're a little girl."

That was the last time his dad had seen him cry, no matter how long the punishment lasted. Jonah leaned back in his chair. Tia had punished him for nine years, and he wasn't crying. But when did the time come to man up and move on?

He opened the file Newly had left, probably expecting to update him verbally on Tom Caldwell. Since the DA had dropped the charges for lack of evidence, they'd kept up a loose surveillance, mainly Newly or McCarthy earning overtime staking out the house after dark. They had little to report.

Jonah closed the file. Someone else had called in the lawyer and cleaned up the property. That was the one he wanted, but no luck. Phone records had turned up no one named Greggor. He hated when a case ground to a halt or got sideswiped by attorneys.

Ruth buzzed the intercom.

"Yes."

"Mayor's on the line."

Jonah answered to City Manager Dave Wolton, but the mayor liked to play in his sandbox too. Owen Buckley had a hearty appetite for attention. Jonah picked up the phone. "What can I do for you, Mayor?"

His father had enjoyed a good-old-boy camaraderie with all the officials, but Jonah still felt like an upstart dealing with the old man's cronies.

———

Tia set up the worktable she had moved into the newly available space near the front counter. She had poured a dozen candles the night before that she could decorate while she watched the shop, replenishing her stock. She tried to focus on that, but seeing Jonah with the vet, sitting where he'd sat with Reba, had upset her.

He had every right to move on, and it shouldn't surprise her that he'd chosen someone similar in type to Reba, but it didn't make seeing it easier. She closed her eyes, then looked up as the fingerprint man came through the door. Wonderful.

He had told Piper he didn't mean to wreck her shop. She'd said the same, assuming she would never see the big guy again, yet here he was. Just in case, she limped to the counter where she'd left her cell phone.

"You're hurt," he informed her.

"The sculpture hit my leg. When you bumped it." The skin had turned purple, and the bruise throbbed with every step. She slipped her phone into the loose pocket of her cotton poncho-style top.

His big hands opened and closed beneath the immaculate cuffs of his starched, blue dress shirt. "You changed things."

"I removed the damaged merchandise and displays."

"It's not so crowded," he said with sincere relief. "That's better. Much better."

She lowered her chin. "Can I help you?"

"The tapers broke. When they fell." His shoulders hunched. "I need them."

"Thankfully that display wasn't damaged."

He turned and headed to the side wall, inspected and chose a pair of linked tapers. He brought them to the counter. "They make a very nice gift."

Was it possible he had blocked out his part in the incident, rewound to the point right before his panic? Could this be a redo? She felt a keen kinship, a stab of hope for his success. "Would you like them wrapped?"

"No." He took out his wallet. "Just like that."

With a sense of déjà vu, Tia saw her hand brushing his, the chaos that had followed. With everything in her she willed this time to be different. If *he* could do it… "Miles?"

He startled, surprised she knew his name.

"Why does touching bother you?"

He stiffened. "People don't touch. People—"

"Touch all the time."

He dropped the wallet and put his hands to his ears.

Was she trying to set him off? He'd taken a chance just by coming back. "I'm sorry." She used her Hopeline tone. "Sometimes talking helps." And sometimes, it obviously didn't.

He didn't know or care about her education, her degrees, or all the good Carolyn thought she could do. He wanted to be left alone. She took the cash for the tapers, put the change into the pouch, and laid his wallet on the counter beside the candles.

Not quite willing to give up, she set a Hopeline card beside his wallet. "I'm here if you ever do want to talk."

He snatched everything up and hurried for the door. She watched him leave, sad that he only knew human contact as a threat. But was he so different from her? Or just more honest.

As if her mood couldn't get worse, Jonah entered the shop, all six feet drawn up taut. "Don't even try to tell me that wasn't the guy who busted up your store."

"Okay, I won't." He must have seen Miles leaving.

"I guess you forgot he's dangerous?"

"I don't think he is."

"Oh, and you're the expert?"

More than he knew. She limped to the worktable and plunked the hypodermic filled with shimmery gold wax back into the hot water. "He's just a guy with issues."

"If you had called when he came in, I could have shown up to determine that."

"Look." She turned. "It was like a seizure that first time. That's how much control he had over it."

"What if he has a seizure at the bakery? Attacks Piper?"

"He can't *touch* people."

"You're still limping from the way he couldn't touch you."

She sighed. "If it was Helen Henratty's shop he'd tossed, would you be this tenacious?"

"Helen Henratty would cooperate. She would want compensation for her losses."

"And you'd feel as personally committed as you do now?"

He crowded her. "You know the answer to that."

"Jonah, I don't want special treatment. Just trust me. He's not the psychopath you're looking for."

Jonah hung his hands on his hips. "Why was he here?"

"He wanted candles."

"He came in to shop?" Aggravation gathered his features again.

"The other tapers broke. He needed to replace them."

"Tia…" He seemed lost for words.

"You're taking it too seriously."

"This isn't only about you. There are other people, other shop owners to consider. If he can come back to shop after what he did to you—"

"He didn't do it with intent, Jonah. And I just…couldn't bring you down on him."

He looked as though she'd struck him. "Bring me *down on him*?"

She swallowed. "I know how you get."

His eyes narrowed. "How I *get*?"

She pressed her hand to her forehead. "Do you hear yourself? Don't you realize how intimidating you are? What it tells people you're capable of?"

His eyes went stone cold. "What am I capable of, Ti? Blowing my dad's head off with a shotgun?"

Her breath came sharp and quick. "No."

"You think I'm too nice?"

She shook her head. "Stop it, Jonah."

"You don't know, do you? You've never asked."

"I don't need to."

"You've kept a nice, safe distance, though."

"That's not why—"

"Ask." The icy demand chilled her marrow.

Tears burned. "I won't."

His teeth clenched down on a cold whisper. "Ask me."

She swallowed hard. "Did you shoot your dad?"

"No. But I got to watch, which was almost as good."

"Don't."

"What?"

"Pretend to be that person you're not."

"What makes you think I'm not?" His temple pulsed. "You see it. Down inside me. The rage."

"There's rage in every one of us."

"Not like mine."

"That's a lie." Her voice rasped.

"But you believe it."

"No, I don't. I have never believed you shot him."

His throat worked. "Then why…" His pain surfaced like blisters on a burn.

She could not let it go on. "You wanted to save Reba from the backlash, told her she didn't deserve to be shackled to a man like you. But the truth is, you shouldn't be shackled to someone like me."

He looked away and swore, then turned back and gripped her shoulders. "This thing, the way I feel, didn't happen because of what we did, it's *why* we did it."

She searched his face.

"I love you. I loved you before we betrayed your sister, before I slid the ring on her finger."

She gulped back tears. "I don't—"

"That day on the ledge, when you followed me to the eagle nest? I wanted to make love to you. I wanted to take off your clothes and let the sun shine all over you. That's what I was thinking while we talked about your sister."

Her tears broke free. *If that were true…* "Then why…"

"I needed everyone to know I was good enough for *Reba* Manning."

Her throat felt raw, her chest hollow.

"*That's* what I'm capable of." He let go and stepped back.

She felt like he'd pulled a stake from her chest and her life was pouring out. She stood unmoving as he walked away.

Fifteen

Loyalty means nothing unless it has at its heart the absolute principle of self-sacrifice.

—THOMAS WOODROW WILSON

Leaving Tia's shop, Jonah's mind reeled. His body shook. He had determined to hold on, but something inside snapped. He had repelled her as surely as if he'd slammed his palms into her collarbones. The ache, the need for her howled, almost driving him back inside, but he had shown her the beast, and she would only recoil.

His phone rang, and he wanted to throw it. "What?"

"Jonah Westfall?"

"Yes." His teeth clenched.

"Sarge asked me to call."

Sarge. It must be the nurse. What was her name? "Lauren."

"Very good."

"What's up with Sarge?"

"His daughters are here. They're moving him to a nursing home."

"What? No." His hand clenched. "I tried to get back to them. They never—" He rubbed his face. "Can you stall them till I get there?"

"How?"

"Tell them you need another test or the doctor has to sign something."

"The doctor's already spoken—"

His breathing hardened. "Just ask them to wait until I get there."

"You better hurry. They want to be done with it."

Done with it. With Sarge. He wouldn't debate the reasons for their decision, but he hoped to change their minds. Shutting the phone, Jonah sprinted to the Bronco. He put on the light and siren and kept the pedal floored.

He'd expended his emotional energy on Tia, and he hadn't prepared for this, but it might be his only chance to give back to Sarge for the things he'd done. Maybe guilt and regret had driven the old man's actions, but the result was the same. With the kind of anger he'd built up, Jonah could be doing time instead of fighting crime, if Sarge hadn't stressed things like taking life head on and making his way through the trenches no matter what the enemy had planned.

Stan had taken credit for his son's decision to join him in law enforcement. But it was Sarge who had encouraged him. "Read the enemy," Sarge told him, "assess his strengths, then do it better, harder, and with a clear conscience."

It all stemmed from the tragedy, from the night in the woods when their souls had intersected. In some ways, Sarge's life had stopped that night. The clock quit ticking. He'd gone into a tunnel where nothing changed. His menu, his schedule. Hiring Piper had been a bigger step than anyone realized, certainly not the daughters who had been gone for years. Hurt, perhaps, by his inability to move out of the past, they had started over without him.

Now Sarge needed a new start, but not the one they planned. Charging out of the elevators, he encountered Lauren, looking drawn. "Where is everyone?"

She pointed to Sarge's room. "Still there. Barely." She looked him up and down. "You really are a cop."

He'd worn the uniform because he was supposed to be in court this afternoon. "Did you think I was making that up?"

"Seeing is believing."

He crooked a smile. "Thanks for calling me."

She smiled back. A lovely, hopeful smile.

Jonah reached the room and entered. The women who turned to him were fifteen or twenty years older. They probably had no memory of him. They might remember his father though, as their expressions suggested. The resemblance was striking. Especially in uniform.

"Hi." He extended his hand. "Jonah Westfall."

"Of course. I'm Billie. This is Stacey. Dad's been hollering for you, but I'm not sure what you have to do with this, unless he's broken the law." A ludicrous thought, her raised eyebrow told him. Sarge laid down the law; he didn't break it.

"He hasn't broken any laws." Jonah looked at Sarge in the bed, shrunken even more than he'd been. "Hey, Sarge." Low simmer, Jonah gauged, by the return stare.

"The hospital is ready to release him to a VA care facility that will continue pain management and—"

"I can manage my own pain. Always have."

Billie rolled her eyes. "The drugs impair balance, cause drowsiness. He won't be able to drive or walk long distances. He's—"

"Not deaf or on my deathbed." A rolling boil.

"He has numbness and slight paralysis in the right leg that will worsen as the spine constricts the nerves. He needs care that my sister and I can't provide."

Jonah nodded.

"We have considered the options—"

"I'd like to discuss one you haven't considered."

That caught her off stride. "Another option?"

"Let him move in with me."

Both women stared at him, slow blinking.

"You want Sarge to live with you?" Stacey tried for an inquiring tone, but it came out incredulous.

"I've just about completed the addition to my home." He hadn't started it with Sarge in mind, but as he'd driven, the thought had come. It was all he could come up with to keep Sarge out of a place where he'd be utterly powerless.

"I don't understand how you're involved." Billie looked more suspicious than her sister. "What's in this for you?"

"Sarge is my friend."

She barely masked her disbelief. "I don't know what he's promised you—"

"I'm not looking for compensation. I'd like to give him a place where he can stay on the mountain and keep a hand in the bakery."

Billie looked at her sister. "We were thinking we'd sell the bakery."

"Over my dead body," Sarge barked.

"It would pay for quality care—"

"My own daughters, digging my grave."

"Sarge," Jonah said mildly. "Everyone wants what's best for you."

"Best for me? Let me live my life. My way."

"We're trying to do that."

"Not those—"

"You're not helping your cause, Sarge. Let me handle it."

Billie scowled. "Has he said he wants to live with you?"

"I haven't invited him. What do you say, Sarge? Want to bunk with me?"

"I don't need to bunk with you. I have my own place."

Jonah hung his hands on his hips. "That's not an option. It's my place or the home." Nursing care was not cheap. The daughters should jump at the chance.

"Dad?" Billie fixed him with the fierce, beaky stare she'd clearly inherited. "For reasons I can't fathom, Chief Westfall is making you an offer."

Sarge looked up. Jonah saw a desperation that could have been interposed on the wounded coyote. *Come on, Sarge.* He waited. *Take the chance you've got.* Sarge would have wanted to fight it, to hold the line and not retreat. He never pretended to be what he wasn't, but right now it was clear he wasn't sure who or what he was.

"I don't have a choice, I guess." His voice sounded thready, but the glare had lost no potency.

Jonah breathed his relief, wiping the sweat from his palms. It didn't seem to matter who was in a vulnerable situation. It always got him in the gut.

"We'll work out the details, Sarge."

Sarge's mouth moved, but no words came. His big hands clawed the sheet.

"I'd like to see you in the hall," Billie said. "Sit with Dad, Stacey."

This apple hadn't fallen far from the tree. Jonah followed her out.

"We will be selling the house. There is no way we can pay for a residence he's not living in—or ever going to again. He should have sold that place years ago and gotten proper care. It's a shrine to the dead."

"It's paid for, but you're right." Jonah nodded. "I'll help him clear—"

"No. Stacey and I are here. We'll clean it out."

Jonah looked toward the room. "He'd like some say in it."

"He'd like to control the whole thing, but that's not going to happen. You think I'm a hard woman. I see it in your face. But I lived with him. Longer than I should have had to. This time, we're doing it my way."

Jonah didn't press it. He'd drop by and collect things Sarge valued when the time came. He'd need to call Jay to complete the finish carpentry. They'd move Sarge's furniture and bring the man in. He wasn't sure who'd be at greater risk, Sarge or the coyote, but he wasn't about to bring that up now.

Lauren touched his elbow. "Coffee?"

He took the cup. "Thanks."

"Who won?" She raised her thick lashes.

"I'll be taking him home, I guess."

Her eyes softened. "Do they issue halos with that badge?"

"If they did, mine's long gone." He sipped the coffee. "This is good."

"The new cappuccino machine. Makes it perfect every time."

"Removes the human element."

She nodded. "So have you thought this through?"

"Kind of freestyling right now."

"I paged the doctor to come talk to you." She signed the chart brought to her by a stocky, male CNA who tried to disguise how much he enjoyed standing in her presence. She turned back. "You're going to need medical assistance with Sergeant Beaker. I could help you get him set up and provide ongoing care."

"It would be a long drive."

"I'm up that direction. My family owns a town house complex in Pine Crest. I have my own unit."

He studied her face. "You have a card?"

She removed one from the slim wallet in her pocket. "My cell's on the back."

"Sure you mean it?"

"I've been inoculated." The corners of her eyes tipped up. "Who else are you going to find to put up with him?"

"That's a very good point."

"I'm a good point maker."

"I'll bet you are." He slipped the card into his pocket. He'd just burned whatever bridge had been left with Tia. Looking at Lauren, he ought to feel something—besides lust. Something like potential. He sighed.

"Call me tonight."

"I'll be getting things figured out."

"Tomorrow then. We'll send Sarge with a walker, but it won't be long before he's wheelchair bound. I can show you what you need."

He had not thought through the details in his rash offer. He'd negotiated the prisoner's release but probably did need help getting Sarge organized. He and Jay could ramp the back entrance, but there were probably a dozen other things he wouldn't think of. "Okay."

She looked up. "Here's the doctor."

Jonah turned, and it hit him that he'd just taken responsibility for another person. God help them both.

———

Piper looked up as Jonah's morning companion came back into the bakery, searching the tables instead of approaching the counter. Piper eyed her curiously. "Can I help you?"

"Oh." Liz turned. "I wanted something from the candle shop next-door, but no one's there. I thought maybe Tia had dropped in over here."

"I haven't seen her. Did she put the sign up? Back in half an hour or whatever?"

"No. But I looked all through. Even the bathroom was empty."

"You mean the store's open, but Tia isn't there?"

"Yes, I found that strange."

More than strange. Tia would never leave the shop unsecured.

"I'm ready to order." The woman who'd been perusing the board decided.

"Can you warm this raisin roll for me?" The squat man behind her queried.

Piper released her breath. "Okay. Sure." She grabbed the roll and asked the woman, "What would you like?"

The microwave took forever, then the register tape jammed, then someone else wanted a coffee refill. When she looked up Liz had gone. She'd have to check Tia's shop herself.

As she started to round the counter, Bob Betters came in with a toothy female companion who wore an embarrassing amount of makeup, trying to look fancy enough for Mr. Successful. Bob had swallowed a canary whole. He would not wait while she searched for Tia.

"What can I get you?"

"No goat cheese?" Bob didn't exactly sneer.

"Just what Sarge has on the board." *Come on, come on, come on.*

"Two cheddar rolls. And warm them up, peach."

Maybe that was what his companion wanted, but she hadn't seen him ask. Piper bagged his order, but he and his date sat down at a table. She didn't like leaving customers in the store but had to check on Tia. As much as Bob annoyed her, she didn't see him ripping her off. She keyed in the register lock, let herself out from behind the counter, and rushed through the kitchen.

Tia's back door was locked, but she hurried around and found the front open. "Tia?" Could she have forgotten to lock her store? The shop seemed undisturbed. The back room looked the same as always except Tia had moved her worktable out front. Piper checked the shelf where Tia kept her sling-back purse. Empty.

Piper speed-dialed her cell phone and got voice mail. "Call me, Ti, okay?" She locked Tia's front door, though she couldn't shoot the bolt without a key, then went back to the bakery.

Bob lounged back. "Everything okay?"

"Yeah." She nodded. "More iced tea?"

"Sure." As she poured the refill, he said, "Thanks, peach."

What was with the peach thing? She filled his date's glass. "I'm Piper."

"Ainsley." The girl had lipstick on her teeth.

"How's the roll?"

Ainsley glanced at Bob and back. "It's good."

Mary Carson came in. "Oh, lovely. You have one last lemon scone."

"Just for you." Piper lifted the flap to get back behind the counter. "To go?"

"Yes, please."

Piper snagged the scone. "Do you know where Tia might have gone?"

"She's not in the shop?"

Piper shook her head. "She didn't turn the sign and forgot to lock the door."

"Maybe she had an emergency."

"Someone on the Hopeline?"

"She's not supposed to make that face to face. Too easy for people to take advantage or misrepresent themselves. Tia knows that."

"Someone from the church?"

"Certainly possible." Mary nodded. "But to leave the shop unlocked?"

Piper swallowed. "It's not right."

"No." Concern furrowed Mary's brow. "Doesn't seem right, does it?"

———

Even with the light appointment schedule, Liz had taken as much time away from the clinic—from Lucy—as she could, waiting for Tia to return. Disappointed that Piper had locked the store, Liz leaned into the glass once more to peer in. She would have liked to walk through again without Tia there, to sense and imagine her, to see what Jonah saw, what he wanted.

She had planned to get a candle for him as a thank-you for the pups—and to see his reaction when she presented it. She wanted him to see that she knew, that she had guessed what he hadn't told her. But it didn't matter. All she needed from him now were the littermates, sweet newborn puppies whose existence thus far had been almost entirely wrapped together inside the mother.

She closed her eyes and imagined them, the closeness, the oneness. She had dared to think she might find that with Jonah when she'd seen the hollows in his eyes. But that wasn't reality. The person she had, the one she'd always had was Lucy.

Nothing mattered now but making things right for her sister, her twin, her other self. As with all identical twins, they'd been one egg that had become two fetuses, their DNA differing only by infinitesimal code changes. But they were closer still. In monozygotic twins, when the egg split in the first two days after fertilization, each fetus developed its own placenta and its own sac. Most of the time the split came later than that, resulting in separate sacs but a shared placenta.

About one percent of the time the splitting occurred late enough to result in both a shared placenta and a shared sac. In that case, the mortality rate was fifty percent due mainly to cord entanglement. In the infrequent instances when the zygote split extremely late, the result was conjoined twins. Mortality was highest then because of the many complications resulting from shared organs.

It was so rare as to be miraculous when such twins survived.

Sixteen

The web of our life is of a mingled yarn, good and ill together.
—WILLIAM SHAKESPEARE

Tia filled the blue plastic bladder with water, stuffed it down into the pack, and pulled the straps over her shoulders. She snapped the strap across her chest and tugged the jacket down beneath the waist belt. Grabbing her walking stick, she limped out the door. Her body was not up to the hike, but her mind insisted.

Jonah had broken her open. She had to go where she felt whole. On the mountain, clouded over as it was, she could ease the horrible pain. The craggy heights had always been her escape. When the weight of inadequacy had crushed in, she charged up the slopes, seeking freedom, release.

She couldn't charge today. She hobbled up from her backyard to the trail running horizontally across the forested slope. The bruise ached with every step. Her chest burned as she pushed up the steep terrain. That much would pass when she found her stride.

Hiking alone without a word to anyone was stupid, especially with a storm moving over the peaks, but she had to. Customers would come to the shop and find it closed. She frowned, a sudden disconcerting thought catching her short. Had she locked the door? She hesitated, then pushed on.

She didn't care. It wasn't even her business. And the candles? What she hadn't lost to Miles's destruction would burn away as though they'd never been. That was how she felt too. Burned up, burned out.

She reached the trail and turned, digging the point of the stick in and striding hard. Aspen groves formed golden bands between the blue-green firs and spruces, but the sight failed to move her. By the time she'd climbed two hundred feet in elevation the clouds filled all the gaps like gray batting, much more aligned with her mood. Her damp hair curled wildly, clinging to her face and neck. She breathed the cold wet air like a needy smoker that first long inhale.

She pressed on, harder, faster, not finding her usual stride but making a new one. Closed in by the clouds, she had only a subconscious awareness of the looming peak on her left, the pitch to her right. As the fog settled around her, she eased the pace and kept it steady.

An hour passed and another, scrambling over boulders and rocks that formed the trail. Her throbbing calf registered distantly, as muscle fatigue might inform a long-distance runner without compromising the goal. The clouds broke open, and sunlight bathed her for a time, before the sky darkened, angrier than before. A far-off rumble called from one peak to another, but she climbed on, needing the summit.

That was one thing she and Jonah had in common, not running away but to a place where her lungs expanded to take in the remnants of atmosphere that worked on her like a drug. Though they'd never climbed together, she had often glimpsed Jonah on treks of his own, and she'd known when she had followed that day, that they would share something on the mountain Reba would never understand. Reba breathed oxygen.

Tia's knuckles whitened on the staff.

"I loved you before I slid the ring on her finger."

Tia shook her head. From the first time he'd looked into her eyes with his own bruised stare, they'd shared a connection. She had thought only she had taken it farther in her mind and in her heart. Now he'd admitted the same, yet still he chose Reba.

Tia stumbled, recovered, and increased her pace. Thunder rumbled, still far but menacing. Her hair clung, a sodden mass. Jonah had to have Reba. He wouldn't settle for the reject. He had desired but not chosen her.

"I loved you before we betrayed your sister."

He had cost her so much. And he dared to call it love. Her hand slid on the wet wood of the stick. Ozone filled her nostrils. Lightning flashed across the valley, deep in the dark heart of the storm.

She should turn back, but she didn't. More than any place else, she felt God in the mountains. Awe. Majesty. Omnipotence. Power that could annihilate her but didn't. She rounded a hairpin and stared up into the cloud, a gray silk cocoon, a womb. If she could really climb back to her inception, would she emerge different? Could she be a milder, more compliant Tia, a Tia someone wanted?

She shook the moisture from her hair. Nature versus nurture missed the point. Any nature nurtured would thrive. Any nature rejected would starve. She'd been born with a spark that could ignite a wildfire. People had feared and resisted it, beaten at it, suffocated it, never seeing the glow or breathing the aroma.

Jonah had seen and craved the fire inside her. But even he wouldn't risk the burn. He'd chosen Reba. Sweet, shining Reba.

Pain speared. Her foot slipped, and the other leg buckled. Her staff tumbled over rocks and juniper, as her hands scraped, her cheek burned, her head and shoulder banged. She grasped for tree trunks, ripping bark and moss and the flesh of her palms before she lodged with a thud in the crook of the ravine.

———

Piper paced. It was way past time for Tia to call or come home. Even if there'd been an emergency, wouldn't she make contact? Piper fingered her phone. She'd left three messages. No response. She looked out through the streaming pane. Rain beat at the windows. Lightning flashed and thunder hollered.

She had searched every hangout, even Tia's church and the library. Nothing. She wanted to tell Jonah, but she had promised Tia not to overreact. If she called the station and said Tia had left without locking up, would they do something? It took more than that for a missing person unless there were signs of struggle or threats or something.

She chewed the nail of her index finger and climbed the stairs. She had not been in Tia's room uninvited, but she pushed open the door now and went in, hoping to find what? A note? Tia would have left it in the kitchen.

The bedroom was in order. No sign of panic, struggle, flight. She went back downstairs, looking again at the darkening windows. Tia could be at someone's house, comforting or encouraging someone. She could be with a friend.

But the unlocked door nagged. To leave her shop unsecured, Tia must have been overwhelmed or distracted by something. Or someone. There wouldn't be signs of struggle if she'd been taken at gunpoint. Her stomach clenched.

Tia had accused her of having a hyperactive worry mode. And it was true. Knowing every time her family members had gone "to work" they might be caught or hurt or thrown in jail had honed her nerves. But she had real cause for concern. Tia unreachable, her shop unsecured.

Piper chewed her cuticle. She'd seen Miles walking by, surprised he hadn't come into the bakery. Had he gone to Tia's? Had she made Tia believe he was safe when he wasn't? She took out her cell and phoned Jonah.

With Jay's help, Jonah pushed the bureau to the wall. After he had testified at the county court, he and Jay had assembled Sarge's bed, collected what they could of his belongings. Billie would be delivering him within the hour. When his phone rang, he guessed it would be Lauren, following up on her offer. But it was Piper.

"What's up?"

"Tia's missing."

"What do you mean missing?" He had a flash of her stricken face as he'd left her stunned and wounded.

"I can't find her anywhere."

He looked at his watch. "She only closed up a couple hours ago."

"She disappeared before noon without locking the door. She left the shop unattended and didn't even secure it. Something's wrong."

He silently cursed himself.

"I think Miles went in there."

Jonah swallowed. "He did, but nothing happened. I talked to her after that."

"Then she's okay?"

He pressed his fingers to his temple. "Are you home?"

"Yes."

"Go down to the mud room."

"Okay."

"I want you to look for her walking staff, hydration pack, whatever she usually takes hiking."

"You think she went hiking in the storm?"

"It wasn't storming at noon." Tia knew better than to set out in bad conditions, but when she got upset, she took to the mountains.

Piper said, "The staff is gone. The hydration pack. Her multipocket jacket and her hiking boots."

He drew a deep breath. She had gone prepared. And she was a competent mountaineer. "Tia's been hiking these mountains her whole life. She knows them like her own bedroom. Have you looked outside?"

The rain had turned to sleet.

"I've tried to reach her. She's not answering her phone."

"She goes up there to be alone. And cell reception is spotty."

"So we, what? Leave her out there?"

He closed his eyes. "I'll call the officer in charge, put them on alert. If she's not back in two hours, let me know."

"What if she's injured?"

The thought punched through his rationalizations. He knew why she'd gone out there. Tia would be furious if he sent out a team. Unless she needed help. Even then, she wouldn't want it from him.

A knock came at the door. Jonah swallowed. "Call me in an hour if she's not back." The trails up there were clearly marked—if she kept to them. An hour would give her time to get down without causing a scene, and he had other concerns.

Jay admitted Sarge's daughters. Sarge shuffled in behind them with a rolling walker. It must be eating him up to be so feeble. He looked bleak but no longer desperate.

Jonah had locked the coyote in his bedroom. She made no sound, but he sensed her awareness. He hadn't mentioned the wild animal to

Billie or Stacey, hadn't put her into the mix when he'd made his offer. He'd have to figure out a way to keep them apart for as long as she deigned to stay, but right now he had another alpha female to placate.

Billie pushed into what would be her father's room, finding it spacious and airy, the windows taking most of one wall with a view of the creek bounded by evergreen and aspen. The attached bathroom might need some modification if Sarge went into a wheelchair, but he doubted she could fault much else. Stacey fussed over him as he lowered himself onto the padded window seat. Sarge growled.

The sooner the daughters left, the better for everyone. They must have agreed, because in fifteen minutes they had pronounced the arrangement sufficient and made their escape.

Jonah sat on the edge of the bed and eyed Sarge. "This all right for now?"

Sarge nodded.

"Up for steak?"

A smile flickered on Sarge's mouth. "Up for anything not reduced to mush."

Jonah nodded. "Three T-bones coming up."

He headed for the kitchen with Jay on his heels. Sarge was his focus tonight, making this transition as painless as possible. Tia's wilderness skills and good judgment would get her back—unless she'd been injured. He called the station and put them on alert.

———

Pelted by rain, Tia raised her head. The scent of mud and piney loam rose up as she assessed her predicament. She had rolled a long way from the trail, and her staff lay farther down the ravine. She didn't have to guess how much she would need it once she'd dragged herself back to the trail. She rose to her elbows, feeling wrenched neck and back muscles. It could have been worse.

She drank from her water tube, then pulled up her hood to block the icy rain. She pressed her scraped hands to the crumbly ground and sat up.

Flashes of lightning darted behind the lumpy oatmeal sky. What daylight was left hardly penetrated. She should have listened to her body, to the pain that had warned her she was weakening. She'd been stupid. And it could cost her.

She tried to stand and gasped. Pain screamed up her ankle to the already bruised calf. She dropped her chin to her chest as the waves passed, then gingerly fingered the flesh puffing up around her ankle bones. Probably a twist or sprain.

Clenching her teeth, she eased down the rocky ravine slick with chipped bark and rust-colored pine needles. She gripped the staff. Dragging it, she crawled up the ravine, her fingers freezing as the rain turned to sleet. Late summer, early autumn, could look like winter at higher elevations—and felt like it already. It began to hail, relentless pellets stinging her. At least no psychopath would be out in this.

The thought should have comforted but didn't. She had hiked alone as long as she could remember. Now someone was torturing animals and leaving them along trails to die. Did that person find them injured and take them at their weakest? She startled and jerked her head to the right. A squirrel scrambled up a fir trunk.

She continued crawling up the slope, rocks and sticks digging into her knees. Breathing hard, she reached the trail and, clutching the staff, got to her feet. She cried out when a bull elk bounded through the trees a short way up the mountain.

What was wrong with her? The chance of a killer being right there right now on a deserted trail in the storm was far less than the danger of injury and hypothermia. This cold front could drop into the twenties or below. She pulled gloves from her pack and tugged them over her stinging hands.

In another pocket of her pack, she activated her phone, but as she'd figured, it found no signal. She pulled the hood over her soaking hair and cinched it around her face. Wincing each time she put weight on her twisted ankle, she worked her way down the rocky trail.

Down was always more precarious. Wet and icy made it treacherous.

Injured, it might be nearly impossible. But she had to try. Piper would worry, and Piper didn't just worry. She called people, called Jonah.

Tia shivered. If she went fast enough—no, she had to be careful. She planted the stick and eased over a sharp rock, reached a level stretch and pulled herself along like a Venetian gondolier.

The hail covered the ground like snow. She tried to recall what phase of moon she'd have, but with the clouds, it didn't make much difference. She prayed. Why was that always a last resort? She ran a prayer line, for heaven's sake.

All things are possible with God. He shall provide all my needs. Ask and it will be given. Out of the depths I cry out, and the Lord hears my prayer.

Lord, help me now. She swiped the moisture from her face and kept on, praying most fervently that she'd be down before Jonah could mobilize. She did not want to see him. Not in this condition. Not in any condition.

Wiping his mouth, Jonah answered the phone.

"She's not here."

He and Jay and Sarge had just sat down to steak and mashed potatoes. He rose and moved to the window, feeling the chill of the storm. Hail had pattered against the roof, bouncing and piling upon the ground.

"Chief?" Piper demanded.

He drew back from his reflection. "I'll send a team out."

The line was silent a full beat. "Did you miss the part where I said it's Tia? And she could be hurt?"

"I didn't miss it."

"And you're not going to find her?"

"I'm handling it."

"What if the psycho is out there?"

The only one crazy enough to be out was Tia. "Piper. I'll take it from here."

She gave a long sigh and hung up. He placed the call. "Hey, Moser. Can you take McCarthy and whoever's on call from the sheriff's office and check out the trails above Sprague Street? Got a call someone might be lost up there, maybe caught in the storm."

"Who are we looking for?"

"Tia Manning."

"Come again?"

"You heard me."

Moser's pause lasted a beat too long. "And you're sending me?"

"You on duty?"

"Well..."

"Are you in charge?"

"Yeah, Jonah, I'm in charge."

"Then take care of it." He hit end.

Both pairs of eyes rose to him when he returned to the table.

"You can go," Sarge said gruffly. "I don't need baby-sitting."

Jonah clenched his jaw. "Moser's got it."

Jay's bicolored stare probed. Jonah rose and went to his room, where the predator in his closet watched no less pointedly.

Seventeen

A part of you has grown in me. And so you see, it's you and
me together forever and never apart, maybe in distance, but
never in heart.

—AUTHOR UNKNOWN

Piper's stomach knotted with anxiety. Every time her mother had put
on a certain dress, or her dad had worn a calculating expression, or
they'd spent a long evening with Uncle Joe, she had known it meant
a new scam. Even when they didn't try to include her, she felt part of it.

She'd been so scared for them, scared her dad would get injured, her
mom would be taken to jail, scared police would come to the door and
take her away to live with strangers. Her hand would go to her mouth.
First she chewed the cuticles, then the nails themselves. She had beaten it
for a while, but now she tasted the blood from her pinkie where she'd
nipped too deeply down into the skin.

Staring into the night, she shuddered. Please let Tia be held up by the
storm and not in the clutches of a sick raccoon killer. Just because she
hadn't been taken from her store at gunpoint didn't mean she wasn't in
the clutches of a psycho. Piper pressed her hands to her face. She had to
do something. She'd be useless in a search. Then what? She closed her eyes
and tried to imagine what Tia would do.

Pray.

Oh, boy. Not the person for *that* job.

Tia had told her praying unleashed power, but what happened if she
did it wrong? It might be wrong to pray at all if she didn't believe in God.
She bit her nail. She didn't so much *not* believe as not know *how* or what
to believe.

What she needed was someone who knew their stuff, who went to
church. Jonah Westfall went to church. He would know how to pray, but
if she called him again, he'd arrest her. She needed a trained pray-er to tell

her how, or better yet to do it for her. That was it. She would call Tia's church ladies.

She rushed for the kitchen, found the slim directory with a picture of the church on the front. She'd start with someone she knew…Mary Carson. Breathlessly she explained, "Remember I told you Tia left her shop? Well, she's lost on the mountain in the storm."

"Oh no."

Thunder rumbled across the sky.

"I need someone to pray. Someone who can. Who knows how."

"You want me to pray with you?"

"No. I mean, I think Tia would want it, but I don't know how. I convinced the police chief to send a search team, and I wanted to do something too, but all I could think of was pray."

"I tell you what. I don't drive in bad weather, so let me call Carolyn. Are you home?"

"Yes."

"Unless you hear back, we'll be there directly."

Piper hoped the tremor in her voice was the palsy. One hopeless worrier was enough. "Thank you." She wasn't sure what she was doing, only that Tia would want it.

Fifteen minutes later, the two women arrived. Mary said, "This is Carolyn Wells, my dear. We would be honored to pray with you for Tia's safety and rescue."

———

Shivering hard, Tia rounded a hairpin turn and saw lights, three strong beams far enough down the mountain that it would still be a long pull to reach them. She drew a haggard breath. She did not look forward to Jonah's scolding, but she would accept their help. Fatigue had become a force.

She slowed her pace. It did no good to rush, now that a team had already come to find her—at least she hoped it was a rescue team and not the animal torture club. She shuddered. Her teeth had been chattering so hard she'd have to check them for chips, but a fresh chill shook her.

She had intended to call out when they drew close enough, but now she wasn't sure. She gripped the staff, biting her lip against the pain in her palms, her knees, her elbows, and most of all her left leg. It felt like a dog had sunk its teeth into her ankle and took a new hold with every step.

She hadn't realized until the cold soaked into her knees that she had sunk to the ground like a penitent. Pulling herself back up seemed tantamount to climbing Mount Everest. But Jonah would not find her on her knees. Digging deep, she climbed the staff and regained her feet as the light beams caught her.

"Tia Manning?" The voice calling was Adam Moser's.

"Yes," she called back. "I'm all right."

She waited for Jonah to stalk up, glaring, but he wasn't among them. She hoped that didn't mean another team was out in the storm searching.

"Are you injured?"

"Not badly. My ankle slowed me down."

A sheriff's deputy wrapped a blanket around her shoulders. She almost collapsed under its insubstantial weight.

Another officer she didn't know said, "Put your arm around my shoulder. We'll get you down." He was short and sturdy as a pony. With Adam Moser on the other side, she hardly had to work at all. Relief rushed in, so potent she shook with it. She'd been closer to collapse than she'd realized.

"I'll run you to Emergency," Adam said when they'd reached the trailhead.

"Can you please just take me home?"

"You should be checked out."

"I'm fine really. There's no one else searching, is there?"

"No ma'am." He unlocked the patrol car.

She slid out of the rain and closed her eyes as Jonah's officer walked around and climbed in with the phone to his ear. "Yeah, Chief, Moser here. We located Miss Manning. Minor injuries, exposure. She's declined the hospital, so I'm running her by the fire station, let them look her over."

She started to object, but Jonah would hear. Besides, the officer hadn't asked; he'd decided.

Moser listened for a beat. "All right then." He signed off.

Tia looked out the slush-soaked window, relieved and devastated. She hadn't wanted to face Jonah, hadn't wanted him to think this a stunt for his attention like the things she'd done as a girl, taking dares and challenging him. She had dreaded him finding her, scolding her, but this new dread seeped in like an infection. Jonah had known she might be in trouble and turned it over to someone else. He'd finally let go.

———

Jonah pocketed his phone. Tia was found, safe and stubborn. He'd made the right call. He relaxed his muscles, working the tension from his neck. Having seen Sarge to bed, he let Enola out once more before she settled in for the night. Her wary eyes and scabby side reminded him how short the time had been since she'd dragged herself into his yard.

He had to agree this might not be her first sojourn in the human world. Maybe she'd been bred intentionally like the wolf hybrids. Leaving the outside door open, he went back to the closet and looked at the little, lumpy pups. He didn't want to swipe them, didn't know why Liz had insisted he bring them over tonight. Being there when the eyes opened might matter, but that was at least a week off.

With a sigh, he lifted and sexed each one. Two females, one male. He turned the last in his hands and studied the face. They looked more like rodents than dogs. No way to tell, yet, if she'd been mated by a coyote or a domestic dog. How could he even think of turning two of them over to a woman who thought she could pattern them like ducklings? She wanted to mother them into pets, but it just—

Jay tapped the door. "The vet's here."

Right now?

She came into the room, her coat and hair slushy, her face determined. "You promised me puppies."

He still cradled one in his hands. "I think it's too soon, Liz."

"You'll have the same concerns six weeks from now, and I'll have lost the chance for patterning."

She cast her gaze around the room he had almost invited her into the other night. That misstep gave her leverage and she knew it, yet in the midst of her resolve, he still sensed her awkwardness, a naiveté that didn't match the outward boldness.

She looked into his face. "We had a deal."

"I know." He nodded. "I was going to bring them to you."

"Sure you were." She half smiled and looked at her watch.

"Tonight got busy."

"So I'm saving you the trip."

He nestled the one he held against his chest. "Those two are female, I think." He nodded toward the closet. If she was determined to have them, they'd better move quickly before Enola returned. "You have something to carry them in?"

She fetched a small carrier from the floor of the hall, checked them over and confirmed his guess, then loaded them in. "This is an opportunity for nurture to conquer nature."

"Nature won't give up easily."

She glanced up sideways. "Neither will I."

Jay murmured, "The coydog's at the door."

She lifted the carrier.

He returned the last pup to the closet. "I'll let you out the back." He led her down the new hall past Sarge's room. As they reached the door, he shook his head. "Why do I feel like I let the fox into the henhouse?"

"The one she has left will get her full attention. And yours." Their eyes met.

At a loss for words, he pushed open the door. Drizzle struck his face. "Be careful, Liz. Don't take risks with them."

"Everything valuable has risks. You either take them or you don't."

He watched her limp away, carrying the pups, then closed the door. Guilt clutched him as Enola walk-ran through the rooms, processing the foreign scents and the trail of her now departed pups. He wished he could explain.

Her pace slowed, became methodical, eyes darting, her tongue hanging to the side. Again and again her eyes flicked over him, but it was not an accusatory glance. She didn't realize he'd surrendered her offspring.

Finally, she returned to the closet, licking his scent off the one she had left.

Jonah watched for a time, then went to the living room and stared at the bottle. He remembered diving down inside its depths, the warmth, the caress, the satiation. The feeling in his brain like softest fur.

Jay came up beside him. "Want to split it?"

Jonah swallowed. "Yes."

They stood, shoulder to shoulder, acknowledging the threat and giving no ground. Jonah sat down. Forearms resting on his thighs, he hung his head. "I wish she hadn't come."

"Your veterinarian?"

Jonah scowled. *His* veterinarian. "Enola. Why did she choose me?"

"Might be the half cow in your freezer." When Jonah didn't smile, Jay shrugged. "Maybe she couldn't go any farther. She got too weak."

"You said she came for a reason, to teach me, to show me things."

"That was the Cherokee answer. This is the Dane."

He preferred to think she'd simply collapsed. But that wasn't what he'd seen. That little drag toward him made Jay's explanation a lie. She had trusted him. His mouth felt parched. His hands shook.

Jay said, "This isn't about the dog, is it?"

Jonah clenched his hands.

"Why didn't you look for Tia?"

He looked at Jay. His friend had never met Tia, but he knew the score, knew they'd reached the bottom of the ninth, just not that earlier in the day he'd made the final out. He had blocked the fear while she was out there. Now that she'd been found safe, it hit. What if they hadn't found her? What if she'd died? He rubbed a hand over his face. "Because it's over."

Jay let the words settle over them. Jonah hadn't said it before now, even to himself. He had gone into her shop intending one thing and accomplished the opposite. "Cold turkey?"

Jonah nodded. He'd beaten one addiction. If he just got her out of his blood…

The rain dwindled and left shredded clouds across a faintly starry sky. Finally Jay stood. "I start a remodel tomorrow. I'll be tied up the next three days, maybe more."

Jonah nodded.

"Six years sober."

Jonah nodded again.

"The Lakota Sioux Chief Yellow Hawk said, 'I seek strength, not to be greater than my brother, but to fight my greatest enemy—myself.' Strength, brother." Jay squeezed his shoulder on the way out.

With each slow beat of his heart, Jonah desired the bottle. Did he even want to fight himself? What difference did it make? So he'd get drunk. Who was there to care? Who was there to harm? He could drown it, cover the pain with the smooth burn. His throat cleaved, dry and needing.

Jay had told him keeping the bottle was holding hands with the devil. Jonah wanted it to remind him he could get burned. He didn't pretend it would be only one swallow. If he opened the bottle, brought it to his lips, they'd make love until nothing remained.

The devil wasn't in the booze. It was in him, driven deep, deeper with every fist, every welt, every searing word that had left his mind as raw as his flesh. And with the blows, the smell of whiskey, the taste of fear in his nose and mouth and lungs.

Lord. Did it ever end?

He had shielded Reba from his fall. But Tia had been there, she'd always been there, in the dark and terror. In the pain. In the shame.

"The worst of it," Sarge murmured, shuffling in behind him, "is going on, day after day. What for?" He spread his hands, then lowered himself into the other recliner. He smelled like an old coat, pulled from a trunk where it had rested too long.

"I hope you don't mind being here, Sarge. It means a lot to me."

"You like to rescue people."

"I didn't—"

Sarge held up a hand. "It's not the first time."

Jonah waited.

"The first was the night Marty died."

Sarge had not talked about it before, not to him anyway.

"When I saw your face, a little boy tormented by a twisted man, I knew. In the moment of my failure, I'd been given a second chance."

"You didn't fail Marty, Sarge."

Sarge shook his head. "I wasn't that different from your old man."

"You're different."

"Hard and immovable. Always proving something. Do you know how it was, being a cook when the others were out there risking their lives? I felt invisible, inconsequential. A poser in uniform." He raised weary eyes. "But at home I was king."

Jonah didn't argue.

"Marty." He tipped his head, looking wounded. "Marty never made waves, not like the girls. He was sensitive. Smart. Introspective. He had a soft heart, and Ellen wouldn't let me harden it."

Billie must not have been so lucky.

Sarge's lips pressed together, his brows gathering. "She was a good mother, a good wife, better than I deserved."

"I wish I'd known her."

Sarge nodded. "She'd have taken you under her wing."

"Your wings were enough."

Sarge looked up. Their eyes held.

"You did well by me, Sarge. Anything I return is because you gave me the chance to be something."

"Then remember who you are. And who you never want to be."

Jonah studied his face, every crag and crevice, every line life had put there. He loved the old man. Throat tight, he nodded.

———

Still shaking with cold but not allowing her teeth to chatter, Tia thanked Adam Moser for finding and transporting her to and from the firehouse where the guys made way too much of it, insisting she sit in warmed blankets with a hot drink while they wrapped her ankle and berated the cop for not including them in the mission.

"Chief's call," Moser said, rubbing it in without knowing.

Now the sooner she got inside, the sooner she would put this whole thing behind her. Using her staff and the officer's arm, she reached her door, then thanked Moser again with a clear finality. "Please go get warm."

"Sure you're all right?"

"Absolutely."

Her calf and ankle were on fire, and her heart had been quarried. She wanted nothing more than to crawl into bed and curl up like a worm. But when she went inside, Carolyn rose from the chair beside the fire. Mary Carson sat on the settee beside Piper. Her heart thumped. "Bad news?"

"What? No, we're here for you. And Piper."

She masked her dismay. "I'm fine. Twisted an ankle. Not my smartest move, but I handled it." Leaning heavily on the staff, she moved toward the fire to combat the chill that still seemed lodged in her bones.

"You're half frozen," Mary Carson said.

Piper jumped up. "I told the chief hours ago that you needed help, but he kept saying you could take care of yourself."

Jonah should know. "The sprain slowed me down, and then the storm moved in and everything got cold and slippery." Tia stretched out her hands, one at a time, hating for these two women to see her in the aftermath of a poor decision. She could have shrugged it off with Piper, but Carolyn's gaze held such concern it hurt. "I'm fine. Really." Her brow puckered. "I'm sorry you had to come out in this."

"We came over to help Piper pray," Mary stated.

"Pray." Tia turned to the young woman who had blithely rejected the notion.

"I didn't know what else to do." Her woeful eyes said it hadn't been enough. "When the chief wouldn't listen."

"Prayer was perfect, Piper. See? Here I am."

"But you're hurt."

"Only a sprain."

"That you should not be up on." Carolyn braced her by the elbow and led her to the settee.

Piper climbed in next to her, pulling a blanket over them both. "They prayed you wouldn't be lost or hurt."

The two things that had driven her into the storm, but she meant it physically. No one knew how soul-sick she'd been. Except Jonah, and he'd told them she could take care of herself. He was also telling her.

"I'm not hurt, Piper. It could have been way worse. A sprain is nothing. Even the firemen let me go."

The kettle sang, and Carolyn left, then returned from the kitchen, not with tea but a cup of hot lemon and honey. The warmth of another hot drink was welcome, but she really wanted to be alone. These women were breaking her heart.

"God loves you, Tia." Mary said. "And you too, Piper."

Piper snuggled in. "Please don't get lost again."

Tia leaned her head into Piper's, but she was lost already, falling, falling into the abyss.

———

Liz set the carrier onto the stainless steel table, toweled her hands and face and hair, then looked in at the amorphous pups, nearly furless, a flat brown without markings. Slits for eyes, snub noses, rounded ears that would peak in time. They curled together in the carrier, and she lifted them out as one when Lucy entered.

"Oh. Oh, Lizzie." Lucy peered at them. "They're so new."

Liz smiled. "Brand-new. Help me fill droppers to feed them. They're going to need very special care."

"Are they from the coyote?"

"Yes."

"Then you saw the chief."

"Only long enough to bring you these."

Lucy beamed. "I've never seen anything so precious. Look how they nestle together."

"Yes," Liz said.

"Did he mind you taking them?"

"A little."

She handed one of the pups to Lucy. They fed them with droppers, then she tucked them into one of the kennels she had padded with receiving blankets.

"Will they be warm?"

"There's a heating pad under the blankets. But we'll have to feed them every hour for a while. And stroke them so they eliminate."

Lucy nodded. "I can do that."

"They can't hear or see anything. But they can smell and feel us."

Lucy raised her hand and laid it over the pups. Softly, softly she stroked them. Liz closed her eyes, overwhelmed by an achingly tender resolve.

Eighteen

One man may hit the mark, another blunder; but heed not
these distinctions. Only from the alliance of the one, working with and through the other, are great things born.
—Antoine de Saint-Exupery

Piper pushed the heels of her hands into the dough. Something had
happened to Tia, something besides getting injured on the mountain, but she wouldn't discuss it, wouldn't say why she'd gone as she'd
gone. Piper rolled and pressed again. She had slipped into Tia's room
before leaving and seen her looking through a drawer cluttered with
empty perfume bottles, filmed and crusted nail polish, children's bracelets,
earrings, lip gloss containers with only a smidgen left around the bottom
edge. A princess paper doll with hand-drawn clothes.

"What's all this?" she'd whispered.

"Reba." Tia put the drawer aside and pulled the covers over her
shoulder.

"I hope you're staying in bed today."

Her silence seemed weary beyond words. God may have brought her
off the mountain, but not whole. Whatever had driven her into the storm
had clung to her all the way back.

Piper sighed, then jumped when the bakery door rattled and swung
open. Her eyes spread wide, her mouth even wider. "Sarge!"

A flush burned into his cheeks as he pressed the walker toward her.
"Don't look so surprised. I'm a POW, not a casualty."

"I'm not surprised; I'm thrilled. You look so much better." He'd been
gone over two weeks, and she'd last seen him writhing in the hospital bed,
ranting like a madman.

Sarge scowled. "Stop fawning. Show some pride."

Piper smiled at Jonah standing behind Sarge. "Back to his old self."

Sarge wheezed as he shuffled closer, pushing the aluminum walker. "What's that you're making?"

"Raisin rolls." She tried not to sound bored. This was Sarge's homecoming.

"Jonah said you've been making all kinds of concoctions."

Traitor. "I've served only regulation since you gave me back my job." The escapade with Miles had been on her own time to clean out the pantry. "Tell him."

"That's true."

Sarge made a slow scan of the kitchen. "And you've been opening Sundays and all sorts of foolishness."

"Well, I thought you'd need to pay some bills."

Sarge pushed through the door to the front of the store like a general inspecting the barracks.

She crossed her arms and frowned at Jonah. "Why didn't you warn me?"

"I wanted Sarge to see you at your natural best. He can't have missed your surprise, and he'll know his inspection is an accurate picture of the job you're doing."

"What if everything was a mess and…and—"

"Only fair for Sarge to see it as it is."

She raised her hand and bit her index cuticle.

"I cured my officer of that little habit."

Piper stuck her hand behind her back. "How?"

"I told her to project the confidence necessary to do the job. Have you done your job?"

"You know I have."

"Then show no weakness under fire."

Easy for him to say. Last time she saw Sarge face to face, he canned her.

By the time Sarge made it back to the kitchen, he seemed pale. His feet dragged, but she couldn't tell if it was fatigue or disappointment. He crooked his face up to hers, stared a long moment into her eyes, then said, "Well done, soldier."

Heat rushed to her cheeks. "Thanks, Sarge."

"And I guess if you're all fired to make something different, a daily special won't sink the place."

It took a moment to understand. "You mean it?"

"You earned it."

If she wore buttons, they'd be popping. She looked from Sarge to Jonah. His eyes held a warmth that melted her.

Sarge extended a knobby finger. "But I don't want you open on Sundays. You need time off."

Piper nodded. "Okey-dokey."

"I'll raise you a dollar an hour since you're in charge."

She bit her lower lip as the smile spread on her face. "Where's Sarge, and what have you done with him?"

Fighting a smile of his own, Sarge turned for the door with a gruff, "Carry on."

———

Still smiling at Sarge's about-face, Jonah went to work. Ruth had a list of things for him to handle before he'd made it three steps inside. Top of the list, *Call the mayor.*

"That color's nice on you, Ruth." Her cheeks and neck flushed a deeper pink above the mint green shirt.

"You miss the note about the mayor?"

"I see it."

"That usually makes you cranky."

"Doesn't mean I have to take it out on you." He moved on to his office. He'd have rather dealt with every one of the petty messages beneath the mayor's, but he picked up the phone and leaned back in the squeaky chair. "Mayor Buckley, please. Jonah Westfall."

He waited in proportion to the mayor's importance. He was head of the council and performed at civic functions, although for the last seven years the city manager, Dave Wolton, had charge of all real business matters.

The mayor came on in a jovial mood. "Jonah. Thanks for getting back so promptly."

"What can I do for you?"

"Well, there's a little matter I'd like to discuss. Have you had breakfast?"

"I have."

"I'd like to talk in person."

"I'll come by your office."

"No, let's say…the bridge at Wesley Park."

The bridge spanned Kicking Horse Creek, which was about twenty feet wide through town. In politics, it wasn't unusual to discuss sensitive matters where fewer listening ears could hear, but Jonah couldn't imagine what sensitive matter there was to discuss. "Okay."

He found the mayor standing on the center of the bridge looking into the creek's stony depths. His silver hair lifted in the breeze of another clear morning anticipating fall, as the cold snap had started the leaves turning. Deep dimple lines indented on each side of his cap-toothed smile. "You remember when the old bridge got wiped away in that flash flood?"

"I do." Jonah looked down through the clear rushing water to the gold-flecked stony bed.

"Imagine standing here and having it all torn out beneath you."

"Luckily no one was on it."

"Still. Can you just feel it in your feet?"

"I guess I can." He glanced at the older man, realizing he was making a point.

"I work very hard to promote this community."

Jonah waited.

"People don't realize how much goes into that, because it's all perceptions. You get me?"

"I think so."

"Perceptions can be swept away in an instant just like that flood ripping out this bridge."

Jonah had already made the connection.

"It takes time to rebuild. Time and resources, which in a bad economy might not be there at all. As you know, this Pine Crest annexation we're negotiating will attract a certain type of resident. You've seen the homes they're building, not just within the Pine Crest gates but throughout this valley. The revenue they'll put into the coffers will pay your salary."

"Should I be asking for a raise?"

The mayor smiled. "You take that up with Wolton, why don't you?"

"So what can I do for you?"

The mayor put his hip to the railing. "It's come to my attention that you've encountered a few bizarre animal mutilations."

"I guess you could call them that."

"Doesn't matter what I call them. If word gets out, we'll have alien abductees cutting crop circles in our meadows, claiming extraterrestrials are performing surgeries on our pets."

"Only one pair might have been pets."

"We'll have PETA breathing down our necks, and trust me, son, it's no foreplay."

Son set his teeth on edge. "Well, I wasn't planning on making an announcement. But I am looking into it."

"You get animal rights groups looking this way, they'll find some endangered mouse that stops folks building and revenue growing—you getting me?"

He got him.

The mayor gave his head a sideways tilt. "Now you know it's probably a prank, kids putting a scare into folks. Why else leave them where they'll be found?"

"This is sick stuff, and I can't see it being kids or a prank. There's a level of proficiency that concerns me. The kind of thing that could escalate, might already have from wild to domestic animals."

"Just a couple cats."

"Cut open and joined."

"What's the vet say? You consulted her, didn't you? At the funeral home?"

Had Morey been his source? "She hasn't seen it before. It could be cult—"

"Don't even start. Think the word 'cult' is going to further our position? We need this annexation."

"Why?" Redford had done fine as a little-known secret all these years.

"For growth and continued prosperity."

"Uh-huh."

"Politics is a balancing act. A high wire, if you will. Lean too far left or right, take too big a step forward, a treacherous step back…" He paused. "If word gets out about cults and animal sacrifice in our fair community, well, may as well wash the bridge right out from under us."

"I can't ignore something that could become a threat to safety."

"Oh, you'd be surprised how many things just…" He spread his hands. "Evaporate. Our jobs, yours and mine, are to balance on that high wire. Your father understood that."

Jonah stiffened.

"I'm not saying he didn't lose sight of things at the end. That business went very bad. The town took a hard hit. That's why we gave you your father's job. Putting the best face on that whole business."

"Nothing to do with my qualifications?"

"Sure. Of course you're qualified. That's not the point here."

"So what are you saying?"

"I don't want anything to cost us this deal. Least of all a few wild animals." The mayor shifted his weight. "Just leave it alone."

"You're asking me to stop doing my job." *Walk away. Just walk away.*

"I'm telling you to balance this potential situation with the greater good." Buckley leaned in. "You get me?"

"I'll consider what you've said."

Mayor Buckley eyed him coolly, then warmth crept into his eyes. "I had reservations about you. But you have the makings of a legend yourself, Jonah. Stan always said so."

———

Tia had made it halfway through the morning before the sickening self-pity forced her out of bed. She showered awkwardly, rewrapped her ankle, and limped down the path to the shop. Summer was ending, all but gone since yesterday's storm had flipped the switch. Even the air felt different.

Autumn was still a good tourist time, with the turning of the aspen and area ski slopes opening. Out-of-state skiers were especially keen on mountain handcrafts. She would incorporate golden aspen and fiery sumac leaves into wax pillars and tie sprigs preserved in glycerin to jars and crocks.

Soon it would be waxed pine cones, juniper and holly accents. The bear and moose and evergreen molds. Hard fingers of desperation strangled her, and when a customer came in, Tia made no move toward her. The woman could decide whether she had anything of value to her.

Apparently, she did. "I'm fascinated with these leaf pillars. But I'm afraid they'll ignite if I burn the candle."

"They're only in the perimeter. The wax at the center melts down, and the flame glows through the leaves. It's a beautiful effect."

"And I just love this one with the pebbles and such clear wax. It looks like a creek bed."

"It's a new glycerin wax." She had made that candle before she'd realized the significance of its scripture: *As the deer pants for streams of water, so my soul pants for you, O God. Psalm 42:1*

Her work had revealed what she had not admitted, even to herself. She was parched, desiccated. The hope that once sustained her had dried up like a creek bed after snowmelt. She could not slake her thirst in it any more than a deer from the rocks.

"I'll take it," the stranger said. "It's so unusual."

"They're all originals."

"Yours?"

Tia nodded.

"You're quite talented."

"Thank you." She wrapped and tied and stickered the purchases. She had told Piper she enjoyed it, but now she hated it with everything in her. How long could her mother expect her to go on?

Forever. Stella Manning had exerted the ultimate control—deep, crushing guilt. But even guilt could not contend with the hollow-chested ache of losing Jonah. She had borne this sentence because he'd borne it with her, even while she pushed him away. Now he'd broken free.

As the customer left, Piper burst in. "You're here!"

She didn't realize the accusation it was.

"I thought you were staying in bed."

"I couldn't." Tia folded her arms. "Look at you. You're completely aglow."

"Am I?" She did a little dance. "Well…"

Words burst out of her. Sarge. Specials. A whole dollar raise.

"So what should I start with? I want it to sell like crazy and show Sarge this was absolutely the right decision."

"I still think the gruyère and sun-dried tomato croissant was your best."

"You don't think the tomatoes were fishy?"

The reminder of Jonah's comment stabbed her. Did even the joyous moments have to hurt? "Not at all. It was wonderful."

"Then that's what I'll do. But Sarge said a *daily* special. Something new every day!"

"Well, that's what you wanted." And God knew it was dangerous to want. "But it wouldn't have to be different every day."

"You're right. Of course." She grabbed her in a hug, then jumped back. "Sorry."

She hadn't meant to wince.

"Tia, what are you even doing here?"

Oh, the answers she could give.

———

Maybe it was a streak of the devil in him, but when Jonah got back, he put aside the administrative paperwork and brought out the file on the animals. Not much new from his initial digging, but—

He looked up as Sue came to a stop before him, arms crossed hard over her chest. The two days since they'd taken Eli into the system had harrowed her. She'd been allowed visits, and she'd made a pretty good case for herself, but no decision had been made. "What's up?"

"Sam took Eli from the foster home."

Jonah laid down his pen. "When?"

"Just now. He walked in and took him."

"That's kidnapping."

Her face contorted. "If he takes him and runs… Jonah." She gulped. He stood. "How erratic has he been?"

"I don't know. We haven't talked. I've been staying at my mother's."

A lot of trigger points. Sam might have snapped.

"How did you find out?"

"Connie called me. She thought I might be in on it, that we could be fleeing."

Connie Wong did her job conscientiously, the only social worker for the region. But if she believed that, she'd read Sue wrong. Fire filled his officer's eyes.

"If I go after him, Jonah, I might use my gun."

"You're an officer trained in restraint."

Her jaw jutted. "And a pregnant woman whose child is in jeopardy. If he hurts Eli, I'll shoot him. And if he thinks he can take him away from me—"

"I hear you."

She drew herself up with a shudder. "Find him, Jonah. Find my little boy."

"And Sam?"

"I guess I'd rather you didn't kill him."

"I'll keep that in mind."

Jonah drove first to their home, guessing Sam might be collecting clothes and things if he planned to take off. The truck was outside the garage. Jonah blocked it in, parking his Bronco sideways between the cedar hedges. He approached the house cautiously, not drawing his gun, but of course a round was chambered.

He rapped on the door. "Sam?"

No answer.

"I'm coming in."

He turned the knob and pushed the door but shielded himself against the wall in case a shot was fired. The door swung to the wall unimpeded. He could see around the door frame into the kitchen. Sam sat at the kitchen table, Eli in his lap. As Jonah approached, Sam looked up, but Eli kept coloring the picture in the book open before him.

"What are you doing, Sam?"

He didn't answer. Eli stopped scribbling with the green crayon and held it up. Sam took it and handed Eli a yellow, a routine they both seemed to know. Sam's eyes were red-rimmed and sagging. "You going to arrest me?"

"You violated the court order."

"I called. I wanted to talk to him, but they said he was too upset already. I heard him crying. You don't know what it's like to hear your kid crying and not be allowed to help him. Not *allowed*."

"Because you're considered a danger."

"I fell asleep, and he took a fall. I don't pretend that was nothing. But I never hurt my kid. I don't know how those fractures got there. Maybe Sue, maybe her mom. Maybe one of the play dates he's had. A while back he was really fussy, and yeah, I dosed him with cough syrup to help him sleep. I didn't know he was injured."

Jonah just stared.

"He's like me. When I was three I broke my leg in a sandbox, broke the other jumping off a couch. Maybe I gave him that. But I never broke his arm."

"People do things when they're using, Sam."

Sam blinked.

A denial now would determine the course.

His chin quivered. "I can beat it. I beat it before."

"Then you were sober. But you know as well as I, you never really beat it."

Sam looked like he wanted to argue. Nothing he said would matter.

"But our concern is Eli."

Sam's mouth worked. "He's my son. You think some foster parents can love him more than I do?" Something stark showed through his eyes, but he was talking to the wrong man. Jonah would have welcomed a foster family.

A tremor seized Sam's chin. "I swear to you, I would never hurt this child."

He sounded sincere. But in the grip of the drugs, could he say the same?

"Right now, Sam, we need to take him back."

Sam shook his head, but there was no real fight in it.

"And I have to take you in." He hadn't expected it to be this easy. He'd envisioned an Amber Alert and highway closures. But Sam didn't have the resources for that. Or the heart.

Jonah watched the words hit him, saw him realize the futility. Tears rimmed the man's eyes as he squeezed his son close to his chest and kissed the top of Eli's head. "I didn't mean for it to come to this."

"We never do." Jonah swallowed.

Nineteen

What I do and what I dream include thee, as the wine must
taste of its own grapes.
—ELIZABETH BARRETT BROWNING

She had to be sure. And so she opened the door to the candle shop,
tinkling the bell as she stepped in.

Tia looked up, braced herself almost imperceptibly, then forced a
smile that didn't reach her eyes. "Dr. Rainer, right?"

"Oh, call me Liz, Tia."

"Liz," she said flatly. "Can I help you?"

"I promised Lucy I'd bring her fresh melts. And I want something for
someone else. I think you know Jonah Westfall?"

Tia formed a neutral expression and nodded.

"I want to thank him for the puppies he gave me."

"Puppies?"

"Coyote pups." Liz slipped a strand of hair behind her ear. "I patched
up the mother when she made his closet her den."

Tia braced her hips with her hands. "Jonah has a coyote in his closet."

"And the remaining pup. Do you have a suggestion?" At Tia's puzzled
look, Liz clarified. "Something Jonah would like?"

"No. I don't know what he'd like." An edge slipped in. She seemed
to realize and regret it.

"I'll just browse then."

Tia frowned. "I can't think why he'd want one of these candles."

Liz half turned. "To go with his collection." She watched it hit the
mark. The woman hadn't known. "Believe me, Tia, he loves your work."
She chose an aspen leaf pillar. It didn't really matter what she bought.
"This will go nicely in his cabin with the others." She set it on the counter.

Tia held her eyes with only a hint of distress. "Did you want melts?"

"Oh. I forgot." She grabbed them off the shelf. Lucy would be glad for them, and it would explain her absence.

"Do you want them wrapped?"

"Yes, separately. It's almost the best part."

Tia's face looked wan, and there could be no doubt. The anguish she'd seen through the window yesterday was real.

—

Tia locked the shop at the stroke of six and began the slow, limping climb toward her house. She could have driven, but she wouldn't give a sprained ankle and a bruised calf the power to limit her. Besides the pain felt good. Every jolt up her leg offered the chance to beat it back, to take another step.

I'm—still—walking.

She didn't know who she was telling. It didn't matter.

Liz had laid her bare, and she was dying, had, in fact, been dying for over nine years. Or if she were truly morbid, since birth. Piece by piece.

Everyone was, she guessed, but most people managed to live in between. She had tried so many times to spread her wings, but criticism and judgment had formed bars she'd flung herself against. Now if all she could do was beat back the pain, she'd beat it back with every step. She might have no wings. But she had legs. She had will. She clenched her teeth against the pain. She—was—still—alive.

—

Walking up the street, Liz watched as Tia came into view, then vanished, then appeared and disappeared between and behind the buildings. Their progress and cadence was ironically similar, a strong step and a weak—mirror images. Though pain furrowed Tia's face, her injury would heal. Liz had healed long ago, yet her injury remained.

She hadn't planned to follow her, wasn't following her now. Their paths had merely found a parallel course. She rubbed her side, her hip. The grade was steep, and Tia's path had veered away from the businesses. Liz took the alley between two shops and paused as Tia moved farther up toward a street with turn-of-the-century houses nestled into the mountainside.

Liz frowned. She would have to climb the path behind her or simply wait to see where she went. It only mattered because understanding Tia would help to understand Jonah. She could not abide suffering, and his pain in seeing Tia had been raw.

The revelation had stung her, but only briefly. He'd given her the puppies, and in that they shared a wondrous task. What could he possibly share with anyone else that would matter so much?

———

Piper all but pulled Tia in the door. "I can't believe you're walking on that leg."

Tia sighed. "I can't let it beat me." She sank onto the settee in obvious pain.

"Really?" Frustration welled up. "Or maybe you can't let it heal."

Tia looked up, surprised.

"That's how you are with everything, isn't it? How you are with Jonah. You want it to hurt."

The pain in Tia's face spoke for itself.

Piper folded herself onto the settee beside her. "Why?"

"I don't know what you're asking."

"Why can't you and Jonah fix what's wrong?"

Tia swallowed. "Because it hurt other people."

"You said he broke your sister's heart—"

"*I* broke my sister's heart." Tia's eyes looked like wounds. "Jonah was the love of her life. They wanted to marry, have kids. He'd finished his criminology courses and become a cop. Reba was studying interior design." Tia's face looked almost fierce. "They had it all planned out."

"But they didn't get married?"

Tia paused, then sighed. "His dad, the former chief of police—you'd have to have known him to really understand—was charming and charismatic and handsome as all get out."

"Like father like son."

Tia looked up, stricken. "It would kill Jonah to hear that. And it isn't true. Stan Westfall was hard and twisted inside. Even I don't know all the damage he did, but trust me, Jonah carries the scars." She'd seen their shadows in his eyes.

"So what happened?"

"A young woman died when Stan Westfall arrested her."

"Died of what?"

"Shot with his gun."

"He shot her?"

"The investigation determined that she went for the gun and they struggled. They cleared him." She moistened her lips. "But Jonah suspected something had not been addressed in the findings. He went to confront his dad, and Stan Westfall shot himself."

Piper gasped. "That's awful!"

"Yeah."

"What did Jonah suspect?"

"He's never told me." Her voice sounded far away. "After that, Jonah lost himself for a while. He started drinking. Reba tried, but she could not get through to him. She didn't have the pieces he'd given me, all the things he'd told me through the years, things he didn't want her to know."

Tia's face contorted. "I knew I couldn't fix it, but I wanted to help. He came to the house, and Reba wasn't home. No one was. He told me he was breaking the engagement."

Tia pressed her fingertips into her eye sockets. "I was only going to hold him, but then we were kissing. He tasted like whiskey and went right to my head. It was the first time I'd ever…" She released a hard breath. "My whole family walked in on us. We hadn't even gone upstairs."

"Omigosh." It came out on a breath.

"What I can't change, what I can barely live with, is the look I saw on my sister's face."

Jonah sat alone on his porch in the dark. Elbows on his thighs, hands locked behind his neck, he stretched the tension from his spine with night-chilled fingers. Dealing with Sam and Eli had taken his mind from the earlier discussion with the mayor, but it haunted him now.

How many times had Buckley and the former chief of police agreed to look away? Stan Westfall had a legendary reputation, the walk and manner of a man who would crush any lawbreaker unfortunate enough to cross his path. Had it been a sham? Was the whole job a sham?

Jonah knew too well the cruelty that accompanied punishment in his father's world. What incentive could Buckley have offered to counter that desire to punish, if indeed they had *balanced* their interests for the good of the town? A reciprocal blindness?

To what? Domestic violence? Child abuse? Not a single investigation. Not one. How much more had Stan Westfall been excused before his son forced the truth? And took his place.

His stomach recoiled. If Buckley thought he could manipulate him, he was sorely mistaken. Scrutinizing the file had yielded no leads, but he would not ignore a dark and potentially lethal threat. Although he had a feel for the method, he hadn't grasped the motivation for the mutilations. He would keep digging until he did, and if it unearthed a cult or extra-terrestrials or, as he expected, a sick and twisted individual, justice would be served.

But still the conversation nagged. One young girl had died. Had there been others? He pressed his hands to his face. He knew the potential pitfall of reverence. He would rather have every move scrutinized than be given a free pass. Stan Westfall's whole life had been a pass. Until the end.

Sweat broke out between his palms and forehead. His breath got shallow. He tasted the rusty smell of blood. Clenching his hands in his hair, he ground his teeth in fury. How could the mayor think he would ever follow that man's footsteps?

From the depths of an exhausted sleep, the sound of a drill bored, paused, bored again until she realized it was her cell phone on vibrate. Tia slitted her eyes to find it, flip it, grope as it tumbled, and raise it to read the display. Short of a death in the family, and maybe not even then, only the Hopeline rang in the wee hours.

"Hello?" She tried to brush the sleep from her voice. "Hopeline."

"And if there isn't any?"

"Excuse me?"

"What happens when there is no hope?"

Tia pushed up to one elbow as the question sent a needle to her heart. "Then we rely on faith."

The scratchy voice was either male or an older woman, or someone who had smoked too long. "And what is faith?"

"The deliberate confidence in the character of God whether we understand or not." Her version of Oswald Chambers, and the only explanation she could manage.

In the silence she wondered if it had sounded glib. Or merely resigned. She'd meant neither. "Without hope, there are only two choices, faith or despair."

The voice rasped. "What about joy?"

"In my experience, joy isn't possible without hope. But with faith there is still the possibility of victory."

"How can you have victory without joy?"

"You embrace what's left to you, not turning your back to the challenge but facing it head on. It's not easy, and it may not feel good, but it's better than giving in." For the first time in years she saw herself as the pirate child, lashed to the rigging as the storm cast itself upon her, tearing at her with vicious fingers and howling in her ears. She felt like howling back. How dare despair devour her?

"I have six weeks to live."

Her heart thumped. She pressed a hand to her chest, groping, and then saying the only thing that came. "Your grief must be tremendous."

"Lung cancer. All my life the kids told me to quit, begged me to quit. But I couldn't. I didn't want to. I never even tried. Never thought I should have to. I'm fifty-nine years old, and I won't see sixty."

"How do you want to spend the time left you?"

Her silence weighed the next two minutes down like lead. "I don't want them to hope when there is none."

"If you didn't smoke these next six weeks, what would that tell them?"

"That I could have done it before."

"Or that you're doing it for them."

"They'll be mad I didn't do it sooner."

"Anger is an expression of grief. You don't get mad when you don't care. Love and anger are entwined."

The woman started to cry, wrenching sobs, then coughs, coughs that seemed to rip the lungs out of her.

When the spasms passed, Tia spoke softly. "There may be no hope to beat this, but there's hope in courage, there's hope in sacrifice and in loving others enough to bring them joy even when you can't find it yourself."

A long sigh, pregnant with emotion said she'd struck a chord.

"Despair will devour every good thing until there's nothing but bitter regret. But if you choose faith—believe that even this has a purpose and grace you can't see—then you may yet find hope, and in both, joy."

An exhalation of breath so deep Tia prayed it wasn't the caller's last.

In barely a whisper, "You've saved my life."

She swallowed. "I pray the peace of God that is beyond understanding will guard your heart and mind in Christ Jesus. And that grace and joy and hope will be your companions until the end."

"God bless you," she gasped, and the call ended.

Tia lay down, eyes open in the dark, stunned and staring. How long had she been locked in the hold?

———

Jonah checked his watch: 6:25 a.m. He'd slept fitfully, but he had to be in court for Sam's arraignment, and he hoped to talk to him beforehand. The shower cleared his mind of the night's residual gloom. Hot coffee and eggs fortified him to go get the job done.

Outside the interrogation room, he eyed Sue. "It's your call." He had relayed the scene in the kitchen with Sam and Eli and watched the anger bleed from her. "He's not trying to hurt either of you. But that doesn't mean he won't."

She nodded.

"With his priors they won't defer. The criminal negligence alone could mean time. The positives for pot and meth trace will require rehab before he has contact with Eli again. If he gives us something we can use, they might drop the kidnapping charge."

Her forehead puckered. "His public defender is young and egotistical enough to hold out for a sympathetic jury, clearing him with no deal."

"Uh-huh."

Sue rolled her eyes. "You put whole conversations into those two syllables."

"I need to know what you want."

She folded her arms. "That gets complicated."

"Don't I know."

"If he could help us get the lab…" Her cop sense kicked in.

"If it's local—and we've had enough indications to make me believe it is—I'll stop at nothing else."

Her face softened. "He's never intentionally hurt either one of us. The meth, if he's using that, it's new."

"There can't be trace if he hasn't used. But it's possible the cannabis was laced. That's how they get new customers." They'd found pot in a search of his truck when he kidnapped Eli. It was at the lab for testing. He checked his watch again. "I need to get in there if we're going to talk before arraignment."

"I guess you need to do what you can to help us fix this mess. And nail the scum that made that drug available."

That meant a deal with the DA. If he could get any sense that Sam would give him what he needed, he'd bring it to them.

He squeezed her shoulder, then went into the interrogation room. Jonah sat down across the table from Sam. He could see fear that hadn't been as visible before, but also a desperate kind of hope. "You're gonna do real time here, Sam, unless you give the DA something to work with."

"Or the jury decides in our favor." His young lawyer had maybe begun to shave.

Sam said, "I don't know what you want. I told you I didn't hurt Eli. His fall was an accident."

The kid lawyer must have pumped him up. "Criminal negligence while under the influence of a drug resulting in injury of a minor child. Possession of said drug. Violation of a court order. Kidnapping."

Sam wilted. He opened his mouth and closed it.

"The kidnapping's bogus." The lawyer smirked. "He simply gave comfort to his son."

Jonah narrowed his eyes. "He removed him from his court-appointed temporary guardians."

"They wouldn't let me talk to him, to calm him down."

The lawyer put a hand on Sam's arm. "Don't talk."

To Sam, "I understand. But you have to give me something to work with."

"What else can I say?"

"Greggor."

"What?"

"You cooperate with another investigation, and we'll work with you on this."

"I don't know any Greggor." Sam spread his hands, a little shaky— from withdrawal?

"Are you tweaking?"

His hands squeezed closed, opened and closed. He looked at his lawyer who said, "No comment."

Sam scratched his forearm. It wasn't the first time.

"Feels like bugs?"

His breath quickened. He grimaced. His teeth, while not pristine, showed nowhere near the decay they would in the not-distant future. "Your toke have more kick to it lately?"

Sam's eyes darted.

"Come on, Sam."

His face screwed up. "Look. I got some weed from Caldwell. I don't know any Greggor."

"I think you do." Sue had told him as much, but he'd protect that if he could.

"No, I'm telling you. It's Caldwell you should lean on."

"You must have wondered what was in the pot. Or maybe you knew, maybe you thought a little extra wouldn't hurt. Then maybe you wanted more, you wanted it straight. Needed it straight."

Sam scratched his arms, leaving welts.

"Maybe Greggor threatened you, threatened your family if you said anything. I mean come on, your wife's a cop."

Again fear flickered. "I can't do it, man."

Sue burst through the door. "Do it, Sam."

Sam stiffened, clenched his hands and swallowed. He wanted to resist, maybe thought he could still handle it all himself, then realized he hadn't a chance. "If I tell you what I know, when you go in, Sue's not with you."

"You can't say that," Sue snapped.

"Yes, he can." Jonah turned to her. "You have the coming child to think about."

Sam turned to her with an ache in his eyes as he took in the bulge of her belly inside the blue hoodie. Jonah gave him a moment to process what he'd just heard. Sam was no hardened criminal. Maybe not even a veteran addict. Prison would change that. And he knew it.

His eyes reddened. He turned back. "I don't want my kids to grow up without me."

Jonah frowned. "There's a greater chance of that happening with meth than anything you say in this room. But that's another story."

Sam squeezed his shaking hands. "I only know Greggor's the cooker."

"Where?"

He shook his head, the slump of his shoulders showing no defiance. "I don't know, man."

"Have you seen him?"

"Maybe. With another guy. Big. Bald. Named Malcolm. Malcolm made the threats."

They might get an ID out of that. Jonah took out a legal pad. "Write what you know and sign it."

———

In the special room they reserved for the puppies, Liz unwrapped the cloth that held them together. Only days old, they barely moved, but whatever adjustments they made, they made together, side by side. Such precious companions. She lifted and nestled them under her chin.

Lucy leaned over her shoulder. "Have you ever seen anything so sweet?"

Liz rested her head against Lucy's. "Never."

"They're okay?"

"Oh yes."

"Should we name them?"

Liz paused. "If you like."

"I'll name one and you the other?"

"You can name them both."

"No, Lizzie. It has to be us together."

"Okay. I'll name mine Daisy."

"Then mine is Bell. Like the song." Lucy wrapped an arm around Liz's shoulders and began to sway. Her voice was pure and high. "*There is a flower within my heart, Daisy, Daisy! Planted one day by a glancing dart, planted by Daisy Bell.* Now you."

Not many knew the introduction to their song, but they'd sung it endlessly whirling on the merry-go-round. "*Whether she loves me or loves me not, sometimes it's hard to tell. Yet I am willing to share the lot of beautiful Daisy Bell.*"

Then together: "*Daisy, Daisy, give me your answer do. I'm half crazy, all for the love of you.*" And then the part they'd improvised: "*It won't be a stupid marriage. We can't afford a carriage. But we'll look sweet upon the seat of a bicycle built for two.*"

Liz laid the puppies down and rewrapped the cloth a little more loosely with room to grow, but not apart, never apart.

———

In the DA's office at the county courthouse, Jonah presented his case and waited. He'd had to wait two days after Sam's arraignment for an appointment with the assistant DA assigned to the case, but because Sam had no money to post bail, he'd be sitting until the trial date anyway.

ADA Ana Ramirez tapped her pen on her chin. She was a small woman, round in a Latina way with black hair cut bluntly at her shoulders. Not traditionally attractive but someone he could imagine spending interesting evenings with, someone who might harbor fires that only blazed in the right conditions. He didn't mind assessing her that way because she did the same of him every time they talked.

Ana said, "I know he's married to your officer, but shouldn't his lawyer be here doing this?"

"His lawyer passed kindergarten and thinks he gets a sympathetic jury."

Ana snorted. "And why do I want to cut this guy a deal? You know how I am about kids in danger."

"I do know." And she knew he blazed with that same fire. "But I think he can turn it around. The fall was accidental, negligence but not intention. Both Sam's and Eli's medical records indicate fragile bone syndrome, mild enough it hadn't been picked up until now. Sam hasn't been hurting him and won't if he's clean."

"You know how that goes." She caught herself. "I didn't mean—"

He pulled a side smile. "I do. Every day."

"Why do I always feel like you have the upper hand?"

"I have no idea."

"I mean you look so macho and you're really so soft."

"Guess that's it."

"Only you seem so soft, when you're really a toreador."

"Too flashy."

She smiled. "See my dilemma?"

"I do."

She cocked her head. "How's Jay?"

"He's good. Still dating your cousin?"

"They'll fly that holding pattern until one of them runs out of fuel."

"Or gets permission to land."

Ana folded her arms over her chest. "You think what Sam gave us is good?"

"If he can make an ID, it'll be better. But even if he testifies, it's enough."

"Okay. I'll have to run it by DA Cutler, but if there's a meth lab out there, I'm guessing he'll deal."

"He'll deal."

Jonah wouldn't tell Sam until the deal was stamped, but he'd bought him a reprieve, given Sue the chance she wanted to put the mess back together. And it felt good. In spite of statistics, he was a personal believer in resurrection. He had to be.

Twenty

Make my joy complete by being of the same mind, maintaining the same love, united in spirit, intent on one purpose.
—PHILIPPIANS 2:2, NEW AMERICAN STANDARD BIBLE

Tia looked up when Miles walked in for the second time since his meltdown almost four weeks ago. Not even a month, yet it seemed like years since Jonah had taken her home, dazed and injured, before he had trashed her psyche as thoroughly as Miles her store.

Her throat locked in whatever greeting she might have managed as Miles made his hulking way between the less crowded displays. Dressed in a pressed corduroy jacket and knife-edge khakis over shined leather loafers, he avoided even the brush of an elbow to a shelf. Others should be so careful.

Certain that Miles was the least of anyone's concerns, even—no especially—Jonah's, she looked back at the supply list she'd been compiling. It was all she could do to fake an interest in oils and tinctures, paraffin, glycerin, and beeswax. The question she asked the woman who'd called the Hopeline had played in her own head ever since. How do you want to spend the time left you?

She wanted to help people the way she'd helped that woman, to listen and understand, to break down hurt and guilt and fear, and restore hope. Yet she'd been so bound up, she had only used that gift stingily on her dial-a-prayer line. If she were called to account today, she'd say, "Lord, I buried my talent in the sand because I didn't believe it was good enough."

She bit her lower lip and watched Miles, trapped inside his fears, staring at the only candles he considered safe, dipped tapers bearing no human fingerprints, believing if he wasn't touched, he would not be hurt. Maybe he was right.

He unhooked a pair by the wick that joined them, ironically the very part she had held to hang them. He brought them to the counter. "I would like these, please."

"Sure, Miles."

He pulled his payment from the wallet, laid the money on the counter, and drew his hand back. She wanted to promise he was safe from her, but how could anyone really keep from touching another life?

She gave him change. "I don't suppose you want them wrapped."

"Yes. Lots of purple ribbon. And the moon sticker."

She raised her eyebrows. "Okay."

"And you can have this back." With a finger, he slid her Hopeline card across the counter.

Her heart sank. So much for gifts and talents…

"I memorized the number."

She stared at the card, then looked up. For one moment he met her eyes. A smile flickered over her mouth. "It's good 24/7."

He picked up the candles. "Your leg is better?"

"Good as new."

He walked to the door and paused, started to say something, then he went out. She looked down at the card, picked it up, and held it to her chest, feeling her heart beat faintly beneath. *Lord.*

———

"Jonah." Ana's voice came through his Bluetooth.

"Hey, Ana." They hadn't talked since striking Sam's deal nearly three weeks ago, and he hoped that wasn't going south this close to the trial.

"Are you driving?"

"I am."

"Do you want to pull over?"

Everything suddenly slowed down. His Bronco in slow motion, the scenery crawling by. His pulse and breaths felt minutes apart, his limbs suspended in water. "What's up?"

"Sam won't be going to trial, Jonah. I'm sorry. He's dead."

His chin dropped to his chest. Sam. Dead. His throat worked over the words before he finally said, "I'm on my way."

They had moved the body to the morgue. Sam's bone structure was indeed small, and he'd lost weight since the day in the ER. With Ana and the coroner, Hao Sung, Jonah stood beside the stainless table trying to internalize the shift to this from the man he'd spoken to just days ago.

"What happened?"

Hao held up a baggy with a syringe inside. "We found this in his cell."

Jonah didn't ask how he'd gotten it. Jails were sieves. The question was who. And why. Had someone heard Sam was cooperating? Or had they hedged their bets, giving him a little something to keep him wanting more, to make cooperating undesirable. Or had Sam just found an opportunity and taken it?

"Anyone hear or see anything?"

Ana said, "The guys on either side say he freaked out and threw himself around like he was hallucinating. He seizured and collapsed."

He turned to Hao. "Would meth alone do that?"

Hao shrugged. "Could. Injecting is a big jump from smoking the stuff. We'll test the syringe. And I haven't opened him up."

"It might have been laced?"

Again Hao shrugged. "When I know, you'll know."

Jonah nodded. It didn't matter. Locked in his cell, Sam had to have injected it. There'd be no resurrection. "I'll tell Officer Donnelly."

This time the drive went too fast. He took Sue into his office and made her sit in his chair. He pulled the only other around and sat.

She said, "It's Sam."

He nodded. "OD or poisoning."

"Poison?"

"He injected something. We don't know what. I'm sorry, Sue. He's gone."

Her face worked through the pain. "You made the ID?"

He nodded. "But of course you can see him. Hao—"

"No." She swiped the tears. "I saw him alive and willing and hopeful. I don't want to see the other man." She pressed a hand to her belly. "Can we still use the statement?"

He held her eyes. "We have it signed and witnessed and videoed. He won't be there to confirm it in court, but…" He spread his hands. "It's something."

"Then"—she cleared her throat—"let's go. Let's get them."

"Sue."

"I want them, Jonah."

"Listen to me." When he got her attention, he said, "I talked to Connie. She wants you to meet her at the foster house and get Eli."

Her mouth fell open. A single word slipped out on her breath. "Now?"

He nodded again.

She pressed her hands to her face, shaking. "Oh, God. Oh my God."

"Yeah," he said, her prayer as pure as any he'd heard.

———

Liz saw him sitting on a boulder at the bank of the creek near the bridge. Wind tossed the pines and willows on either side, but he seemed somehow removed from the physical world. His fingers drove into the sides and front of his head as he held it from falling to his chest. A monument of dejection.

Quietly she approached, sat on a boulder beside his. He rocked his head to see her.

She smiled thinly. "It must be bad."

"Yeah." Did she imagine him stiffening, pulling up the walls? He frowned. "I'm sorry. Did you need something?"

She sniffed a laugh. "Do you ever let someone help you?"

He pressed his tongue between his side teeth. "It's not me. One of my officers lost her husband."

And yet the wound seemed to be within him. "You knew him well?"

"Hardly at all. She kept her work and family separate."

Then it was the wife he hurt for.

"It must be hard to have so many depend on you."

"I wouldn't say that."

"It's not hard, or people don't need you?"

He pressed his hands to his face and rubbed. "I just wish it hadn't come down this way."

"Are there kids?"

"Two-year-old. One on the way."

Liz shook her head. "I wish I knew what to say."

"Yeah." He looked at his watch. "Sorry, Liz. I have to meet with the mayor."

"Like seeing a man about a horse?"

He glanced down. "Uh, as I understand that phrase, you're not far off—between you and me." He formed a dry smile. "At least I can tell him there have been no more mutilations."

"Like the raccoons, you mean."

"Yeah. He's afraid word will get out that aliens are operating on our pets."

She stared at him. "Are you serious?"

"He doesn't want animal rights groups interfering with the growth and health of our community. It's just politics. One part of my job I hate—although today it's a tossup." He stood, lanky and lupine with an inner agitation behind his weary eyes.

"Take care now."

She said, "I will." But who would take care of him?

She stood and watched until he was gone, then pressed a hand to her heart. Lucy was waiting.

———

Piper slipped out from the counter and into the kitchen to check the sourdough sponge she had proofing in the big glass bowl. Never guessing Sarge would lift the ban, she had created the starter at home, assuming she'd have to learn anything new on her own time in Tia's kitchen. She fed the starter like a pet for three days until it developed a bubbly froth, then brought it to work. She had mixed up the sponge six hours ago. Now it was white and frothy with a sour beery smell.

The bell on the front counter would alert her if someone needed service, but she hoped the lull lasted long enough to make the dough. After measuring out enough sponge for the recipe, she put the remainder back into the cleaned jar, added fresh flour and warm water, and put it in the walk-in to grow the natural yeast for the next batch. To the sponge, she added sugar, salt, and oil, and, using the enormous dough mixer, kneaded in the flour.

It was brainlessly easy, and yet she got such a kick out of it. She wasn't sure her mother had ever made a meal that wasn't microwaveable. Almost always they'd eaten out, almost always finding something wrong so some or all the ticket got comped. Piper shook her head. This simple thing of making bread from flour and water, sugar, salt, and oil was as big a statement of independence as anything she'd done.

No one rang the bell, but as she tipped the mixer bowl to the rising board, she thought she heard the door. She gently patted the soft-as-baby-skin dough and covered it with a crib-sized cloth, giggling at how often she compared her loaves and buns to babies. Maybe all creativity stemmed from a generative urge.

She washed her hands and went out front. No one. She started to turn back to the kitchen when she saw the package on the counter. Puzzled, she lifted it, recognizing Tia's wrapping at once, but not finding anything to explain its appearance.

Piper frowned, noticing a slip of paper that must have fallen to the floor. The hand printing looked typeset and said only, "For Piper." She went to the front and searched the street through the windows. People milled along the sidewalks, though no one she knew. She pulled open the paper. Two pale golden tapers of natural, honey-scented beeswax. She locked the register and hurried next-door. "Tia?"

Tia straightened up from behind one of the displays. "Hey."

"Did you wrap these for someone?"

Tia looked at what she held. "He brought them to you?"

"Someone left them on the counter."

"It was Miles."

"Miles?"

She nodded. "He seemed very pleased with himself."

"Miles bought these for me?"

"I think you have a friend."

"That is so sweet."

"And no fingerprints. He gave you the germ-free candles."

Warmth filled up inside her. "I wonder why he didn't stay and have me open them."

"Guess it was a surprise."

The warmth became a glow. "I didn't know he could think in surprises."

"Underneath his phobia, he seems very intelligent."

"Oh, you should have heard all the scientific explanations he gave me for why the dough rises and how heat and pressure and oxygen and whatnot affect food and cooking and how the body processes energy. He went on and on like a talking teddy bear that swallowed an encyclopedia."

They laughed.

Piper rewrapped the candles. "I'm glad he's not a psychopath."

"He still has issues." Tia forked the mane back from her face. "I'd love to work with him, get to the bottom of it. Although it might require medication I can't prescribe."

"What do you mean, work with him?"

"I mean therapy. I have degrees in counseling and clinical psychology."

"You do?" Piper searched her face. "Then why aren't you doing it?"

"I was just asking myself the same question."

Piper shook her head. "You keep surprising me."

"Not many people know. I had to take the courses online since I was responsible for the store. I still need clinical hours and a license to practice."

"But you could be helping people. More than the Hopeline."

"I see that now. I kept waiting for things to change." Tia turned. "But only I can."

———

Jonah had called in his entire force except for Officer Sue Donnelly. The conference room where they assembled smelled of bitter coffee and McCarthy, who'd just come from the gym. They looked curious and a little uneasy. He briefed them. Moser put a hand to his face when he explained about Sam.

Newly said, "They got to him? In the jail?"

"Someone got something to him." He didn't express what they'd all realize at some point, that Sam still made a choice to use. Unless he'd been forcibly shot up before lockdown? He'd talk to Hao, have him look beyond the obvious. Hand or fingerprints where he might have been held. Trauma at the needle site.

"This is our top priority. I want 24/7 surveillance on Tom Caldwell. I want you all through town checking vacant properties, trailers, motel rooms where there have been odor complaints."

"That would be most of the places I've stayed," Newly lightened the mood.

"Especially when you've had burritos." McCarthy flicked his head with a backhand.

"Nah, that was his girlfriend." From Moser, cracking up Beatty, the rookie.

Jonah let them get it out. They had to hate what this meant to their fellow officer. "I'll be calling the sheriff for support. And guys? Everything by the book. I don't want one count inadmissible because we scratched the wrong armpit. Beatty, you shadow Moser. He's been a cop since Moses brought the tablets down from Sinai."

"I wrote the tablets." Moser ran his fingers down his perfect facial hair.

Jonah looked around the table. The worst they'd dealt with were domestic calls. He had a feeling they'd all be growing up.

Twenty-One

My twin and I were wombmates and then roommates. Some
day our bodies will be tombmates.
—CLARA TAIPALE

She shouldn't leave Lucy, miserable and distressed by her increasingly frequent absences. It broke her heart to see her confusion, but how could she explain? She couldn't do it alone, and now there was someone else who bore others up, who carried the weak without complaint.

"It's him," Lucy rasped. "I know it."

She sighed. "I won't be long."

Lucy didn't believe her.

"I promise." She pressed a hand to Lucy's pale cheek and turned away.

It had been two and a half weeks since she bought the candle, no knowing if she'd ever give the gift. Seeing him at the creek, open once more and sharing his true feelings had been a sign, an invitation to treat him as she would any wounded creature. But a different vehicle sat beside the Bronco in Jonah's driveway. If someone else was there, maybe she should leave.

But she grabbed her package and went to the door, her heart jumping when he hollered, "Come on in," as though he'd been expecting her.

A less robust voice barked and swore. Curious, she moved through the cabin to the back rooms he and Jay must have completed. From a chair beside a single bed, an old man, bent like a shepherd's crook, let loose on the young woman who held her hand just out of reach, urging him to stretch farther than it seemed he wanted to.

Providing a counterforce with a hand to the man's chest, Jonah sent a glance over his shoulder. "Liz?"

"I didn't realize you were busy. I can come back."

"We have, what?" He turned to his companion. "Ten more stretches?"

"Ten more."

The old man growled.

"Just ten more," the woman urged.

Jonah murmured, "There's hot chocolate in the kitchen."

A reminder of the evening he'd opened his heart? Liz smiled. "I'm fine, thanks."

"Again." The woman held out her hand, and the old man stretched.

His ill temper reminded her of the surly old dogs people brought her to put down. They assumed the animal preferred death, because they didn't want to watch it live in anything less than perfection. Not Jonah. His patience and affection warmed her more than the space heater in the corner.

When they finished stretching, the woman said, "You did very well, Sergeant Beaker. Opening the upper spine allows the lower lumbar some flexibility, and building strength between the shoulders will relieve more tension." She began to lightly massage the muscle group they'd worked, flicking Jonah a glance. "We'll just finish up here."

"All right." He tipped his head, and Liz preceded him out. As they walked away, the woman murmured something Sarge responded to with a laugh. Jonah shook his head. "Nimue wooing Merlin."

"Excuse me?" She turned, confused.

Jonah jerked a thumb over his shoulder. "*Le Morte d'Arthur*. If Sarge doesn't watch out, he'll end up smitten." He searched her face. "Never mind."

"Is he your father?"

Jonah opened his mouth, then closed it. "My dad's dead. Sarge is an old friend."

"Sarge, who owns the bakery?"

"You have a good memory."

"You took him in?"

"He's living here, yeah."

They had reached the kitchen.

"Did you want some cocoa? SoBe? water?"

Why couldn't she think? "Do you need to see the therapist off?"

"Lauren? She's Sarge's nurse. She'll be a while."

Liz noticed three plates next to the Crock-Pot of rich roasting meat, red-skinned potatoes, and onions. Turning, she formed a tentative smile. "I brought you something." She held out the package.

He looked from it to her.

"A thank-you for the pups. Since you've collected Tia's work, I thought…" Again she lost what she had thought.

He took the package, untied the ribbon, and let the paper fall away. The aspen leaves cascaded in a spiral to the bottom of the candle, just the way they swirled to the ground in an autumn breeze.

"Do you like it?"

"It's great. But, Liz, you took care of Enola—"

She shrugged a shoulder. "I just wanted you to have it. Tia didn't know you liked candles. Hers, I mean. She said she couldn't imagine that you'd want one."

His brow lowered. "You told her?"

"Was it a secret? They look so nice." She looked past the café counter to the main room mantel, then turned back, heart rushing. This was what she'd come for. "She's the one, isn't she? The one you can't get over?"

His face darkened dangerously. "I'm not sure what we're doing here."

"I'm saying I know, Jonah, and it's all right."

"I don't understand."

But he did. "You said we could start something, but it wouldn't be fair because I didn't know about Tia. Now I do. I understand, and I don't care."

He jammed his hand through his hair. "That was…a bad day. I shouldn't have said any of it."

"Why? You found a better choice? Sarge's nurse, maybe?"

He stiffened. "That's enough."

"Jonah, I *know* you. I get it. We have…so much in common."

"Liz."

"You loved two sisters, and I—"

He raised his hands, palms out at her. "I need you to stop. I can't deal with this now." His flinty face was all sharp edges.

This wasn't the man she'd seen hurting by the creek, who'd come to her for help, who'd needed her. He was a stranger, a liar, a thief. He had stolen her trust and thrown it back. She snatched the candle from his hands and pushed past him out the door.

———

He stood, fists clenched, until a hand on his arm released the tension.

"Jonah?"

When he turned, Lauren searched his face.

"Bad news?"

He controlled his breathing with difficulty.

"Do you need to sit?" The nurse taking charge.

"No."

Her touch was gentle, her expression caring. They had shared a few meals around his table, cooking for her the least he could do after putting Sarge through his paces.

"I take it that wasn't your girlfriend."

"I don't have a girlfriend."

"Your former fiancée?"

"Not even close."

Her gray-green eyes shimmered like shady pools. He could imagine her as the enchantress Tia had read aloud from Malory's tales, enamored with knights and kings and magic. He'd gladly be enchanted, beguiled, bewitched, even betrayed if it meant an end.

"Your pulse is racing."

When had the anger kicked in? When he pictured Liz in Tia's shop, describing the whole pitiful scene, and Tia wondering why he'd sent someone to buy candles for his home, surrounding himself with parts of her. Pathetic.

And Liz. He pressed a hand to his face.

"Can I help?" Lauren held his arm.

"No, I don't think so."

"You don't have to do everything alone."

"Well, it's a lot smarter that way."

"Smarter? Or safer."

He expelled his breath. "Yeah, that."

———

The scent of butterscotch from the waxed pine cones mingled with the wood fire was one of the best mood-setting aromas she knew. Tia glanced over at Piper curled up on the opposite end of the settee with a novel. Tia would have liked to read, loved reading, but she couldn't find solace in imagination now. It was time to face reality.

The doorbell rang. Piper pried her eyes from the page. "Are you expecting someone?"

"No." Tia got up and opened the door to the last person she would have imagined. "Liz?" She looked from the woman to the candle she held. "Is something wrong?"

"I want my money back."

Tia stared for a moment as a chill crawled up her back. "This is my house, not my store. How did you—"

"Jonah didn't like it."

Oh, the irony. "Why don't you just come by the…"

"I paid twenty-eight dollars plus tax." Liz looked past her at Piper.

Irritation rose, lacing the words, "That included the melts for your sister. Do you have your receipt?"

"No, I don't."

"You know what? Never mind. Let me get my purse."

"Tia?" Piper sent her a disbelieving glance.

What difference did it make? As she moved toward the mud room where she kept her sling-back purse, she heard Liz saying, "Why are you here?"

And Piper, "I live here."

This was surreal. Tia took out a twenty and a ten. Liz had stayed at the open door, and the cold that swirled in around her might have emanated from the woman's body. Tia handed over the money, feeling invaded.

Liz thrust the candle at her. "He told me he wasn't over you, but he is."

Tia drew the candle to her chest. "I could have told you that."

"He has someone there, right now."

"That's not my business. Or yours."

Something shifted in the woman's face. "When we first met, I wanted to be friends." A fleeting poignancy touched her voice. "Before I knew."

"Knew?"

"What you'd done to him. How you've wounded him."

Tia swallowed. "Well, that's what we do best." She probably should have held her tongue.

Liz's eyes narrowed. "Are you so hateful?"

Apparently. "I'm sorry I've offended you."

One nostril and the side of Liz's mouth flickered up. "You would have to matter to offend me."

Tia barked a soft laugh. "Okay. We're done here." She closed the door.

"What was that?" Piper half whispered.

Tia rubbed her temples. "Fallout."

Piper grabbed her shoulders. "You have to tell him."

"Who?"

"Jonah."

"Tell him what? His scorned girlfriend whacked out on me because he's with someone else?"

"Tell him she's…weird."

Tia's mouth pulled. "I imagine he knows. And so what? You know what I think, Piper? Everyone's weird. Everyone's got stuff. She was just hurting enough to let hers show."

———

Early the next morning, Liz watched Tia set out. To the mountain, of course, passing through the chilly mist like a wraith. Pressed into the side of the house next to Tia's, Liz stared after her. She'd heard from Catrin

Draper, whose chocolate lab, Monster, had required forty stitches, that Tia had been lost in the storm on that mountain. Lost and injured. Only a sprain, Catrin assured her. *"But I'd have been terrified. Mountains are not forgiving."*

Neither were people. Confronted with Jonah's pain, Tia had not even defended herself. Wounding each other was what they did best. Liz clenched her hands. She'd called it hateful, but could there be anything more honest? Could it be that bare honesty that drew her again and again to the woman she wanted to despise?

Appearing through the mist where the trail bent back around, Tia stopped, leaned her head back, and stretched out her arms, a mythical being who stood for long beats of the heart as the fog passed over and around her like tattered gauze. When Tia slowly raised her head and lowered her hands, Liz breathed, as though released from a trance, and saw only a woman climbing farther up the mountain.

———

After a long day including two domestic calls, Jonah exited the courthouse with a warrant to question a punk who'd been peddling crank at the middle and high school. With any luck they'd tie him to Caldwell or Greggor or both. He was ready to get home, but when he reached his vehicle, Ruth's voice came over the radio. "Jonah, you know I hate to pile on."

"Go ahead."

"We had a 911. I think you'll want to respond."

"What is it?"

"The address is your mother's."

"Medical?"

"EMTs are en route. Sounds like a heart attack. I'm sorry."

"Who called?"

"Laraine called it in herself, but she collapsed in the process."

He put the Bronco in gear, hit the lights, and took off. He had not seen this coming, but who ever did? He activated his Bluetooth and called Jay. "I might be tied up awhile. Can you check in on Sarge and Enola?"

"I'm not sure I can get away."

"Then don't worry about it. They've got to make friends at some point."

"What's going on?"

"My mother's had a heart attack." Strange it should come now. Why not during all the years of heartbreak? Except it was never really her heart breaking.

"You're going over?"

"She's my mother."

"Don't take this wrong, Jonah."

He braced himself. "But what?"

"Is it in her best interest?"

"You mean, will I make her worse?"

"To put it bluntly."

Jonah considered that. "I'm not sure who else she has. I don't want her to be alone."

"No, you should go. But remember, if a circle tries to bend too far, it's no longer a circle."

"Where do you get this stuff?"

Jay didn't laugh. "Just remember who you are."

And also, as Sarge had said, who he never wanted to be. At his family home, more than anywhere, the lines blurred. He saw himself in the old man and the old man in him. It was like the story Jay had told amid the sweats and potions.

"There is a fight going on inside of you, a fight between two hungry wolves. One wolf is fear, envy, sorrow and regret, greed, spite, arrogance, and self-pity. It is guilt, resentment, false pride, superiority, ego, and unfaithfulness. The other wolf is joy, peace, love, hope, humility, kindness, and forgiveness. It is integrity, benevolence, friendship, empathy, generosity, truth, compassion, and faithfulness. The fight goes on and on, each one trying for control. Which wolf wins? It is the one you feed."

He reached his mother's house and parked beside the ambulance. The team was inside, and Jonah joined them. Curtains were drawn, making the house dim. Stacks of mail and magazines covered most surfaces, cups and dishes on the corners of tables and lining the counters. He moved through the rooms to her enclosed porch where his mother lay on the brick-red pavers. She was conscious, pale, and trembling, wearing a blood pressure cuff, finger monitor, and oxygen.

She said, "What are you doing here? It's not Sunday." Splotches appeared on her cheeks.

"How're you doing, Mom?" When she didn't answer, he asked the EMT, Mack Dougal.

"Pulse is thready."

"I shouldn't have to put up with you more than one day a week. Shouldn't have to do it then." The clear plastic mask fogged.

"Take it easy, Mom," Jonah murmured.

"Easy," she snarled, her irregular heart tones increasing.

Jay had been right to worry. Jonah knew the team, knew she would receive the care she needed. He stepped back. "You're in good hands."

"No." She gripped her left arm until the flesh turned white. "You made sure I'd never be." This conversation would dredge up old suspicions. The EMTs were friends of a sort, but that wouldn't stop them spreading it.

Jonah caught Mack's eye and read his rising concern.

"Let's move," Mack said. "Riding along?"

He shook his head. "I'll follow separately."

"Don't," his mother hissed.

Her rancor had steeped in resentment and curdled with rage. The wolf she had fed was sated, and it looked out at him now. He started to shake, seeing in her eyes what he'd seen that night, when he'd staggered back, spattered with blood and more. As they wheeled her into the back of the bus and pulled the doors closed behind them, his hands clenched.

He locked the house, intending to get into his vehicle. Instead, he moved around to the back and stared at the shed. An agony of fear and loathing seized him. His legs moved forward like mechanical shanks he couldn't control. He wrenched open the door and smelled or imagined the rank odor.

Wood spiders had woven netting across the ceiling. Crackling black-widow webs clogged the lower corners. But his mind skipped over his childhood fears and centered on the steamer trunk near the back, the black stains thick with dust.

The former police chief materialized, standing tall, legs spread, hands on hips. *"I told you to walk away."*

"You know I can't."

"We stick together on these things. That's the first rule I taught you."

"Stacie Williams is dead."

"A drunken pothead got out of control."

"You took the call and went out to the party. When Stacie got belligerent you arrested her, put her in your car."

"Blah-blah-blah."

"You stopped a mile and a half from the arrest location."

"She got sick. I let her out of the car, unfastened the cuffs so she didn't fall on her face when she puked. It's all in the file."

"I ran a rape kit."

"You what?"

"One of the samples matched your DNA."

His glare was not ice; it was nitrous oxide. He knew better than to argue DNA, given the rest of the story. So he justified. *"She wanted a deal."*

"Sex for leniency?" He couldn't keep the disgust from his voice.

His father's nostrils flared. *"You think you're better than I am."*

"I need your service revolver, Dad."

"You don't know when to quit."

"You taught me that." He held out his hand. *"Your gun."*

With a low growl, the chief removed the gun from the holster and held it out grip first. *"So you're the big shot now. Think you can do the job better than your old man. You'll see how the mighty fall."*

Jonah took the weapon and, as he removed the clip, his father reached back for the shotgun, chambered a shell. For an instant Jonah believed his father would kill him.

But Stan Westfall rammed it under his own chin and pulled the trigger. Choking with shock and splatter, Jonah staggered back, ears ringing.

Horror engulfed him with the smell of death, his mother's screams splitting the night.

Remembering, Jonah's legs gave way. He dropped to his knees in the silent musty space and stared at the dirty sunshine spilling over the floor where his father had fallen. He tasted bile. He'd hated the man, and yet…

Twenty-Two

*Perseverance is more prevailing than violence; and many
things which cannot be overcome when they are together,
yield themselves up when taken little by little.*
—PLUTARCH, *LIFE OF SERTORIUS*

Tia locked the shop and walked home. Her early morning trek and a
day at the store had brought clarity. Entering the house through the
mud room, she looked for and found Piper in the kitchen, sucking
honey off her finger. "Miles would be horrified."

Piper giggled, turned to the sink, and scrubbed. "What he doesn't
know can't hurt him." She stirred the tea, then sipped. "Perfect."

Tia threaded her fingers through her unruly hair. "I'm leaving town
for a while. I don't want anyone to think I've been abducted or gotten lost
in the mountains or dissected."

Piper paused with the cup almost to her lips. "Anyone meaning me?"

"I'm pretty sure if you don't worry, no one else will."

"Hey. Every time I've called for help, you needed it."

"This time I'm going to be fine." She kept the tremor from her voice.
This would be harder and riskier and probably more painful than a crip-
pling injury on a mountain. "I'll be gone a few days, max."

"Do I get to know where you're going?"

"Arizona."

"You're going to see your sister?" Piper's excitement lit her eyes.

"I'm going to try. Amanda's watching the shop, but you'll have to
hold down the home front."

"I think I can manage. Do you need a ride to the airport?"

"I'm driving."

"Now? It's almost dark."

"Great invention, headlights."

Giggling, Piper set down the cup. "Will you call when you get there?"

"Sure." Tia laughed.

"Are you telling Jonah?"

She sighed. "Let it go, sweetie."

Piper stretched out her arms and hugged her. "Be careful, okay?"

Tia hugged her back. "I'll see you soon."

"I'll be here."

"Good. Because you know I'm not letting you go, right?"

Piper laughed. "Right."

She packed quickly, some overnight things and a couple of changes. She would drive it straight and face things in the morning. With as little rest as she'd had the last week, she ought to be exhausted. Instead, she felt as though she were waking from a very long sleep.

In the foggy glow of the street lantern outside the bay window, Piper saw Jonah exit his Bronco and approach the house as though someone had blown the ground out from under him. She wrenched open the door, rasping, "Is it Tia?"

He stopped, confused.

She pressed a hand to her racing heart. "Did her car crash?"

He frowned. "She's not here?"

Piper collapsed against the door frame. "She drove to Phoenix."

He blinked, the news adding weight to his shoulders. Even all ragged edges, he was still a million bucks plus tax. He wore calamity like cologne, evoking not sympathy but a primal feminine instinct to attach and defend.

"When did she go?"

"A couple hours ago. I think she's trying to make up with her family." The lines deepened between his brows. "You could call her cell."

He shook his head.

"I could call for you."

"No, don't bother her."

"It isn't Sarge, is it?"

"Sarge is fine. I just wanted to…" He spread his hands. "I don't know what I wanted, tell you the truth."

He was obviously hurting. "You want to come in?"

"No." His smile was thin. "Thanks, Piper. You take care."

He started for his car.

"Jonah?"

He looked over his shoulder.

"She'd want you to call."

His eyes narrowed pensively. "I don't think so."

As helpless as she'd felt with Tia lost on the mountain, she watched him drive away. Once again, there was nothing to do—except pray?

———

Jonah climbed the steps and hunched into the chair on his porch. Despite the damp cold, he didn't go inside. Neither Enola nor Sarge would matter. He'd down the bottle and not stop until he'd saturated every cell.

Funny thing, alcohol. It made some erudite, others contrite. Too many took it straight to their fists. Some could take it little by little, even work a buzz and walk away. To him it called from a hollow in a bottomless well, the voice of a siren in the drowning deeps.

Same with love, it seemed. Most people moved in and out of relationships with the same ease they left a half-empty glass on the bar. He would lick the rim and sides if that was all there was left for him, then wait, hoping for a refill that might never come.

His extended affair with booze had probably been an attempt to sacrifice his life for the life taken. Had his affair with Tia been the same? He acknowledged a self-destructive streak. But the longing he felt for her, the connection he'd experienced with her seemed like his one sure chance at survival.

He closed his eyes, then looked down at his shaking hands. His mother's heart might stop, and she didn't want him there. He'd apprised his brother, Pete, who'd said, "Keep me posted," which meant, "Let me know if she dies." Neither faked an affection they didn't feel.

Pete had taken him aside at their dad's funeral and said, "Stan Westfall did whatever he intended to and nothing else. If you think Mom's any different, you never learned anything."

Jonah dropped his head back against the chair and ached for Tia. He hadn't spoken to her in weeks, but stunned by the experience in the shed, he'd staggered to the one person who'd understood. He clenched his hands, hearing the bottle's sibilant song. He could call Jay, reaffirm their mutual commitment to sobriety. Or he could toast his mother's health in a tribute worthy of Chief Stan Westfall, pillar and legend.

A single scratch sounded on the door behind him. He stood and opened it, letting Enola pass by. He looked inside and caressed the bottle with his eyes. The smell of drink permeated his nightmares. He'd hated it, hated the smell of himself as it had seeped from his pores.

He jerked the door closed and returned to his seat, lowering his face to his hands. He watched through his fingers as Enola disappeared, then emerged from the shadowed edges of the yard beyond the circle of porch light. He would have risen to let her back inside, but she came to a stop beside him with a measured stare.

He waited. Normally he didn't make lengthy eye contact, not wanting her to feel challenged. But something in her stillness, in the way she didn't move past, caught and held him. Carefully he let his arm slide down the side of the chair, his hand dangling.

Almost imperceptibly she extended her nose, taking his scent. He had not before offered his unclosed hand, but she stretched and tucked her nose under the edge of his palm. An inexpressible joy bloomed inside. Centimeter by centimeter, he slid his hand over her face and worked his fingers into the stiff fur of her forehead.

In all that time they had not lost eye contact. As he slid his palm over the side of her face, he hoped, truly hoped, the wild would not call her back.

———

Tia had gotten in around four in the morning and caught a few hours of ragged sleep. She showered, tamed her hair with finishing lotion and left it to air dry. Hoping the latest address she had for Reba was current, she got directions from the motel clerk.

Gangly palms graced some of the yards in Reba's nicely manicured neighborhood. All seemed to have a citrus tree in the front, lemon, orange, even a few grapefruit. Minor variations differentiated the ranch-style bungalows with pools in the backyards and tall plank fences. Tia pulled up to the slate blue and blond brick home and parked in the lollipop shade of an orange tree.

She didn't know whether or not her sister worked outside the home. Their three kids were still young, and Mark would have a solid income. She had known him a little, but after he and Reba had started dating, she didn't see him much. Reba rarely brought him to the house, and was there any wonder why?

Closing her eyes, Tia wondered if she could get out of the car. What if Mark answered and said Reba had told him to never, ever allow her sister through the door? What if Reba answered and did the same? Only one way to find out.

The inner door was angled halfway to the wall, and the screen allowed a view into the front room and hallway. Reba called out when she rang, "You know you can just come in."

No, she definitely didn't know that. But she went in. The screen snapped shut behind her. Unwilling to advance under false pretenses, Tia stood there and looked left and right. The room had a south-of-the-border flair she would never have imagined Reba choosing, and yet she had pulled it off wonderfully. Clay pots in the corner held black mesquite branches and another sort that spiraled up like knobby, gray smoke.

The couch was upholstered in sage green suede with a red, gold, orange, and black serape tossed over the back. The red side chairs flanking it had legs made of what looked like webbed stovepipe cactus skeletons. A slice of petrified wood formed the low tabletop where two big-wheeled trucks and a stuffed dog waited for playtime.

With quick steps, Reba strode in, her silky blond hair straight to her midback, highlighted to diminish most of the red tones, her clear blue eyes registering shock, if not dismay. "Oh. I thought you were Mom here early."

"Nope." Tia formed a tentative smile.

"I never noticed how much you look like her. Now that you're older, I guess it shows."

"I hope I haven't interrupted."

"No. I mean Mom's going to watch the kids while Mark and I— What am I saying? I can't believe you're here."

"I'm here."

"You've changed."

"I was eighteen when you left." In spite of her efforts, her voice cracked.

"Yeah," Reba said faintly.

"But you. No one would know you've had three kids."

Reba flushed. "Four actually. Robbie was born three months ago."

Stunned, Tia masked the pain of not being informed. "You've lost the weight."

"Running after the others. I meant to send an announcement. Actually, Mom did them for me since my hands were full."

Tears stung the backs of her eyes. "It's all right."

"I'm…I'm glad to see you."

"Maybe." Tia's smile twisted. "Maybe not so much."

"No, really. Sit down."

"I know you're busy."

"Always. You know how it is, running here and there and someone needing something every minute."

Tia smiled as though she knew.

"But what are you doing here?" Reba slid the hair behind her ear, a simple yet elegant gesture.

And now it came to it. "I wanted to ask your forgiveness."

Reba searched her face, then looked down at her hands. "That was a long time ago."

"I apologized then and understood why you couldn't accept it. If anything, I understand more now. But…"

Reba looked down. "I don't want to dredge it up."

"Of course. I'm sorry." Tia pushed up from the couch. "Then I'll go. I need to tell Mom—"

"How is Jonah?"

Tia swallowed. "I don't know."

"You're not together anymore?"

"We've never been."

Reba shot her a disbelieving look.

Tia tipped her head. "Did you think we were?"

Reba's eyes widened. "Why would I think anything else?"

Tia's breath made a slow escape. "Mom thinks so too?"

"We don't talk about you."

She was truly dead to them.

"So all this time…" Jonah had been right. They neither knew nor cared what she'd sacrificed.

Reba's voice softened. "I'm sorry, Tia."

"You have nothing to be sorry for."

Reba stood up. "I suggested Mom ask you to watch the store."

Tia stared. She'd been certain it was her mother's ultimate punishment. But Reba knew how she'd wanted to break free. As much as she couldn't bear to leave Redford now, she'd yearned for a fresh start back then, a place where she'd stand or fall on her own merit. To be loved and accepted as she was.

Reba spread her hands. "I thought—"

Footsteps approached, and Mark, lean and blond, appeared with a fussy baby sucking his fist. Mark smiled at her without recognition. "Sorry to interrupt, but he's ready to eat."

Reba turned. "You remember Tia, Mark?"

A jolt of recognition. "Oh. Wow. Yeah, of course."

"I'll let you go." Tia turned for the door. "Mom lives three blocks away?"

"Yes, but—" Robbie's fussing intensified, and Reba took him from her husband. "She'll be here any—"

The door opened, and Tia faced her mother.

"Good Lord." Stella actually pressed her hand to her breast.

For a horrible moment, Tia almost laughed. She could hardly have been more poorly received by them all if she'd arrived on cloven hooves.

"What on earth are you doing here?"

"Don't worry, I'm not staying. I wanted to say you'll need to find someone else to run the store. I'm not a shop girl anymore."

Her mother let the screen close behind her. "What are you?"

"A counselor."

Stella expelled her breath. "What could you possibly know that would help someone?"

Tia looked away, deflecting the pain. "I learned a little getting my degrees."

"Degrees?"

"Believe it or not." Her mother could not argue her academics. How she must have leaped at the chance to make her brighter daughter a shop-keeper. Reba's request.

Stella's brows rose and fell. "If I'm selling the store, I'll be selling the house as well."

Tia's heart sank. The mortgage payments she'd made for her parents these nine years were far below the escalated prices she'd find now. And with the house in their name, she had established no credit of her own. Even if Piper moved with her, what could they afford? "Would you like me to list it?"

"Your father will handle it."

Robbie started to wail.

"I'm sorry. I need to feed him." Reba gave her a rueful look.

"Go take care of the baby," Stella said. "I'll take care of this."

Her tone set Tia's teeth on edge, and for the first time she did not envy her sister. "There's nothing to take care of. I just wanted you to know." Tia moved toward the door like an animal scenting freedom. She had hoped for at least a glimpse of her father, but it wouldn't make any difference. He marched to Mother's drum.

She had already checked out of the motel. Now there was nothing between her and the road—a road to upheaval. She had not realized how dependent she'd been, how even from a distance with no real contact, she'd still been controlled like a marionette on their strings. Never again. She had broken down the cage and she—would—fly.

Twenty-Three

If we have no peace, it is because we have forgotten that we belong to each other.

—MOTHER TERESA

As the morning rush passed, Piper cleaned out the case in preparation for the lunch offerings in the oven. Hopefully, since Tia hadn't called, the visit was going well. Thinking about a happy reunion made her fish her phone from her pocket. She speed-dialed and said, "Hi, Mom."

"Piper!" She then hollered to the side, "Reg, Archie. It's Piper. I'm putting you on speaker, honey. How are you? Where are you?"

"Redford, Colorado. I'm a baker."

"A baker! How nice."

She could hear the smile, but her mother had no clue how nice it was. "At first I had to make only the same old things, but now Sarge—he owns the bakery—lets me run a daily special, so I get to try out all kinds of things."

"Well, isn't that just great. Did you hear that? Daddy wants to know when you're coming home."

"Where's home?" She heard a room full of laughter.

"We're in Dallas."

"I'm kind of settled in here. I've made some friends, and I really like my job."

"You just always were a curious kitten. You know we'd have you in the business."

"If I didn't throw up?"

Again the laughter. Piper ached. One day they could all be laughing behind bars.

Her mother's tone sobered. "Are you doing all right? Do you need any money?"

"I'm earning enough."

"We're pretty flush right now. Uncle Archie—"

"Don't tell me, Mom. I just wanted to say I love you. I love you all." And she wished, how she wished they were not who they were. "Bye now. Be careful, okay?"

She wanted to say stop it, stop it all.

"Good-bye, sweetheart," her dad called. The others chimed in.

"You just let us know if there's anything you need," her mother said.

"Bye, Mom."

The ache passed when Miles came in and stood before the counter. She looked up into his goofy face. "Did you leave me those candles?"

He turned and stared at the board. "You made lemon curd tarts today."

"You liked them best when we baked."

"They were tied for first with the oat nut muffins with cranberry glaze."

"I'll bake those tomorrow."

A smile tugged at the corners of his lips. "Did you like them?"

"I like how nutty we made them, and the golden raisins did go well with the cranberry."

"The candles. Did you like the candles?"

"I like them very much, Miles. I put them in my room, on my dresser. Tia lent me candle holders."

"They smell nicer than other candles, but they burn faster. Beeswax is softer than paraffin. It melts at a lower temperature. You have to tell me when they're gone."

"Okay, I'll tell you."

He looked at her. She looked back.

"Do you want a lemon tart?"

"I want to not be what I am."

She could almost feel her heart swelling and breaking inside her. "Have you tried?"

"Phobias don't just go away."

"Not by themselves. But maybe it's like baking. You have to start somewhere."

His larynx rose and fell. "I'll have a lemon tart."

She slipped on a glove, grabbed a tissue, and handed one over. "You know what I like? You're a compulsive truth teller. Like me."

"You're beautiful."

"Thank you."

"Everyone wants to be with you. I see how they look at you. That guy who sells cars looks at you like you're a juicy steak he wants to gobble up."

Piper laughed. "Doesn't he just."

"He doesn't tell the truth."

"How do you know?"

"I can tell."

"Miles. There might be things you can do to get over it. Tia's a therapist. Maybe she could help."

He lowered his chin and shook his head. "I've tried."

"Some of the things I've tried have not turned out. But I keep trying."

"It's not the same to make a stringy goat-cheese roll. That doesn't hurt people."

"Unless they have to eat it."

He didn't laugh, just sighed.

"All I know is the dough has to rise," she said. "If you bake it before it's ready, it won't turn out. But if you wait too long, the holes get too big."

He gave her a slow blink, then went to a table with his tart—just as the police chief came in. Miles could hardly bolt right in front of him, but he didn't even try.

Jonah slid him a glance, then came to the counter, looking even more ragged than yesterday.

"Are you all right? It seemed like you needed to talk last night."

He paused, then shrugged. "My mother had a heart attack."

"Oh, I'm so sorry!"

"It could have been worse. They've cleaned things up now."

"Tia will wish she'd been there."

"Don't bring it up, okay?"

"Why not?"

"Please. She's dealing with things her own way."

And maybe that was the problem in a nutshell. "Can I get you something?"

"Bear claw. Coffee. To go."

Jonah carried his bag to the table where Miles sat.

Miles slumped like an old stuffed bear. "I didn't mean to hurt her."

"There's still the matter of restitution."

Miles looked up at him, then to where she watched, then back. "You're not taking me to jail?"

Jonah stared at him. "Take care of it yourself, and we won't have to talk again."

A timer rang, and Piper hurried to the kitchen. When she came back, neither man was there. Tucked beside the register, she found an envelope with Tia's name. Inside, ten one-hundred-dollar bills.

———

Four more hours, Tia estimated, and she would be home. They hadn't discussed details, but she supposed she could live in the house until it sold. She told them she'd be counseling, but she would need to fulfill the licensing requirements, complete an internship of supervised experience, pass the NCE, and of course find a place to work—or start her own practice.

Her hands clenched the wheel. Even if she had a doctorate—an MD in brain surgery—her mother still would have said, *"What could you possibly know that would help someone?"*

At first she had taken courses to keep from losing her mind, then to understand her mind and the minds of others. But that wasn't enough. Faith had found a place, and with it the Hopeline and all the people she'd listened to and prayed with.

What did she know? That it didn't matter what she knew. God put a spark inside every person and gave her the desire and insight to help them ignite it. If all she did was keep one spark from guttering, then that was enough.

God! The heart cry came without words. She didn't care about a career, about letters behind her name. She wanted to help people break free of the cages of condemnation, abuse, and fear. To heal their wings and watch them fly. That was the stream of living water from which she'd drink.

She almost laughed out loud when her cell phone played the tone for a forwarded Hopeline call. At some point she'd really need to earn a wage, but right now, she drew a breath and answered. "Hopeline."

"You said talking helps."

She hadn't recognized the number, but she knew the voice. "It certainly can."

"I want to make an appointment."

"You don't need an appointment. I'm listening now."

"It would be better in person."

"This is the Hopeline number, Miles. It's a prayer line.

"Piper said you're a therapist."

"I have a counseling degree, but I'm not licensed to practice yet."

"I don't care about that."

"But I don't have an office or…"

"I'll come to the store. To the candle store."

She stared at the great hulking shoulders of the mountains drawing nearer. "I'll meet you there tomorrow, and we can talk about it. Nine o'clock?"

"The store doesn't open until ten."

"That will give us an hour before I have customers."

"Piper liked the candles."

Tia smiled. "She liked them very much."

———

"You're back!" Eager to hear it all, Piper rushed to Tia and took the overnight tote from her shoulder. "I can't tell if you're happy or sad." She followed Tia up the stairs to unpack.

"Both I guess. Mostly relieved. A little scared."

"You?" Piper heaved the tote onto the bed.

"I told my mother I was through watching the store."

"Wow. How'd that work out?"

"She didn't seem to care." Tia unzipped the bag. "But when she sells the store, she's selling the house too. That's the part that affects you. I don't know how long we'll have here."

"I thought it was your house."

"I've been making the mortgage payments and renting out the room, but my parents hold the title. They'll make a killing selling it, the way values have escalated, but I won't see a dime."

"What will you do?" She removed Tia's hairbrush, toothbrush, and toothpaste.

"I was hoping we could find something together."

Her heart rushed. "I hope so too."

"But honestly? I won't have any income to speak of for a while."

"What about counseling?"

"I have to get licensed. Then I'm starting from scratch, building a client base."

"Miles wants help." Piper stashed the items in the bathroom.

"I talked to him. We're meeting tomorrow to discuss a strategy. If he'll agree to work with me under Carolyn's supervision, it would be a start."

"Do you think he will?"

"He seems motivated." Tia formed a sly smile. "Any guesses why?"

Piper flounced on the bed. "Can you help him?" It surprised her how much she hoped so.

"Phobias can be symptoms of psychosis or trauma. If it's the first, then no. But therapy can be effective for the other."

Piper leaned one ankle against the opposite knee. "He's goofy, but… he couldn't ever swindle someone."

Tia's eyes softened. "I just hope you're not trying to rescue him to compensate for your family."

"Gosh." She stared up at Tia. "You mean all the people they've taken unfair advantage of?"

"Something like that."

She didn't dismiss the possibility. "Miles is sweet and funny and wants to dump his junk. I just hope he can."

Tia put the last of her clothes into the laundry hamper and zipped the empty bag.

"So…how did the rest of it go? Was Reba glad to see you?"

"Maybe a little. We didn't have much time. She has a new baby— which I didn't know."

Losers. Creeps. Dolts.

"Anyway, I apologized. Again. Then my mother arrived and showed me the street."

Piper stared into her face. "What is wrong with those people?"

Smiling through the tears, Tia sat down beside her on the bed. "I'd say I committed the unpardonable sin, but they probably think my sin was being born."

"Well, I'm sure glad you were." Piper wrapped her arms around Tia.

Tia hugged her back. "I wish my decision wouldn't mess things up for you."

"We're not there yet."

She nodded. "I have some savings and the merchandise in the store. Miles says a single candle can keep a person from freezing to death."

"Miles!" Piper jumped up and snatched the envelope from the dresser.

Tia took it, puzzled.

"For damages."

She frowned. "I didn't ask—"

"Jonah did."

Tia fingered the bills. "This is a thousand dollars."

"I know."

"It's way too much. Jonah must have put the fear of a billion germs in him."

"He wasn't in any condition to put fear in anyone."

"What do you mean?"

"Well…I sort of agreed I wouldn't tell you, but Jonah came looking for you last night."

Tia searched her face. "Why?"

"His mom had a heart attack. I think she's doing all right, but he looked awful. I even prayed, but you know I might have messed it up."

She said, "You can't mess up a prayer, goof," but she was obviously distressed. "He came here, then asked you not to tell me?"

"He thought you were kissing up to your family and didn't want to interfere."

Tia closed her eyes. "This is so messed up." She got up and paced. "I need to call him."

Piper's heart rushed. "I'll be downstairs."

"You don't have to—"

But she was already halfway out the door.

Twenty-Four

Rest springs from strife and dissonant chords beget divinest harmonies.

—SIR LEWIS MORRIS, "LOVE'S SUICIDE"

Jonah approached his house quietly so as not to disturb Jay, sitting cross-legged on the porch, and Enola, circling and sniffing. She looked up and caught sight of him, then half loped down the steps. Jonah held out an open hand, and she nuzzled it, quivering when he ran the hand over her head. Someday she might express pleasure, but for now the stakes were too high.

"I tried to call you."

"I know," Jay said, not leaving his position. "We were practicing silence."

Jonah nodded. Sometimes it was better not to ask. He let Enola back in to her pup, then settled on the top step. His day had been grueling and wasn't done yet. But for this moment, he might practice a little silence himself.

Or not.

The vibration preceded the ring. Noting the caller ID, he braced himself and answered. "This is Jonah."

"Where are you?"

No preamble. "I'm home."

"Can I come over?"

"Yeah, Tia, you can come." He closed the phone and looked at Jay.

"Guess I'll be going."

"It'll take her a while."

"Yeah. But you'll want to pace and work yourself up." Jay rose and moseyed down the steps.

He would if there were even a chance this could be good.

"You know," Jay said over his shoulder, "some chances you just take."

Some you didn't get to. But he paced anyway until tires turned into his drive and Tia's Xterra appeared between the trees.

She got out, as crazy beautiful as ever. He went to meet her.

"Piper told me about your mom." No preamble again.

"I asked her not to."

"Why aren't you with her?"

He hooked a hand on her car door and cast his gaze away. "She doesn't want me there. The look she gave me as the EMTs loaded her up was exactly the same as that night." He swallowed. "In her mind, I killed him."

Tia shook her head.

He looked back, finding in her eyes a sympathetic anger. "After they took her, I went into the shed to see if she was right."

"Jonah."

"I had him cornered. I confronted him with what I knew." His voice rasped. "His DNA in the rape-kit sample."

She slumped. "Oh no."

"I'd disarmed him. But I didn't see the shotgun." His throat constricted. "He was…all over me, and I kept thinking, I will never get his blood off."

She gripped his arm. "I'm so sorry."

"In the days and weeks after, I could hardly look anyone in the eye. I couldn't stand the pity, the doubt, the condemnation, and worst of all, the admiration. It made me sick, and all I could think was to drown it. But that didn't help. What I needed—you know this already—what I needed was you." His voice scraped his lower register. "So if you came—"

"I came to apologize. To say I'm through trying to please people who don't care. To tell you I quit the store, and they're selling the house."

He caught up to her. "Selling your house?"

"It's not mine. I've only been paying the mortgage. Now I don't even know if I can stay in Redford."

"You're not leaving."

"I came here to say I don't blame you. For anything."

His breathing shallowed. The warmth of her hand sank into his arm.

"Everything, even that day, was my choice."

"You were a kid."

"I knew what I was doing."

He raised an eyebrow, and she pinched him. "Don't sidetrack me."

He slid his hand under hers, flopping the fingers as Enola did, then closed it tight. "I thought you were coming here to dump me for good."

She looked into his face. "I don't seem to have it in me."

"So where does that leave us?"

"I don't know."

"You want to come in?"

She shook her head.

"You don't have to worry."

"Yeah, Jonah. I do."

"It's been nine years. We have talking to do."

She looked from him to the door behind him, as tentative as Enola. He tugged her arm like a bellpull. "Where's that pirate kid?"

Her eyes flashed up.

"Oh yeah. There she is."

———

Tia paused at the door. She had never been inside Jonah's house. Going in felt irretrievable. She tipped a glance at him, then stepped through the threshold.

"Not so bad, was it?"

She gave him the point of her elbow—but gently—in the ribs and took in the log walls, the stone in the kitchen and fireplace, the gathering of candles along his mantel. "How did you get those?"

He followed her gaze. "Ruth."

"I never suspected."

"She's my undercover go-to gal."

She surveyed the rest of the room, the hall that led to more rooms, furniture that looked well made, comfortable seating. A smile formed on her lips. "I can see you here, Jonah."

"Sarge is back that way. He's not doing great today."

"I'm sure there's a story there."

"Lots of stories there. You hungry?"

"I ate on the road."

"Something to drink?"

"I'm fine."

He motioned her to a recliner angled toward another.

She shook her head. "I shouldn't stay."

"You came inside to tell me you have to leave?"

She wrapped herself in her arms. "I don't know how to be."

He reached out and clasped her elbows. "You always know how to be."

"I've imagined this too many times, too many ways."

"Pick one."

"No, that would not be good."

He slid his hands up her arms with a smile in the corners of his mouth. "Then take a seat before my imagination kicks in."

She crossed to the recliner and, once seated, drew her knees up and fit herself sideways in it.

"So tell me how bad it was. In Phoenix."

"You really want to hear?"

"Every heartless word."

Her mouth crooked up. "The refrain was 'Hit the Road Jack,' with verses of 'You're No Good.'"

"I could have saved you the trip."

"You tried to. And the funny thing? Reba thought we'd been together this whole time."

"You're surprised?"

"You're not?"

"I never did get what you were trying to prove. Or who you were proving it to."

———

Tia woke to the smell of steak and coffee and a pair of golden eyes. She didn't dare move until the animal brushed past with a furtive gait no one would mistake for tame. A small version of the mother wobbled up behind on stumpy legs.

Coyotes. Liz hadn't lied.

The moment the animals passed, she shot upright in Jonah's recliner, a blanket slipping to the floor. The last thing she remembered was telling Jonah about Reba's new baby and their inadvertent nondisclosure. She dropped her face to her hands, massaging her eyes—and froze at the touch of Jonah's hand on her neck. She turned. Rumpled and ragged, he looked achingly irresistible.

He whispered, "Sarge sleeps in, so let's take our plates out to the porch and let the dogs roam."

He acted as though it were nothing, having her there in his kitchen in the morning, handing her steak and eggs that wafted a glorious aroma and a mug of coffee creamed blond, the way she had drunk it as a teenager—and still did when she didn't have tea.

"Come on." He balanced his mug on his plate to open the door and motioned her silently out into the misty mountain morning.

A stream that would eventually feed Kicking Horse Creek burbled in its bed, while jays and chickadees hopped and twittered in the trees. He held the door for the coyote and her offspring. When the puppy whined at the perilous ledge of the first step, Jonah set his plate on the half-log railing and carried the pup down, carefully setting it on its wobbly legs. Enola knocked it over with her tongue.

"Now was that necessary?" Jonah put his hands to his hips.

The dog must have thought so since she kept licking. Jonah came back up.

Tia set her dishes on the railing, the end of her nose and fingertips chilling, her jeans and brown ramie sweater barely warm enough. She could just imagine her hair. "People will think we slept together."

"We did."

"I mean—"

"I know what you mean. You need to stop worrying what people think."

"Right." She expelled her breath. "Jonah, I've worked hard to repair my reputation. I've been scrupulous about appearances, but people haven't forgotten. There are plenty out there just waiting for me to show my stripes."

"Like who?"

She looked over her shoulder. "Like Sarge for one. If he sees me here, he'll know everything my mom said about me is true."

"You misjudge him."

She dropped her head to the side. "Jonah, I know exactly what he thinks of me."

He frowned. "I'd have expected this conversation if we'd done something last night. But I'm having a hard time seeing what I should feel guilty about."

"I'm not saying you should feel guilty. But I don't have the luxury of everyone's respect. I've had to overcome years of my own rebellion and others' judgment. Now it looks like—"

Jonah spread his arm. "Who's going to see?"

She looked around at the dark trees and aspen. Maybe she was overreacting, but, "All it takes is one word, and the whispers start again. The looks, the raised eyebrows. People thinking they know." She glared. "I've had to live down what we did, on my own. I can't risk—"

"Being with me?"

"Being with anyone in a way that dredges it all up again."

"We're having breakfast. And by the way, I like it hot." Scowling, he lifted his plate and stabbed a bite of eggs, the yolk running down his fork.

"I didn't know you're grumpy in the morning."

"You'd know a lot of things if you hadn't kicked me to the curb."

Touchy too. She cut a sliver of thin, rare steak. "You'd know some things also."

"Like what?"

"I prefer my steak medium." She'd been joking, but he grabbed her plate and swept back inside. She stared at the swinging screen, jaw slack. Obviously neither were at their best today.

Gripping the hot cup, she took a sip of coffee and watched the coyotes sniff around the base of the porch. The puppy could not be more than a few weeks old, still tumbling off his legs. She could see what looked like German shepherd markings in the mother, although her shape was all coyote.

Jonah came back, returned her plate, and took a bite from his own cold steak. He chewed in silence.

"I was joking."

He washed his bite down with coffee. "Let me tell you about appearances, Tia. My father sat in a pew every Sunday with his lovely wife—except for the times when her bruises would have shown. He and other respected officials chuckled together as they wove their webs and slept with other men's wives and decided who should be punished and who got a pass." He speared her. "So guess what? I don't care about appearances."

"But that's your world, Jonah. You haven't had it held over you for nine years."

"The hell I haven't."

"Not by everyone you lost."

"By the one who mattered." He put his half-eaten breakfast on the porch floor and turned to her. Leaning one arm on the post, he said, "I need to know if you're in this with me."

"Or what? You have someone else?"

His face darkened. "Yeah, Tia. I have them waiting in line."

She looked down. "That's what Liz said."

He grabbed her chin and raised her face. "The only women in my life are that four-legged one and you." His eyes pierced. "If there's no chance—"

"I wouldn't be here." The words wrenched her emotion out with them.

He searched her face, then buried his hands in her hair and kissed her. Eyes closed against the tears, she kissed him back with nine years of loss and longing.

They both stiffened at the snarling growl, and Jonah's fingers slackened, coming to rest against her cheek. "Don't panic."

She tried to look around him at the coyote.

"Hold still." He slowly lowered his hands, moving back inches at a time from her.

The animal's hair stood like a spiny ridge, her hackles quivering.

Jonah said, "Easy," to the dog, then, "Tia, look at me. Don't challenge her."

"Challenge *her*?"

The snarl rose in pitch.

He took a half step back and pivoted, his back to her, facing the animal. "Easy now."

Hard to say which of them he addressed, but she drew a long breath through her nose and dropped her shoulders. Slowly, slowly he went down on one knee, his hand out, fingers curled under. He held his hand there for three long beats, before the curl left her lip and she stretched her neck to butt his hand with her nose, then sniffed.

"She's taking your scent with mine."

"Lovely."

"You're the first female she's had to accept."

Tia cleared the fear from her voice. "What about Liz?"

"Liz only had contact when Enola first came, too injured to strike. I lock her up when Sarge's nurse comes over. She and Sarge can get contentious."

"The nurse or the dog?"

He chuckled. "Both."

Tia looked into Enola's hard golden eyes. "Does she like anyone but you?"

"Jay."

"Who's Jay?"

Giving the dog's head a slow stroke, Jonah looked over his shoulder. "We have a lot of talking to do."

"Didn't we do that last night?"

"About ten minutes. Then you dropped off midsentence."

She sighed. "I drove twenty-one hours on four hours' sleep."

"That's why I didn't send you back out on the road." He stood up.

"You could have driven me home like a responsible officer."

"Yeah." His mouth pulled. "I could've." He looked at his watch. "Speaking of which, I have guys on surveillance I need to relieve."

She hadn't even thought about the time. And then suddenly, "Miles!"

Twenty-Five

"Forget thee?" If to dream by night and muse on thee by day;
If all the worship, deep and wild, a poet's heart can pay;
If prayers in absence breathed for thee to Heaven's protecting
     power....
If this thou call'st forgetting, thou, indeed, shalt be forgot.
—JOHN MOULTRIE, "FORGET THEE?"

Piper excused herself from the couple sampling her morning special and pushed open the bakery door. "Miles."

Dressed in pressed khakis and a crisp white shirt that hurt her eyes in the morning sun, he turned from Tia's door. "She said nine o'clock."

"I just talked to her, and she's on her way. Come in and have something while you wait." The brisk morning air had brought in an early rush eager for hot rolls and coffee, but the crowd had thinned now.

When she'd left the house before dawn, Tia's door had been ajar, her room empty. In her brief call, Tia made it clear she had merely dropped from exhaustion in Jonah's recliner. Piper was just glad they'd made it through the night without killing each other. She served up the couple's to-go order and thanked the three that got up from their table to leave.

In the doorway, Miles looked back over his shoulder. "I told her the shop didn't open until ten, but she wanted to meet at nine, before she had customers."

"Things happen." Piper moved back behind the counter. "What can I get you?"

"Surprise me."

Smiling, Piper slipped on a glove and used a parchment to hand him a sour-cream cinnamon puff. He paid her with four crisp single-dollar bills. None of the bills in his wallet appeared to be hundreds, and she wondered if the ten he'd given Tia had wiped him out.

He said, "Keep the change. Some places have a tip jar."

"Thanks, Miles." She pocketed the extra dollar and ten cents.

"What happened to Tia?"

Before she answered, Bob Betters pressed the door with thick, gold-bedecked fingers. "There she is, a vision of loveliness." In his lavender shirt and white tie, every blond hair and smile in place, he looked like a spanking new Ken doll.

She did try to smile. "What would you like?"

"One Piper to go." His chuckle was high and nasal. "Excuse me," he said to Miles still standing at the counter.

Miles didn't move.

"You've been served, mister. Go have a seat."

Miles took a bite of his puff, chewed carefully, and announced, "Needs more cinnamon."

"You think?" She watched it register in Bob's face that this was the guy who had gotten the last fig roll and held him up last time.

"The sour cream is nice."

She turned again to Bob. "Are you ready?"

"Honey, I've been ready since you brought your pretty face to town." He looked again at Miles. "You mind?"

Miles took another bite. She had the crazy feeling he was trying to protect her.

"You can sit down and wait, Miles."

"I'll stand."

"Okey-doke."

"Hey. Buster. She doesn't want you blocking the counter."

She shook her head. "There's plenty of counter."

A woman came through the door holding a bald baby who was happily sliming the eyeglasses that hung on a woven lanyard around its mother's neck.

"What can I serve you, Bob?" It wasn't easy coming up with an innuendo-proof line.

"Hey." He swatted Miles's arm with the back of his ringed fingers.

With a holler, Miles flung his cinnamon puff, banging into a table that tipped over into Bob. Two chairs toppled, napkins and sweetener packets flying.

"What the—" Bob shoved the table back and raised his fists.

"No. Don't. He can't help it." Piper rushed around the counter.

The baby wailed as his mother shot out the door.

Bob had the front exit blocked, so Miles burst through the swinging door into the kitchen, knocking over yet another chair.

Bob hurtled after him.

Piper grabbed his suit coat. "Let me handle it."

"You?" He spun, shaking her off. "You stay out of harm's way."

"No listen. He's fine. You just can't touch him."

"He's not fine." Bob pointed a thick finger at the kitchen door. "*That* is not fine."

She got between him and the door.

He scowled. "He assaulted me with that table."

"He bumped into it."

"I'm calling the police." Bob pulled out a fancy phone.

"No, please."

Bob's finger hovered over his phone. "I won't call, peach, if you explain *over dinner* what you see in him."

She swallowed hard, but there really wasn't a choice. "Okay."

A broad smile pulled his mouth. "Where do I pick you up?"

"I'll meet you there."

"Peach, the ride is half the event."

She glumly revealed her address.

"Six o'clock for cocktails."

"I'm not old enough to drink."

"Oh yes you are. Unless that's a fake ID you've been flashing around."

She wished it were. "Six o'clock."

"Now I'll have those two frosted raisin rolls."

When he'd gone, Piper pushed through the swinging door. "Miles?" She hoped he'd run straight through, but she found him crouched in the pantry. "You all right?"

He shook his head, despondent. "No matter how hard I try."

"You want to come out?"

He shook his head.

"Okay."

When Tia hurried in a while later, Piper nodded toward the kitchen. "In the pantry. Bob Betters touched him."

"Oh no." Tia checked the place for damage.

"I straightened up. The only damage is dinner tonight with Bob."

Tia raised her brows. "I *am* sorry."

———

Tia moved through a kitchen scented with yeast and butter and cinnamon, to the open pantry. Miles sat in the corner, knees pulled to his chest. Even though Piper kept the place clean, a true OCD germ phobic obsessed with filth and germs would not sit on a floor. He seemed to have very specific triggers and patterned reactions.

"Miles?"

"Don't touch. Don't touch people."

He'd reversed the phrase from *people don't touch*. A reprimand or reminder instead of an explanation? His distress level seemed higher. Because of Piper's involvement?

"May I join you, Miles? Or would you rather come out?"

"Don't touch. People. Don't touch."

It could be a means of reminding himself of the rules as he saw them. She went into the pantry and leaned against a shelf that held bags of flour. "Piper told me what happened. I'm sorry Bob touched you. He had no right to invade your space."

He flicked a glance, then pulled his knees in tighter.

"I know how much it upset you when our hands touched."

He stared at the floor, saying nothing.

"You know, Miles, everyone has things that make them uncomfortable, make them feel bad or scared. That mechanism is built into us for our protection. It's a good thing."

He swallowed.

"Chemical or communication problems in the brain can affect that natural sensor, make it react disproportionately to the threat. One result is obsessive-compulsive disorder."

His forehead twitched.

"Have you been diagnosed with that disorder, Miles? Or Asperger's?"

"I've been called a lot of things."

"I'm not calling names. Those are medical terms that help identify areas in people that aren't working right."

Miles put his head in his hands but didn't cover his ears.

"I'm not a psychiatrist, not an MD. But I should know if you've had medications prescribed and whether you're taking them. It's part of a profile I'll keep for our work together."

"Not taking drugs."

"Should you be?"

"Didn't help. Made me sick."

"The doctors took you off?"

He nodded. "Long time ago."

"That might mean it's not a chemical issue. If that's the case, therapy might be able to resolve the root of this problem. Do you want to pursue that?"

He stared at the floor, then nodded.

"I would need to work under the supervision of another counselor. Most likely a woman named Carolyn. Would you be all right with that?"

"I don't know Carolyn." He put his arms up against his head, weaving his fingers in the back and breathing hard.

"We would all sit down together and decide if you want to go forward."

"And do what?"

"We'd put together your profile, things like your last name."

"Forsythe."

Okay, if he wanted to answer now. "How old are you?"

"Twenty-seven."

Her age, and they were both just breaking free. "Where do you live?"

"Nineteen Pine Crest Lane." The facts. The simple facts.

"Pine Crest's a nice area. What do you do for a living?"

"I invent things. Hardware and software solutions for companies. I got my first patent at sixteen." His breathing slowed.

"That's amazing."

His hands came down to his knees. "I'm not that smart. I just had a lot of time."

"You're not fooling me. I can tell you're smart."

"Not like a child genius or prodigy. I had tutors. You learn faster when you're not in a herd."

"You didn't go to school?"

His knuckles whitened on his knees.

"We'll talk about that later. Who do you work for?"

"Lots of people. Someone tells me a problem. I make a solution."

"That's wonderful, Miles."

He looked up. "Why?"

"Because we've identified a problem. Together let's make a solution."

———

From her place between the trees, Liz had watched Tia leave, watched Jonah go inside, leaving the door cracked open for the animals. She had told Lucy, had tried to tell herself he didn't matter. She despised him for leading her on, his thumb on her cheek branding her, claiming her. He had loved two sisters. If he'd given her the chance, she'd have explained her plight, Lucy's plight. He'd have embraced them. Even Lucy believed it.

Liz closed her eyes. When she saw Tia's car heading toward his cabin last evening, she had known it would be there this morning. She burned, imagining them together. Of all the men Tia could have, she had taken the only one Liz dared hope for.

Lucy would remind her that Tia had him first, that it was Jonah who couldn't let go. Fair-minded Lucy. She didn't understand that women like Tia were poison to men, seeping into their senses and paralyzing their wills. Clenching her hands, she groaned.

She shouldn't be here. The less she saw and thought about Jonah

Westfall, the better. The less he saw and thought about her as well. But she couldn't walk away.

Enola had sensed her now. She would remember the scent, but that wouldn't be enough to get close. She'd be hyperalert and guarded with the pup nosing the brush around the porch. The risk was terrible. But if he saw her, she had a plan: she would say she wanted to apologize.

She unbuttoned and put her hand into the large pocket, drew out what she needed. It would daze Enola only for a moment, so when the dog stumbled and dropped, she hurried over. Jonah's pup was bigger and stronger than her two. He'd sucked the teats of the mother and grown fat and healthy. He'd known Jonah's touch and grown trusting. He had no struggle, no suffering. He knew no fear.

———

Showered, dressed, and armed, Jonah attached his badge and peeked in at Sarge, still sleeping. He silently closed the door, got his keys, and went outside. Enola loped around the yard, swinging her head side to side, sniffing the ground. He whistled through his teeth.

She kept loping, then suddenly raised her head, the pointed ears hard upright. Just as he realized the pup Scout was nowhere in sight, she bolted into the forest. He bolted after her.

A sharp whining pierced his ears. Over a ridge in a shallow ravine, Enola nudged something that must be Scout, then raised her head and howled. He hurried down, cautiously moved her aside, and reached for the bloody pup. Cradling it, he started back, heart aching.

Enola pressed into his legs, but there was nothing she could do. He needed Liz. He pulled the hem of his shirt free and tugged it up around the pup. He closed Enola into the house, then broke every speed limit in town, hoping as he banged the clinic door with the toe of his boot that their bad blood wouldn't keep her from letting him in.

"Liz! I need help. Liz!"

She came forward, looking startled and annoyed. "I'm not open."

"It's my pup," he hollered through the door. "He's hurt."

She unlocked the door, and he pressed through with the bleeding pup still wrapped in his shirt.

"This way," she said.

He followed her to the surgery and laid him on the stainless steel table. The pup shuddered feebly.

"Something got him," he rasped. "It's bad."

She went to the sink and started washing her hands. "Did you see what?"

"Enola must have scared it off."

She dried her hands on paper towels.

"Can I help?"

"Scrub your arms and hands. He's lost too much blood to anesthetize. You'll need to hold—"

"I've got him." He was weak enough it took hardly anything to hold him still. He followed the directions she gave, holding Scout still while she disinfected and stitched the gashes. The rents were not ragged, but sharp and straight, one deep enough to show white rib bones. Could claws or teeth do that? Eagle talons?

"Has he been dropped?"

"You mean from a distance?"

"Could it have been a hawk or eagle? I found him in the trees, so the branches might have broken a fall."

"I can't tell without x-rays, but I don't think so."

"The cuts are sharp, not ragged. A badger?"

"I don't know, Jonah. I'm not really experienced with predators." She gave him a look he would unpack later.

"Will he make it?"

"He's lost a lot of blood."

"Can you transfuse?"

"A large veterinary hospital might have blood on hand, but I collect from donors as needed for preplanned surgeries. I'm not sure we could match his type."

"Enola?"

"How would you get her here?"

"DOW might have a tranquilizer gun." He hated the thought.

"Her blood may or may not match, and testing would take time and a lab."

"Your pups?" He was grasping and knew it.

"Just because they were in the same litter does not mean the same sire. We would have to test the blood or a transfusion could kill him. That's days or weeks for results, Jonah." Liz stroked a finger up the pup's oversize ear. "You'll just have to wait it out."

Scout made a small movement of his head. Jonah pressed in. "Did he move?"

"The wounds are serious, but there's no organ damage. If he can recover the blood loss, he should survive."

A rush of relief.

She said, "I'll watch him overnight."

"No, I'll take him. If you don't have blood anyway, I'll return him to his mother."

"She could damage the stitches, licking the wounds."

"I'll watch." He cradled Scout's head.

From a cabinet, she gave him a bottle of antibiotics.

"Thanks. Do you want to send a bill, or can I pay you now?"

Her eyelids hooded. "I'll bill you."

"Thank you. I mean it." He lifted Scout, wrapped him again in the hem of his bloody shirt, and went out.

—

Liz stared after him, stunned.

"Lizzie?"

"I've never hurt something on purpose." She looked down. Her hands were shaking. And why not? They were streaked with Scout's blood.

She scrubbed and disinfected her hands, her arms to the elbow and above. She scrubbed the table, her eyes stinging from the bleach, until no molecule of blood remained. She found a drop on the floor and scrubbed the entire floor until her knees ached and her knuckles throbbed. Then she washed her hands again.

"You can't get rid of it."

She turned and glared. "Rid of what?"

"The bad feeling."

Shaking, she toweled her hands dry. "I'm cleaning up the mess."

"But the damage is done."

"Why are you saying that?"

"You should have left him alone."

She knew it.

"But you wanted him to come."

"Yes." Liz seethed. "Is that so wrong? For me to want something? I've given you everything. My whole life."

"That's not true." Lucy's voice was weak. "You know it's not."

Liz sank to her knees, her head reeling. Lucy faded in and out, and Liz was sure she'd faint. She gripped her head, swaying.

"But I love you. I'll always love you." Lucy came close and held her. "Even when I'm gone."

Liz wrapped her sister in her arms. "You're not leaving. I won't let you go."

"Oh, Lizzie. How much longer can we do this?"

"Forever."

Lucy sighed. "I don't have forever."

With Scout cradled in his lap, Jonah drove home, knots of tension in his muscles. "Jonah." Ruth came over the radio. "Are you on your way in?"

"I have to go by my house first. What's—"

"I'll meet him out there. Tell him—"

Ruth broke in. "The mayor says he'll meet you there."

Jonah scowled. "What's up?"

"He'll talk to you there."

Mayor Buckley was waiting when he climbed out. "You'll have to give me a minute."

The mayor took in his bloody shirt and the animal he clutched. "Anything I can do?"

"I wouldn't recommend it. His mother's half coyote, and she's already frantic. Just give me a few minutes to deal with this."

Enola came out of his room, hackles raised, growling.

"Easy, girl." He knew she could smell the puppy's blood, the vet, and his own fear. "I'll just bring him in where it's safe and quiet." He moved past her to the closet, squatted down, and laid Scout on the blankets inside. He backed away to let her in, watching for any sign that she might harm her offspring.

She shot a look over her shoulder, then moved into the closet and started licking. Liz had been concerned about the stitches, but they looked—his breath caught—no. He gripped his head, staring at the sharp, straight cuts, neatly stitched. No!

Enola looked up, sensing his sudden fear. Dread filled his chest. He'd need a sample of that thread to send to the lab for a match. And if it matched the raccoon thread, what did that mean?

Experimentation? Research? She must have a reason for not voicing it when he'd shown her the animals. Another cog turned. If she could do that, then—Scout?

The breath left him. Sharp slices, like a blade, a scalpel. He had no proof, no evidence. He didn't want to believe it. Why would she hurt— Tia.

He had told her no one would see, but what if someone had? What other reason could there be? He stared down at Scout, barely responsive. His chest felt cold.

And then he remembered the mayor in his yard. He went out, barely hiding his scowl. "Sorry to keep you waiting. What did you need?"

Mayor Buckley handed him an embossed invitation. The Founders' Luncheon. He could not be serious. Jonah looked up.

"Noon today."

"I'm not a founder."

"Neither are half of them on the board. It's about solidarity. About caring for Redford. I want you to hear the speakers so you'll understand the big picture."

"I have two investigations that require my attention. I don't have time—"

"Have the sheriff back you up on that if the officers we pay aren't enough." The mayor flashed his smile. "I'll see you there."

Cursing, he went inside and changed into his full uniform, armed himself again, then stopped when Sarge came out of his room. "I know you never saw combat, Sarge. But did you ever want to kill?"

Twenty-Six

All are good and happy. The blessing of unity still dwells
amongst us and oh what a blessing, it should make all else
pass into nothing.
—CATHERINE MCAULEY

Tia went into the shop, amazed that it could feel so foreign already.
She moved through it to the back room, like a ghost that had once
occupied a space and couldn't understand why it was still there. She
grabbed card stock from a shelf and started making signs. Once her merchandise sold, she wouldn't enter this store again.

She put the big sign in the window, the smaller ones around on the
shelves. Then she started making calls, Mary Carson first, then the others who had faithfully supported her. With the hint of a smile, she
included Ruth. In the back room, she sorted and discarded everything
she would have no use for, going to the front when Mary and others came
in to buy out her stock.

"So," Mary said. "A new direction."

"I hope it's the right one. It's taken me long enough to find it."

"Well, nothing is wasted. The Lord is infinitely resourceful."

Tia tipped her head. "Where have I heard that before?"

"You mean Carolyn's pet phrase?"

They laughed.

Mary cocked her head. "When I got your message, I thought you
might be depressed, but you seem…joyful."

"I'm peaceful even though I should be frantic."

"A good indication you're on the right path."

"Thanks, Mary. Thank you for all the candles you've bought all the
years I've been open. And for your example. And your friendship."

Mary's eyes teared. "I'll thank you for those last two right back. But
you sound as though you're leaving."

"I don't know. When the house sells and I have no income…" She shrugged with a rueful smile. "See why I should be frantic?"

"Just look for that open door." Their hug lasted moments longer than any before.

She went into the back and pulled out bins of wick and scents and dyes. When the bell signaled another customer, she went forward and paused. "Liz."

She sent her gaze around the store. "You're closing?"

"Yes."

"Why?"

Not her business, especially after the other night, but maybe Liz still needed a friend. "I've done this a long time. I need a change."

"Why now?"

Tia shrugged a shoulder. "Have you ever been going along and suddenly you realize it's all wrong? It's as though you've awakened from a paralyzing sleep and what you believed, everything you thought you knew, is different."

Liz shoved out her arm like a traffic guard. "Stop it."

Tia raised her brows.

"You can't know how it is. You are not like me. You are not special, not…"

"I wasn't trying to speak for you, Liz. I'm speaking for myself."

"You're a liar." Her eyes narrowed. "You lied when you said you and Jonah were through."

How would she know they weren't? "It's complicated with Jonah."

"No. It's simple. He told me he'd stop it if he could."

That had a ring of truth.

"You think he can't love someone like me." Pain reddened the fair skin around her pale blue eyes. "But he said if it weren't for you, he would."

How would she handle this if it were a Hopeline call? "Liz—"

"Why couldn't you let him go?" Her face contorted, but before tears came, it went flat as a mask. "You should have let him go."

The disembodied tone chilled her.

Liz turned and went out the door Piper had pulled open.

Head cocked, Piper pressed in. "Was that as freaky as it sounded?"

Tia bound her hair back with her hands, more shaken than she'd realized.

"Like *Fatal Attraction* freaky?" Piper hugged herself. "We won't find a dead—omigosh."

Tia's jaw fell slack. "Don't. Don't go there. It can't be."

"The raccoons, Tia. She's a veterinarian. And she's whacked."

Her head spun.

Piper gripped her arm. "We have to tell Jonah."

Tia shook her head. "He's been with her. He'd have seen it."

"He didn't see her like this. It sent a shudder up my back."

Tia paced. "Why would a veterinarian torture animals?"

"Maybe it's not torture."

"You don't think clawing and chewing themselves apart is torture?"

"Of course. But maybe that wasn't her intention."

"We don't know for sure it was—"

"Tia. Who else would know how to surgically remove and reconnect organs?"

Tia pressed her hands to her face. It made some horrible sense—unless she thought about Liz and tried to imagine. "It can't be."

"What I just saw, the way she looked at you, there's one word." Piper shuddered. "Malevolent."

———

Jonah had never heard such blow-hards. He should be doing his job, not feigning a starry-eyed interest in the droning erudition. When at last it was over, he shook the mayor's hand, told him the event had been enlightening, and made his escape. Noticing a missed call, he returned it.

"Hello?"

"Sorry I missed your call. I was enduring the Founders' Luncheon at the mayor's command and am now properly illuminated."

Tia laughed. "I've missed that dry humor."

He reached his Bronco and got in. "What did you need?"

"You don't think I called just to hear your voice?"

"My ego would say yes. My highly developed cop sense says no." He started the engine.

"I know you're really busy—"

"Actually, I was coming to see you."

"You were?"

He backed out of the slot. "I have to tell you something you won't like."

A pause. "I guess I do too."

That did not sound good. "I'm just up the street. I'll see you in a minute."

"Okay."

He parked outside her shop, and she met him at the door with Piper by her side. Past closing time for the bakery, he still hadn't expected her there. "Talk to me."

"It's about Liz, Jonah. I don't think she's handling your breakup well."

"Breakup? I told you—"

"Her perception at least." She held his eyes with a sober intensity.

"Why don't you tell me what happened."

Tia recounted the conversation, then Piper jumped in. "You had to see it to understand. Her face was livid, then went all flat like it didn't belong to her. Totally freaky."

Back to Tia. "Did she threaten you?"

"No."

Piper added, "She didn't have to. It was like *Fatal Attraction*. And then we thought—well, I thought—she might boil a bunny or something and then we remembered the raccoons. And think about it. She's an animal surgeon."

For the second time that day, he went cold.

Tia pressed a palm to her temple. "I know it sounds psychotic."

Piper turned to her. "You should know. You're the expert."

He canted a glance. "Expert?"

"Hardly."

"She has a master's degree in clinical psychology."

Jonah stared. He couldn't help it. "When did that happen?"

Tia glanced up. "I took courses online."

Somehow that was harder to digest than Liz. Not that she couldn't do it, but that she'd done it without him knowing. Nine years of things he didn't know. "So what do you think? Is she psychotic?"

"I'm really not qualified to say. That takes all kinds of tests."

"Tell me your gut."

She raised and dropped her shoulders. "I was concerned enough to call."

He glanced at Piper. "Can you give us a minute?"

She beamed. "I can give you a minute and more." She headed for the door. "I'll be hanging at Java Cava."

When she'd gone, he took Tia's hands, drew a breath, and said, "I think Liz was watching us this morning."

"What?"

"I guess your Spidey sense is pretty hot."

She tipped her head. "How do you know?"

"I don't." He swallowed. "But…I think she cut Scout."

"What?" She squeezed the blood from his hands.

"I found him in the woods. She must have immobilized Enola long enough to get at him."

"Please tell me Scout's okay."

"He was alive when I left him. I brought him to Liz before—" He beat back the emotion. "Before I had any idea. But the wounds were sharp, not ragged, and have the same neat sutures as the cats and raccoons."

She slumped. "If she hurt a helpless animal to punish you, that's escalation, right? You can arrest her?"

"I don't have enough for a warrant."

"You have Scout."

"Who was neither disemboweled nor joined. The only physical evidence might be the thread, but even if it matches, it's not enough for a warrant. Anyone could get that kind of surgical thread. Anyone can sew stitches."

"But you know she was there."

"I didn't see her. Did you?"

Tia turned away and paced. "Why was she there? Has she been watching you? stalking you?"

"That's a weird thought."

"By hurting Scout, she forced contact. She knew you'd bring him to her, that you'd need her."

It sickened him to think it.

"Maybe even the raccoons were to get your attention." Something bizarre enough for the chief to take notice.

He shook his head. "I can't see that."

"You don't think someone could set up scenarios that prompted interaction?"

"She didn't initiate it. I went to her with those raccoons." Then he realized what Tia meant. If she'd set that up—no, too complicated. She couldn't have known Piper would bring it to his attention. Whatever had developed, it happened after he initiated contact. He was the one who'd kept calling, kept asking for assistance. He was the one who had made it personal. But she'd taken it too far.

"You talked to her, Tia. Is she angry enough to hurt you?"

"Me? I was worried about you."

He brought his palm to her cheek. "You should know by now, I'm indestructible. So answer my question."

"She didn't seem angry as much as sad—a deep, soul-weary sad. Like she regretted…"

"What she did?"

Tia pressed her cheek into his hand. "Or might do."

He tipped her face up. "Is she a danger to herself or someone else?"

"I don't know, Jonah. I haven't had clinical experience. I talk to people on a prayer line. I don't know what crazy looks like."

The bell over the door rang. "You're not really closing, are you?"

She drew back. He brought his hand to his side. Tia turned to a small, middle-aged man.

"Your candles are my wife's favorite thing. Without you, what will I give her?"

"Mort." Tia turned with a smile that sent a spear to Jonah's heart.

For nine years, in countless ways she had impacted people's lives, and he hadn't been part of it. He watched her now, treating a customer like an old friend—and maybe he was. The spear sank deeper. She had college degrees, a prayer line, a thriving business, and more people than she realized who appreciated her. If something happened to her...

No way. He'd spend the rest of his life—he expelled his breath. Yeah—the rest of his life taking care of her.

She sent Mort out the door with a box full of candles.

Jonah took her hands. "I want to marry you."

Her lips parted. Her eyes kindled, but with what, he couldn't tell.

"We lost the last nine years. I can't get that back, but I want to be the guy who knows what his wife loves—and gives it to her."

"Jonah."

"Remember the first time I saw you?"

"On the playground?"

"I was on the slide. You were standing there, so tiny, your hair like a dark flame, your eyes looking right through me."

"Yours were black and blue."

"I looked down at you, and it was like the earth shifted."

Tears welled up in her eyes. "But you chose Reba."

He pressed her knuckles against his mouth, then tucked both hands beneath his chin. "I'm not calling that insignificant. For whatever reason, that's there and I can't change it. But you're the one who's always been inside me."

A tear broke free and slid down her cheek. She was shaking her head when his pager went off. He checked it and frowned. "I have to go." He raised and searched her face. "Dinner tonight. Seven thirty?"

"You're asking me out?"

He bent and kissed her lips. "It's time we had our first date." He left her with the retort still trapped in her mouth.

———

Liz lifted the pups into her lap, cuddling and murmuring as she administered the antirejection drugs to suppress their immune systems. Everything would be better. They'd been so young when she started patterning. There would be no emotional struggle, no false need for distance. They'd never known distance.

"Lizzie, are you sure?"

"This time will be different." She turned and studied Lucy, misshapen, pale. So small and fragile. "For you, Lucy."

Tears streamed down Lucy's wan face. "It's the only way?"

"I have to be sure."

Gulping, Lucy nodded. "I'm here. I'll help."

Jonah strode into the conference room. "What do we have?"

Moser rose and addressed the wall where the case was diagrammed. "We got Sean Bolton peddling at the school, released on bond, did not give up Caldwell, Greggor, or his muscle, Malcolm. Must have got the message that talking wasn't healthy."

Jonah felt gratified that none of his officers snickered. He glanced at Sue, every bit as intent on Moser's briefing as the others. Though he had initially put her on leave, her participation in this portion of the investigation had merit, for her and the case.

"Caldwell's been a choirboy. Knows he's on *Candid Camera.*"

"Candid what?" Newly rocked his chair back.

"Before all your reality TV," Moser explained, "*Candid Camera* caught people kissing their elbows and such."

As expected both Beatty and Newly gave it a try.

"Kids?" Moser snapped his fingers. "If I may have your attention."

As Moser laid out the investigation to date, Jonah forced himself to focus. The pieces seemed to be all there. If only they could put them together, they would get these guys. Jonah thought of Sam, and his blood heated once more. But thoughts of Liz and the pups and Tia kept pressing in.

When the briefing ended and the officers had dispersed, he took Moser aside. "I need to throw something at you."

"Okay."

"It goes back to the raccoons." He gave Moser a chance to catch up, then laid out his suspicions.

"Liz Rainer? The vet?" Moser's face reflected his own doubts. "What's the evidence?"

He told him what little he had.

Moser shook his head. "You know Judge Walthrup. You don't have physical evidence? Even one eyewitness? No way."

"The stitches match. At least the parts that weren't torn out."

Moser gave him a stare.

"I looked close while you were losing your lunch. I don't think I'm wrong."

"But you can't prove it. And, Jonah. I've seen her with Marlene. Not getting that sense at all."

He nodded. That was why they needed proof.

Back in his office, he called Jay, who was either practicing silence again or too busy to answer. He'd have to trust Enola to give Scout what care the pup needed. Frustrated, he dove into the work that couldn't wait. Ruth brought him coffee that he drank without tasting. Clearing his desk of administrative backlog would eliminate the mental clutter of undone tasks. And sometimes, in the mundane, he found clarity.

———

She had been forced into this date, but Piper took her agreements seriously. She dressed nicely in white jeans, a fitted green tee, and a gray sweater that tied around the waist. She applied mascara and curled her hair. She knew how to play fair.

Bob could have made trouble for Miles and hadn't. For this she was thankful. If he wanted to know how she could befriend someone so weird, she would explain. She'd also make him understand it would be only one date.

He picked her up in a Camaro convertible she had to admit was smokin'. She had a feeling the drive would leave the rest of the date in the dust.

"Here, put this on." Bob reached into the backseat for a black leather jacket. "We'll take a little spin, and the wind can get cold."

"Thanks." That was thoughtful but probably part of the schmooze. The jacket smelled like his cologne.

He sped up the mountain highway, cornering and maneuvering like a Grand Prix driver. "Tell me you don't like this beauty." His hair blew free of its style, and he grinned.

"I like it fine." She leaned her head against the rest and let the ride take her.

The curl had been blown out of her hair by the time they reached the restaurant, and she felt a little dizzy getting out, like after a roller coaster. But he was a good driver and, well, a Camaro? "Nice ride, Bob."

He flashed his perfect teeth, flicked out a comb, and unfortunately reset his do. "You probably won't need that inside."

He locked the leather coat in the trunk and ushered her into Redford's fanciest restaurant in the lobby of the Tarleton Hotel. He wore a blue dress shirt, open at the collar, and cream-colored Dockers. The flat gold chain around his neck was a half inch of shimmer, and his loafers probably cost more than all her shoes together. If she wanted money, he'd be a catch.

When the server came, Bob eased back in his chair. "What are you drinking, peach?"

She told the server, "Chardonnay, please." She could nurse that awhile.

Flushing, the server said, "ID?"

She gave Bob an *I told you* look but showed a valid ID.

"Thanks. I have to ask."

"No problem." She flashed him a smile.

Bob ordered a martini, then studied her appreciatively. "They'll probably card you until you're thirty."

"Probably." She slipped her hair behind her shoulder.

"You are a puzzle." He stared like a cat at a fishbowl. "Now tell me, cutie, why on earth do you give that big nut a second thought?"

Right there was the reason this test drive would not end in a sale.

Twenty-Seven

Union gives strength.
—AESOP, "THE BUNDLE OF STICKS"

When Jonah came for her in a black crew-neck shirt and khakis, his hair still damp and a little tousled, Tia almost couldn't walk through the door. How had she functioned nine years with him in the same town?

He took in her filmy layered skirt, tights and boots, her soft sweater. "You look great." The kiss he brushed where her jaw met her neck sent a jolt straight through her. "Smell nice too. Like your candles."

"I was cleaning out scents." True, but she hadn't needed to tell him that. "Is Scout—"

"He's alive."

"Liz?"

"Not enough for a warrant." His frustration formed a piece of common ground.

She had felt more pity than anger, but if Liz hurt a puppy to punish them… "How will you know unless she hurts something else? Do you have to wait until something or someone else—"

"I have no proof. All I can do is put together the pieces I get."

The whole thing left her prickly and agitated. Or was that Jonah? "Can't you make her tell you?"

"I'd need grounds to interrogate."

"But you could talk to her, draw her out. Let her think—"

"What? I want her?" His face darkened. "Get her all warmed up, then ask if she attacked my pup?"

She shook her head. "I hate not knowing. What if she *isn't* guilty?"

"That's why we have due process. Now can we have dinner?" He slipped a hand behind her back and eased her out the door.

As a cop, he might be able to shift gears like that, but she couldn't shake the uneasy thoughts as they drove the short distance to the Tarleton Restaurant. "Really?" She hadn't eaten there since Reba's sixteenth birthday, and her uneasiness grew.

"I go all out on the first date." He parked beneath an old-fashioned gas lantern. "It's burgers and fries after that."

"So many first dates, you developed a strategy?" She climbed out, gathering her skirt in the wind.

He came around, head cocked. "I was joking, Tia. We can eat here every night, if you like."

"On your salary? On mine?"

"Or go somewhere else if you'd rather." He was picking up her mood. She reined it in. "I wouldn't."

"Then our table is waiting." He took her hand.

For a moment she lagged, then with a slow transfer of weight, stopped resisting. As they followed the manager through the elegant, meandering dining room, she caught sight of Piper with Bob Betters at a table by the windows. It seemed Bob went all out too.

A waiter appeared to take their drink order. Tia ordered a glass of Shiraz.

"Coffee," Jonah told him.

She looked over when the man had gone. "Not even wine?"

"Six years sober."

"Is Jay your sponsor?"

"How'd you know that?"

"You gave his name weight."

"Pretty good police work."

The compliment peeled one layer of the tension in her chest. "Nothing to it."

His eyes crinkled. "Uh-huh."

"You've said that exactly the same way as long as I can remember."

"Okay."

"And that." She opened her menu. "So what's he like? Jay…"

"Laugersen. Half Dane, half Cherokee."

She cocked an eyebrow. "Is that what defines him?"

"Wait and see."

"Will I?"

"He's eager to meet you."

She bit her lip. "How much does he know?"

"He pretty much saved my life."

So everything. Skidding off that thought, she sipped the wine, then glanced up. "Will this bother you?"

"Never was a wine fan."

"You haven't slipped in six years? Not even once?"

"Have to start over if I do." He took a sip of coffee. "Can you live with that?"

"Of course." But then she wondered how he'd meant it. "If it became relevant."

"Oh, it's relevant."

"I meant that living with each other's frailties implies a future together."

"I guess I wasn't clear before."

"You were." She looked up. "But just because you have some organic hold on me doesn't mean everything goes away."

"I know that."

"I need to do this right." She moistened her lips. "I need time."

"I'm not going anywhere."

Another layer peeled away.

He glanced past her. "What's the story on Bob and Piper?"

She ran a finger down her glass. "If I tell you, will you not overreact?"

"No promises."

She frowned. "Miles had an episode at the bakery. Bob was ribbing him, and then he tried to get his attention—tactilely."

"He touched him?"

She nodded.

"And Miles went ballistic."

"He bumped a table into Bob, who got really upset, then said he'd get over it if Piper went out with him."

Jonah nodded slowly. "Which part am I not overreacting to, Miles, or Bob extorting a date?"

With a rush of warmth, she leaned in and squeezed his hands. "Good answer."

———

Jonah glanced across the room again. He couldn't hear the conversation, but from the continuous flapping of Bob's mouth, Piper was paying big time. Her plate was nearly empty. Bob paused now and then to shovel in his own food, then took up where he left off.

The server brought new glasses of wine. Piper dabbed her mouth and escaped to the ladies' room. Jonah slid his gaze back to Tia, but a shift in Bob's posture caught the corner of his eye. Bob leaned, then settled back in his seat.

"Jonah?"

"Sorry."

"Is something wrong?"

"I'm not sure." When their server came over, Jonah motioned for her to order.

"I'll start with the glazed pear and walnut salad and then the pan-seared rainbow trout."

"Very good. Chief?"

"That salad sounds good. Make my entrée lobster. Thanks." He checked Piper's table. She had rejoined Bob and was downing her wine for reinforcement.

"I thought you were a red-meat man," Tia said.

He turned back to her. "At places like this, I order things I don't cook myself."

"You don't like dropping the wiggly fellows head first into boiling water?"

"Thanks. I'll enjoy my meal much more now."

"I think it's just the tail here. He's already passed on."

At least she seemed to be coming out of her funk. Bob was holding forth again, and Piper had made it halfway through her wine. He studied her face, saw her blink.

"Not that I'm sensitive, but are you staring at Piper?"

"I need to watch for a moment."

"What's wrong?" Tia looked over her shoulder.

"Don't draw attention."

She turned back, drilling him with her gaze. "Is something wrong with Piper?"

Jonah folded his napkin and set it beside his fork as Piper put her palms to the table and gave a little shake of her head. He stood up, walked over to their table, and removed the glass from her hand. "I'll take this."

Bob looked up, a flash of irritation, followed by concern, followed by jocularity. "Hey, Chief. She's a little tipsy, but I'm looking out for her."

"I don't think so." Jonah signaled the server for Bob's bill. In a moment the woman in black and white stood the leather folder on the table. Jonah said, "Pay it."

"Okay, sure." Bob took a credit card from his wallet and slid it into the slot in the folder.

Piper blinked. "Jonah?"

Bob spread his hands. "Look, what's this about?"

"It's about what you put in her drink."

Bob pushed back with a schmoozy grin. "You're not serious."

Jonah lifted the goblet. "Blue Chardonnay?"

Bob blanched. "It's a wine cooler. With Curaçao or something."

"No," Piper slurred. "White. White wine."

"Didn't know about the dye in the new pills, did you?"

Bob looked from Piper to the glass Jonah held. He started to say something and stopped. Jonah called the station, reached McCarthy, and apprised him. Less than ten minutes later, McCarthy, dark Irish and wiry, and Newly, towheaded and fleshy, had Bob Betters cuffed and marching out of the dining room between them.

Tia had come to Piper's side, and Jonah asked her to find the server and cancel their order. "Tell him I'll come back and settle up the bill."

"That won't be necessary, Chief." The manager spoke softly, approaching from behind.

Jonah nodded. "Thanks. I'll return the goblet once the lab has it processed."

"Let me seal it in plastic."

He shook his head. "I can't let it out of my sight. Chain of custody."

"I didn't drink that much." Piper's words slushed. As slight and young as she was and with the alcohol she'd already had, the drug had hit hard and fast. "Why am I…"

Tia crouched down beside her. "It's all right, sweetie. We'll take care of you."

Tia helped Piper into the Bronco as Jonah opened his kit, poured the liquid into a sterile container, then bagged and labeled the goblet. Tia climbed in back with Piper.

He glanced over his shoulder. "Sorry about dinner."

"Are you kidding?" She stroked Piper's hand. "If you hadn't seen this?" She shook her head, jaw cocked.

He debated driving Piper to the hospital but took out his phone instead. "Hey, Lauren. Have you finished up with Sarge?"

"A while ago."

"I was hoping you were still in town."

"I'm still in town."

"Can I ask a huge favor?"

"You can ask."

He glanced in his rearview mirror. "A guy slipped someone a roofie. I hate to take her to emergency. Could you draw some blood for the lab?"

"Hold on a second." She talked to someone in the background, someone whose voice he recognized.

Lauren came back. "Where do we go?"

"Is that Jay?"

"Mmm hmm."

Huh. He gave her Tia's address, then pocketed his phone. Tia murmured assurances all the way to the house. Jonah scooped Piper up and carried her to an overstuffed recliner that looked more comfortable than the antique settee. Tia went into the kitchen.

Lauren arrived in Jay's truck. Jonah looked from one to the other, then told Lauren, "The first glass of wine was clean. She had about half the doped glass."

Lauren prepared for the task, inserted the needle, and drew blood into a vial. She pressed a label onto the vial and gave it to him. He initialed beneath Piper's name, the date and time, then bagged the vial.

"Can you check her vitals?"

Lauren cocked an eyebrow. "You think?"

Right. He stepped back and looked at Jay. Jay looked back. Jonah cocked his head, and Jay's mouth quirked.

Lauren spoke up. "You're not very observant, Jonah."

"Tell that to Piper." Did he only notice criminal behaviors? To Jay, he mouthed, *"Dena?"*

Jay shrugged. Jonah rewound the past weeks. Had Jay been there the nights he'd invited Lauren to stay after working with Sarge? Probably. Jay was like furniture, always there when you needed to sit down. He'd obviously been there when Lauren recalculated her odds with the chief of police.

"Sorry I interrupted your plans."

Tia came in with a tray of cheeses, flatbread, and pear slices. She set it on the table and sank to her knees beside her semiconscious friend.

Lauren said, "She probably shouldn't eat or drink until she's over the side effects. Rohypnol is a sedative and muscle relaxant." She lifted Piper's limp arm. "She'll be like this for four to six hours, and then she'll probably be confused and hung over."

Tia's features tightened. "Will she be okay?"

"The drug increases intoxication, causing imbalance and impaired speech. I don't detect respiratory depression, and I wouldn't from a half glass of doped wine." She looked up. "It's a good thing you stopped her finishing it. Even so, she may experience vomiting and insomnia. And she probably won't remember this part of her night."

"So it is the date-rape drug."

Lauren seemed confident, as he was, but said, "The lab will tell for sure."

Tia's eyes were burning embers. "Bob won't get away with this, right?"

Jonah shook his head. "Not if I can help it."

"You're the chief of police."

"The DA brings charges."

"There are witnesses. There is evidence. Tell me—this time—you can do something."

"I already did." He hadn't seen her so shaken in years.

She gripped Piper's hand and murmured as the girl's head lolled.

Lauren gathered her things. "Seizure is possible, so I wouldn't leave her alone. If she doesn't wake up after eight hours, rouse her. If you can't, get her to the hospital."

He nodded. "Thanks, Lauren."

She gave him a slow, knowing smile, then followed Jay out.

———

When Jay and Lauren left, Tia stood up, hands to her hips. "Sarge's nurse?"

He spread his hands. "What?"

"Were you two serious?"

"We never got started."

"Did you want to?"

"What is this?"

"I saw that look between you."

"That look was her identifying the love of my life."

Tia's whole body shook. Piper's helplessness and the fear of what could have happened ripped through her protective layers to a vulnerability that terrified her. She felt as powerless, as defenseless as Piper. And there'd been heat in that look, whatever Jonah claimed it meant.

"Liz. Lauren." She huffed out her breath. "Nine years, a husband and four kids, yet I'm not convinced Reba's over you."

"What are you saying?"

"I don't want to be hurt." She pressed her hands to her face. "If these nine years have shown anything, it's how much we can hurt each other."

"Yeah, it hurts." His eyes went black as obsidian. "Because we love harder, we can also cut deeper. The happier—"

"You think I'll make you happy? I'm the *other* Manning, remember? The one you didn't choose."

"I've been in love with you a long time, Tia."

She looked away, fighting what she saw in him.

"Even Reba knew it. She had just been programmed to believe no one could prefer her renegade sister. And yeah, for a time I lost sight of it too."

"How can you say she knew? She was devastated."

"Yet she made a way for you to stay here with me."

Tears burned her eyes. "What? Why would she—"

"You were the one they rejected. But did you ever think how it was to be her? Trapped in their smothering love."

Her unwilling mind filled with the thought of Reba still obeying Stella's imperious commands, adored and...accursed? She'd almost seen it in Phoenix, almost realized.

Jonah gripped her elbows. "She didn't desert you, Ti. She set you free."

No. Please. Why wouldn't he stop? Didn't he know that would break her heart? For Reba to have given in the midst of her betrayal...

Shaking, she slipped her arms free. "I need to be alone. I'll take care of Piper."

———

Frustrated, Jonah left the house. He'd gone from hero to heel with one look, condemned for something that never happened but sure dredged up everything that had. Maybe they couldn't get past it. Maybe there was so much water under the bridge, it had washed the bridge away.

His Bronco roared to life. The desire for drink kicked in. He'd expected that, unfounded accusations a trigger every time. Yes, Lauren was attractive, and he had entertained thoughts of her. And resisted.

That's why it mattered. What use was fidelity without temptation?

What good was resisting anything you didn't want anyway? His throat cleaved. His palms sweated. He jammed the vehicle into gear. She wouldn't hear him now. Not when the rest of what she'd said had weight.

He'd chosen Reba over the one who had the power to lay him open. Never mind, Liz. His attraction to Tia was the fatal one. How much longer—

His radio came alive with Sue's voice. "All units alert. Caldwell's on the move."

"Officer Donnelly, where are you reporting from?"

Silence.

"Answer my question, Sue."

"I'm tailing Caldwell. He made Beatty and Newly. He hasn't made me."

"I want you to stand down, Sue. Back off now."

"I'm not going to lose him, Jonah."

"I put you on leave. Then I let you sit in. Now I'm ordering you to back off."

"I'm sorry, Chief. I can't do that."

Twenty-Eight

Fidelity is the sister of justice.
— HORACE

Every tendon tightened. He rechanneled his frustration. "What's your location?"

"Heading up Godfrey."

The only undesirable part of town, a street named for a notorious trapper who'd wiped out the beaver population for half a century, homes like warrens tucked into old pines with dirt roads and dumps of old rusty cans and appliances. Survivalists, whom he didn't mind, and slobs, whom he did.

They had patrolled there, but nearly every dwelling could conceivably house a meth lab. Now Sue was in pursuit of a dangerous man in a dangerous area. She was a good officer, a great one for talking down domestic disputes. Short, compact, swaggering—she loved it when guys thought they could disabuse her of a traffic ticket. But she had no experience with this kind of trouble.

"Sue, listen to me. I promised Sam."

"I made him talk, Jonah. I made him give up what you needed to nail this slime. I did that."

"We did it. And there was no way we could know."

"He was just a scared man. I'm a cop."

"You're a good cop, Sue. But this is not your collar. I need you out of the way."

"I'm not going to lose him."

Clenching the wheel, Jonah put out a call for all available officers. The sheriff came back with the news that the local office had been hit by flu. County support would have some miles to cover. Newly and Beatty checked in. No word from McCarthy or Moser. He gave the location. "Code two. I don't want them scared off."

"Copy, Chief."

Then directly to Sue's car. "I've got cover cars coming. Do not engage, do you copy?"

"I'm staying back."

"If you see him, chances are he sees you."

"We may not get another chance."

Jonah gunned it through town to the fringe where she'd gone. He pulled the weapon belt from the lockbox between his seats. The second gun rested against the small of his back. Moser called in. He briefed him. "I'm code eleven on Godfrey."

The pavement ended. The trees pressed in. Night was darker in the warrens. He had his window open, listening. Crickets. Dogs. Distant hollering. A lot of silence in between.

Sue came on. "Turning. No marker."

"Coordinates."

She gave them. He plugged his GPS. "Wait for backup."

"Negative. I'm keeping a visual."

Tension pulled his neck tendons taut. He raised his guys to confirm they'd heard. "Do not engage. You copy, Sue?"

No answer.

His heart pounded. But the rest of him grew calm. He understood physical threat, knew with every fiber how to resist the fear of whatever came. His father's legacy. But the others were green. He clenched his jaw, then slowed his quickened breath. *Lord. Protect my people.*

Branches rasped against the Bronco's sides, moonlight catching in the overhang. He turned where Sue had said. Creeping along with no headlights, he caught a flash of taillights about two hundred yards ahead and almost hit a vehicle half off the road. Sue's. He yawed off behind it, parked, and radioed his location, suggesting they look for an alternate route.

He attached the weapon belt and pulled on his Kevlar vest, then disabled the dome light before opening the door. He crept as silently as the needle-strewn ground allowed. The Jeep was empty. Fists clenched, he moved forward, searching the trees.

"Jonah." Her whisper carried sharply from behind a half-buried stove. "Shack."

He nodded and squatted beside her. She was not in uniform. In her dark hoodie and ball cap she looked more like a high-school girl hoping to score dope than an officer of the law. No wonder Caldwell hadn't picked her out.

Jonah swallowed. "Where's your vest?"

"The station." Her voice quivered. "But I'm armed." She held the gun she'd never fired outside the range.

She was not thinking as an officer. He jerked his chin. "Get back in the car."

She shook her head.

Caldwell opened his door, the dome light illuminating the immediate area. They froze. As Caldwell leaned down and fiddled with something, Jonah removed his vest and slipped it over her. He'd confiscated Caldwell's guns, but they may have been returned when charges were dropped.

Caldwell climbed out. Sue clutched her revolver. Jonah pressed her arm down and jerked his chin once more to the vehicles behind them. She recognized the order but shook her head again.

In one swift motion, he disarmed her. No clearer way to show he meant it.

Her face twisted. The truck door closed, casting them in darkness. He pressed his mouth to her ear. "Get back to my car and direct the others to circle around." If she disobeyed this, she was through.

Her motion made Caldwell pause and search the darkness, but he moved on.

Weapon drawn, Jonah crept closer and crouched. He needed backup, and he needed it now. Almost smothered in pines, the shack blended into the slope. The door opened when Caldwell approached. A large, bald Caucasian with an assault rifle searched the area, hindered, Jonah hoped, by the light behind him.

Another man with a rifle came around the far side of the shed into the light cast from the doorway. Sean Bolton, a lowlife since his teens, probably strung out. The other guy looked unimpaired. Malcolm? Or Greggor himself? "What are you doing here?"

"They pulled the morons off me. I need product."

"Greggor told you to keep away."

That made the bald one Malcolm.

Caldwell said, "Come on, man. Let me talk to him."

Jonah heard a rustle. He reached down and clicked his radio button, got a return click, then two more. Either Moser or McCarthy had joined Beatty and Newly. He looked back at Caldwell. Thanks to Officer Donnelly, they had not only the lab but the operators—and no plan.

Jonah sensed someone behind him. "Where's your vest?" Moser breathed.

Jonah shook his head. Sound carried too easily. He motioned Moser to the right, then caught a glimpse of someone flanking Sean on the far side of the shack. Newly?

A voice spoke from inside. Malcolm raised his weapon.

"No," Caldwell dove and rolled at the same moment Jonah shouted, "Freeze!"

Bullets sprayed.

Jonah spun, feeling a punch. The door slammed, casting them into darkness for only seconds before return shots caused a *whump* of flame and an explosion that tossed him like a straw man. Landing hard on his spine, he lost his breath, then rolled to his knees. Choking on the caustic chemical smoke, heat crisping his skin, he charged the flaming, fleeing man who'd fallen out the window. He covered him to smother the flames.

Not large enough to be Malcolm the shooter, and not Sean who'd been outside, he guessed he'd just extinguished Greggor. Jonah searched and cuffed him, stuffed a large-caliber handgun into his own waistband, then dragged him farther from the flaming shack. By the light of the blaze, he saw his rookie, Beatty, cuffing a wounded Caldwell.

Distant sirens pierced the night. She must have called it in. He hoped they could contain the fire before acres of forest and half the town went up. Surrounding trees already held dripping pockets of flame. Coughing, Moser staggered up, a gash on his forehead.

"Moser, you okay?"

"I can't raise Newly."

"I'll find him. Take this one."

He ran to the far side of the blaze where he'd last seen Sean and Newly. Fire licked the forest floor. A dark figure lay beneath a log plank. Eyes stinging, Jonah heaved the plank aside and found Sean. No pulse, only blood all over his ragged throat and chest.

He hollered, "Newly?"

A groan from his left. "I think my leg's broken."

Jonah hurried to where Newly had landed on a rusted car chassis. As the fire climbed up around them, he fitted his shoulder under Newly's arm and hauled him up. Newly hollered, then stifled it.

"We've got to get past the flames." The smell of burnt grass and leaves joined the chemicals. The shack was burning like a torch, the meth gases a smorgasbord for the ravenous flames. Jonah hooked an elbow over his mouth and nose, blinking as he hauled Newly through the knee-high flames. "Don't breathe it in."

Newly bobbed his head. Sirens shrilling, lights swirling, the first fire engine pulled through the narrow passage. While some of the crew uncoiled hose, Jonah directed Walsh to the torched Greggor, then hollered, "Got a body. Far side." No sense looking for Malcolm. Only one had come out of the shack.

Jonah eased Newly onto the big metal truck step and gripped the door handle, swaying. "Want to wait for an ambulance?"

Newly shook his head, coughing. Jonah gathered himself and helped Newly to the Bronco, got him into the back, then motioned Sue out of the driver's seat. She'd pulled her hood over her mouth and nose, but even at this distance, her eyes were running.

Glancing to make sure her Jeep had access, he ordered, "Meet me at the station."

Jonah climbed behind the wheel. With his hand pressed to his side, he braced himself against the searing pain now making an appearance. He looked back at Newly. "Hold on."

"You hold on, Chief." Newly grinned. "What a night."

When Piper whimpered, Tia took her hand.

Piper's eyes blinked open. "I don't feel good."

"That's because Bob drugged you."

A second's delay. "What? With what?"

"The date-rape drug."

"Unh." Piper lurched up and rushed for the bathroom.

Almost 2 a.m. Piper had been out five and a half hours. She came back and sank down beside Tia, rubbing her temples. "How do you know?"

"Jonah saw him do it."

"Did he—"

"Bob never got you out of the restaurant." Thanks to Jonah. Remorse stabbed her. He had not deserved the things she'd said.

Piper moaned. "I need to lie down."

"Do you want to go upstairs?"

"I'm too woozy."

Tia settled her into the recliner. Two in the morning or not, she had to talk to him. She moved into the kitchen and phoned, surprised that it went to voice mail. On or off duty, even sleeping, he should answer. Unless he was out on a call.

She tried the station, and a woman said, "Officer Donnelly."

"I'm looking for Jonah Westfall. This is Tia Manning."

"I'm sorry, Tia." Sue Donnelly's voice hitched. "Chief Westfall's been shot."

Tia almost dropped the phone. *Oh, please God.*

"They took him to Tri-County Hospital."

"Then he's alive." Her heart kick-started. "How bad is it?"

"He got to the station and collapsed. They took him by helicopter."

Tia thanked her and hung up. She snatched her purse but didn't rouse Piper, who'd fallen back to sleep. He'd only been gone a few hours. Not *gone.* She trembled. *Away.* They'd been apart six hours. And he'd been shot? She stifled a sob.

The road was too winding, the night too dark. The hospital looked like a movie set for M. Night Shyamalan, disturbing, fraught with impending storm. She ran through the automatic emergency doors, halting at the counter. She spoke through the small window. "Jonah Westfall?"

She held her breath while the man checked his screen.

"He's in recovery."

She took her first full breath as the man directed her to the surgical waiting room. She ran for the elevators, ended up in the closed cafeteria, backtracked, and turned into the pass-through with the elevator bank.

Adam Moser looked up when she approached. Taller than Jonah, he unfolded from the chair, a bandage taped on his arching forehead. "He's out of surgery. Newly too, though I guess you're here about the chief."

"Did they tell you anything?"

"The bullet passed through the tissue in his side, nicked his colon, and broke a rib getting out. Barring complications, he should be okay." He rubbed a knuckle into each bloodshot eye. "I guess if you're here, I'll go home to my wife."

When he'd gone, she found a nurse and asked, "Jonah Westfall?"

"Are you family?"

"I'm his…"

"He's in recovery. I'll buzz you through."

She must have looked stunned. She *was* stunned. Jonah. So vital just hours before, then shot. She went through the wide wooden doors and saw him lying on one of the gurneys, eyes closed. He smelled like disinfectant and looked pale and fragile. Even as a battered kid, he'd never seemed breakable. Trembling, she drew close and pressed her hand to his face.

His eyes flickered.

"Jonah?"

They opened slowly, streaked red and bleary like Adam Moser's. "Hey." His voice rasped.

"Thank God."

"Good idea."

"What happened?"

He blinked. "Later."

She gripped his hand between hers, tears filling her eyes. "Jonah, I'm so sorry!"

His throat worked, but no words came.

"We're moving him to a room now," an older nurse said. "Do you want to follow?"

Tia stood back as the woman rolled him to the elevator and then to a room, not in the ICU, she realized with relief. A younger, plumper nurse joined the first. They transferred him to the bed, and the older nurse said, "He did well through surgery. He's strong."

He was strong. And brave. And good. Tears formed again. "Thank you."

The other nurse checked his IV, connected his oxygen, and replaced the clip on his finger to monitor his oxygen. She took his blood pressure and made notes on his chart. "The chair's a recliner if you're staying." She wrote "Nancy" on a small whiteboard. "That's me if you need something."

"Thank you."

The blue-gray chair next to the bed pulled out into something like a bent cot. She could feel the frame through the cushioning. At home with Piper, she had been too upset to sleep. Beside Jonah, she drifted into a raw and anxious semiconsciousness where Piper ran blindly, hands outstretched. Jonah chased a shadow, blood streaming from his side, as Lauren waited with bandages, and Enola snarled at something dark and menacing in the woods.

With a gasp she woke to Jonah's open eyes.

He moistened his lips. "Can't stop sleeping together."

Curled on her side facing him, she reached through the bars and grasped his hand. "I don't want to."

One side of his mouth pulled. "I don't either. You're the only one whose hair looks worse than mine in the morning."

She pinched him.

"Ow."

"Sorry." She rubbed the spot. "And I'm sorry about last night." Then realizing last night was pretty broad for him, "What you said about Reba, about us."

She massaged the muscle of his unbandaged forearm. "I didn't want it to be true that she could love me that much when I hurt her so badly. Then I realized she'd done it for you."

"For both of us."

She brushed her fingers down the arm. "When I thought of it that way, I could understand."

"You don't see how people love you." He blinked. "But you will."

When she realized he'd fallen asleep, she phoned Piper, who sounded a little more like herself. "Are you doing all right?"

"I guess. I'm done throwing up and walking into things."

"I'm sorry I had to leave."

"It's okay, but where are you?"

"The hospital." She looked at Jonah's sleeping face, drawn and pale. "Jonah got shot."

"What?"

"He's going to be okay." No other outcome allowed.

"What happened?"

"I don't know. He's pretty out of it."

"Do you need me?"

"No. Just take it easy, okay?"

"I'm going to shower and try to eat. Might not make it to work, though."

"Me neither."

"Take care of Jonah and don't worry. If I decide to kill Bob, I'll give you time to get there."

Tia laughed. "It's a deal." She settled back down beside Jonah, feeling an oncoming repose that, in the chair, would probably maim her.

Together we sit. Together we stand. The cameras flash.
A voice says, "How do you tell them apart?"

Apart? We are never apart. We don't run away to separate places, separate games. We are one.

"What are you thinking, Lizzie?" Lucy's voice was hardly a breath.

"About the TV people who filmed us that first time, remember?"

"Why the funny look?" Lying across her lap, Lucy tipped her head up.

"The cameraman who asked how to tell us apart."

"And Mom said, 'Well, one is on the right, and one is on the left.'" Lucy's giggle rasped.

Liz raised an eyebrow. "As though we might rearrange ourselves."

"Silly, silly, silly."

"Very silly." Liz stroked her hair.

"I'm glad you're back. I hated you leaving."

"I know." The sadness passed before Lucy looked up again. Liz stroked her sister's cheek. "I know."

She had awakened from her sleep, and soon, everything would be different.

———

Under the warm, streaming water Piper realized, thought by thought, what could have happened to her. She soaped her body, feeling the intended violation. How dare he?

After toweling off, she stepped out of the claw-foot tub. She pulled on stretchy shorts, a sports bra, and tank, then turned on her Turbo Jam DVD workout. Throwing the punches felt good, kicking out in controlled power even better. Before she'd finished the final stretches, she heard a knock at the door.

Her heart thumped. Bob was in jail, wasn't he? She swallowed. It might be a friend of Tia's or someone about the house. She'd never before been afraid to answer. Slowly she made her way to the door and looked through the cut glass. *Miles?*

She pulled open the door as he raised a bouquet to her face. Laughing, she lowered the flowers to see him. "What are you doing here?"

"You didn't open the bakery."

"I'm taking a sick day."

"Are you sick?" He paled.

"Not contagiously. I promise."

"I brought you these."

She took the mums and daisies. "They're pretty."

"They're from my garden. But they want water." Miles shifted from foot to foot.

Last night she had put herself in danger without realizing a thing. She hesitated, then motioned him in with her head. "Come on."

He closed the door carefully and followed her to the kitchen. "This house is old."

"It's one of the originals. Part of Old Town, if you include the residential district." Piper put the flowers in the sink and searched for a vase. She settled on a glass pitcher, filled it halfway with water, then added the stems. "There. Kind of still-lifey."

"I have a book about Dutch still-life painters."

She smiled. "I'd like to see it sometime."

"I could bring it over."

"I could see it at your house."

He searched the kitchen to avoid her gaze, then blew air through his lips. "People don't come to my house. It's a safe zone."

"But you might get my germs here and take them back with you."

He nodded. "It doesn't make sense."

"Do you want some tea or coffee? I have a half an orange-mango coffeecake."

His brow puckered. "You're not upset?"

"That I can't come over?"

"About last night."

How could he possibly know?

"You didn't want to go out with Bob."

"Don't get me started on that." She filled the kettle with hot water and turned on the stove. "I'll just get mad all over again."

Miles looked stricken. "What do you mean?"

She cut the coffeecake and put the slices on two plates, anger welling up. "Bob drugged me. He planned to—"

Miles backed into the pantry door, hands gripping his head. "No!"

"Miles."

"It's my fault. My fault you were with him."

"Nothing happened. Jonah caught him."

"But you wouldn't have been there if I hadn't—"

"Miles!" She gripped his wrist. "It's not your fault."

He froze.

She could feel him shaking.

The Adam's apple jerked up and down in his throat. "You're touching me."

"I know."

"People don't touch." He sounded strangled.

"Do you want me to let go?"

"I don't know." He slackened against the door, keeping only the arm she held stiff.

She stared into his soft brown eyes. "Can you help me understand the touching thing?"

He blinked, blinked, then sighed. "I was too big. A pituitary gland tumor. It causes gigantism in children."

"You're not that big." Six feet seven maybe, a burly, round-shouldered build.

"I was four feet ten in kindergarten. My hands and head were huge. Big clumsy feet. I banged and bumped everything. Auntie Beth said, 'Don't touch, don't touch.' But I couldn't help it."

"Oh, Miles."

"The kids were so mean."

"I just bet."

"Not the five-year-olds like me, but the older ones. They pushed. They made me fall down in the dirt, in the mud. They made my clothes dirty, my hands dirty." His chest heaved. "Aunt Beth said, 'Don't touch people.' But one time, that *one* time, I couldn't stop it. I pushed back."

Piper ached.

"I had big strong bones, big long arms. They hit, and I hit harder."

He hung his head. "I didn't mean to hurt them. I just wanted them to stop."

"Of course you did."

"I never went back to school."

She melted. "You didn't need school."

"But now I'm this." He raised his clasped wrist, and she could see his hand shaking.

She softly let go. "You're going to be okay."

He looked at his hands. "Can I use your sink?"

Twenty-Nine

And when I sue
God for myself, He hears that name of thine,
And sees within my eyes the tears of two.
—ELIZABETH BARRETT BROWNING

Jonah pressed through the fog as voices penetrated, Tia telling some-one he was sleeping. But he'd done enough of that. He opened his eyes to Jay, looking confused.

"You're not bulletproof?"

Jonah pulled a wry smile. "Now you know."

"Gotta watch him," Jay told Tia as she pushed up from the chair. "He does this stuff."

"Gets shot?" She tried to tame her crazy mane.

"Anything for attention." He extended his hand. "I'm Jay. You were preoccupied with your friend last evening, then Jonah goes and pulls a stunt like this. You'd think people were conspiring."

Tia smiled. "Nice to finally meet you."

He watched her take Jay's measure, watched them take each other's. Jay glanced over. "Now I see."

Jonah guessed he did.

"They think you'll live?"

"Last I heard."

"Then you guys don't need me hanging around."

Tia objected, but Jay quieted her with a hand.

"I'll go fraternize with the nurses. One in particular."

Jonah sank into the pillows, pain making an edge inside him. He wouldn't be much good if it got hold, so he depressed the morphine pump.

Tia noticed. "Is it bad?"

"Bad enough." He brushed her hand. "Are you okay?"

"Me?" She looked incredulous. "No." She paced beside the bed. "My emotions are trapped in time warp. I'm an eighteen-year-old girl in over my head with the boy I've adored pretty much always."

"Is that so bad?"

"I want to be the woman I am now with the man I can't live without."

He'd take that. But last night he'd seen the chasm. "How do we get there? Intact."

"I don't think we can." Tears sprang to her eyes.

"Tia."

"No, Jonah. It's bigger than us. All this...stuff. We're like the raccoons, utterly dependent and still ripping ourselves apart."

"So what—"

Someone tapped the door and entered, a bushy-bearded man who amply filled his clericals. His voice boomed like Friar Tuck. "I heard someone's catching bullets."

Jonah looked at the bandages on the side of his torso. "This one got away."

"Even better." He extended his hand. "I'm Chaplain Casey."

"Jonah Westfall. And this—" He turned to Tia, who stood staring. "Tia?"

She startled. "I, um, I'm Tia." She gathered herself. "And I don't think you're here by accident."

"At God's disposal, I hope," the big man said.

She brushed a tear, huffing a soft laugh. "I have no doubt."

Jonah frowned. She'd been saying the connection between them was killing her as surely as the animals tearing their bodies apart. What could she want from the chaplain?

Tia searched his face for something, permission maybe, then started to tell their story. His chest swelled and constricted with the memories, things he'd forgotten, things he hadn't realized she knew, things he wished she didn't. He hadn't known her feelings went so deep so young. She was feisty and loyal and tough and sensitive, and he filled himself with her, more intoxicated than any bottled spirit could render him.

She stopped pacing. "The crux of it is, we can't go on like this. We need..."

"Christ in the middle?" the chaplain said.

Eyes sparkling with tears, she nodded.

———

When they had finished the coffeecake and drunk their tea, Miles washed and Piper dried the dishes. "There's nothing at all you would change?" She slid the last plate into the cabinet.

"It was perfect. Not too much orange, not too much mango. Just perfect."

She handed him a fresh towel to dry his hands as the water gurgled down the sink. His story had broken her heart. But she was thankful he wasn't soul-damaged by abuse. A growth disorder, a traumatic incident reinforced by repeated admonitions—they could work with that, couldn't they?

Bob's bullying as much as the contact might have set him off. That jerk. He'd probably already talked or bought his way out of trouble. And why not? He was only half to blame. She'd been so desperate to dull the maddening monologue, she hadn't even noticed the wine turning blue. That kind of stupid got taken advantage of. She'd seen it her whole life, the way her family identified the marks.

People not paying attention. Complacent. Distracted. She shuddered. Bob hadn't touched her, except for a brief fondling of her knee when they drove and a clasp of her hand on the table. She'd pulled away after each contact. Touching should mean something.

She looked at Miles, recalling the taut tension of his wrist, his pulse against her fingers, his life in her hand. That meant something.

"Miles? You only mentioned your aunt. What about your mom and dad?"

He smoothed every wrinkle from the towel he'd hung on the rack. "My dad was a high-level executive I never met. My mother worked for him before she died of leukemia."

Her heart melted all over again. "How old were you?"

"Almost four." His brow rippled. "Everyone wore masks and gloves and said, 'Don't touch her, you'll make her sick.'"

Talk about reinforcement.

"Aunt Beth took me home to her house. So many pretty things." He sighed.

"She told you not to touch."

"She wasn't mean."

"But didn't she ever hug you?"

His big shoulders rose and fell.

"You listen to me, Miles. Before we're done—you and me and Tia? You're going to give me the biggest bear hug ever."

He studied her like a program that had developed a fatal glitch.

"I don't mean now, and I don't mean tomorrow. But you better run if that's not okay with you."

He gulped. "Can I use your sink?"

"No."

He startled.

"You're not dirty. And you won't make me sick."

Her ringing phone broke their eye contact. "It's Tia, and I have to take it. The chief got shot last night."

His jaw dropped.

She brought the phone to her ear. "Tia?"

"Piper, do you feel up to driving? To the hospital?"

"Um, sure."

"Room 312."

She looked over at Miles. "We'll be right there." She hung up. "Come on. We're going to the hospital."

Miles bent his arms like a pretzel over his chest, his two fists framing his neck as though he had a bad chill. "No, no, no, no, no. No hospital."

"Tia needs us."

"People die in hospitals."

"Some do. But most get well." She snatched her purse. "Are you driving, or should I?"

"Do you know how many germs are in a hospital?"

"You can tell me as we drive."

She dug for her keys, but Miles formed a deep sigh. "I will drive."

She shot him a brilliant smile. "Come on, then." She locked up and stepped into the brisk morning. Half a block down the leaf-strewn sidewalk, she realized what car he was leading her to. Her mouth fell open.

"The engineering makes it very safe on mountain roads." He touched the handle, then opened the passenger door of the deep blue BMW Z4 Roadster.

"Omigosh." She slid into the buff-colored leather as she would a feather bed.

Miles fit surprisingly well, as though it had been formed to him.

"Miles…" she breathed. "How rich are you?"

He slid her a look. "That's relative. And it fluctuates."

She laughed. "And you could probably tell me down to the penny. But I don't want to know. Bob went on and on about the money he makes. I almost puked."

The big hands clenched.

"Don't get upset."

"It's my fault. Every other time you said no."

"Maybe I did do it for you, but that was my decision. Now fire it up, and let's feel this sweetness."

Miles looked at her. "I don't think you're real."

"You haven't seen me on a bad day. Well, I guess this was a bad day, but it's better now, so just get me to the hospital."

Obediently, Miles made the motor purr, and it was sexier than any roar. Last night she'd been tossed about, but Miles took the curvy highway with such precision she hardly moved in her seat. Her teddy had talent.

"My name is Forsythe," he said. "Miles Forsythe. Corny, I know."

"It's not corny. It's distinguished."

"If we don't die at the hospital, I'll show you my house."

The smile almost hurt her face. "I'm hoping real hard we don't die at the hospital."

Outside Jonah's flower-scented hospital room, Tia paced a hall that smelled of canned peas and tomato soup. Inside, the chaplain questioned Jonah. He'd been shot last night—she still didn't know how. He had burns and cuts and respiratory problems. Was he in any condition for this?

She moved closer to the wall to let a staff member with an instrument cart pass. Jonah had started it by proposing in her store. He'd been proposing in little ways this whole time, every time he tried to keep her safe, tried to make her see, to break her free of the blinders. He'd been saying he wanted her in his life a million different ways. But would he say it now?

The door opened, and the chaplain motioned to her. "He'd like to talk to you."

Quaking, she went in. Jonah's face was far too serious.

He reached for her hand. "This isn't what I wanted."

Her heart fell hard.

"I intended the whole big deal, the dress, the flowers, the string quartet."

She blinked back tears. "I think you have me confused with Reba."

He searched her face. "I want everybody to know you're the one."

"Jonah, it's always been you and me. Everything else would be extraneous."

He pulled her close and kissed her.

"I love you," she breathed.

"I love you more."

"You are so not going to win that one."

His eyes crinkled. "Wanna bet?"

She sniffled. "Are we doing this?"

"I need to know it's not because of this bullet hole in my side."

"You think almost losing you had no impact?"

He tightened his hold on her hand. "You're not losing me."

She brought his hand to her heart and pressed it there. "I need you. Every day. You fit all my ragged edges. And I believe this…covenant…can mend the places we've torn apart."

He nodded. "That's all I needed to know."

"Tia?"

She turned as Piper came in with…Miles?

Piper looked from Jonah to her. "What's the emergency?"

Tia swallowed the sudden tightness. "I need a maid of honor."

Piper squealed, "You're getting married?"

The chaplain came in with Jay. "This the one you wanted?"

Jonah nodded. "That one'll do."

Tia squeezed Jonah's hand. Maybe this wasn't how he'd wanted it, but nothing had ever felt so right.

———

He hadn't intended to cry. Not in front of Jay and the chaplain, Piper, and Miles, of all people. He could blame it on the pain, but that would be a lie. *"I pronounce you husband and wife"* undid him. Eyes filled, he kissed his bride long enough to drive the tears back, but they had all seen it. He didn't care nearly as much as he could have.

First order of business once he got out was to buy her a proper ring. Piper's aquamarine birthstone and Jay's silver wolf head—which they'd already returned—had only temporarily served. He would have made the ceremony as big and fancy as Tia wanted, but she only wanted him. Man, if that didn't start the tears again. He blinked hard and fast, but all eyes were on his beautiful wife.

Tia and Piper squeezed so long, he wasn't sure they'd separate. Miles looked like he might pass out. Jay eyed him as though he'd performed a shape change, then shook his head, smiling.

"No Cherokee wisdom?"

"No. But the Danes say, 'If envy were a fever, the whole world would be ill.'"

———

Hands clasped at her throat, Piper beamed all the way to the car. "I can't believe they did that. After all the pining and fighting, they're actually married. I'm so happy." She hugged herself.

Miles said, "I'm happy too."

"That we didn't die?"

He looked across the car top. "Not exactly normal, am I?"

"Oh, normal. Normal's overrated. Has your blood pressure dropped yet?"

"Probably."

"That's good."

He still looked pale, but he hadn't fainted or panicked or knocked anything over. She tipped her head. "Are you letting me into the car?" When he didn't move, she said, "You make a good statue, something titled *Cast in Stone*."

He swallowed. "More like *Petrified*."

She giggled. "We don't have to go to your house. We could just drive."

"Okay."

The highway back to Redford wound through one of the most ruggedly gorgeous panoramas she'd ever seen. Glacial ice streaked the stony reaches where the crevices stayed cool. The creek widened and narrowed, wending through the canyon, flanked by gold and russet and copper leafed trees and bushes. So beautiful. She sighed.

"What's the matter?"

"I was hoping I could put roots down here. Now Tia's married and the house is for sale. I guess I'm out."

"Can't you rent another room?"

"Maybe." She leaned her head back. "Miles?"

"Yes?"

"Can we just keep driving?"

"No."

She turned surprised.

"We're almost there." He put on his signal for the Pine Crest exit.

She held her breath as he wended past one marvelous home after another. His house nestled into a grove of golden white aspen with multi-colored shrubs and evergreens. A pond from the golf course lay sedately to one side with a carpet of lawn rolling over a slight hill. The house had clean lines and a contemporary style that managed to complement its setting.

"Wow."

"It's very nice inside."

"I imagine it is. But, Miles, if you don't want me in there, it's okay."

"We can wash off all those hospital germs." He shuddered. "Sick people with sick germs. We'll wash up."

She pictured an anticontamination chamber in his entry, but it was like any other except bigger, brighter, and more amazing in architectural design than anything she'd seen. "Wow," she said again.

"I designed it."

"Miles, you're amazing."

"My shower's upstairs. I'll use it now."

"If you're not back in three hours, I'm coming after you."

He gave her a troubled look, then turned and walked upstairs. She spent the next forty-five minutes walking all over the main level of his house. There was no dedicated library, but each area had shelves of books and cutting-edge electronics. As far as she could tell, that was where his spending money went.

That and new clothes. He came downstairs in fresh khaki slacks and a golf shirt, put the clothes he'd worn earlier into a plastic bag that he cinched and sent down a chute to a dumpster under the massive deck that looked over the gorge behind the house. She waited quietly while he performed his ritual, then he said, "There's a guest shower at the far end of the hall upstairs. It's never been used."

"That's fine, but I don't have a change of clothes."

"I'll bring you something from the ladies' boutique at the club."

"You belong to the country club?"

"It's required. I've never used the membership. But I toured the facility."

He would not relax with her wearing contaminated clothing, so she shrugged. "Size four, long."

"I'm going to set the alarm so no one can get in while you shower. If I'm not back, don't open an outside door."

"Will it yell at me if I do?"

"The noise is not pleasant."

"Well, thanks for keeping me safe."

She went up the stairs and along the inner balcony to a massive bath, steam sauna, and shower room. It might be overboard, but it was overboard in style. If he was going shopping, she may as well make this maiden flight worthwhile.

Later, in the flirty, flowered slacks, yellow silk shell, and three-quarter-sleeved jacket, she felt chic and pampered. She looked down at the beige, beaded-leather, moccasin-style sandals and splayed her toes. If she wasn't careful, she'd get used to this. "You have good taste."

"I described you to the salesclerk."

"Oh yeah? What did you say?"

He sent her an enigmatic glance from his seat beside her on the deck. "Enough for her to choose that."

She pouted. "You're not going to tell me?"

"It's called teasing."

"No, teasing would be, 'I told her you weigh four hundred pounds and have hairy warts.'"

"I would never say that."

She sipped the lemonade he had poured from the glass pitcher in his stainless steel french-door refrigerator.

"I said you have golden skin and sky blue eyes, a bubbly personality, and sunshiny smile. All clichés, but they are true."

Her mouth curved up. "Oh."

"I could have told her more, but she got the idea."

"You're sweet, Miles."

He stared out over the gorge. "I like you so much it makes my stomach ache. I know that isn't romantic, but there's a hole inside that gets bigger every time I say your name or think of you or…" He spread his hands. "Anything."

She stood up and walked to the galvanized metal rail, looking down the narrow, forested gorge, then glanced back, seeing his misery. "I won't lie to you, Miles. I need hugs."

His face drooped.

"Do you think you can learn to like it?"

He took ages to say, "I might hurt you."

"No." She shook her head. "Hugs don't hurt."

In spite of the brisk fall temperature, sweat beaded his hairline. "Could I…touch your hair?"

The smile broke over her. "Sure."

His hand might have been made of lead, but the big fingers came up, slowly extending from his palm. He brought them trembling to the hair hanging over her ear, a more intimate touch than a big bear hug, but she didn't say so.

Pressing his forearms to his head, he stepped back and looked down at her. "Someday," he said hoarsely, "I'm going to hug you."

Thirty

Let those love now who never loved before;
Let those who always loved, now love the more.
—THOMAS PARNELL

Chafing at the pain and confinement, Jonah leaned back in the bed. Earlier, the doctor had closed the ceremony by shooing everyone but Tia out and conveying the cheery news that he would not be released for several days at least, longer if infection developed in the bowel or surrounding tissue—a real possibility with gunshot wounds, Dr. Vargas had reiterated, even one that passed through. Foreign matter had repercussions in the human body that took time, rest, and care to heal.

Duly chastised but still impatient, he stroked Tia's hand. "This is not how I pictured our wedding night."

"I'm thankful you lived to have one." Tia frowned. "Have you seen the news?"

"I was there."

"A flaming meth lab? Assault rifles?"

"Redford's growing up. The mayor should be proud."

"The mayor tried to see you. So has every news outlet in the area. *'Police Chief Jonah Westfall was critically injured by gunfire in the meth lab incident that claimed the lives of two others.'*"

"I wasn't critical."

"Yes, Jonah, you were. And a half inch to the side might have been fatal. Not to mention toxic smoke, bruises, and burns."

"Hey." He pulled her close to him. "Enough."

"You said you were indestructible."

"I'm here, aren't I?"

"Why weren't you wearing a vest?"

"Someone else had it."

She shook her head, incomprehensibly. "Would you allow your officers—"

"No. It was stupid. The situation unfolded without a plan."

"Oh well, if that's all."

"Wife."

She raised her brows and jutted her chin.

"Don't tell me how to do my job."

"No, of course not." Only she could abuse those words so thoroughly.

"I apprehended an entire drug ring." He winced as the tiny shift in position shot pain through the rib.

"About that...I should have said *three* dead." She stroked his arm. "Officer Moser came to tell you Greggor didn't make it. Shrapnel from the explosion and burns."

Jonah looked down. "When?"

"About an hour ago. You were sleeping."

Three dead. And she was right. Besides the gunshot and the pursuant blood loss, he had a minor burn and cuts on one arm, a bruised spine and kidney. Kevlar would have been prudent.

"Officer Donnelly came with Officer Moser. She's desperate to see you."

Jonah scratched his jaw. He'd have to deal with that, but right now he'd leave her to Moser. He lay back and closed his eyes. "Ti?"

"Hmm?" She ran her fingers through his hair.

"Did you marry me? Or am I dreaming?"

"If it were my dream?" She leaned in and whispered in his ear.

Suddenly very much alive, he gripped the nape of her neck, his kiss long and deep.

———

Liz formed a smile for the woman who came in Monday morning with her Himalayan cat in a fancy carrier.

The woman smiled back. "Mary Carson. I have an appointment for Chelsea."

"I'm all ready for her."

Mrs. Carson glanced at the small television playing the news. "We've certainly hit the map with that story, haven't we?"

Liz had watched the aerial shot of flames, the burnt shack, and of course Chief of Police Jonah Westfall in the hospital, saying, "Redford doesn't tolerate crime." Again and again.

"We're lucky he wasn't killed. But I must say I'm less surprised by that whole affair than his getting married."

Liz stiffened. "His what?"

"Wedding. Right there in the hospital room. To my dear friend, Tia. I guess in life and death moments, you realize what really matters."

Life and death moments. What really matters.

The woman prattled on as Liz administered Chelsea's shots and performed the physical. She must have made the appropriate responses because Mrs. Carson paid and left, satisfied that her pet had been properly cared for. And it had. She was a good vet.

"I'm sorry, Lizzie." Lucy's voice was hardly more than a breath in her ear. It was the first time she'd risen from her bed in a long while.

"He deserves her. They deserve each other."

She would have cared for him as she cared for Lucy, unflinchingly, unsparingly, selflessly. She had seen the haunting in his eyes, yearning for what should not be. Now he had succumbed to Tia as to the bottle, sating himself, oblivious of the wreckage to come. She could have saved him.

"It's all right to cry."

Liz turned. "I would never cry for him."

Lucy stroked her face. "So strong. So brave."

"You're the brave one, Lucy." She had almost lost sight of that, so brave and precious, so indispensable.

"It's easy to be brave when I have you."

They embraced. Lucy had her, but how much longer would she have Lucy?

⸻

After seeing that Scout and Enola had everything they needed and that the pup was at least responsive, Tia brought Sarge his egg salad sandwich.

She sat down with a mug of hot chocolate, wishing her husband had sent her anywhere but here. Dying a thousand deaths, she said, "I don't know if Jonah told you—"

"That he went and married you?"

"Yes, that."

"I suppose you'll be taking over here now?"

"I certainly hope not."

He frowned at her. "I know you."

"No, Sarge, I don't think you do. You know my mother's version. And guess what? She never knew me either."

He growled, "What's your point?"

"My point is I think we both deserve to be taken at face value, where we are now, who we are today. Jonah will be more peaceful if you and I find a way to get along."

He studied her. "You love him?"

"I always have."

"Then I accept your recommendation. He's one of the few people I admire."

"He feels the same about you."

Sarge looked away. "Guess this wasn't how you imagined starting out together."

"I'm learning to take whatever comes and be glad for it."

"One tough cookie, huh?"

She shrugged. "When I have to be."

He turned back and studied her even harder. "You're more like your mother than I realized."

"Why would you say that?"

He shrugged. "She took things head on, just like you. After the affair, I thought she'd end the marriage."

"Affair?"

"But, being pregnant, she chose to stick it out, showed some real—"

"Are you saying my dad cheated?"

"Well, that depends." Sarge scratched his bristled jaw. "Which dad you mean."

Tia sat mute, unable to request clarification.

He grasped his mug and drank, then set it clumsily down. "I assumed you knew."

She started to shake. "My *mother* had an affair?" A dark shade seemed to come down, while at the same time everything grew clear. Her mother's hatred, her dad's disinterest. The projection of immorality onto her before she even knew right from wrong.

Why had Sarge sprung this on her the second day of her own marriage? But she saw in his face that he had believed she knew, had not intended to insult her. She pushed back from the table, went outside, and staggered to the creek. She looked up through the pines, to the leaden sky, drawing damp air into her lungs, at once dazed and vindicated.

It had not been her behavior or her nature or anything about her Stella rejected. No matter who she was, her mother would have hated her, the reminder of her sin—or of what she'd given up because of her. She pressed her hands to her face. Daughter of infidelity, destined to the same?

No. She would not put her sin on her mother as her mother had on her. She and Jonah had failed and paid for it. But she had paid for her mother's sin as well. How cruel and unfair was that?

She blinked back tears. "Lord." What would she tell someone calling for prayer? God is bigger than the storm, his grace a haven from the tempest. If life throws you overboard, then swim! She clenched her fists.

God had loved and forgiven her. He had given her hope and wisdom and purpose. With Jonah, she'd already found joy. How could she possibly care who had impregnated her mother? And yet...

She went inside and, gripping her mug, sat across from Sarge, who looked as if he wished he'd beaten a quick retreat. She appreciated that he hadn't. After releasing her top lip from her teeth, she asked, "Who was it?"

———

At the bakery counter, Piper placed the last selection into the box, drew a deep breath, and looked up at Miles, the only person there after closing time. "Tell me if I've completely lost my mind."

"Not completely. I could make a logarithm to determine the percentage of mind loss at any given time, but it's a constantly shifting, dynamic variable."

"What percentage of crazy am I now?"

"Just enough."

"I want Sarge to still feel a part of this. It's his business."

"He put you in charge."

She slid the box lid on. "Yep. And raised me one whole dollar every hour."

"That makes you the manager."

She beamed at him for not belittling her wage. It was ridiculous, she knew. But she was proud of that dollar.

"When he came in that one time, it seemed like he was telling the bakery good-bye. I hate that. It's hard enough knowing Tia won't be working next door."

"You should expand."

"What?"

"You could open the wall and triple your seating and add more menu options."

She looked at the brick wall between the businesses. "Make it a bakery bistro?"

"Soup and salads."

"And quiche."

"And desserts."

She bit her lower lip. "And hire someone to work the counter and wait tables. Want a job?"

He looked aghast.

"Kidding."

"I know. But it's no less horrifying."

She took the money pouch out of the safe. She'd make the deposit on the way to Jonah's—Tia's—the Westfall's house. "With that kind of business, I might make tips or have a real salary. I could afford to stay."

"You shouldn't delay. Once something else goes in, the chance is gone." Miles looked ready to take the wall down the minute she said the word.

"Sarge will have to love the idea—and he'll need money to expand."

"Or have a partner."

"My three cents won't go very far."

"What about your family?"

She shook her head. "They offer all the time, but I can't take it. You know why." Since he'd been so open with her, she'd given him the same.

"A silent partner then. Someone who finances but isn't involved in the business—unless you wanted him to design the expansion and give an opinion on menu items."

Her mouth dropped open. "You?"

"Is that going too far? Did I overstep?"

"No, it's…it's… I don't know what it is."

"I make investments."

"I appreciate the offer, Miles, but…"

"I want you to stay."

She released a slow breath. "It's a long shot that Sarge will even consider it. Change is hard for him."

"Change is hard."

They went out, and she locked the bakery, then took the box from him.

He said, "Can I see you tonight?"

She smiled. "Okay. We could try out some soup recipes in your big sterile stainless steel kitchen."

"Okay."

She drew a deep breath. "Well, wish me luck."

"You don't need luck. Everything you need is right inside you."

"What a nice thing to say."

"I don't lie."

Tears rose. "I know." She held his gaze like an eye hug, then jumped when a car skidded in the street.

"What the—"

Bob Betters hung an arm out the Camaro window, glaring. "You really do prefer that freak-tard."

She turned stiffly. "He's smarter than you with his brain on hibernate."

He pointed his thick ringed finger. "You caused me a lot of trouble. I haven't forgotten." His tires squealed as the smell of burnt rubber engulfed them.

Coughing, she noticed Miles's bone-white knuckles. "Don't bother. He's just a bully."

———

Leaning forward in the bed, Jonah stared. "Buckley?"

Tia nodded. "She confided in her good friend Sarge." He was almost crushing her hand, and she wiggled it looser. "What does it change? Neither one of them cared two fish for me."

"Does he know?"

That gave her pause. Maybe he didn't. She looked so much like her mother; neither the mayor nor her erstwhile dad would know by recognizing himself. Would Stella tell Sarge and not Owen Buckley? "Maybe that's why he cut it off—if he was the one who did. The point is, I don't care. I only told you because you're…the one I've never kept things from."

"Except for two college degrees. A prayer line. EMT certification…"

"That's just stuff I've done. The EMT isn't even valid still. That was way back when Reba first left, and you were hunting every female that walked."

"I was out of my head, Ti. Self-destructive."

She stared at their joined hands. "I've never had anyone but you."

"Once I got sober, there's been no one but you."

She met his eyes.

"That's the truth. Jay will tell you. I hung on to what I couldn't have rather than settle for someone I didn't want. Even for a night."

"And Reba?"

He shook his head. "No. I wanted her for all the wrong reasons and…truthfully? We weren't even compatible."

"And you know this because…"

"I went looking for you. If you hadn't pushed me away—"

"What was I supposed to do? Start dating you? They *hated* me. You talk about shunned? They did everything but wear garlic. I slept on the mountain instead of my bed because the freezing night was warmer than my home."

Tears filled his eyes. "I didn't know."

"I didn't want you to."

"I should have seen. But I was too messed up, thinking I'd killed the bastard I'd dreamed of killing for so long."

Through her own tears, she whispered, "How did you make it?"

"God. And Jay." He rolled her fingers one by one. "And the hope of you."

She wiped a tear. "I thought you hated religion."

"I hated the sham."

"But you go to church. The same one even."

He leaned back, nodding. "God…found me there. In my confusion, my disgust, my hatred—God said it doesn't matter what anyone in these pews says or does. I am."

Tia blinked. "That's profound."

"Jay pulled me through a bender that should have killed me. I was…so empty. I had nothing left. So I offered that. And in return? Unconditional love." He huffed a breath. "I had no concept."

"Oh, Jonah."

"That's how I held on. It's how I'll make this marriage work."

"How we'll make it work." She kissed his mouth, salted with their tears. "I won't doubt you again."

"I won't give you reason to."

She pressed her hand to his heart. "This is better than how we would have spent this time."

"No."

Laughing, she kissed him again. "Well…"

He stroked her cheek. "You're the love of my life."

Thirty-One

Nothing is more noble, nothing more venerable than fidelity.
Faithfulness and truth are the most sacred excellences and
endowments of the human mind.
—MARCUS TULLIUS CICERO

Following Tia's directions to Jonah's cabin, Piper could not stop thinking about an expanded bakery bistro. There weren't that many restaurants in Redford. The hotel, and the diner, and the Summit Saloon. Hers—Sarge's—would be completely different. She chewed her cuticle. If he'd even consider it.

For the first time she had the urge to pray for something *she* wanted. Was that okay too? Tia had said she couldn't mess it up. *So, God? I'd really like to stay. Could you give Sarge just a wee little nudge?*

She bit down on the nail and remembered Jonah. Show the confidence to do the job. She pulled the fingernail out from her teeth and knocked on the door.

Jonah's cabin was nothing like Miles's home, but no less appealing. She could smell the lumber of the new part built onto the back. She smelled the wood smoke from the chimney. Gripping the box, she knocked again.

She heard the scrape and bump of the walker long before he opened the door. "Hi, Sarge."

"Where's the fire?"

"Sorry. I wasn't sure you could hear the knocking in the back."

"What's that?" He zeroed in on the box.

"This is a sampling of specials I've made since you said I could. I want you to decide which ones should be keepers."

"Why should I decide?"

"Well, I thought I'd know by which ones sold and which ones didn't. But they all sell out, so I thought you could judge."

"Oh, you did, did you?" But he moved aside to let her in.

She opened the box on the table, and the fresh, mingled aromas rose like ambrosia. "Willing to try?"

He sat down, growling. "You won't go away unless I do."

She beamed. "Start with the wild huckleberry maple sugar coffeecake." She cut a corner and handed it to him. "I might not be able to get huckleberries all the time, but I bet good old blueberries would work too."

He ate the piece with a shifting emotion that was the polar opposite of Miles's poker face. Brow buckled, he closed his eyes, chewing and swallowing, then groaned.

"Sarge?"

He put his palms flat on the table and opened his eyes. "What tomfoolery did you pull to make something so…"

"Yummy?"

He glowered. "What's next?"

She had started him on her very favorite—Miles's too—so he'd be likely to continue. "Why don't you choose?"

"What is this, a game?"

"This is serious business, Sarge." And she hadn't even broached the most serious part. "Try the sage and lemon salmon puff."

"Fish pastry?" He scrunched his face. "No, thanks."

"Then the apple smoked-turkey arugula croissant."

"Croissants are too time consuming." But he accepted the part she cut for him and popped it in his mouth with another attempt at disinterest. Humoring her.

"They are complicated, but I've got the process down so it's not unreasonable. I think the results are worth it. But you're the judge."

"Sure I'm the judge," he grumbled. "Don't think I can't see mutiny."

"No mutiny, I promise. But I want to talk to you about something. You know how Tia's closing the shop next-door?"

"Closing her mother's store." He shook his head.

"What would you think about expanding? We could knock down the wall and make it a bakery bistro serving breakfast and lunch, with your old favorites and my new specials."

He stared at her as though she'd told him he had three days to live.

"If the Pine Crest annexation happens and with all the new development, we'd have the population to support another restaurant. We're already known for the best baked goods—"

"Were known. Not sure that's still so."

"You bet it is."

He scowled. "Even if you're right, you think I'm made of money? Paying you is all the expanding I can afford."

"What if you had a partner?"

"You?"

She shook her head. "A silent financial partner investing in both of us."

His eyes reddened. "That store has served this community for thirty years. Now you want to change it."

"It would be a change."

Sarge slumped. "Who's this silent partner?"

"Miles Forsythe. He's an inventor whose first patent at sixteen kind of set him up. And he's a whiz at architectural design. He could…"

Sarge looked up, clearly distressed.

Piper patted his hand. "You just think about it, Sarge. If someone else snaps up the Half Moon, then that's our answer." She tried not to show how badly she hoped it wouldn't be. "But it wouldn't hurt your retirement to have—"

"What do I care about retirement?"

"Well, then a new venture."

"I'm too old for that."

Piper crossed her arms. "That's playing both sides."

He glowered. "Watch your step, soldier."

"Yes sir."

"You talked your way into this outfit, but you have a lot to learn."

"Yes sir, I do."

"Takes more than fancy recipes to keep a business on its feet for the long march."

"That's your job, Sarge."

He rubbed his jaw. "You really want this? You want it so much you can taste it?"

"Tastes as good as that huckleberry maple sugar coffeecake."

His mouth spasmed as he fought off the smile and lowered his brow. "Tell your investor to put together an offer for the Half Moon. We'll see where it goes."

Squealing, Piper threw her arms around him, not easy the way he was bent. "Oh, Sarge, you won't be sorry."

To her surprise he didn't say he already was, but rather, "Make me proud, soldier."

———

Recognizing the distinctive throat clearing, Jonah opened his eyes. Through a new row of "get well" plants on the swing arm table, he saw Moser—and Sue.

"If you really need to sleep, we can come back." Moser's careful elocution assured they would be back, they would deal with it.

He sighed. "Leave us alone, Moser."

Moser looked at Sue. "I'll be outside." His shoes squeaked on the mopped linoleum.

She waited until the door clicked, then dove in. "I'm sorry, Chief."

"I'm sure you are."

"I couldn't stop myself. Every time I thought of Sam dead and those scumbags passing more and more drugs, Sean Bolton selling at the school—where Eli will go one day—I just couldn't let it go."

"We had leads. We had an active investigation. We had manpower."

"I know." She paced. "But Caldwell knew Beatty and Newly had tagged him. When I relieved Beatty—"

"How exactly did you do that?"

She gulped. "I told him you were mixing things up. He took my patrol."

With a slow blink Jonah added that to the cauldron.

"Caldwell didn't notice me. He made his move, and I couldn't miss the chance. We couldn't miss the chance."

"To blow up a meth lab? Incinerate three people? Injure fellow officers? You went in unprepared and forced the action."

"I knew once you were there—"

"You disobeyed direct orders."

"I know. I was so mad when you sent me back, but…" Her face contorted. "I could have been killed. And Eli would have had no parents." She pressed a hand to her belly. "You were right every step of the way."

"Law enforcement involves risk. Any traffic stop can prove fatal. It's my job to minimize the risk to my officers. It's your job to use proper judgment and trust me."

She stood straight. "If this costs me my job, I understand."

He scrutinized her, weighing and sifting. "You're on three weeks' suspension. Use that time to decide if you want to be a cop, or if you're just a vigilante."

Her breath came in a gasp. "I will. Thank you, Chief. Jonah. Thank you."

"Send Moser in." Then to Moser, "What's the word from Hao on Sam?"

"The meth was laced with PCP. At that dose, a fatal cocktail."

"Sam might not have known. Can Hao give us homicide equivocal or accidental?"

"Already did."

Jonah settled back in the bed. "She'll get the life insurance?"

"Far as I know."

"Is my wife outside?"

Moser nodded. "And I might say about time, Chief. About time."

———

Propped up in the bed, Lucy's lips were blue-tinged violets, her forget-me-not eyes overlarge in sunken sockets. In just the last hours, her skin had grown so pale it glowed, thin threads of veins at her temples. She looked up from the puppies in her lap. "They're so still."

Liz felt her chest constrict as though bands were crushing the breath from her. She had thought, really thought… "They love it when you hold them."

Lucy smiled. "So soft. So sweet." She labored over the words, drawing a rasping breath that caused a sympathetic rasp in Liz's throat.

"You should rest." She saw the fatigue in every part of her twin.

"No use."

"Don't say that." Liz crouched down beside the bed, taking Lucy's hand between hers. "You need to fight. You can't give up."

"I'm so tired."

Liz searched Lucy's face, willing her to continue. Fear and fatigue had settled deep inside her as well. But she wouldn't give up. "I'm going to fix everything."

Lucy looked away, fighting for each breath. "Lizzie, you should…let me go."

She is part of me, my own self and not me. I feel her dying.

"Lucy. Do not let go." She gathered the pups into her arms, crying. For them, for her. No more experiments, no more attempts. It had to be now.

"Do you remember the park?" Lucy whispered.

Arm in arm, we prance across the park. We are special, rare, priceless. No one knows what we share so purely, so completely, so without regret. What do we care for the stares on the lonely faces?

"It had a merry-go-round." Lucy's voice had a small child's singsong tone.

"I remember." Liz smiled.

Swings and slides and seesaws had been unaccommodating, but they'd ridden the merry-go-round endlessly, Lucy's head against her shoulder, eyes closed. Liz had kept hers wide open and watched everything spin. In a whirl, she'd seen the faces staring, the fingers pointing, the whispers hidden behind hands. They didn't know. They could not imagine the joy of plurality, of complete unity.

Only we know, our minds so synchronized we hardly need to speak, our delight in each other complete.

Yet into that joy had come needle pricks of desire to run without Lucy holding her back, to fling out her arms and fly solo. Shame dizzied her. Lucy had needed her then and needed her now. "It won't be long. I've found the one I needed."

"Oh, Lizzie," Lucy breathed. "Who is it?"

Liz clutched the lifeless pups.

"A friend of Tia's. She's perfect."

———

"He said yes!" Piper shrilled, one hand on the steering wheel, the other on the cell phone. "At least, he said put together an offer and we'll see where it goes."

Miles said, "It will go."

His confidence boosted her already buoyant mood. "I sure hope you were serious."

"Have I ever not been?"

"Umm, yes." She laughed. "I went by the hospital to make sure Tia didn't mind if we took over her shop, but she's happy too."

"That's good."

"Anyway, I know we said your house tonight, but I forgot to water the plants. For, like, two weeks. Tia just reminded me."

"That's okay."

"Can you come over? We can still try out some recipes."

"I could make dinner."

"Really?"

"I do know how to cook."

She used her signal to pass someone on the highway. "I should think so with that gourmet kitchen. Or we could go out."

"I don't eat out if I haven't seen the kitchen."

"So that's why you scoped out my pantry?"

"I'd rather not remember that."

"It's one of my treasured Miles moments." She slowed as she entered the city limits. "I'll be home in about five minutes."

"I'll shower and see you there."

"Okay." He could have come straight over, but who cared if he liked getting clean? A lot.

She parked beside the house and got out. She might not be living here for long, but if their plan worked—

She felt the sting and thought the monster of all wasps had stung moments before her limbs got spongy and her head rushed.

Thirty-Two

When our two lives grew like two buds that kiss
At lightest thrill from the bee's swinging chime,
Because the one so near the other is.
—GEORGE ELIOT

n the waning western light, Jonah reflected her surprise. "Let me get this straight. Piper, Sarge, and Miles?"

Tia nodded. While the nurse had changed his bandages, she had slipped into the hall to hear Piper's news. "It sounds like Sarge is excited. He told Piper to make him proud."

"And Miles."

"Piper thinks he's something special. All the boys in town buzzing around her like bees…" She smiled.

"How does that even work? With no touching?"

Incomprehensible to Jonah Westfall—thank God. "They'll have to overcome the barriers." She sat on the side of the bed where they'd lowered the rail, frustrated by their own barriers. "His affection for Piper and hers for him should be powerful incentive."

"I'm experiencing powerful incentive." He clasped her knee.

"Because you thought about touching."

"Come here." He caught her face and kissed her, causing a buzz that she realized belatedly was the phone in her pocket.

His lips moved against hers, "Ignore it."

"It could be the Hopeline." She drew back and checked, then curious, answered, "Hello, Miles."

Her heart thumped when he said, "Piper's missing."

"What do you mean?" She'd just seen her, just sent her off, beaming with her good news.

"She said to meet at her house, but she's not here."

Tia checked her watch. More than enough time for Piper to get home, but that didn't mean trouble—except maybe in this man's precise world. "Maybe she didn't hear you at the door."

"I tried all the doors."

"I guess she's late."

"She isn't just late. She's in trouble."

Trouble? "Hold on a minute." She pressed a button. "You're on speaker with Chief Westfall, Miles. Tell us what's wrong."

"Bob Betters threatened her. Outside the bakery. He said she caused him trouble and he wouldn't forget that."

To Jonah, "Is Bob out?"

"He made bail that first night."

She rolled her eyes.

Miles again: "He threatened her, and she said I should come to her house and she's not here."

"Don't panic, Miles. There are a lot of possibilities."

Jonah said, "I'll call in, have them check Bob out."

The jerk. He would deserve the hassle for the threat alone. But her chest squeezed. "She was driving home from the hospital. Can the highway patrol—"

"I'll get that too."

"Miles, I'll come over and check the house, but she might have stopped for something. Maybe you beat her there."

"She said five minutes. She had to water the plants. I took a shower. And I picked flowers."

"I'll be there as soon as I can." If it proved to be nothing, she could at least calm him. But it didn't feel like nothing.

She hung up, and Jonah caught her wrist. "What are the chances he'll freak out?"

"Miles is the least of my worries. She told him five minutes. That's specific."

"Things happen."

"Jonah, Bob drugged her once, intending sexual assault."

"I'll send someone to the house."

"Exactly how many officers do you have with no broken legs or bullet holes who aren't suspended?"

His hand tightened. "Don't go inside until an officer arrives."

"Are you kidding me?" She punched the callback on her phone. "Miles, there's a key in the birdhouse. If Bob has Piper inside—"

Jonah spoke over her. "Use only what force is necessary to subdue him. Do you hear me, Miles? Tia?"

But she had shut the phone off and run for the door.

———

Jonah put the calls through to dispatch, but something didn't sit right. Bob was a sleaze, but he was also a sneak and a coward. He might make a threat, but would he—

"How are you doing, Chief?" Nurse Nancy raised his arm to apply the cuff and take his blood pressure.

"I'm good to go."

"Where would you place your pain, one to ten?"

He answered her questions. The pain had lessened. No excessive bleeding, swelling, burning. His sluggish body functions were what they were. Breathing better. Eyes still stung from the toxic smoke. "But listen. I should be out of here. I have a job to do." And precious few others available to do it.

"I'll pass the word to Dr. Vargas."

The doctor with the stone ear. "I tried him."

"I'm sure you did."

He returned to the ruminations that had not ceased the entire time. Bob Betters had snuck Piper a roofie and might have assaulted her if he hadn't been caught. But he probably could have gotten away with that. This was different. Acting on a threat made in daylight with witnesses?

He shook his head. An accident on the highway was more likely. The state patrol would check that out. He took a sip through the bent straw, the water almost room temperature. Tia had surely tried Piper's cell phone, but he called it himself and got no answer. If she hadn't stopped somewhere, then what? Miles? What did any of them know about the guy?

He reached for the laptop Moser had brought him, set a search for Miles Forsythe. Rubbing his burning eyes, he read one and then another article, searched an impressive Web site, then the law-enforcement database and found no complaints or arrests, not even a citation.

The highway patrol called with an all clear on accidents along the stretch of road between the hospital and Redford. She had not crashed or broken down. He called Beatty again. The rookie officer on duty—and overtime as Tia had pointed out—had been code six on a domestic disturbance. He came on now.

"Go ahead, Chief."

"Have you located Robert Betters?"

"On my way now."

"Anyone on shift with you?"

"Negative." With only Beatty, Moser, and McCarthy, they'd been pulling what backup they could from the sheriff's department that still had crew out with flu.

"I'm redirecting you to Sprague Street, house number 18. We're looking for a white female, approximate height five-nine, blond hair, age twenty-one, eye color blue."

"Would that be Piper, Chief?"

"It is." He shouldn't be surprised the officer knew her name and address. It suddenly struck him they hadn't checked for her car. If she'd made it to the house and wasn't there, he'd be concerned.

"Check that location for a vehicle. If it's there and she's not, put out an APB. Be advised of an incident of harassment around 3 p.m. today."

"Copy, Chief. Would that be Robert Betters?"

"Affirmative. Beatty, I want you to scope the location for any sign of struggle. What's your ETA?"

"Leaving a domestic on Marburry. ETA ten minutes."

"You've got two people possible on the scene—" if Tia had arrived by the time Beatty did. "Miles Forsythe witnessed the earlier threat, also the last person to speak to her."

"Okay."

Receiving a call back, Jonah asked the deputy sheriff to help locate Bob Betters, gave her the background on the previous arrest and the current harassment. If Bob was unaccounted for, they'd focus there—when they got there—if they got there. He clenched his hands in frustration and reminded himself this could be nothing. Nowhere near enough time to consider her missing.

However, he still asked himself who else would have cause to bother her. He'd seen her with a group her age and sometimes, as on the night Sarge fired her, with one or another in particular. No indication of animosity. He had a hard time picturing it.

The only time he'd seen her worked up or heard a bad word toward anyone was when she defended Tia from…Liz.

———

Pulling up to the house beside Piper's car, Tia heaved a sigh of relief. But then Miles came around from the back, shaking his head.

Tia frowned. "She's not in the house?"

"I checked everywhere. And the plants aren't watered."

"But…her car's here." She moved around to the driver's side and froze. Keys lay in the dirt and, just behind the tire, a beaded leather sandal. Tia pressed her hands to her mouth, dread descending.

"Something's wrong. Something's really wrong." Miles bent and searched around and under the car, but she was already running for the door. If Miles had looked or even called out, he still could have missed her. She might be too scared to answer him.

Yanking open the door, she called, "Piper, it's Tia. Are you here?"

No response.

Where would she hide? She pulled open all the doors on the ground level, the kitchen, the mud room. A terrible foreboding sank in as she climbed the stairs with Miles just behind. Please God, don't let them find her dead.

Miles seemed to sense it and emitted a high-pitched hum.

"Miles. What were your plans?"

"We were going to discuss the bistro. I was making dinner. Everything I brought is on the porch. She didn't answer the door. She would have answered the door."

Quaking, Tia went into Piper's room. The bed was neat, the springs high enough she could see the wooden floor and nothing else beneath. Holding her breath, she opened the closet. Nothing but clothes.

"I looked there. I looked everywhere."

She pressed a hand to the tear that streaked down her cheek. "I'm not doubting you, Miles. I just have to see for myself." They searched the other rooms, including the attic accessed by a pull-down ladder. No Piper.

She jumped when the doorbell rang.

They shared a look, then Miles preceded her into the hall and down the stairs. Seeing a uniform through the glass, he froze. Had they found her on the highway?

She swallowed her fear, then remembered. "Jonah sent him." She reached around Miles and opened the door to a fresh-faced officer maybe no more than Piper's age.

"I'm Officer Beatty, ma'am. The chief requested I search the premises."

"We already did. She's not here. But there's something you need to see." She took him around the side and showed him the keys and sandal.

"Did you touch anything?"

She shook her head, waiting while he photographed the items where they lay.

"Did you see anything else out of place or missing, besides...Piper?"

Tia jolted. "You know her?"

The officer nodded. "From Java Cava." He looked up, squinting in the shafting light. "You're Miles?"

Miles looked troubled.

"She's mentioned you."

His hands squeezed and unsqueezed. "I was supposed to meet her here. She said five minutes, and she had to water the plants." He had fallen into the speech pattern of a high-stress episode. This qualified.

"Mrs., um, Westfall?"

She turned. "Tia, please."

"I do need to look inside."

"Of course."

"If you'll wait here."

She nodded, knowing he was following orders but chafing at the delay. Piper was not in the house. She looked at the bag of groceries Miles had brought to make their meal. Piper would have enjoyed that.

After searching, at length, Officer Beatty came back outside. "Would she have walked somewhere?"

"Not without her sandal." Tia's voice broke. "Please. Is someone looking for Bob Betters?"

"Let me check with the station." He went down the walk and into his squad car. A good kid, no doubt.

She closed her eyes, wishing, *wishing* Jonah were not incapacitated in a hospital bed. How many times had she resented his supercompetence, his overprotectiveness? She needed him now. Piper needed him. Miles shifted from foot to foot, needing Jonah too.

Officer Beatty stepped out of the car, "Deputy Faulk questioned Robert Betters. He's been at the dealership since three with witnesses."

Tia pressed a hand to her heart, relieved and frustrated.

A voice came over the radio. "Unit two, come in."

The officer grabbed his radio. "Unit two, go ahead."

"We have a B and E in progress. 217 Brockhurst. Code three."

"Responding code three." Officer Beatty looked over the roof of his cruiser. "I put out an all-points bulletin for Piper. You two could canvass the neighborhood, see if she's at a different house. And don't worry, we'll find her." He swung into his car and hit the lights and siren.

Tia stared after him. Don't worry? Piper wasn't his only concern. The depleted force was stretched so thin, how could they hope to find her? If Piper had run to the neighbors, she would answer her cell phone. She would have called for help. Or called Miles. Or her. Tia paced.

Think. If not Bob, then who?

Please God. Why would someone take Piper? Unless it wasn't about Piper but the people who loved her. Without thinking, she gripped Miles by the arm. "Quick. Come with me."

With the laptop burning his thighs, Jonah searched Liz/Elizabeth Rainer. In the search he'd run of the criminal database when he first suspected her of the animal mutilations, he had found no arrests or warrants, no juvie record sealed or unsealed. Now it occurred to him there could be something else, an accident or incident that had caused her injury and the emotional instability he'd seen that night looking into her eyes. The chance it had made the news was slim, but he followed his instincts—and found it.

Conjoined twins Lizzie and Lucy Rainer—Controversial separation surgery. He stared at the photo of blond pigtailed girls, one resting her chin on the other's shoulder.

A stone sank down inside him.

He read under his breath, "From birth, eight-year-old conjoined twins Lizzie and Lucy Rainer have been inseparable. However, Lucy's failing health has driven the controversial decision to separate the twins, even though the girls have expressed no desire to live apart. Doctors say the complicated and risky separation surgery would give Lizzie a strong chance of survival."

Only Lizzie?

"The twins, who were featured on *Good Morning America,* are literally joined at the hip, at which point their spines diverge. Lizzie has all major organs while Lucy's incomplete complement are underdeveloped. Her poor health has weakened both twins, and survival of either is unlikely without separation.

"Controversy has spiked over the decision to forfeit one twin to save the other. Dr. Marcus Verigo admits Lucy's chances of surviving separation are remote. 'Lizzie controls her two arms and two of their three legs. Her pulmonary and digestive systems have predominately supported both girls, but her ability to maintain that has reached a critical point. Without the surgery both twins will die,' says Dr. Verigo. Representatives of the family say they will deeply mourn the loss of their daughter Lucy if the surgery proves fatal."

This had to be behind the animal experiments. Understanding what happened? Finding a way to help other conjoined twins? He read the brief follow-up article.

Conjoined twin Lucy Rainer dies in surgery. Proponents on both sides launch debate on the moral and ethical repercussion... He skimmed down to the final sentence. *The family asks to be allowed to grieve privately.*

Jonah looked at the second photograph, how playful and innocent they were. His first impressions of Liz were that she was strong and confident and compassionate. He imagined her literally carrying her sister, being strong for both of them—but ultimately not strong enough.

Had they gone into surgery knowing only one would come out? He didn't know which would have been worse, for Liz to know Lucy would die or to lose her unprepared. Certainly Liz was wounded and unstable, but what could it possibly have to do with Piper?

He traced back through all their interactions up to Scout. His chest went cold. If she'd hurt the pup to punish him, what would she do to punish Tia? He shoved the laptop onto the table, reached down, and disconnected his IV.

Thirty-Three

We were two and had but one heart between us.
—FRANÇOIS VILLON

Two steel surgical tables side by side. Just like when they'd wheeled her, sedated but not yet anesthetized, into the bright room. She had stared at the two tables thinking that for the first time they'd have separate beds. With Lucy's arm wrapped around her chest, her head nestled into her neck, fear had formed a taste on the back of her tongue, a bitter taste like tears held too long.

"Lizzie?" The word came into her mind since Lucy had grown too weak to speak.

"Don't be scared, Lucy."

"I wish I were you. You're never scared."

But she was. When Lucy had gone into the deep sleep the night before the surgery, they had told her, "Lizzie, the separation could give you a normal life." And the scary, scary thing was she had wanted it—but only for a moment. Until she remembered she had a special life. They had said so from the start. She and Lucy would always have each other.

"I don't want to be alone, Lizzie."

"You won't, I promise."

Someone moaned. Liz shook herself. The horse tranquilizer was wearing off. She hadn't intended it to take Piper through surgery. That would require anesthesia. She dragged the tarp to the nearer table, untied the thin rope threaded through the eyeholes.

Even lame, she was strong, and Piper, though taller, was slight. She looked to the other table where her mutilated sister lay, one leg hanging from a concave torso, so many missing organs. How she had survived so long was a mystery, a miracle. But they'd been miracles from the start.

Unconscious, she had felt no pain, no cutting, no untangling. But she had felt Lucy leave. She had felt the separateness begin.

———

As Tia drove, Miles hunched beside her, gripping his big knees. Over-whelmed with concern for Piper, he had not reacted to her touch but rushed with her into the Xterra. In a calmer voice than she could have pro-duced, he said, "If she wanted to hurt her, why did she take her?"

Tia frowned. "What do you mean?"

"She cut the pup, but she didn't take the pup."

"She wanted Jonah to bring it to her."

"She could have cut Piper. But you wouldn't take her to a vet. You would go to a hospital."

"So you think"—Tia turned too sharply, and the tires squealed—"she wants me to find her?"

"She could have just hurt her, but she didn't."

Tia tried to put herself in Liz's place. The woman had come to the house and to the store. Both times she'd seen her with Piper. *"What are you doing here?"* And Piper's *"I live here."* Liz must have hoped she would guess, known she would act.

Tia drew a deeper breath than she had yet. "It does her no good to hurt Piper. If she wanted to lure me—" Or was she the real target? Maybe… "It's Jonah she wants. She despises me."

Miles turned. "You would call him to help Piper."

Her knuckles whitened. "Doesn't she know he's in the hospital?"

Miles shrugged, miserable. "To help Piper, maybe…"

"He's been shot, Miles. What can he do?"

"But if you called him, he might help."

Lord. Groping, she raised her phone, speed-dialed and, when he answered, said, "Jonah. I think it might be Liz."

"I think so too." He sounded winded. "And pathology could be extreme."

"What do you mean?"

"She had a sister."

"Yes, I know. She's ill. Liz buys her scented melts."

"No listen. They were twins, conjoined twins. Her sister died in separation."

"What?" She thought of Liz shopping, the tenderness in her eyes, her brittle smile. "Did you know about a sister?"

"She never said a word. Whatever she's doing, Ti, it stems from that. The raccoons. All of it."

The raccoons. The cats. The…pups. "I thought it was like Scout. That she was luring us—you—to her again."

"I don't know what it is. But you keep away from her. I'm on my way there now."

"Well," Tia turned in and hit the brakes. "I'm already there."

———

An antiseptic smell filled the room as Liz sterilized the instruments, light glinting off the stainless steel. Attaching Lucy's damaged organs to Piper's would be the most tenuous part. But without that Lucy would die.

She took her twin's limp hand and kissed it, then laid it gently back. "I wish this could be me, Lucy, but I have to perform the surgery. I've done the best I could." Her twin was so small, had hardly grown at all. Piper had strong legs, a strong back, healthy organs. She could carry her, sustain her. She would not let Lucy die.

Piper stirred. Liz bent and slipped her arms under the young woman's back, clasping her wrists over the breastbone. She pulled her up to sit, and Piper's head lolled. She had found Lucy a beautiful body. Only the best for Lucy.

And when her twin had someone else? What then?

Rest.

She pushed the thought away. With all her strength, she rolled Piper's upper body onto the table, pushed her hips and legs until she lay on her side. Piper blinked. Should she sedate her again? She had hoped she wouldn't have to. Anesthesia was tricky enough, but Piper gripped the edge of the table, fighting for consciousness. She had no choice.

Liz reached for a needle, just enough to keep her still until all was ready. "I'm doing this for Lucy. She'll die without you."

"Liz," Tia said behind her.

Liz snatched a scalpel from the sterilized tray and held it to Piper's neck. She turned to Tia, frozen beside an enormous man.

"What are you doing?" Tia's voice was calm, caring, but she knew better.

"I'm saving Lucy." She looked at the table, saw Lucy's pleading eyes. "She can't make it on her own. She isn't strong enough."

She expected a harsh response, but Tia's eyes softened. "You love her so much."

"More than you could know."

Tia took a step toward her. "But you can't save her, Liz. As much as you want to now, as much as you wanted to then."

Liz jerked. *She's awake. Doctor, she's looking.* Coming out of anesthesia. Seeing her sister, what was left of her sister… Then darkness.

"Lizzie," Lucy moaned.

Liz shook her head. "They took you once, Luce, but they won't take you again."

Tia took another step. "You've done everything you can to keep her alive. But I know you're tired."

"No."

"That's why you needed Piper. Because you can't do it alone. It's too much."

"I'm the strong one." Liz shook away the flashes of Lucy on the operating table. She had been a whole person before they cut her away. "Stop it."

Tia moved in again. "It must have been like losing yourself."

"My other self," Liz breathed in a voice closer to Lucy's.

A siren sounded outside, another farther away.

Her whole body quaked. "I have to save her."

Tia's voice came soft and low. "The only way you can is to save yourself."

Liz shook her head. "Why should I?"

"You're as valuable as Lucy."

She clenched her jaw. "They cut her off like a tumor, a malignancy." She heard someone at the door, saw Jonah with a gun held down along his leg. Would he shoot her? End it now? Liz trembled.

"Step back, Tia." His voice was firm, commanding.

But she didn't. Tia held out her hand. "Give Lucy the dignity she deserves. Let her die in peace."

Liz looked over, expecting Lucy's pleading eyes, the rasping breath, but the table was empty. A racking sorrow started deep inside, wrenching her apart with an animal groan more primitive than words.

The scalpel clattered to the floor. She stared at Tia, a woman whose friendship she had coveted, at the young woman on the table who had known that friendship. She felt Jonah's grip on her elbow, the man she had hoped to love, saw the deep concern in his eyes. Maybe it was real, but how would she know? How would she ever know real again?

———

Confused and disoriented, Piper pressed up from the table.

Tia stood beside her asking questions, but before she could answer, Miles crossed the room, pulled her into a hug, and squeezed her tight.

"Wow," she breathed. "Wow."

Thirty-Four

For if they fall, the one will lift up his fellow; but woe to him
that is alone when he falleth: for he hath not another to help
him up.

—ECCLESIASTES 4:10, KING JAMES VERSION

Seeing Jonah wince as he eased out of the Bronco, Tia shook her head. "You should have listened to the doctor."

He paused to get his breath. "I don't want another night with bars between us."

She couldn't argue, even if all they did was hold each other. She needed the connection of arms and hearts after witnessing the haunting solitude of Liz Rainer.

Supporting Jonah up the porch stairs, she drew in the scent of pines, of coming winter, of her incredible, obstinate husband. "If you won't go back to the hospital, you at least need to rest."

"I have to do one thing first." He made his way inside to the corner shelf near the fireplace and stared at the bottle of Kentucky bourbon. She'd wondered what it was doing there, but she held her tongue when he raised his hand and stroked the long neck and fancy label. He took the bottle into his hands, then, turning, started back outside. Aching or not, if he was ending six years sober, he would do it where he felt most alive, outside on the mountain.

Clutching her shoulders, she followed, unsure how to be with him in this. They slowly crossed the clearing to the creek. He loved the water—they both did—running icy cold and tumbling golden aspen leaves over moss-slick rocks. Its burbling told the tale of long and endless travels, its voice springing from ancient stone that would stand long past their time on earth.

Jonah removed the lid, held the bottle under his nose and breathed the fumes. His throat worked. "I've kept this to remind me I could crash and burn."

He closed his eyes, then drew himself up. She held her breath as he slowly tipped the bottle, sending an amber stream into the frigid creek until nothing remained.

"From now on, I want to remember I can live." He stooped to fill the bottle from the stream, then twisted on the lid. He set the bottle on the ground and took her hands with his creek-chilled fingers. "I want what happens now and tomorrow and every day to fill me, to fill you."

Tears pooled in her eyes. She had no bottle to pour away her past, but she let the water carry it too, down and away in its quest for the sea. She brought her fingers to his jaw and kissed him, then pressed her forehead to his chin, his neck between her hands. She felt his pulse.

The wind came through the pines, bracing, invigorating. They were alive. They were together. They would do this crazy thing. She drew a deep, hungry breath and laughed.

From somewhere in the house came the long and wild song of a coyote.

Acknowledgments

I can do nothing without the grace and power of the Holy Spirit and the love of God and of Christ my Savior. I am shored up by my family and friends and, in this endeavor, by those who pray for, read, and support my writing. Particular thanks to readers Jim, Jessie, Devin, and my mom for feedback and insight, to David Ladd for law-enforcement expertise and longsuffering through multiple revisions, and to the Minturn Police Records and municipal court clerk Lisa Osborne. My gratitude to the wonderful WaterBrook crew, especially editors Shannon Marchese and Jessica Barnes, and to Stephen Parolini and others who fine-tuned and improved this work. Special thanks to all who purchase these books and keep me writing.

About the Author

While homeschooling her four kids, Kristen wrote her first novel. It became one of a five-book historical series. Since then, she has written three more historical novels and eight contemporary romantic and psychological suspense novels including *The Still of Night,* nominated for the Colorado Book Award, *The Tender Vine,* a Christy Award finalist, and Christy Award–winning *Secrets.* She lives in Colorado with her husband Jim and sundry family members and pets.